BELIEVERS

Love and Death in Tehran

راز سربستهٔ ما بین که به دستان گفتند

هر زمان با دف و نی بر سر بازار دگر

Raaz-e-sar-basteh-ye-maa bin, keh be dastaan goftand

Har zamaan baa daf o nei, bar sar-e-baazaar-e-diger.

See our deepest secrets, now told by storytellers,

With flute and tambourine, from morning till night, at
the gate of yet another bazaar

—Hafez

BELIEVERS

Love and Death in Tehran

A NOVEL

Marc Grossman
and
John Limbert

انتشارات مزدا
Mazda Publishers
2020

Publication of this book was made possible in part by a grant from
The A. K. Jabbari Family Trust

Mazda Publishers, Inc.
Academic publishers since 1980
P.O. Box 2603, Costa Mesa, California 92628 U.S.A.
www.mazdapublishers.com
A. K. Jabbari, Publisher

Library of Congress Cataloging-in-Publication Data

Names: Grossman, Marc, 1951- author. | Limbert, John W., 1943- author.
Title: Believers : Love and Death in Tehran : a novel / by Marc Grossman
and John Limbert.
Description: Costa Mesa : Mazda Publishers, Inc., 2020.
Identifiers: LCCN 2020013893 | ISBN 9781568593807 (paperback)
Subjects: LCSH: Women spies—Iran—Fiction. | Espionage,
American—Iran—Fiction. | IranPolitics and government—Fiction. |
GSAFD: Spy fiction | Suspense fiction.
Classification: LCC PS3607.R6725 B45 2020 | DDC 813/.6—dc23
LC record available at https://lccn.loc.gov/2020013893

Cover design: Nosrat Tarighi, DC Multimedia Productions,
(www.dcmulti.media).
Original calligraphy: Sharif Sharifi Shahrivar.
Model:Stefanie Vale.

We dedicate this book to our colleagues, the men and women of the U.S. Foreign Service. Along with their coworkers in the civil service, the intelligence community, and the military, they proudly serve the people of the United States of America.

We also honor those Iranians who have endured so much loss and still seek a better future for their families and their country.

CONTENTS

Acknowledgments   ix

Chronology of Real-World Events   xiii

Prologue: The Present. Middlebury, Vermont   xvi

Part One: A Time to Act

1. Nilufar   3

2. Massoumeh   33

3. Porter   63

4. Beheshti   78

5. In Plain Sight   119

Part Two: A Time to Love

6. Ruzbeh   145

7. The Two Rafsanjanis   188

8. Behnam Alley   219

9. Sarhaddi   236

Part Three: See Our Deepest Secrets

10. Two Conspiracies   275

11. Nazanin   309

Epilogue: Vermont, One Year Later   355

About the Authors

Acknowledgments

Writing a novel, like so much else in life, turns out to be a team sport. We wish to express our enthusiastic thanks to the many people who supported our effort. We hope they will recognize how and where they made the story and characters better. The many things that can be improved are of course solely our responsibility.

We thank those who read the book in its various drafts. We are especially grateful to Doug Thomas, a dedicated reader of espionage and historical fiction, for his honest and detailed review just when we most needed it. We also thank Secretary William Cohen, bestselling novelist in his own right, for reading an early draft and for his encouragement.

We thank Sam Marquis, another accomplished author of both fiction and nonfiction, for an informative telephone call early in our quest. We are indebted to Amy Bernstein, who was very generous with her time and advice in an enlightening phone conversation. We thank William Reynolds for his expert guidance.

For help giving the story credibility, we thank Joe Benkert, Mark Brunner, Michael Goldfein, Shelby Stone, and Frank Trippett. For their technical wizardry, we are grateful to Alan Krieg and Terrill McCombs.

We thank Kamron Jabbari of Mazda Publishers for his patience, suggestions, and support. He introduced us to the fascinating memoirs by Iranians of their experiences from the years of war and revolution. Noël Siver of Mazda Publishers did a superb job of copyediting, and saved us from many inconsistencies of names, relationships, places, and times.

We had invaluable help from journalist friends. Barbara Slavin and her husband Mike Ross, both added excellent insights from their experiences in Iran and the Middle East. Professor Ernest Tucker, a valued colleague from the United States Naval Academy's history department also shared excellent suggestions.

Mark Bowden, prizewinning author of *Guests of the Ayatollah*, gave valuable guidance on combining fiction and history. Patrick Tyler, *Washington Post* correspondent in Iran during the 1980s, generously shared his observations from the Halabja tragedy of March 1988.

The Washington office of the Kurdistan Regional Government, in its annual observation of the Halabja events, provided first-hand accounts from survivors, including some of the orphans – like Kazhal – adopted and raised by Iranian parents.

Doyle McManus of the *Los Angeles Times*, who covered Iran during the hostage crisis, told us about the "rehabilitation center for alcoholic foreign journalists" noted in chapter six. Scott Peterson of *The Christian Science Monitor* shared observations on Sadeq Ahangeraan, "Khomeini's nightingale".

For the cover art we are most grateful to Nosrat Tarighi, the highly creative photographer based in Washington. Sharif Sharifi Shahrivar provided the calligraphy on the cover.

Neither of the authors has been in Iran since 1981. We relied on many friends' willingness to share their firsthand observations of conditions in Iran during the harsh years of the 1980s and in more recent times.

We had the benefit of excellent work by journalists and scholars who helped us link history with the fiction of our narrative. Below is a selection of works we consulted and which we highly recommend to readers interested in learning more about this tumultuous period.

Ervand Abrahamian. *A History of Modern Iran.* Cambridge University Press, 2008.

Ervand Abrahamian. *The Iranian Mojahedin.* Yale University Press, 1989.

Said Amir Arjomand. *After Khomeini: Iran Under His Successors.* Oxford University Press, 2009.

Said Amir Arjomand. *The Turban for the Crown*. Oxford University Press, 1988.

Mohammad Ayatollahi-Tabaar. *Religious Statecraft: The Politics of Islam in Iran*. Columbia University Press, 2018.

Shaul Bakhash. *The Reign of the Ayatollahs: Iran and the Islamic Revolution*. Basic Books, 1984. A superb account of the bloody infighting in the first years of the Islamic Republic.

Joost Hiltermann. *A Poisonous Affair: America, Iraq, and the Gassing of Halabja*. Cambridge University Press, 2007.

Mehrangiz Kar. *Crossing the Red Line: The Struggle for Human Rights in Iran*. Blind Owl Press, an imprint of Mazda Publishers, 2007. A valuable memoir by one of Iran's leading human rights activists. Includes the story of "Haji Orgaani" in chapter six.

Peter Kornbluh and Malcolm Byrne, editors. *The Iran-Contra Scandal: The Declassified History*. The New Press, 1993.

Samuel Segev. *The Iranian Triangle: The Untold Story of Israel's Role in the Iran-Contra Affair*. The Free Press, 1988. Description of the role of the mysterious "Ayatollah Hassan" of Iran-Contra, related in chapters six and seven.

Nahid Siyamdoust. *Soundtrack of the Revolution: The Politics of Music in Iran*. Stanford University Press, 2017. Excellent discussion of Sadeq Aahangaraan, "Khomeini's nightingale."

Patrick Tyler. *A World of Trouble: The White House and the Middle East – from the Cold War to the War on Terror*. Farrar, Straus and Giroux, 2009. Includes a valuable firsthand account of the 1988 Iraqi attack on Halabja.

Nahid Yousefian. *Red Olive: One Woman's Account of Survival, Revolution, and War.* Translated by M. R. Ghanoonparvar. Mazda Publishers, 2015.

Coleman Barks kindly allowed us to use his beautiful version of a Rumi quatrain in chapter ten. The other translations – be they songs, poems, or obscenities – are by the authors.

To tell the story of Iran Air 655 in chapter nine, we relied on the United States Navy's *Formal Investigation into the Circumstances Surrounding the Downing of Iran Air Flight 655 on 3 July 1988* (the "Fogarty Report") and Pierre Razoux's, *The Iran-Iraq War.* The Belknap Press of Harvard University. 2015.

Last, but hardly least, we thank our wives and families for their patience, guidance, and perseverance. Marc's spouse, Mildred Patterson, read the manuscript when it was still less than a "work in progress" but always believed we would get to the finish line. John's spouse, Parvaneh, added much of the Iranian flavor, including the relationships, the Persian phrases, the food, and the atmosphere in prerevolution days. We would be nowhere without them.

CHRONOLOGY OF REAL-WORLD EVENTS

February 1979. Iranian monarchy collapses. Victory of Islamic Revolution.

Summer-Fall 1979. Fighting intensifies among revolutionary factions and in ethnic minority regions. Religious ideologues gain strength.

October 1979. American government admits deposed Shah of Iran for medical treatment.

November 1979. American Embassy seized and staff held hostage for return of the Shah. Ayatollah Khomeini endorses the occupation, provisional government resigns, and Iran hostage crisis begins.

January 1980. Abu'l-Hassan Bani Sadr elected first president of the Islamic Republic.

January 1980. Six American diplomats escape from Iran with help of CIA and Canadians.

March 1980. Failure of United Nations mission to release hostages.

April 1980. US breaks diplomatic relations with Iran. Eight American servicemen die near Tabas in failed attempt to rescue hostages.

April 1980. Islamist gangs attack opponents at Iranian universities.

May 1980. Akbar Hashemi-Rafsanjani elected to Iran's first parliament. Becomes Speaker (until 1989).

June 1980. Universities closed as part of "Cultural Revolution." Reopened 1983.

July 1980. Deposed Shah dies in Egypt.

September 1980. Iran-Iraq War begins.

January 1981. American hostages released. Ronald Reagan becomes US president.

June 1981. Ayatollah Mohammad Beheshti and others assassinated in bombing of Islamic Republican Party headquarters. Reign of terror against MEK.

June 1981. President Bani Sadr dismissed.

December 1981. Ayatollah Abu'l-Hossein Dastgheib, Friday prayer leader of Shiraz, assassinated.

1982–86. Mohammad Khatami serves as minister of culture and Islamic guidance.

June 1982. Iranians expel Iraqi forces from Iranian territory. Khomeini rejects Saddam's cease-fire proposal.

July-October 1985. Meetings in Europe of Iranians, Israelis, and Americans to arrange supply of US weapons to Iran.

November 1985. Ayatollah H. A. Montazeri appointed successor to Khomeini as supreme leader. (Removed March 1989.)

November 1986. Lebanese newspaper breaks story of arms-for-hostages deal (Iran-Contra scandal).

May 1987. American frigate USS *Stark* hit by missiles fired from Iraqi aircraft.

June 1987. Iraqis attack Iranian town of Sardasht with chemical weapons.

July 1987. UN Security Council Resolution 598 calls for cease-fire and withdrawal of troops. Accepted by Iraq; rejected by Iran.

September 1987. Mehdi Hashemi, brother of Montazeri's son-in-law, executed.

March 1988. Iraqis kill thousands of Kurdish civilians in poison gas attack at Halabja.

July 1988. American cruiser USS *Vincennes* shoots down Iranian civilian airliner (IR 655) over Persian Gulf. 290 killed.

July 1988. MEK, with Iraqi support, launches invasion of Western Iran. Invasion fails with heavy MEK casualties.

July1988. Iran accepts UN Security Council Resolution 598. Cease-fire goes into effect in August.

July-December 1988. Mass, secret executions of MEK and other leftist prisoners.

June 1989. Ayatollah Khomeini dies. Ali Khamene'i becomes supreme leader. Hashemi-Rafsanjani becomes president.

PROLOGUE

The Present
Middlebury, Vermont

"*Mama Nilu. Telefon.*" Nilufar looked at her grandson Ruzbeh with endless adoration and sorrow. At eight, his every innocent motion, word, and gesture told a story of love, death, pain, deception, and of that universe of madness she fled thirty years before. His dark brown hair, his deep eyes, and his smile all spoke of this world of love and loss.

"*Kiye, junam?*" (Who is it, my dear soul?) Nilufar desperately wished to keep her grandson's Iranian heritage alive and insisted on using Persian during his summer visits to Middlebury. In Vermont she socialized with a few Iranian families – like Nilufar, associated with Middlebury College – and a small community of doctors and academics in nearby Burlington. Her son Behnam and her American daughter-in-law Anita did their best, but an all-English school and environment in their North Carolina home made it hard. Still, Ruzbeh was naturally quick and curious, and would do anything to bring a smile to the face of his beloved *Mama Nilu.*

"*Nemidunam. Nagoft. Mardeh.* (I don't know. He didn't say. It's a man.)," Ruzbeh replied in his one-word Persian sentences, doing his best to imitate the musical rhythms of his grandmother's speech.

"Nilufar. It's Alan Porter. Do you have time for a relic of the past?"

"Mr. Ambassador. What a surprise. Of course I do. How are you?" She could never use his first name. She had met him as "Mr. Ambassador" forty years earlier and he had remained so eternally. And, unlike too many of his colleagues, he had earned and kept her respect.

What could he possibly want after so many years? He belonged to a buried life she had long abandoned with no regrets. Since leaving US government service thirty years earlier, she had isolated herself in this peaceful corner of Northern New England to deal with the pleasures and jealousies of academia. In her classes she taught her undergraduates a humane version of international relations completely different from her own bitter experience.

Porter was the exception to her chosen exile, her solitary tie to a previous life. She had politely rejected others' attempts to recreate links and networks she wanted no part of. She had put her previous life in a box and sealed it. With Porter, the contact was rare, but always cordial. She appreciated him – his age, his experience, his humanity, his judgment – too much to lock him out. He was perhaps the single person who understood the hurt and disillusion that had made her leave public service and choose a reclusive life raising her son in the genteel obscurity of classroom and library.

His voice was still clear and decisive. "Nilufar, I regret this is not a social call. I need to see you."

"Mr. Ambassador, you know you are always welcome for a talk or a visit. But you also know I made my choice years ago after Tehran. I will never go back to your world. And you of all people know why."

"Yes, of course I do. What happened to you was inexcusable and you did the honorable thing. You made the right decision. I believed that in 1988 and I do today. But Nilufar, please believe me when I say something has changed."

"Changed? I've heard that before. I never expected to hear it from you."

"I can't say more on the phone. We need to meet. As soon as possible. It's beyond urgent. I can't give you orders any more, but I can ask you to indulge your old boss and your greatest fan."

"For anyone else, it would be a quick 'no.' Where and when?"

"I can be in Vermont tomorrow. A United flight from Dulles lands in Burlington about noon."

Nilufar made some quick calculations of travel times and day camp arrangements for Ruzbeh. "I will pick you up at the airport. Can you stay over? Do you still like Iranian food? I can make a fair *khoresht-e-karafs* (celery stew) although not as good as my mother's. It's also my grandson's favorite."

"I'm afraid not. I'll need to get back on an evening flight. We should talk somewhere quiet." His voice grew serious. "And as much as I enjoy seeing you, I'm sorry it has to be rushed this way. You'll understand when we meet. Can I bring anything for you?"

Nilufar thought of all the delicious Middle Eastern products in Washington markets like *Yas* and *Yekta* and answered, "No, but many thanks," and added the lie, "I can find everything I need here."

"Good. See you tomorrow. Will we recognize each other after so long?"

"Not many undersecretaries of state pass through Burlington."

After she ended the call, she asked herself, "What can bring an eighty-year-old man out of retirement and running to me here? It can't be good."

For Nilufar, now in her sixties and with her late Iranian mother Farzaneh's elegance, the memories and the bitterness persisted despite her success at building a new life for herself and her son, and her devotion to her cherished grandson. Whoever was sending Alan Porter on this mysterious errand had read her well. For no one else would she face those long-buried memories and agonies.

PART ONE

A TIME TO ACT

NILUFAR

WASHINGTON
JUNE 1979

"David, Nilu, look at these rooms. They're a disgrace," Farzaneh Hartman whispered to her husband and daughter. "Look at these Naugahyde sofas, the worn carpets, the faded drapes. They belong on a low-budget cruise ship to Nassau. It must be embarrassing to bring foreign leaders here."

She paused and continued, "But the paintings, the china, and the sculptures are superb. They just need proper light and display space. Someone should raise the money to show off these treasures."

Nilufar Hartman, dark-eyed like her mother, missed nothing. "Enjoy them while you're here. These rooms are showplaces compared to the rest of the building. 'Utilitarian' would be the polite description."

Farzaneh continued admiring the badly displayed art in the State Department's eighth-floor ceremonial rooms. Nilufar's father David, well-dressed, compact, with a quick and often mischievous smile that both the women in his life adored, found the "Americana" artwork a jumble. "Too many howling coyotes," he thought. He walked onto the south balcony and watched the planes make their final approach to National Airport over the Lincoln Memorial and Potomac River in the late afternoon. "They could fill those rooms with unsold junk from a yard sale and never ruin the view," he said to himself.

3

Forty-five new Foreign Service Officers made a semi-dignified scramble for seats in the front rows of the Benjamin Franklin Room. The important and the self-important found places on the podium. Guests, family members, and friends filled chairs in semicircular rows behind the new officers.

Swearing-in ceremonies for new Foreign Service Officers at the State Department came on Friday afternoons at the end of a ten-week course optimistically called "orientation." It was designed to indoctrinate the new officers in the values and principles of their new profession. Specific training in languages, area studies, consular affairs, or trade promotion would come later. Just as drill instructors turned civilians into marines in three months, this program took graduate students, lawyers, academics, military officers, and journalists and – with fewer curses and push-ups – turned them into "FSOs." Few people used the term "diplomat," which seemed pretentious given the work most of the new officers would soon perform.

Nilufar had enjoyed these last ten weeks. Highlights included peeing into a cup for a drug test, selecting insurance options, and lively discussions of current world problems – China, Afghanistan, arms control, Iran, human rights, the Camp David peace accords between Israel and Egypt, rising oil prices – that were keeping thousands of dedicated people working long hours in dismal offices.

She liked her new colleagues. There were men and women who had spent years learning Chinese or Russian; ex-lawyers fed up with the money culture of large firms; a few very brainy people with advanced degrees in math, science, and engineering. Most of her class had studied the amorphous subject of "international relations" at Georgetown, George Washington, Fletcher, or Johns Hopkins.

The male, WASP, east coast, Ivy League stereotype of the Foreign Service Officer was changing. It had taken lawsuits from courageous women and pressure from Congress for more blacks and Hispanics, but Nilufar was now part of an emerging new meritocracy.

Each new officer – properly sworn in – would be sent to more training and eventually to an assignment abroad in an embassy or consulate. Nilufar, twenty-five years old with an MA in anthropology from the University of Virginia, looked forward – as did most of her colleagues – to dealing with the unsolvable problems she and her classmates had debated. For the next two years, however, her job was to be more routine but no less important. After a six-week course in consular affairs, she would join the US embassy in Kingston, Jamaica, as a vice-consul. There she would issue visas and passports and take care of American citizens in trouble.

Most of her colleagues would go to similar jobs or to postings as "general service officers," dealing with the logistics of embassy life: housing, furniture, appliances, plumbing, electricity, motor pools, and shipments. One colleague, on receiving such an assignment, said, "I've studied to be president of General Motors. Now I'll be running the parts department of a used car lot."

Nilufar did not mind. She had joined the Foreign Service out of curiosity and a wish to serve the United States. For her, it didn't matter where or how. She was certain she would find the unusual and the new almost anywhere. If the Foreign Service believed it needed her as vice-consul in Kingston, then that's where she wanted to be.

Her own background was unusual. Her mother, Farzaneh Rastbin, came from an upper-middle-class Iranian family. Recessive genes, probably from Georgian soldiers serving Iranian kings in the seventeenth century, had made Farzaneh taller, with lighter hair and fairer skin than most Iranians. Other, nomadic, ancestors had given her dark eyes a Central Asian shape. Her complexion and striking eyes had earned her the family nickname "*Tork-e-Shirazi*," the renowned fourteenth-century Persian poet Hafez's famous beloved.

In Tehran Farzaneh had been an outstanding student in science and math at the select public girls' high school, *Anushiravaan-e-Daadgar*. Fending off marriage proposals from wealthy men at least fifteen years her senior, her family was progressive enough to send her to the University of

Pennsylvania. Her talent in math drew her into economics, which became her passion despite being tagged the "dismal science." Now she was a respected officer of the World Bank in Washington.

At Penn in the fifties, Farzaneh met and married law student David Hartman. Although some relatives were disappointed at this marriage to a foreigner, her parents supported her. They knew her independent spirit would never accept the restraints and expectations of marriage into an Iranian family. As her father put it, "With us you always marry the tribe. And our tribes always have too many in-laws with too many demands."

She was drawn to David's quiet openness. His Czech-German ancestors had settled in Iowa in the late nineteenth century. Both his parents had been professors at the University of Indiana, and he grew up in an environment of personal modesty and common sense, midwestern liberalism.

David treasured Farzaneh, this brilliant, exotic beauty. He encouraged her passion for economics. They were two professionals without competition or jealousy. He showed great respect for her family and their traditions. The Persian language, however, with its double and triple meanings, defeated him. His logical mind, well suited to the law, could not fathom a language in which a slight shift of accent changed "seed buyer" into "donkey's balls."

Nilufar's looks were a throwback to other ancestors. She was shorter than her mother, dark-haired and dark-eyed, and was often taken for Greek, Italian, Spanish, or Palestinian. In Iran she did not stand out. Iranians called her coloring *sabzeh* (olive-skinned).

Farzaneh insisted, and David agreed, that Nilufar should know her Iranian side. She belonged to two cultures and should be at home in both. Farzaneh had seen too many alienated Iranians in America who denied their origins and either pretended not to speak Persian or spoke a version that loaded English words into Persian sentences. She had seen Iranian teenagers who spoke fluent English but who spoke Persian like six-year-olds. Farzaneh would not have that for her child. The

Iranian Nilufar would be as literate and educated as the American one.

Nilufar learned her mother's language as a toddler. At about five, when children begin to favor the English of school and playground, Farzaneh began taking her daughter for long visits to her family in Iran. She would leave her there for months, and Nilufar spent her elementary and high school years alternating between schools in Tehran and suburban Washington.

In Tehran she was the special darling of her great-aunt Zahra who became her guide to Iranians' traditional religious culture. Others taught Nilufar Persian grammar, calligraphy, Iranian history, and the great poets. Zahra taught her the Qur'an and the stories of sacrifice, devotion, and martyrdom that are the essence of Iranian Shia Islam. Nilufar especially loved to hear the story of the revered Abu Fazl-e-Abbas, the half-brother of Imam Hossein, who, when the soldiers of the cruel caliph cut off his arms and legs, crawled with a water bucket in his teeth to relieve the thirst of his brother's followers on the bloody plains of Kerbala.

Zahra taught her rituals, prayers, and fasts. She took her on pilgrimages to the saints' tombs found in every Iranian town and village. When Nilufar turned nine, Zahra instructed her in *taklif*, the obligations – including fasting and prayer – that came with puberty. She took her to *he'yaat* (neighborhood mourning associations), to recitations for martyred Shia saints, and to passion plays that reenacted the seventh-century martyrdom of Imam Hossein.

Zahra, like many Iranians, mixed her piety with a dislike for clerics and an unfocused distaste for Arabs – the same people who brought Islam to Iranians. Nilufar once asked Zahra, "*Khaleh jun* (dear auntie), wouldn't you like to go on pilgrimage to Mecca some day?" Zahra sighed and answered, "Well, if God wills it. But honestly, I'm not so interested. Our neighbor went a few years ago and said the place was hot, dirty, expensive, and full of Arabs. Maybe one day I can go to Iraq and visit Karbala and Najaf, but there are Arabs there too –

maybe the same ones whose fathers betrayed Imam Hossein at Kufa."

Zahra had actually never met an Arab in her life. And Nilufar knew better than to remind her aunt that those beloved imams and saints – Ali, Hossein, Reza, Abbas, Fatemeh, and Zeinab – were all Arabs. Zahra's faith left no room for questions. Such inconsistencies were better left unsaid.

As Nilufar Hartman grew up, she moved easily through three worlds: an American world of studies, sports, and dances; her mother's modern Iranian world of cafés, movies, music, picnics, and vacations on the Caspian coast; and her Aunt Zahra's Shia world of prayer, fasting, pilgrimage, and mourning ceremonies. In Tehran, in the morning she might cover herself carefully in a *chador* and visit Shah Abdul-Azim, a shrine a few miles south of town. In the evening, wearing the fashions of the day, she would meet her friends at Ray's Pizza or at the popular, upscale sandwich shop on Pahlavi Avenue called, for some reason, "Moby Dick." With her arresting looks, her long black hair and her unaccented Tehrani Persian, she appeared to be just one of the thousands of stylish girls who filled the streets, shops, and cafés of northern districts of the capital.

As a graduate student at UVA, she wrote her thesis on traditional religious practices among women in Shiraz and the surrounding towns of Fars Province. With Aunt Zahra and her friends as guides, she attended the women's gatherings at the Shiraz tombs of Amir Ahmad and Amir Mohammad, brothers of the eighth Shia imam.

She visited shrines in remote valleys near the towns of Fasa and Neyriz. No one knew exactly who were buried there, but all were certain the occupants had been holy and that a pilgrimage would bring blessings. She transcribed religious and folk poetry both in classical Persian and the melodic dialects of the countryside. She sat with fellow pilgrims near shaded pools, sharing tea, fruit, and roasted watermelon seeds, and listened as the women exchanged stories – sometimes off-color – of the buried saint. There was always someone with a good voice who would recite verses of Hafez or Rumi for twenty or thirty minutes from memory.

Nilufar had a gift for languages, and to her fluent Persian she added French, German, and some Arabic. When she first joined the Foreign Service, she earned the highest marks on the State Department's Persian fluency test. For most of the test she and the instructor discussed the use of the past and present perfect conditionals and the differences between the colloquial and formal languages.

Once the formal swearing-in was over, Farzaneh introduced herself to undersecretary of state Alan Porter, the main speaker at the ceremony. Without hesitation – Nilufar was now a Foreign Service Officer after all – she asked Porter, "Mr. Undersecretary, I don't understand it. I would have thought you could use Nilufar's language talents in other places. In Iran, for example. The country is in crisis, and how many people do you have like Nilufar?"

The forty-four-year-old Alan Porter was a Foreign Service prodigy. He had joined the service at age twenty-two, and had advanced quickly after assignments in Vietnam, Turkey, Poland, Senegal, and Washington. Of tall-to-medium height, attractive, and well spoken, Porter had the diplomat's gifts of patience, a good memory, and the ability to listen. Those gifts he combined with a fluency in written and spoken English and in French, Turkish, and Polish, which he had learned growing up in a Polish-American family in Cleveland.

At a young age he now occupied the most senior post normally open to career officers. Porter, himself a veteran of the State Department's impenetrable personnel system, did not understand Nilufar's posting any better than did the Hartmans. Drawing on his experience arguing for sometimes questionable American policies to skeptical foreign officials, he concocted the best explanation he could. His lack of conviction belied his words, and Farzaneh remained gracious, but unconvinced. They both knew that in the summer of 1979 – with Iran in turmoil – the Kingston assignment made no sense.

But he was not yet ready to fight another battle over Nilufar. He did not tell the Hartmans that the department's security masters had tried their bureaucratic best to keep their daughter out of the Foreign Service altogether, let alone serve in Iran. They argued that her background showed "very close links to a foreign country" and that they could not verify her accounts of what she had done in Iran. With such ties, they were not certain of her loyalties. "Yes, her passport says she's American," they argued. "But she's too Iranian."

Porter had confronted Bill O'Donnell, the department's chief of security, in a discussion full of undiplomatic language. Porter argued that the same rare, rich background that made security officers uneasy and made them dig in behind walls of bureaucratic obstinacy also made Nilufar a superb candidate for the Foreign Service. "How many of our applicants have done what she has?" he asked. "How many of them have her languages and experience? We need her. Especially now. Are we going to exclude those with firsthand knowledge of foreign societies?"

The head of security surrendered, but with reluctance and bad grace.

FALLS CHURCH, VIRGINIA

That evening, Farzaneh's younger brother – Arash Rastbin – and his wife Farideh came to dinner at the Hartmans' house off of West Street in Falls Church. At the door, the aroma from fish and rice steamed with herbs greeted the visitors.

The stated reason for the gathering was to honor Nilufar after the ceremony. Such occasions usually included spirited games of hearts, *hokm* (Persian whist), or rummy. But Arash, a diplomat at the Iranian Embassy in Washington (another point against Nilufar, Bill O'Donnell had argued), was preoccupied and increasingly worried by news from Iran. He was suspicious of his embassy colleagues, and could speak freely only with his sister, brother-in-law, and niece.

"*Mobaarak basheh, Nilu jun* (Congratulations, dear Nilu)," he greeted her. "It's good we have another diplomat in the family. We already have too many Rastbin engineers and doctors. And now with me working for Iran and you working for America, we cover all sides."

"*Lotf darid, da'i jaan* (You are too kind, dear uncle). I hope I can do a tenth as well as you in this career. It looks like both countries are going to need all our skills in the next few years. Did you ever do consular work?"

"Actually I did. I think you'll like it. In my entering class at the foreign ministry, those with connections went to Paris and Rome. There they would even get to kiss the hands of the Shah and the Empress. As for me, I became vice-consul in Sofia."

"What was that like?"

"In 1960? Poor, shabby, dark, and hungry. But the Bulgarians are very nice people. Almost Middle Eastern in outlook. Despite Communism, religion ran deep. We had some difficult consular cases of Iranian Communists who had fled Iran in the late 1940s and early 1950s. Many had Bulgarian wives and were living in miserable conditions. We helped them, their wives, and their children get Iranian documents and Bulgarian exit permits. We worked with our ministry for amnesty, so they and their children could visit relatives in Tehran. They hadn't seen their Iranian families for years. It was heartbreaking. In many cases embassy people helped pay for their bus tickets home. After so long, the Iranian authorities were willing to overlook their past sins."

Nilufar admired her uncle. He spoke fluent English, and an elegant, idiomatic Persian free of the English and French expressions that many educated Iranians used. He had been a top student at the Tehran law faculty and had earned a graduate degree from the Woodrow Wilson School at Princeton. He and his foreign ministry colleagues represented the best of modern Iran: well educated, broad-minded, patriotic, and professional.

Before the Islamic Revolution he had complained privately about the abuses of the Pahlavi system: the excesses, the nepotism, the mismanagement, and the corruption. He had seen the top positions in Iran's diplomatic service filled with well-connected incompetents chosen for their ability to flatter the Shah and his relatives. In Washington he watched a parade of shady wheeler-dealers, both American and Iranian, attach themselves to the embassy and the ambassador.

For Arash Rastbin and most of his colleagues, Iran's revolution – in one form or another – could not have come soon enough. He considered the royal courtiers mostly pimps and parasites who had enriched themselves with kickbacks from unneeded arms purchases and show projects, and squandered Iran's vast oil wealth on palaces and bizarre international festivals. Things only got worse after 1972 when quadrupled oil prices brought a deluge of cash. An insecure monarch ignored sensible advice, silenced dissent and criticism, and allowed the media to print only extravagant praises of his wisdom.

Now they had their revolution. And their second thoughts. Four months after the Shah's fall, they were not sure the revolution had been a good idea. Maybe they had been wrong. Able to speak openly with his relatives, Arash said, "Perhaps it's best Nilufar is going to Jamaica and not to Iran. Things there are not going well. The embassy here has become a herd of squabbling donkeys. We now have a leftist faction and an Islamic faction. The first says we shouldn't let any American travel to Iran. We should cancel all their visas. They just want to spy on us and steal our money. The second group says we should all grow beards and throw away our neckties. Our wives and daughters should start wearing at least a headscarf, and preferably a full *chador*."

David turned to Farideh and said, "Well, Fari, I think you'd look attractive in a headscarf. Very mysterious and exotic. Nilufar was expert at covering when she was doing her research. I thought she looked good. Auntie Zahra could teach you."

Farideh put aside her usual courtesy and turned on her brother-in-law. She was not amused. "Never joke about this, David. For us it's serious. It's not about just headscarves. We've had to fight for our rights as human beings for fifty years, and now we could lose them. As for Auntie Zahra, don't mention her. The language she uses about our new leaders, from Khomeini on down! Mostly about their mothers and sisters. You'd blush to hear it. She doesn't care who listens, but her tongue could get her in trouble."

"What about the new provisional government?" asked Farzaneh. "Most of them seem like reasonable people. They're not going to let the Communists or the *akhund*s (clerics) steal the revolution."

Arash answered carefully, "Most of them – the ministers, heads of universities, governors – are decent and well-educated people. But we were naïve when we marched and shouted for an Islamic Republic. Remember our slogan, 'Independence, Freedom, and an Islamic Republic.' Everyone could agree on the first two. The problem is the third. We did not understand just what we would get with an Islamic Republic. We nationalists had our ideas, but others had different ones."

Farzaneh asked her brother, "So where is the country going?"

"I fear not to a good place. Mehrdad Dashti, who's married to our cousin Pari, works in the Foreign Ministry legal department. He says that the ministry still operates, and the minister has promised there will be no wholesale purges or witch hunts. Those whose records are clean and served honestly will not be harassed or dismissed. I just don't know if he can keep that promise."

"Why not? The minister's very close to Khomeini, isn't he?"

"It would appear so, but nothing is certain now. We imagined once the Shah was gone, things would settle down, the clerics would go back to their mosques, and leave us technocrats to run things rationally without the corruption of the monarchy. We could continue our middle-class lives, although we might have to give up drinking alcohol in public. But things have not settled down. The infighting is getting worse."

"How does all that affect your work at the embassy here?"

"Well, I mentioned the factions and the embassy being in chaos. But matters are a hundred times worse back home. In Khuzestan we barely put down a rebellion of the local Arabs, who had Iraqi support. Can you imagine what would happen to

Iran if the oil revenue from Khuzestan were lost? In Kurdestan the only good news is that the Marxist and non-Marxist Kurds hate each other more than they hate Tehran."

Nilufar asked her uncle, "And what about the leftists?"

"It's hard to know. They're well organized, especially in the universities and in state radio and television. They demand more purges, more confiscations, and more executions. Have you listened to Iranian radio recently? After a lesson on Islam, there are long denunciations of 'feudals,' probably written by some idiot with a doctorate in Marxism-Leninism from Patrice Lumumba University.

"In Paris Khomeini talked about open debate, but there is no sign of it. Those of us who believe in a free, independent, and democratic Iran are being squeezed. Islamist gangs attack liberal newspapers and rallies. The leftists cheer them on. Goons who call themselves *Hezbollahi* attack women's rights demonstrators with clubs, knives, and acid."

Farideh added, "You remember our friend Aazar, who worked at the liberal magazine *Ayandegan*? Last month a gang of thugs trashed their offices and she was lucky to get away. Most of the writers' groups protested and wrote letters, but those leftist bastards, particularly the *Mojahedin-e-Khalq*, said nothing."

Arash continued, "Everybody hates everybody. The clerics still don't trust the leftists even when they cheer on the *Hezbollah* gangs against the liberals. Some *komiteh*, acting on someone's orders, even arrested two sons of a prominent ayatollah for leftist connections. Then another *komiteh* arrested a leading *mojaahed*, Mohammad Reza Sa'adati, and claimed he was spying for the Soviets. When that happened, the leftist papers went berserk and accused our minister of engineering Sa'adati's arrest on American orders."

Farzaneh asked, "What about everyday life?"

"On the surface, life goes on. There's no anarchy. The police have disappeared but security is still pretty good. Traffic is no better or worse than it always was. People come and go as always, and at night families are out walking, eating kababs and ice cream. Beer and vodka are a little harder to get. A lot of young men with advanced degrees have lost their jobs and are now running chicken kabab stands in the public parks. The quality of the kababs has gone up. Every neighborhood has a *komiteh* of armed vigilantes who more or less keep order. They seem to have the power to set up checkpoints anywhere and arrest anyone."

Farideh said, "Well, it sounds like we have thoroughly fooled ourselves and there's no going back. It's all too depressing. Let's play cards."

WASHINGTON, JUNE-OCTOBER 1979

Nilufar began her consular training the next Monday in Rosslyn, Virginia, across the Potomac from the main State Department building. Rosslyn, once home to pawnshops, was now filled with dreary buildings rented to government agencies. She was drilled in the multiple categories of visas. She learned about issuing passports to American citizens and was surprised to discover she would attach their photos with Elmer's glue and an electric iron. She learned about protecting American citizens, visiting those in prison, and what she could and could not do for them. She learned about the infinite varieties of consular fraud and learned that in many countries almost all "official" documents – marriage certificates, bank statements, birth certificates, property titles, and school records – were manufactured in workshops next door to the embassy.

From veterans of consular work she heard stories over coffee or drinks after work. Consular officers always had the best tales to tell: harrowing accounts of American women losing their children in foreign divorce proceedings; consuls rescuing beaten American spouses and how – too often – they were back with the abusive husband two weeks later. She heard about ingenious schemes, like the entrepreneur in a West African country who told visa applicants that – for a fee of $3,000 – he would intervene for them (and divide the money) with his "close friend" the American consular officer. Furthermore, he offered a money-back guarantee: no visa, no money. Of course the self-appointed middleman didn't know the consul and would do nothing. If there was no visa, he returned the money to the victim. But if the visa was issued, he had earned himself a nice sum for no work at all. Best of all, he didn't need to divide the money with anyone.

She heard sad stories about a few colleagues who had succumbed to the lure of easy money and sold visas, usually splitting the proceeds with a local crook. It had seemed almost too easy. If one saw 100 applicants a week, who would notice one or two bent visas sold for $10,000 each? Even after dividing the loot, officers who earned $20,000 a year could make money. These schemes usually went bad (and the disgraced officer went to jail) when someone got greedy, someone informed, or the corrupt officer could not hide or launder the cash.

In one class she met two couples – Mark and Cora Lijek, and Joe and Kathy Stafford – who were going to Tehran after their consular and Persian language training. She helped them and others create a game called, "Let's do this in Persian." Nilufar would play the role of an Iranian visa applicant or police official, and the others had to function in Persian. Some of her new friends picked up the language quickly, but others struggled. When Nilufar became a young Iranian applying for a student visa, a future vice-consul wanted to tell her, "I cannot give you the visa. Your grade point average (*mo'aadel)* is too low." The phrase, however, emerged as, "I cannot give you the visa. Your mother (*maadar*) is insufficient."

Thinking of her uncle's unsettling news from Iran, she admired her new colleagues' courage and spirit. They were going into chaos but were full of curiosity and optimism. She invited them to her Dupont Circle apartment for Persian meals and gave them tips on shopping and daily life in Tehran: where to find pork products, seafood, pizza, the best men and women's tailors, and how to navigate the city's chaotic traffic. She also supplemented their language lessons with phrases such as: "The power is out. The pipes are blocked. The gas capsule is empty. The tire is flat." (Situations unfamiliar to the department's aristocratic Persian instructors.) She gave them names and telephone numbers for some friends and relatives in

Tehran. She wanted the Americans to meet people outside the embassy and knew that a contact in the consulate could be very helpful for the Iranians.

One day, after a boring class on notarizing documents, she found a telephone message in the central lounge of the consular training division. "Call Undersecretary Porter. Very important." When she called, Porter's secretary told her, "He wants to see you. Can you come now?"

Nilufar now knew enough about her new Foreign Service culture to recognize this was, despite its polite wording, a command and not a question. She quickly made her way to the State Department shuttle bus from Rosslyn and, thirty minutes later, she was in Porter's spacious office on the seventh floor of the state building.

"Nilufar, good to see you. I hope the consular training isn't too tedious. It is important work."

"It has its ups and downs, sir. I'm looking forward to getting to Kingston."

"When do you leave?"

"In about another month."

"That's why I wanted to speak to you. I've had a message from our chief of mission in Tehran. Last week they reopened their visa section after six months. It was closed in all the confusion earlier this year."

"I have been helping some of my classmates get ready for their assignments to Tehran."

"Well, now the consulate is swamped. There's a huge backlog of applicants – probably over twenty thousand – and they can interview just a few hundred a day. They desperately need help, particularly a consular officer who speaks Persian. I'd like to send you there for a few months. I know the situation is difficult, so if you are at all concerned about your safety or the safety of your relatives in Iran, and say no, I will understand. On the other hand, you'll be doing us a great service."

Again, Nilufar recognized an order when she heard it. One did not say "no" to an undersecretary. "Of course I will help, sir. For how long? What will happen to my Kingston assignment?"

"For now, you'll keep the Kingston posting. You'll be assigned to temporary duty to Tehran for four months until we can get some more officers assigned and trained. Don't worry about being late for Kingston. I'll talk to the people there. They'll manage."

He paused, and in a softer tone asked, "Nilufar, are you sure about this? I don't want you to feel obligated. I mean that. Conditions in Tehran are difficult. We hoped they would settle down after the revolution, but so far they haven't. We're scrambling to find the right people to deal with the uncertainties there. We have a few political officers and a press officer with good Persian, but we don't have nearly enough."

Nilufar appreciated Porter's show of concern. But she also knew the Foreign Service valued those who were positive and flexible – not those who saw their postings as prison sentences and left heel marks on the pavement as they were dragged to an assignment. No one would ever tell her, but she was expected to show how delighted she was to be serving in the most difficult and dangerous places.

She told herself she could be much more effective in Tehran than in Kingston. She would be home, and not have to struggle with a new culture and life in an unfamiliar city. Tehran would never be dull. She would have the chance to be with family there and be helpful if things got difficult.

To Porter she said only, "I can't think of any place I'd rather be. When do they need me?"

"Finish your consular course. Then I'd like you to spend time in the department with both the Bureau of Consular Affairs and the Iran office. And with Diplomatic Security. If you can get to Tehran by late October or early November that will be fine. I know your coming will make the embassy very happy."

"I look forward to it."

"And Nilufar. Come and see me before you go. And whatever you do, please be careful."

Porter had not told Nilufar that the previous day he had endured another disagreeable meeting with security chief Bill O'Donnell. When he learned about Porter's idea of sending Nilufar to Tehran, O'Donnell – still seething from his earlier defeat in the Nilufar wars – was furious.

"Sir, first you overrule us to bring her into the Foreign Service. Now, against all good practice, you want to send her to Tehran. I don't have to list the reasons why that is a lousy idea."

"You don't, Bill. I know all the arguments against it. There just is one argument for it: we don't have anyone else like her and the country needs her there. I know we're making brave public statements about Iran – I write most of them. But the reality is, the revolution was a disaster for us and it's getting worse. If the president changes his mind and lets the Shah into the country, our people there are finished.

"It's bad enough that we've lost a major ally. Every day the president takes a beating from the press for 'losing Iran' and every day he chews out the secretary for our being blindsided by the revolution. The new phrase in Washington is 'I told you so.'

"We've already lost billions in commercial and military sales. I don't have to tell you the other awful possibilities: the Soviets, the PLO, the Iraqis are all ready to pounce. Look at the chaos in Afghanistan. Crude oil prices are going through the roof. And the Saudis think we're responsible for the whole mess in their neighborhood because we didn't act decisively. What we could have done, they don't say."

O'Donnell said, "Sir, we all know it's a complete fuckup. I wouldn't want your job of having to pretend in public that it isn't. But about Ms. Hartman – what happens when the security service there – whatever they call it now – tries to turn her by bringing pressure on her mother's relatives? Can she stand up to that? Can her family? When the shit hits the fan, we'll see the usual witch hunt. I for one don't want to be called to testify in Congress and be asked, 'Who approved this posting? What were you thinking?'"

"Bill, you're right of course. But the stakes are so high, we have to take the risk. I'm willing to send her there on a short-term, temporary posting and not cancel her assignment to Kingston. She goes for, say, four months, helps the consular section dig itself out, and then moves on to Kingston. Can you accept that?"

"Do I have a choice, sir? If I say, no, you'll do it anyway."

"I knew you'd see reason. Can you make sure she is well briefed on security and counterintelligence? She needs to know what to do if something is not right."

"Of course. You and I agree on one thing: it's an awful mess there. I just pray that she is as savvy as you think she is."

"So do I."

Nilufar finished her consular training with top marks. She found the need to apply both law and compassion in visa cases challenging and fascinating. Her father had always said she would make a skilled and humane lawyer. She also realized that as a consul she would have the ability to help people navigate their way through an opaque bureaucracy for virtuous ends: uniting a family; beginning a new life; or getting an education in the world's great universities. She appreciated the authority that – as a most junior Foreign Service Officer – she would have in visa cases. The instructors told her repeatedly: NOT EVEN THE AMBASSADOR CAN OVERRULE YOUR DECISION IN A VISA CASE. SOME WILL TRY, BUT THE FINAL AUTHORITY IS YOURS. In every other way she would be at the bottom of the hierarchy; but here was a welcome reversal.

Her classmates, the Staffords, Lijeks and others, had left for Iran before she learned of her new assignment. She had little news of them, but she did hear that the Tehran consular officers were facing a crowd of visa applicants. The backlog was growing by the day.

She met mixed reactions when she told her parents of the Tehran posting. They were worried for her safety in a place of growing chaos. Arash's accounts were becoming darker. Friends and relatives had little good news to relate.

David and Farzaneh were proud that the United States government had finally recognized Nilufar's unique abilities and was sending her to one of its most important diplomatic stations. They knew their daughter was special. Now others confirmed their opinion. Nilufar in the embassy could be a potential lifeline for Iranian friends and family if matters there went seriously wrong. There were now frequent reports of high officials dismissed, arrested, or simply resigning and leaving the country. Yesterday's ministers became today's fugitives. Farzaneh did not need to say so, but part of her was thankful Nilufar would, in extreme cases, be there to help her relatives.

In August, after the consular course ended, she began working in the department's Iranian affairs office on the fifth floor. The walls in the crowded and dingy spaces were painted a bilious green, and the fluorescent ceiling lights turned everyone's skin consumptive yellow.

She found bedlam: officers drowning in a tidal wave of unsolvable problems. One day it was, "Georgetown University claims Mashhad University owes it $100,000 for services. How can we help it collect?" On another, "a congressman demands we do something to help Iranian Jews, Armenians, Assyrians, and Baha'is." Nilufar thought, "What about the Zoroastrians? Probably nobody has heard of them. Without a lobby, they're out of luck." Another day it was, "Mr. Felani (so-and-so), with important American friends, has been arrested in Tehran. How do we get him released?"

Officers arrived at 7:00 a.m., after long commutes from distant suburbs, and rarely left the building before 8:30 p.m. Nilufar admired their dedication but found that few had any experience with Iran, much less with its new realities. The iron whims of the State Department's personnel system assigned a talented Spanish-speaking officer who had just left Venezuela to help settle outstanding claims of American companies. In that office only Nilufar spoke Persian. Lunch for most was a sandwich devoured in a few bites at a desk washed down by a soda from the machine down the hall. Telephones rang constantly with calls from Iranian-Americans desperate to help their relatives. The embassy in Tehran sent salvos of messages demanding more of everything: security, people, money, and answers.

Nilufar went through the prosaic steps of moving, which were a comfort after the chaos of the Iran office. At least she could accomplish something. She cancelled her lease, sold her car, bought new, conservative outfits for herself and gifts for her Iranian relatives. She packed lots of books and music and sent her new diplomatic passport to the Iranian embassy for a visa. Arash told her that because she had an American father and Iranian mother, the Iranian government considered her American and would give her a visa as a diplomat.

In late October, on her last day in the department, she had lunch with James Branson, the director of Iranian Affairs. He had just returned from Tehran where he had told the prime minister and foreign minister of the deposed Shah's admission to the United States for cancer treatment. Like most of her colleagues, Nilufar was appalled by the decision and wondered whether an American embassy would exist by the time she arrived. Branson, speaking in an Alabama drawl, described the meeting at which he and Bruce Laingen, the chief of mission in Tehran, had told the Iranians of President Carter's decision.

"They seemed to take it in stride," he said. "They weren't happy, but they repeated their commitment to keeping the embassy and our people safe. So far there hasn't been any strong reaction either from the government or the public."

Given what Nilufar knew about the feeble provisional government, she found little comfort in its assurances. She kept her doubts to herself. "What else did you find there?" she asked him. "What's the mood in the city? What's the mood at the embassy?"

"It's not easy there, but the embassy people seem OK. After the decision, no one asked to leave. In the consular section, however, there's a big problem. The chief is a veteran consular officer with years of experience in the Caribbean. He's never been near the Middle East. He ignores the department's instructions about easing visa issuance to help the thousands of frightened middle-class Iranians. He insists on applying the same rigid standards he used in Santo Domingo."

"Can't the chief of mission intervene?"

"He has to be careful before he overrules a senior officer. Most of the first-tour consular officers go along because they feel they have to. There are a couple of more experienced officers who ignore him and issue visas to just about everyone. One of them told me he now understands what it was like working in Nazi Germany in the 1930s. People seem desperate. I don't know if he's exaggerating. In any case, it's not a healthy situation.

"As for the city, what can I say? A few days after the decision to admit the Shah was announced, I went to Friday prayers at Tehran University. I had called on Ayatollah Montazeri and he invited me. He was to deliver the main sermon. I went with a Persian-speaking embassy officer and an escort from the foreign ministry. My Persian isn't very strong, but I understood enough to know that Montazeri never mentioned the United States or our decision to admit the Shah. Our embassy people think the senior clerics are afraid things could get out of hand and want to cool the anti-American rhetoric."

"So the ceremony wasn't a 'Death to America' festival? I guess that's encouraging."

"Things got tense at the end. After the sermon there was a sort of pep rally. A cheerleader with a microphone would chant a slogan and the crowd would repeat it and wave their fists. It all started out safely enough with slogans like, 'The Kurds are our brothers' and 'We shall triumph through unity.'

"With a million people shouting, you can imagine what we had to do. Well, then he shouted something in which I heard the name 'Carter.' I asked our embassy colleague what he had said, and he told me, 'Don't ask, James. Just wave your fist and shout.' Later he told me that the slogan was, '*Marg bar seh mofsedin, Sadat o Carter o Begin* (Death to the three agents of corruption, Sadat, Carter, and Begin).' There we were, with a million others shouting for the death of our president. I hope no one filmed us!"

Nilufar could not contain her laughter. "Well, you were serving your country. I'm sure the president will understand."

Later that afternoon she met Porter. "Laingen and the others at the embassy are all good people with an awful job. Their mission is to create some kind of relationship with the new reality in Tehran, whatever that is. They won't give up. It may be impossible, especially after we've admitted the Shah, but they are professionals and are doing their best. Frankly, what we do in Washington doesn't always help them."

He continued, "In public we're always hopeful, but I am worried. When we admitted the Shah I argued that we should evacuate all or most of our people from Tehran. The assurances of the provisional government ministers are worth nothing, and we've become the scapegoat for everything that goes wrong in Iran.

"The secretary agreed, but the White House wouldn't hear of it. They told us, 'For over thirty years we have fought to keep the Soviets out of Iran. Now do you expect us to leave and tell the Soviets they can have the whole country?' I can understand their argument, but I can't help thinking we've hung our colleagues out to dry."

"Mr. Branson told me the clerics want to keep the lid on."

"I hope he's right. In any case, here's what I want you to do. These are my personal numbers: office direct, pager, and home. If none of those work, the operations center can always find me. You will see and hear things there that others do not. If something is going wrong, I need to know. Call me immediately anytime here or at home. I mean that. I want to know what you're seeing. Others may be too polite or too cautious to be frank. Plus, they want to succeed and won't admit that their mission is hopeless."

Porter had confirmed Nilufar's suspicion that he was sending her there to do more than issue visas. "Sir, I'm flattered by your confidence in me. I can tell you now that my uncle Arash in the embassy here is just as pessimistic. Probably more so. I cannot repeat the language he used after he heard about the Shah's coming to the US."

Porter smiled and said, "You mean he doesn't believe our statements about a purely humanitarian action to help an ailing Shah, with no political motives? I'm shocked. Shocked, that he would not trust us." He did not tell Nilufar that he was already meeting privately with her uncle Arash at least once a week. Nilufar and Porter shook hands. Downstairs, she collected her things from her desk, said her farewells to colleagues, and headed to Falls Church for a meal of her mother's squash stew and last advice from her parents and her uncle.

"Remember, Nilufar," Arash told her. "Our cousin's husband, Mehrdad Dashti, is in the foreign ministry legal department. He's a veteran and knows everyone. You may not need him, but he can be useful. Be careful."

"Everyone is telling me that. I will be."

TEHRAN, NOVEMBER 1979

Pan American 055, like most international flights, landed in Tehran after midnight. Nilufar had not been in Iran since the revolution, but conditions at Mehrabad Airport at first did not seem so different. There were fewer foreigners coming to Tehran, and she noticed young men in Banana Republic revolutionary garb standing around with submachine guns. The passport and customs officials – more bearded than usual – were courteous and respectful of her American diplomatic passport. Since she looked and spoke like an Iranian, she had to explain her having an American passport – that her nationality came from her father and her looks and fluent Persian from her mother. Several officers asked her about getting an American visa. They also asked about her marital status, but there were no outright proposals -- only hints of future visits by mothers and aunts.

Even at that hour the arrivals area was full of waiting relatives with flowers for their loved ones. In Nilufar's case, the reception committee was her aunt Minu, her husband Ahmad, and their oldest son, her cousin Babak. Apologizing for the sparsity of the welcoming group, they explained, "More are waiting for you at the house. The children couldn't stay up, but they are very excited to see you in the morning. Auntie Zahra is on pilgrimage to Mashhad, but I know she'll want to see you as soon as she gets back. You know you're her special pet."

She asked them, "Did you see anyone here from the American Embassy?" They might have sent a car and driver for me. Perhaps they never got notice about my arrival."

Ahmad answered, "No one here that I can recognize. No matter. You can check in with them in the morning."

On the ride home they passed a checkpoint on Mosaddegh Avenue. Nervous, armed young men in civilian clothes checked Ahmad's ID, and, when asked about his relationship to his women passengers, he explained courteously that he was bringing his wife's niece from the airport. Addressing them as "brother," he thanked them for keeping the capital's streets safe. As they drove on he told Nilufar, "I meant it when I thanked them. They're volunteers and they've kept Tehran a safe city, even when the police have disappeared. Just don't get caught with alcohol or the wrong man in the car."

As promised, there were more relatives at Ahmad and Minu's apartment in the upscale Yousefabad neighborhood. The narrow, shaded streets were lined with three- and four-story buildings, usually with a spacious apartment on each floor.

Inside there were kisses, flowers, tea, and fruit. Nilufar, the "American cousin," was always a favorite in the family and she made a point of keeping up with the children and their progress. The gifts she brought – blouses, children's picture books, sweaters, shirts, and music cassettes – were quickly distributed to obligatory cries of *"chera in hameh zahmat keshidi* (Why did you go to all this trouble?)" to which she would reply with the equally obligatory *"Qaabel-e-shomaa nadaare* (It's not worthy of you)."

Ahmad's nephew, her cousin Iraj, was blunter than the others. "What are you Americans doing? First you get rid of the Shah and bring Khomeini to power. Now you've taken the Shah to New York with some crazy story about cancer. What have we done to you to deserve this?"

Ahmad interrupted. "Not now Iraj. Can't you see she's exhausted? She wants to see everyone and get some sleep, not argue about politics." He refrained from saying, "Shut up, you idiot. Why are you arguing with someone who has the power to save your neck with a visa?"

Nilufar said, "Iraj dear, in the next few weeks there'll be plenty of time for us to argue politics. That's a promise. I can't imagine there's much going on at the nightclubs now."

Iraj laughed and said, "Actually there's a lot going on. You just have to know the secret knocks and passwords. Just say the word, and I'll give you the 'Revolutionary Tehran by Night' tour."

Nilufar slept until nine o'clock the next morning. It was Sunday and a workday in Tehran. Ahmad had left for his office at the National Oil Company, and Aunt Minu had prepared her favorite breakfast items: warm *barbari* bread with butter, white sheep's milk cheese, walnuts, sour cherry jam, boiled eggs, and plenty of strong hot tea served in large glasses. Nilufar planned to call the US Embassy after she ate.

She luxuriated in the hospitality and the affection of her relatives. Nilufar knew that the revolution had thrown shadows on everyone's future; but there was a tacit agreement that they would not let their worries undermine the family fortress.

It was difficult to explain these ties to Americans. Her relatives might or might not like each other; but likes and dislikes were irrelevant, as were political views. Her mother's extended family included communists, nationalists, royalists, and devout Moslems. Whatever their views, they depended on and supported each other. The family was a combination bank, employment bureau, and marriage and family counselor. Her grandparents were deceased, and her senior uncle lived in Isfahan from where he acted as family patriarch *in absentia*. Minu's husband Ahmad was widely respected, and was usually consulted on major decisions: schools, investments, marriages, and jobs.

Respect extended even to Nilufar's father, David the American. His in-laws admired him for being a devoted husband to the brilliant Farzaneh and for always welcoming relatives to their Virginia home for long or short visits. The whole family appreciated how he had supported Farzaneh's efforts to keep Nilufar attached to her Iranian roots. They paid him a huge compliment when they said, "He is one of us."

The women in the family – smart, focused, and practical – exercised enormous influence. The men understood that they had best listen to the women's advice. Not for Nilufar's family the stereotype of the meek, quiet, and submissive Middle Eastern woman. Most of the men in the family preferred to play backgammon, drink tea, recite poetry, and argue politics. Tough, determined, and practical women ensured the family's survival.

Nilufar also knew her relatives speculated about a marriage with one of her cousins. Her education, her prestigious career as a diplomat, and her American nationality made her a very desirable prospect. They were even willing to waive demands for the virginity essential in an Iranian bride. In that department her American side was the perfect pretext.

Her mother advised her, "Your cousins are fine young men. I cannot tell you what to do, but I would advise against such a marriage. There would be too many expectations. When and where I grew up girls had to be very strong. I married not only outside the family, but outside the culture. I could never have been happy as the wife of an Iranian. You may find the perfect Iranian husband – there are many good men there – or someone from elsewhere. I just hope you will be as happy as I have been."

She was on her second glass of strong tea when the phone rang. Minu said a few words and told Nilufar, "It's Mehrdad from the Foreign Ministry. He says turn on the radio. There's trouble at the American Embassy."

"Can I talk to him?"

"He says he can't talk now. He'll call later."

The radio reported that demonstrators had broken into the American Embassy compound and had occupied the buildings. The fate of the American employees was unknown. Large crowds had gathered outside the embassy walls and were blocking traffic. So far there were no reports of gunfire, deaths, or injuries. The radio had not broadcast any official statement from the Iranian provisional government.

Nilufar first thought she should call the State Department's 24-hour Operations Center to tell them where she was. Some warning voice, however, told her not to. The fewer people in Tehran or official Washington who knew about her the better. She made two calls. First a brief one to her parents to reassure them she was safe. The second to Undersecretary Porter. She thought, "It's three a.m. Sunday morning in Washington. He told me to call any time. Now I'll find out if he meant it."

There was no hint of reproach when she reached him at home. "I was just talking to the Operations Center. The line is out to the embassy. Our last message from there was that no one's been hurt. We are talking to the Iranian Foreign Ministry and pushing them to clear the compound. They are promising it will be done in the next few hours. Stay away from the embassy for now. Are you safe where you are?"

"Yes, sir. Everything is calm in this part of town. The reports on the radio are sketchy. My cousin at the ministry couldn't talk this morning. I'll speak to him later today. If you need to reach me, here is the number at my aunt's house."

"You did well to call me directly. The fewer people – American or Iranian – who know you're there, the better. Did you speak to anyone at the embassy?"

"No. I suspect the embassy never got the message about my arrival last night. There was no one at the airport."

"That's probably for the good. Lie low for now until we see what happens. You can call me anytime, but be careful about doing that as well. For public consumption we're saying we expect the Iranian authorities to protect our people and clear the compound in the next few hours. I wish we were that confident."

Then there were calls from family members, who added little to the radio reports except rumors: the prime minister and the foreign minister were at the embassy with an armed group to expel the demonstrators; Ayatollah Khomeini had ordered the Revolutionary Guards to secure the embassy and its people; gunfire was heard near the embassy; demonstrators had attacked other foreign missions.

She stayed indoors with her aunt the rest of the day reading newspapers and listening to the radio for news. Tehran Radio's bulletins gave little information and the story got scant coverage on the BBC and other foreign stations.

By evening it was clear only that the occupiers, who called themselves "Moslem Student Followers of the Imam's Line" were still in control of the embassy and that provisional government officials had done nothing to remove them.

About eight o'clock her cousin Mehrdad came to the apartment. With disgust in his voice he ranted, "What a mess. What a country! Sometimes we Iranians *ajab gohi hastim* (are truly shit). When the attack started, someone from the US embassy called us for help and the idiot secretary kept asking him about her visa. *Mordeh-shureshro bebare*! (May she go to her grave unwashed!) We think only of ourselves and our damned visas to get out. Even people with high posts are making sure their passports and visas are up-to-date. We test the winds and play both sides. And we won't even protect foreign diplomats."

"Is anyone in charge?" asked Ahmad.

"Who knows? If it can't fix this mess, the provisional government is finished. Whatever power it ever had, it has already lost to neighborhood vigilantes who answer only to clergymen no one has heard of. In the provinces power is in the hands of Friday prayer leaders and 'Imam's representatives' who answer to no one and ignore the local governors. In Khorasan the cleric Tabasi is all-powerful. He controls the Mashhad shrine endowment and is now virtual king of Northeastern Iran."

"Who comes out on top? The clerics? The leftists?"

"Hard to say. Remember that the leftists helped overthrow the Shah. Now I think the religious groups are terrified that those same leftists will steal the revolution. The leftists are supporting the embassy attack, presenting themselves as the only true revolutionaries and denouncing us and our nationalist friends as 'accommodators' and 'American agents.' If they make that charge stick, we're finished."

"What's the foreign minister doing about the embassy?" Nilufar asked.

"He can't do anything on his own. He traveled to Qom this afternoon to persuade the Imam to act. He called us from there. The Imam told him to go ahead and kick the students out. How he'll do that is anyone's guess." Minu and Ahmad interrupted. "Listen to the latest on the radio."

The announcer read, "The office of Imam Khomeini has issued the following bulletin: 'In the name of God. A group of devout, brave, and patriotic students have taken the initiative and acted to foil the plots of the world-devouring American imperialists. By seizing the den of spies – the so-called embassy – they have undertaken a second revolution more profound than the first. I approve their action and praise their pure spirit. I also endorse their just demand for the return of the criminal Shah for trial. I expect all God-fearing Moslems and patriotic Iranians to do the same. Ruhollah Mousavi Khomeni.'"

Everyone went white and mute from disbelief. Mehrdad swore, "*Pedar sag!* (Son-of-a-bitch!)" And that after he told our minister to kick them out. Nilufar, unless I'm completely wrong, this business is about to get a lot worse."

"There's more," said Ahmad.

The announcer continued, "This evening, members of the provisional government submitted their resignations to the Imam. After accepting, he asked the Revolutionary Council to take charge of ministries and government offices."

Nilufar asked her cousin, "What does this mean? Why would he do it? It makes no sense."

"I'm not sure what his plan is. He may seem crazy but he's not. My guess is that he sees an opportunity to preempt the anti-Americans on the left. At the same time, he creates a crisis, fuels hysteria, mobilizes the mobs, and destroys anyone who questions his vision of an Islamic state – the carping intellectuals, he calls them. As for the nationalists, he needed them during the revolution, but never liked them. Now he's given them the death blow."

Minu asked, "And what about our Nilufar? Is she safe? People who don't know her think she's Iranian, but some of the neighbors know her as "our American."

Mehrdad answered, "For the moment she's safer here than anywhere. She mustn't be seen by anyone in the neighborhood who knows her. If we can't resolve this mess in the next two days, I'll find a solution for her. I'll know more tomorrow when I go to the ministry."

"With no minister, who's going to run foreign affairs?" asked Ahmad.

"Good question. That opportunist Qotbzadeh has had his eye on the ministry for a long time. He's not stable. You see how he's destroying Iranian Radio-TV. In his office he keeps a portrait of Hanifnezhad, the executed 'Islamic Marxist' from the *Mojahedin-e-Khalq*. He's been furious ever since posts were distributed. He keeps whining, 'This one's a minister; that one's a governor; another's head of the oil company; and they made me boss of a band of *mezqun-chi* (street musicians).'"

Nilufar called Porter at his office. "You've heard the news, sir? The Imam has backed the occupiers and the provisional government has resigned."

"I just heard. The president is sending a personal appeal to Ayatollah Khomeini. There's no one else to talk to and there's no one else who can do anything. Any suggestions?"

"Not now. I first thought the adults in the room would sort it out. Now I don't see that there are any."

"Nilufar, very few people here know you're in Tehran. We're going to keep it that way. I'm the only one at the department who knows exactly where you are. The only others are your parents and your uncle Arash at the embassy."

"Thank you, sir. I'm probably in the best place I can be. Any news about our people at the embassy here?"

"As far as we know, no one's been hurt. Beyond that we don't know much. Let's hope this all gets resolved soon and you can leave with them. Otherwise we'll have to make sure you stay safe. Please keep our contact open. Take care of yourself."

2

MASSOUMEH

Porter was right. Things got worse. Khomeini refused to receive President Carter's letter or allow his envoys into Iran. Encouraged by the Imam's defiance, huge crowds marched and shouted outside the American Embassy. The students inside strutted around waving weapons and issued declarations full of bombast. They declared themselves heroes and loved the attention from the international press.

Everyone competed to confirm Mehrdad's description of Iranians as members of the "party of the winds." Merchants' associations, boy scouts, student groups and writers' unions sent the occupiers messages of support. State Radio and TV aired the students' communiqués with great fanfare and denounced anyone who questioned the occupation.

Porter had never told Nilufar about his meetings with her uncle Arash. Their rendezvous of choice was the Zebra Room, a dive on the edge of respectability near the toney Cleveland Park neighborhood in Northwest Washington. The indifferent food, watered drinks, and persistent musty smell ensured no other diplomats would be there. Both men came directly to the point. No one lingered at the Zebra Room.

They had begun meeting in the summer of 1978 because Porter knew conditions in Iran were going sour and that official sources were not providing a coherent story. The Iranian ambassador in Washington put out only reassuring pap, and the US embassy and the CIA station in Tehran talked to the same

33

clueless Iranians. Porter recalled a comment on the Tehran Embassy from a University of Texas political scientist and Iran expert. Paraphrasing Churchill, he said, "Never for so long have so many [American officers] known so few [Iranians] who knew so little."

Porter was blunt. He told Arash, "I want Nilufar to stay in Tehran for a while. We need her there. Is there a way to arrange that? And keep her safe, of course."

"Alan is this your request or does it come from others as well?"

"Let me put it this way. It is an official request."

In Washington, letting your boss be surprised even by the smallest thing is a cardinal sin. Porter was taking a huge risk by not telling the secretary of state or anyone at the White House about Nilufar's presence in Tehran. He wanted arrangements set before confessing, because telling his bosses now would ensure their opposing his plan. No one in Washington wanted to take more risks in an Iran that was bringing nothing but misfortune.

"I like the way he calculates," Arash thought. "They could smuggle her out of Iran tomorrow, but she's much more valuable to them there. The Americans are in the middle of a crisis, are desperate for information, and have no sources. I also like the fact he has such a high opinion of Nilufar. She is like my sister in so many ways: smart, determined, resourceful, and completely honest. If the women were running Iran, we wouldn't be in the mess we are."

Arash knew that to cooperate with Porter, he would need to talk about Nilufar with his cousin's husband, Mehrdad Dashti in the Iranian Foreign Ministry. They had been corresponding secretly for months and had set up a secure channel to exchange messages. Without revealing his source, Arash had shared many of Mehrdad's comments on conditions in Iran with a very appreciative Porter.

"Give me a few days. Let me talk to some people. In the meantime, you and Nilufar must keep your contact to a minimum. Fear and suspicion rule Tehran."

Two days later Mehrdad called Nilufar. "We need to talk. Come to Nayeb's Kabab for lunch today. Around one o'clock. During the day you won't have to worry about checkpoints." Nilufar changed into a long dress, stockings, and a headscarf. She ordered a taxi. Nayeb's Chello Kabab restaurant was on the former Pahlavi Avenue, now Mosaddegh Avenue. She wondered how long the new street name would last. Telling the driver where she wanted to go, she was careful to keep her accent as Tehrani as possible.

The restaurant was noisy and crowded. The smoky, sweet smell reminded her of those times she had spent in Iran as a child. Mehrdad was already inside. He had ordered two *sultani*, a combination plate of grilled lamb filet and ground beef with a mountain of aromatic steamed and buttered rice. There was her favorite yoghurt drink called *dough,* fresh bread, and the obligatory plate of raw onions and fresh greens.

The always well-dressed Mehrdad, who had a reputation for honesty, patriotism, and excellent connections across the political spectrum, was sporting a two-day beard and had chosen a shirt with a buttoned collar and no tie. At least on the outside, people were going along to get along.

On the inside, Mehrdad was agitated. The walls of repression were closing in. The revolution was not building a humane and open Iran where citizens and government respected each other. Instead, he saw that violence, intolerance, and brutality were becoming facts of everyday life. Iran's new order answered its critics with fists to the mouth, kicks in the stomach, and acid in the face.

In Nilufar he saw an opportunity for him and others to assert a rival vision. They could get their message out. If the Americans knew the reality, perhaps they would intervene and end this madness. But should he use Nilufar to promote his fantasies? He was going to try.

"Nilufar, I hope you're comfortable at Minu and Ahmad's. You know how much they love and admire you. Like their own daughter."

"They couldn't be kinder. It's hard not being able to go out. I'm a burden on them. To say nothing of the danger of my being there. If I'm discovered – if some nosy neighbor decides to tell the local *komiteh* – they will have real problems."

"That's why I want to talk to you. I don't know how much you know, but your uncle Arash in Washington has been meeting quietly with Ambassador Porter. They have talked a lot about you. Porter wants you to stay in Tehran for a while. In all this chaos he is desperate for information and no one else can supply it."

She was furious but kept her face still. She asked herself, "How can Porter and Arash have been meeting and deciding my future and no one tells me? I have no say?"

Straining to stay calm, she asked Mehrdad, "How can I do that? I'd think they would want me out. I certainly can't stay here on my American diplomatic passport?"

"I think I have a way that you can stay and even work. If you're willing, of course. We can give you a new identity as an Iranian. I know someone who can make you an identity card with a new name and family details. We'll make sure no one discovers your American passport."

Nilufar now faced another order from Porter clothed as a request. She was flattered that he would offer her a part in such an adventure. At the same time, she felt Porter, Arash, and Mehrdad all pushing her onto dark and unknown paths.

What did Porter expect she could do in Tehran? How long did he expect her to stay? She also knew Mehrdad could not tell her. But now any arrangement that let her live even a little more openly in Tehran and maybe do some good for the United States – that's why she chose the Foreign Service after all – was welcome.

With Khomeini endorsing the embassy occupiers, chances for an early resolution of the crisis were getting slimmer by the day. She could go along with Mehrdad's plan – with all its uncertainties – or stay hidden at her aunt's house until someone found a way to get her out of the country.

"Mehrdad, what do you think? If I can't leave soon, what choices do I have?"

"Nilu, there's a madness at work in Iran, and it will drag the country God knows where. If you stay it will be dangerous;

but it could also be very useful both to your American bosses and for those of us trying to limit the damage of all this stupidity. If I thought the plan was crazy, I would have told Arash directly and we would not be having this talk. As things are now, every day you stay you're in greater danger – unless we can protect you with a new identity."

Mehrdad did not need to say that her presence also threatened her family.

He tried to lighten the mood. "Any preference for a new name? I'd suggest something more Islamic than 'Nilufar.' Changing names is very popular these days. It's like growing a beard or changing your shirt. Many Fereshtehs have become Fatemehs."

"So, I'll need to change my name to fit in. How about 'Massoumeh'? Very Islamic. I'm sure Auntie Zahra would love it. Massoumeh, the sister of Imam Reza, is her favorite saint."

Mehrdad grew serious again. "Nilu, this is important. If you can't do it, say so now and we'll figure out another way to protect you. If you agree, you'll need to change much more than your name. If you're going to be a Massoumeh in our crazy new world, you'll have to live and dress like one. Can you manage that?"

"Mehrdad, you know I can. I've had lots of practice thanks to Auntie Zahra's pilgrimages and mourning ceremonies."

"We'll keep most things the same. You can keep your mother's family name and become Auntie Zahra's granddaughter through her late son Yousef. It's fortunate that Zahra's late husband Mehdi, may he rest in peace, was a cousin and a Rastbin. On your education documents we'll just change the name. A lot of foreign-educated people are Islamicizing themselves, sincerely or otherwise. We Iranians are good at hypocrisy and reinventing ourselves. Look at me.

"One more detail. We'll add a husband to your ID card. We need to keep suitors away and give you at least the relative freedom of a married woman. If people think you're an unmarried girl, they'll never leave you alone. They'll want to know all about you and will monitor everything you do. We will say that you've signed a marriage contract but are waiting on the ceremony until your husband comes back from his assignment in Dubai and you can live together. We'll make him an engineer working for a contractor there.

"Any preference for your husband's name? You'll need someone Islamic. How about 'Abbas' or 'Ali Reza'?

"Too many of them. Let's try 'Hadi.' The tenth imam. Family name Reza'i in honor of the eighth."

"Hadi Reza'i it is. I like Hadi too. He's the greatest imam we've never heard of. *Mobarak basheh* (congratulations) on your marriage. And Hadi Reza'i, whoever he is, is a very lucky man."

Two days later, with her new identity card and doctored education documents, Nilufar officially became Massoumeh Rastbin, MA (UVA), born in Tehran, with Hadi Reza'i as her registered husband living in Dubai. Minu and her husband Ahmad spoke to Auntie Zahra and arranged for Nilufar to move to a vacant apartment in a two-unit building she owned off Asiya Lane in the pleasant downtown neighborhood of Amirieh. The other unit Zahra had rented to two middle-aged widows, Zeinab and Fahimeh, whose children were abroad or in the provinces. The building had an elderly doorman who did odd jobs and, while he wasn't a eunuch, made sure the women's virtue and reputations were protected.

Zahra had accepted Nilufar's new identity without question and was overjoyed that her beloved granddaughter would be staying in Tehran and living in her place. Her only question was, "Couldn't you find a real husband?" Then she answered, "Of course not. Most of our men are garbage. My late husband Mehdi, may God pardon him, was probably the best of them. But he was still garbage."

Mehrdad called her and said, "Once you are settled in, I have a meeting set up for you. I'll tell you more later."

It took Nilufar a few days to move her things and the cat adopted from the street from her aunt's place to her new apartment. She put up pictures of the Shia saints and shrines, along with some specimens of calligraphy in Arabic and Persian. The apartment was already furnished, so she had to buy only sheets, towels, a radio and TV, and a few kitchen items she found in shops on Manouchehri Avenue. She arranged with the neighboring tenants to share services of a cleaning woman. Near her apartment, located on a shady, narrow street of older homes, were small groceries, bakeries, a pastry shop, a dry cleaner, a bank branch, a mosque, a newsstand, and some sandwich and kabab shops. Her neighbors invited her to a women's devotional group in the neighborhood, where "Massoumeh's" combination of piety, religious knowledge, and Western education made an excellent impression. There was great disappointment, however, when the women – perpetual matchmakers – learned she was already married.

Everyone in that corner of Amirieh feared and respected the devout, blunt-spoken Zahra. With such a pedigree, Nilufar soon became accepted as Massoumeh, the modest and pious young woman, recently returned from studying in the US and with a husband in Dubai. Even the swaggering young men of the local *komiteh* were careful to act properly around the granddaughter of Zahra, whom they called by the honorific *haji khanom* and whom no one, revolution or not, was going to cross.

The identity change came just in time. A day after Nilufar moved out, a group from the local *komiteh* came to Minu and Ahmad's house asking about reports of "a foreign woman" someone had seen there. When Nilufar went to her aunt's for dinner, Minu told her, "A bastard of a neighbor must have snitched to the *komiteh*. I told them, 'There's been no foreigner here. You must be asking about my devout niece Massoumeh, who just returned from study in the US. She doesn't live with us but comes to visit. Please remind whoever told you this nonsense about a foreign woman to mind his own business and to stop wasting your time by being so nosy. We're very grateful that our brothers at the *komiteh* are keeping our neighborhood secure. You don't need a bunch of stupid people spreading stories about their neighbors.'"

Mehrdad told Nilufar, "Now we need to take the next step. Tomorrow I will send a car and driver for you at ten. He will take you to Ayatollah Mohammad Beheshti's office at the Constitutional Assembly. I will be waiting for you there and introduce you. Beheshti's title is vice-chairman of the assembly, but in fact he controls most everything. If he doesn't write the new constitution, he'll shape it. The chairman, Ayatollah Montazeri, is a decent man but is completely incompetent and cannot control the delegates.

"I know Beheshti from Hamburg. He was director of the Islamic Center there in the late 1960s when I served in the Iranian consulate. At the time, few people knew about our friendship. I also have a second cousin married to his nephew."

"What does he know about me?"

"He's heard about my wife's devout cousin Massoumeh recently returned from America and looking for work in Iran. I think he'll be anxious to help you find a place in the new order, which is short of educated, religious women. Women lawyers, judges, managers, teachers, journalists – tainted by the old regime – are either quitting or being purged. At the last women's rights demonstration, the thugs chanted, '*Ya ru-sari, ya tu-sari* (Either the head scarf or a crack on the head).'"

"Not a welcoming message. Obviously, the new system doesn't want them. Isn't Beheshti head of the Islamic Republican Party (IRP) as well?"

"He is. No one else has half his political smarts. He's only fifty, which makes him young for an ayatollah. He's well educated, a skilled organizer, and his IRP is on its way to dominate the new system, whatever it is. He is determined that the new constitution establishes an Islamic state as the Imam intended it, not one infected with Marxist or liberal ideas. You can read all that in his party's newspaper *Jumhuri-ye-Islami*, which I would normally use to wrap fish."

"What has he said about the hostage-taking?"

"Publicly not much. Like everyone else, he is looking for ways to exploit it. The difference is that he's always ten steps ahead of the competition. I suspect Beheshti's people are already giving orders to the occupiers and that he will steer events to his advantage. In the coming weeks and months, follow the students' communiqués and watch carefully who gets denounced."

"You're assuming it will go on that long."

"It will. Who is going to end it?"

TEHRAN
NOVEMBER 1979

The next morning Nilufar, carefully covered with a long black robe and a *maghna'eh* (face cowl), left her apartment at 9:45 and walked through the alleys of Amirieh until she reached Moayyeri Street on its northern edge. She was aware of the curiosity she aroused as a young woman newcomer in this close-knit neighborhood where everyone knew everyone's business. Now the neighbors and shopkeepers were watching to see how she walked, where she bought her bread, where she bought groceries, who she greeted, and how she spoke to whom. Between her house and the main street, it was clear from peoples' reactions that they had their orders: "Don't mess with Haji Khanom's granddaughter."

She got into the back seat of a dark-green Iranian-made *Peikan*. She smiled as she recalled the jokes about this car – a 1960s underpowered Hillman assembled at an Iranian factory. Her favorite story was how the car body collapsed whenever it collided with a donkey. "Our cars may be shit, but our donkeys are the world's toughest" was the proud conclusion.

The driver took her uptown to the old Senate building, now the meeting place of the "Assembly of Experts" who were writing a new constitution for the Islamic Republic of Iran. Mehrdad was waiting at the gate, and the two of them entered the building through separate men's and women's checkpoints. The women guards looked approvingly at Nilufar's modest dress that covered everything but her hands and face.

The day's session had not yet begun, but the building was thronged with journalists, television crews, and people talking and drinking tea. An aide escorted them to the vice-chairman's large, ceremonial office in a busy corner of the building with extra security. He then took them through a side door into a small, private office with wood paneling and flowers in vases scattered on the side tables. After a few minutes, a tall, confident Mohammad Beheshti, wearing a well-tailored robe and a neatly trimmed beard, arrived. He shut the door, ordered tea, and embraced Mehrdad saying, "We should see each other more. Friends should not let friendship slip away."

Mehrdad said, "That is true. But we all know what responsibilities you have. I have come today to introduce my wife's cousin, Mrs. Massoumeh Rastbin, about whom I have told you so much. She recently finished her graduate studies in America and is the daughter of the late Mehdi Rastbin and his wife Fatemeh. They both unfortunately died young in an auto accident. She was raised by her pious grandmother, Zahra Khanom, who is famous in Tehran as the 'sheriff of Asiya Alley' in Amirieh."

He turned to Nilufar. "May God have mercy on the souls of your parents. I welcome you home to the Islamic Republic." He did not offer to shake hands. "Mehrdad told me you were married. If you were not, we could do a *sigheh mahramiyat* (paper marriage contract) between you and my three-year-old grandson. That would make me legally your grandfather-in-law. Then we could shake hands."

Nilufar knew this form of contract. Religious families used it to create family ties and free women from the need to veil in the presence of men who, thanks to this legal fiction, were now immediate family.

"Mehrdad speaks very highly of you. It is very important that you have chosen to return to Iran at this moment. Our enemies claim we are getting rid of the educated. That's not true. We need our young, educated people, both men and women, to build this new Iran free of polluted ideas from East and West. Do you know how you want to serve the Revolution? How can I help you?"

She realized Beheshti had no need in this setting for the flowery circumlocutions so common in Iran, preferring instead to get to the point. "Thank you for receiving me, sir. I know how busy you are with the vital work of the Constitutional Assembly. I have been abroad for over six years, but I have never lost my love for Iran, Islam, and our traditions. After all my time away, and all these changes, I need to get to know my own country again. Thank God, it's not the same Iran I left. I seek your guidance about how I can help build a new, strong, healthy Iran free of foreign influence and true to its Islamic roots."

Beheshti was prepared for her request. "Bravo, my sister. I think I can help. First, stay away from the universities. They are hopeless – thoroughly infected by leftists. We may have to close them. In a few months, whenever the rowdy delegates finish writing our new constitution, I will need someone like you to help us work on relations with foreign parliaments and foreign political parties, especially those with revolutionary ideologies like ours. Mehrdad remembers the useful contacts we had in Hamburg with sympathetic German political parties and religious groups.

"In the meantime, we can use someone with your languages to join the women's *komiteh* at Mehrabad Airport. It's vital that foreign passengers entering or leaving Iran – especially women passengers – are treated professionally so they have a positive impression of our country. According to the reports I hear, that is not always the case, and a simple misunderstanding – exploited in the foreign press – can do our country's reputation great harm. This is not the most glamorous of jobs, but you said you wanted to learn about the new reality here. And you would be doing us a great favor until we can train our *komiteh* members."

By now, Nilufar was expert at obeying men's commands disguised as requests. "Sir, that sounds ideal. As I said, I'm ready to help any way I can. When do you need me at the airport?"

Beheshti rang a bell on his desk and an aide entered. "Write a note from me to Gholam-Hossein Sarhaddi at the Mehrabad *komiteh*. That will serve as sister Massoumeh's introduction. Also send Sarhaddi a copy of her identity card. Turning back to Massoumeh, he said, "My aide will give you a copy of my note. I suggest you go there in about a week.

Turning to Mehrdad, he asked, "Dear friend, what do you think?"

"Very good indeed. Of course, she's my wife's cousin so I shouldn't praise her too highly. But she is exactly the sort of educated young person we need to rebuild our country after the corrupt Shah and his cronies ruined it."

"How are things at the Foreign Ministry?"

"Difficult. This business with the American Embassy has brought a deluge of questions down on us, both from foreign governments and journalists. What advice do you have for us?"

"Well, I'm sure that our brother, His Excellency Foreign Minister Qotbzadeh, can handle the matter with his usual skill," he said, the sarcasm dripping from his words. "We can't say so publicly, but the reality is these naïve students may have saved us from a leftist putsch. The Marxists were beating the anti-American drums and they had an audience, especially among young people. We risked being outflanked and being labeled 'American agents.' We had to do something to preempt them, and the students – misguided as they were – took the initiative."

"But it's a high-risk game. If things go wrong – if a hostage is killed for example – then who knows what could happen."

"Mehrdad, it's a risk we have to take. Between us, I can tell you that I have delivered a message directly to the students from Imam Khomeini. His orders are that under no circumstances is any American to be harmed. If the students want to scream, shout, march, and denounce, well and good. All that can be useful, especially when they denounce the right people. But they have clear instructions to keep the Americans safe."

"Can they do that?"

"My assignment from the Imam is to make sure they do."

After they said their farewells and were leaving the building, Nilufar asked her cousin, "Do you think he bought the story about serving the new Iran? I hope I didn't lay it on too thick."

"You did beautifully, sister Massoumeh. I almost believed you myself. With us Iranians you can never lay it on too thick.

I'm not sure he bought it all, but I think it suits his purpose to pretend to believe it. We cannot hope for more than that."

She asked him, "How is he going to keep the students from injuring a hostage?"

He answered, "He'll never say so, but his main job is to make sure the leftists – particularly the MEK – don't infiltrate the embassy. They are his most dangerous enemies."

They rode together back to Amirieh. As she left the car he told her, "Nilufar, I will get a message to Arash in Washington. Porter will be pleased to hear about your new situation. As for what Beheshti said about the hostages, you should report that however you can. That's your job now."

WASHINGTON

Three days later, after Porter told the secretary of state about Nilufar, the secretary asked him to brief the national security advisor, the CIA director, and the secretary of defense. To draw the least attention, they met in the secretary of state's inner office. Each official was driven into the State Department's basement parking garage and then escorted by a security officer to the secretary's private elevator to the seventh floor. From there it was a few short steps to the office.

After the discreet, long-serving office assistant brought coffee, Porter began. "Gentlemen, we find ourselves, by a stroke of luck and an individual's courage, with a well-placed source in Tehran. It is close to one of the most powerful officials in the regime. If the Iranians had any idea of its existence, the lives of the source, the source's family, and even those of the hostages would be in great danger. My plan is to establish a secure reporting channel with the help of a friendly, third-country embassy in Tehran. I ask you to accept that I cannot and will not identify this source."

The secretary of state spoke next. "I support Alan's decision to pursue this source and to exploit it. I know the dangers. He has identified the source to me only in a general way," he lied. "I do have enough information, however, to know that we must pursue this opportunity. We simply cannot lose it given the stakes for our country."

The CIA director was unconvinced. "How can you trust an untested, unvetted source? We have dozens of people beating on our doors every day claiming to be close to this or that ayatollah. They claim to have inside information about the hostages and the students at the embassy. It turns out they have nothing and just want money, attention, visas, or God knows what."

The secretary of defense was next. "I don't know about the agency, but I can tell you that our covert reporting from Tehran is now zero. Our sources have gone into hiding and are terrified that the intelligence services will identify them from all those embassy documents that were never destroyed. We're desperate. The president keeps asking for information and we don't have anything worth a damn to give him."

The CIA director was still not convinced. "Alan does this source have any experience or training in clandestine work?"

"No. But it has access and a very strong cover identity. We call it "Miriam." That's a woman's name, but I won't identify it to you as either man or woman. You're right about those damn self-promoters peddling their junk and their fantasies. Miriam is not that. I wish I could tell you more, but I am asking you to take my word. We are talking about a unique source with a unique background. I'd like to set up the reporting channel as soon as possible and see what we get from it."

The national security advisor said, "We can agree that we're desperate for information from Iran and we're not getting any. Draft a memo for the president. I'll get a decision quickly. He may want a briefing, but I suspect he'll agree, and then you can go ahead and set up the channel."

TEHRAN

The following week Nilufar received a message from Mehrdad to pick up some sweets ordered in the name of Miriam Shirvani from the *Shirini-ye-Danmarki* (Danish Pastry) shop on Villa Avenue. The middle-aged female clerk gave her two kilos of mixed pastries in a exquisite box of Isfahani *khatam-kari* (inlay), saying "There's a 1000-*toman* deposit for the box, which we'll refund when you return it empty. Is this for a special occasion?"

"Yes, I'm giving a party for my uncle's wife. She has just returned from a pilgrimage to Karbala. Since the revolution it's been harder to travel there, but she was lucky. All her life she has waited to make this trip and visit the blessed shrine of Imam Hossein, the Master of Martyrs."

"May her pilgrimage be accepted. My name is Shahnaz. When you return the box you should give it only to me or to my colleague Nahid. One of us is always here. Do not give it to anyone else."

At the bottom of the sweets box she found the following note in English:

> Miriam,
>   Please know me as Sara. I will receive and send your messages through our friends at the pastry shop. When you return the box to the shop Shahnaz or Nahid will notify me to collect it. They are friends and you can trust them. There is a loose bottom in the box where we can conceal our messages. If there is any problem, I will write your name as Miryam and you should write mine as Sarah. Thank you for what you do.
>
>   Sara.
>   P.S. Mr. Porter says hello and be careful.

Two days later Porter received the following message. It had come to him via an empty sweets box, a pastry shop, an intelligence officer in a friendly embassy in Tehran, and an embassy in Washington.

> From Miriam for Undersecretary Porter,
>
> Met Ayatollah Mohammad Beheshti last week. Expect to begin working in his office within two months. In meantime will be stationed at *komiteh* at

Mehrabad Airport working at women's security checkpoint.

Beheshti said the embassy occupation was primarily an effort to block leftists' bid for power and stop them from monopolizing the anti-American ideology of the revolution. He (and by implication the Imam) view the Iranian leftists – Tudeh, MEK, FKO, etc. – as the most serious threat to the new order. He implied that if the students had not acted when they did, a more militant and more violent group would have attacked the embassy. He has given clear orders from Ayatollah Khomeini to the occupiers that the American captives are not to be harmed.

It appears that Beheshti and his allies in the Islamic Republican Party (IRP) are gaining control of the embassy occupation. They are using the event to eliminate their rivals – both leftists and nationalists – within the coalition that made the revolution. At Beheshti's orders, the students are using embassy documents to discredit the IRP's opponents.

Beheshti gave no indication when the American hostages would be released. He implied that they would remain captives until he and his faction solidify their control. He made no mention of the deposed Shah.

Beheshti is also exploiting his position as effective leader of the Constitutional Assembly to shape the Islamic Republic to the wishes and ideology of Ayatollah Khomeini and his closest followers.

My new identity and situation is working. Look forward to hearing from you.

Respectfully, Miriam.

TEHRAN AND WASHINGTON
NOVEMBER-DECEMBER 1979

In late November Nilufar – in her persona of the revolutionary and devout Massoumeh – arrived at Mehrabad Airport to begin work at the women's security checkpoint. In the airport's administrative wing, she found the *komiteh*'s dingy, unmarked office.

An unshaven, bleary-eyed, twenty-eight-year-old Gholam-Hossein Sarhaddi slouched behind a desk chewing on bread and a raw onion. Unsteady hands had spray-painted revolutionary slogans on the walls. Nilufar noticed how many of the Persian words were misspelled. Unanswered telephones rang constantly. Files overflowed from dented, rusty metal cabinets or were piled randomly on chairs, tables, and cabinets. Armed, half-bearded, teenaged Revolutionary Guards in pieces of uniforms – trying and failing to look fierce – wandered in and out and hung around the door. Flies feasted at uncovered sugar bowls and unwashed tea glasses. No one had emptied the ashtrays in weeks.

Without rising from his seat and with his mouth still full, he snapped at Nilufar in a thick Shirazi accent, "Yes, sister, what do you want?" He clearly resented her disturbing his snack. When she mentioned Beheshti and his letter, his manner became respectful. "Ah yes. Welcome, sister. I've spoken with the ayatollah's office and we're glad you can join us. I'll take you to the women's section."

He took her down the hall, knocked on another unmarked door while calling out "*Ya-allah,*" warning the women to cover themselves. This office was smaller than the first, only much cleaner and neater. The floor had been swept, desks dusted, and a steaming samovar stood on a counter with clean glasses inviting one to take tea. Files and papers were orderly and there was no army of hangers-on.

Massoumeh thought, "This is clearly an Iranian women's realm. Left to themselves, Iranian men will drown in their own filth. Most of those spoiled brats have never lifted a finger at home but leave the housework to their mothers and sisters. I pity their wives."

Sarhaddi introduced her to Nazanin Dowlatabadi, the twenty-five-year-old chief of the women's section, who gave Nilufar a comradely embrace. Nazanin was no more than five feet tall, very thin, and with dark complexion that suggested origins in Southeastern Iran. Her face and manner conveyed a fierce intensity and intelligence. Sarhaddi said, "Ms. Dowlata-badi. This is our sister Massoumeh, who comes to us with the special recommendation of Ayatollah Beheshti himself. She has just come back from studying in America and speaks perfect English."

Turning to Nilufar, he said, "Sister Dowlatabadi is a veteran of the revolution and a graduate of the Shah's prisons, where her husband was martyred. She spent four years in jail for distributing leaflets and lost two cousins during the fighting in Mashhad last January. Just a month ago a relative in the Revolutionary Guards was martyred in Kurdestan by American mercenaries. Her commitment to the holy cause is an inspiration to all of us."

"I'm honored to meet you," said Nilufar.

Sarhaddi left. Nazanin gave Nilufar a shift schedule and told her, "You can leave your coat and purse here. It's safe. Most of the time there are no men in this room, so we don't have to cover so strictly. As you saw, the men's office is a disgrace. They expect us to clean it for them, but I'll shoot any woman who touches a broom over there. We didn't make this revolution to become housemaids."

Nazanin never spoke of her history, but Nilufar soon learned more about her from the other women. She was originally from Rafsanjan, a medium-sized town of Kerman province in Southeastern Iran. Nilufar detected few signs of a regional accent in her educated speech. Before the revolution, she had been on a path to be the top graduate from Tehran University in electrical engineering. She was looking forward to a full scholarship for advanced study abroad.

At the university she and her husband Farid were part of a clandestine Islamist student group when they were betrayed and arrested. Her husband had been a member of a bomb-making team. He died in prison after two weeks of torture. He had refused to talk. A few of the guards had quietly told Nazanin how much they admired his courage. Nazanin gave birth to her son in prison, and when she came out, as a young widow, she devoted herself to raising her child and to the cause of the revolution.

Nilufar quickly mastered work at the checkpoint. She checked documents, hand baggage, and the appearance of departing and arriving women passengers. If a woman wore too much makeup, they sent her to the ladies' room with a cloth to clean her face. If a woman's outfit was too revealing, they told her to put on a *chador*, a floor-length body and head cover. Foreign passengers usually made an attempt to conform to the new rules. Many of the Iranian women, however, insisted on showing open defiance by wearing short skirts, sleeveless blouses, and heavy makeup. They did not care if anyone objected. They had a point to make.

Opposing groups of Iranian women waged daily class warfare at the checkpoint. Most of Nilufar's *komiteh* colleagues were from traditional, lower-middle-class families – daughters of conservative south Tehran shopkeepers and *bazaari*s who had been the backbone of Khomeini's revolution. Under the Shah's regime, the North Tehranis, upper-middle-class women wearing the latest European fashions, had ridiculed them and their ways, treating them as servants and labelling them backward and ignorant. In North Tehran veiled women were excluded from fashionable hotels and restaurants and treated as servants or prostitutes. Revolution or not, these "modern" women were not going to obey or conform to the standards of those they had despised for so long.

The two worlds collided at the Mehrabad checkpoint. The inspectors carried grudges from years of being mocked. Now the revolution had put them in charge and they were going to make up for all the slights they had endured. The other side was not going to admit that those they had reviled were now in control. Every day, an appalled Nilufar watched as the two sides screamed insults at one another: *jendeh* (whore), *kolfat* (servant), *bi-savaad* (illiterate), and *olaaq* (ass).

Nilufar tried to calm the storms. With her educated speech and manners she could usually pacify the angry North Tehranis, who first assumed from her appearance that she was just another spiteful zealot. Often, however, the gulf was too deep and, unable to stop the barrages of abuse, she could only let both sides vent their grievances, real and imagined.

Many of the foreign women leaving Iran were bitter and traumatized by events of the revolution. The whole country appeared to go mad and turn on them. The kind and friendly Iranians they had known had disappeared. In translating, Nilufar would alter stories to please her colleagues, telling them, "This German woman is crying because she is so sad to leave Iran. But she needs to visit a sick grandmother in Berlin. She hopes to come back soon to this beautiful country she considers home." The woman had cursed everything Iranian and had wept when describing how a mob had lynched a neighbor suspected of working for the Shah's secret police. Nilufar recalled the poet Sa'adi's sage advice: "A white lie is better than a mischievous truth."

Nilufar came to empathize with the *komiteh* women. They led difficult and complicated lives completely different from hers. Rarely educated beyond the sixth grade, they were usually married by sixteen and were now mothers of two or three small children. Their husbands had left school by the ninth grade and worked as drivers, shop assistants, or factory workers. The turmoil of the revolution had left the men unemployed or forced them into underpaid day labor. The women's modest income from the *komiteh* made them their family's breadwinners, a fact their husbands resented. They struggled with demanding in-laws, unemployed and demoralized husbands, transport, childcare, and daily searches for essential goods that would mysteriously appear and disappear from store shelves.

They came and went irregularly because of frequent family demands and emergencies. Relatives from the provinces could show up and stay for months. A doctor's appointment could consume a whole day. They stood in line for hours to buy detergent or onions. Nilufar admired their spirit and understood that their work at the airport, demanding as it might be, was a precious respite from homemaking and child-raising.

They admired Nilufar for her education, piety, mild temper, patience with difficult passengers, and her willingness to cover for their absences. They came to trust her with their problems and she became advisor on matters of finance, health, law, and family. Without hesitation they shared their most intimate secrets and complaints. They called her "Mollah Massoumeh" because she could give them opinions on whether an action was permitted under religious law. She also quietly made small emergency loans, so they could buy diapers, medicine, and formula. Among the women discussion of sex was frank. Many complained about their husbands' constant demands for sex while they were exhausted from cooking, cleaning, and taking care of children. All sought advice on stopping pregnancies, since their husbands showed no interest in taking precautions. One asked her, "When I'm having my period my husband wants to take me from behind. Is that legal?" Another complained, "My husband found a religious scholar who says that in Islam oral sex is permissible. Now that's all he wants. It's disgusting!" Another asked, "Since my husband lost his job, he cannot perform in bed. What should I do? Do I have grounds for divorce?"

Some of the women wanted divorces but needed either specific legal grounds or their husband's agreement. In the latter case, they would often need to surrender any claim to their marriage settlement – an arrangement that would leave them destitute and a burden on their struggling families.

It didn't take long for these sessions to degenerate into crude jokes about impotent men, damaged virgins on their wedding night, elderly husbands with eager young wives, lecherous mollahs, and couples with chronic gas.

When their boss, the austere Nazanin, was absent, the women competed to shock modest Massoumeh with their stories. Her colleague, Amira, who would recount her previous night's sexual adventures in colorful detail, once told the others, "We should be more discreet around her. She's very pious and still naïve and inexperienced." The others agreed, and then launched into still more explicit accounts.

Nilufar did her best to play the shy Massoumeh, preoccupied with prayers, fasts, and honoring the Shia saints. In fact, little could shock her after the frank talk of Auntie Zahra's friends. To pass the time during their pilgrimages, those women had traded stories about their own sex lives and those of the saints they were visiting. Their stories reminded Nilufar of her college English course on *The Canterbury Tales*.

Nilufar played her part well. The women accepted her performance as Miss Proper but still longed to know more about her sex life. They kept asking if she and her legal husband had already consummated their marriage or were they waiting, as was customary, for the *arusi*, the formal wedding ceremony. If they had, they wanted details. "What was it like? How many times? Was it painful?"

Nilufar blushed and deflected their questions, which only increased their interest. Amira, realizing Nilufar was not going to satisfy their curiosity, told her own story. "Once Hossein and I signed our marriage contract (*aqd*) we couldn't control ourselves. We knew we should wait, but we figured we were legal (*halaal*) to each other, so why not? We found a storage closet and went at it. Our families are both very traditional and expected to see a bloody sheet after the ceremony as evidence of my purity and my family's honor. Hossein took a fruit knife and cut himself. There was enough blood to satisfy the relatives. I loved him more after that."

In gloomy official Washington, no one was joking about damaged virgins. November became December and there were no signs of freedom for the hostages. Newscasters were counting the hostages' days in captivity and the initial unifying effect of the crisis had worn off. Competing pundits and instant experts were advising the president to "be tough" or to "listen to what the Iranians say." Khomeini had caught the mood in both countries by his defiant statement, "America cannot do a damn thing."

Porter met regularly with key officials in the White House Situation Room. On the wall were clocks set to the times of hot spots around the world. One was always set to Tehran.

"Gentlemen, you have seen the reporting from 'Miriam.' What has happened confirms what Beheshti told her a few weeks ago. It also reports the students are making selective releases of embassy documents under the title of 'Revelations from the Nest of Espionage.' Director Pearson correct me if we're wrong, but I gather the CIA sees Beheshti's hand behind these revelations."

"That's right, Alan. Our analysts see precise targeting. The students go through the embassy files, find a name of some nationalist figure and enemy of Beheshti's IRP and denounce him as an American agent. The document may be crap and the context innocuous, but it doesn't matter. Just having your name on an American document will destroy you. About two dozen officials have had to resign and some have gone into hiding, fearing arrest. Source Miriam also reports that when the students find names of IRP allies, or even of Beheshti himself, they bury the documents. It's a very sophisticated operation. They obviously have help."

The national security advisor asked, "What about the leftists? Didn't source Miriam report Beheshti's saying they were his real targets? Can or should we encourage him in that direction?"

The secretary of state answered, "I think we should. If he can weaken the left, that's less chance for the Soviets to meddle. If Beheshti isn't lying, the sooner they crush the left, the sooner they'll release the hostages. In the meantime, the president has sent a message directly to the Iranians warning them against injuring the hostages or putting them on trial. That message will reinforce what Beheshti said were Khomeini's orders."

As the meeting broke up, the national security advisor said, "Alan, the president asked me to thank you for your work with this source. He won't speak to you directly because if he does, he will ask about Miriam's identity. He doesn't want to put you on the spot. You can imagine how hard it's been for him to stay out of the details. Miriam's reporting is the one bright spot in this disaster."

WASHINGTON AND TEHRAN
DECEMBER-JANUARY 1980

Tehran and Washington are at the same latitude and early winter was miserable in both places. Snow gave momentary relief, but it quickly melted into black slush. Americans marked

Christmas and New Year's without good news, and mumbled wishes of "Merry Christmas" and "Happy New Year" failed to lift anyone's spirits. Out-of-focus videos of the hostages and visiting American clergy at the embassy just multiplied frustration and anger. Christmas parties at the State Department were especially depressing.

In December Iranians celebrate *Shab-e-Yalda* to mark the winter solstice and the hope of longer days. Senior clergymen, in their Friday sermons, denounced the holiday for its pre-Islamic origins. Nilufar and her relatives quietly gathered and ate the customary out of season cantaloupes and watermelons. "I suppose they would prefer us to weep and wail for some dead Arab," grumbled Minu.

As if to reinforce the long nights, restrictions were mounting. The authorities were closing liberal and leftist newspapers; they were making veiling compulsory and uncovered women risked attacks from gangs of thugs on motorcycles. Tehranis, who never lost their sense of humor, named these gangs "heaven's angels." The universities were scenes of open warfare between leftists and Islamists and the authorities were intervening on behalf of the latter. The embassy occupation dragged on, and Ayatollah Khomeini rejected all attempts at mediation, enjoying his role as defier-in-chief. Iranian travelers – who two years earlier were welcome everywhere – now found themselves unable to get visas anywhere.

In the United States gangs attacked Iranian students in Houston, Denver, and other cities. The American government cancelled thousands of Iranians' student visas, and those who stayed pretended to be Italian or Spanish. Speaking Persian in public was dangerous. Nilufar's uncle Arash remained at his post in Washington, but everyone knew it would not be long before the Iranian embassy was closed permanently.

Nilufar, as Massoumeh, continued her work at Mehrabad Airport. Every day she saw more chaos and incompetence. A rival militia, connected to a powerful clergyman and lured by the money to be made, ignored the existing *komiteh* and set up an extortion racket at the airport. Surly young men with automatic weapons shook down travelers, drivers, and airport employees. When negotiations failed, and international airlines threatened to end service to Tehran, Ayatollah Beheshti sent a unit of Revolutionary Guards to drive them out.

At Nilufar's station the screaming class wars continued. She heard the other women say, "For forty years they crapped on us. Ridiculed us. Why should we put up with it anymore? We made the revolution. Our brothers were martyred. Now it's our turn. If they can't accept the new ways, to hell with them. This is our country now, not theirs. We make the rules. They can leave and good riddance."

One day three veiled women loaded with baggage pushed their way through the checkpoint, ignoring the inspectors. When asked for documents they cursed Nilufar and her colleagues saying, "Mind your own business, idiots. Don't you know who we are?" Nazanin called Sarhaddi at the main *komiteh* office and learned that the women were relatives of the notorious "Sheikh Mohammad Ringo," the unstable son of Ayatollah Hossein Ali Montazeri. Sheikh Ringo (named for the "Ringo Kid" in the John Wayne 1930 movie classic *Stagecoach*) and his entourage of armed thugs bullied their way past the men's checkpoint and commandeered an Iran Air 727. They were taking suitcases of cash to allies in Lebanon. No one dared stop them. The women were along for the boutiques and nightclubs of Beirut.

On a Thursday evening in late January, the Rastbin clan gathered at Ahmad and Minu's apartment for food, cards, backgammon, and gossip, which by now was 90 percent political. Pushed by darkness, cold, and repression, Tehranis had moved their social lives indoors. Nightclubs and most cinemas were closed. In public places, self-appointed morality squads were harassing men for long hair and women on any pretext. They pestered couples to prove all was proper in their relationship.

As soon as she arrived, Nilufar took off her Massoumeh outfit and put on the Western clothes she cached at her aunt's place. Beer, wine, and vodka made their appearance. Iranian music played at low volume. Ahmad and Minu kept on good terms with the local *komiteh* but knew from experience that neighbors were always ready to inform.

Mehrdad drew Nilufar aside and said, "I have an urgent message from Porter via Arash. It's gotten difficult for them to meet. In Washington everyone is watching everyone, especially at our embassy. The whole place is in chaos. They have to make the government's case, but no one knows what it is. Imagine having to defend the hostage-taking in Washington. At the same time, many of the staff members there are looking for ways of staying in the US if they are recalled. No one in the ministry trusts Qotbzadeh. I don't know what Arash will do."

"It must be awful for him. He's a professional and a patriot. The best of Iranian diplomats. What is Porter's message?"

"He wants you to be at the airport the day after tomorrow. You need to be there early – around six a.m. That's Sunday, January 27. He didn't say why. Only that it is most urgent."

"It must be if he tells me this way and on such short notice. There's a shift that begins at four a.m. and ends at noon. I will be on it. Does he need an answer?"

"No. Our channel is not safe. It must be important if he's willing to take the risk. He said that other means were too slow."

"Any idea what it's about? Did he say anything to Arash?"

"No. Only that it's critical."

On Saturday Nilufar convinced Nazanin to adjust the women's work schedule to put her on the four a.m.-to-noon shift the next day. She told her boss, "I'm sorry for the late notice. I just learned that Ayatollah Mahdavi-Kani is giving a lecture to the Fatemeh-Zahra Women's Association in Amirieh. I don't want to miss it."

Nazanin liked the friendly and modest Nilufar, who never missed a shift and was always happy to work extra hours while the other women dealt with their personal problems. Nazanin didn't tell her that some of the *komiteh* men, including the chief Sarhaddi, had asked her to take marriage proposals to Nilufar.

Nazanin sympathized with the younger single men but reminded them that Nilufar was married to engineer Hadi Reza'i and was waiting for his return from an assignment in

Dubai. She promised them she would look for eligible girls from religious families.

Nilufar booked a taxi to Mehrabad for 3:15 a.m. Sunday morning. Her work ID took her through the guards' checkpoints, which were multiplying across the city. Passengers on international flights had to be at the airport three hours before scheduled takeoff. They needed that much time to pass through the multiple circles of purgatory run by police, Revolutionary Guards, customs, passport control, and unidentified groups that enjoyed showing their power and harassing passengers. The system – if there was a system – was designed to be the most arbitrary imaginable and to inflict maximum mental abuse on guilty and innocent alike. A passenger never knew if he would be on a flight, be sent home for some flaw in his documents, or be carted off to prison because his name – or something like his name – was on a secret list.

Just after six a.m. Nilufar heard a commotion. Her colleague Amira was shouting at two foreign women. They seemed not to understand Persian, and Amira was getting louder and angrier.

Nilufar asked, "Amira, what's going on here? Is there a problem?"

"Massoumeh, thank God you're here. Maybe you can make them understand. They don't seem to comprehend human speech. These two foreigners are on Swissair 363 to Zurich. I think they're Canadian, but something's wrong with their baggage. We should hold them for more questioning. You stay here, and I'll call the main *komiteh* office."

"What's wrong with their baggage?"

"They're carrying cameras, film, and all sorts of photographic equipment. When I ask them why, they can't understand and give me business cards I can't read. It looks like spy stuff to me. We should definitely question them."

Nilufar took the Canadian passports and looked at the two women. To her astonishment she saw Kathy Stafford and Cora Lijek, two vice-consuls from the American embassy and her former classmates from the consular course in Washington. Cora's passport belonged to "Teresa Harris" and her business card identified her as a writer for a Canadian film company called "Circle Six." Kathy's passport name was "Rachel Dewort" and her business card said she was a photographer and graphic designer.

Nilufar spoke to Cora and Kathy politely. "There is a misunderstanding here. Will you ladies please explain what you have been doing in Iran?"

The two Americans at first did not recognize Nilufar in her Massoumeh disguise. To them she was just another veiled, hostile Iranian woman. But when she spoke to them in fluent American English they looked again. Recognition became disbelief and then silence.

"Holy shit. It's Nilufar."

Keeping the tightest hold on their emotions because they knew their lives depended on it – and now so did Nilufar's – they showed no sign of knowing her. They told the cover story they had rehearsed a thousand times. They were part of a Canadian film crew scouting location shots for a Hollywood science-fiction movie.

Nilufar interpreted.

Amira, who still wanted to call Sarhaddi at the airport's main *komiteh*, asked her, "What do they say about the cameras? Why do they have all that spy equipment?"

"Amira, you were right to question them. They are with a Canadian film crew looking to shoot a space movie in Iran." Indicating some of Kathy's albums, she said, "Here are some of their shots of mosques, palaces, and parks in Tehran. It's clear they're professionals."

Amira admired the photos and seemed mollified. "They are good pictures. Ask them what they think of Iran and Iranians."

Nilufar translated as Kathy said, "The country is beautiful, the food is delicious, and the people are very kind. I'm looking forward to returning in a month to do more exploring and photography. Next time we'll visit Isfahan and Yazd to shoot desert scenery and the ancient mosques."

Nilufar said a silent "Bravo" as she duly translated the nonsense. Amira asked Kathy, "Can you take a picture of us as a memento?"

"I can do that, but I'd have to send you the print from Canada. It might be weeks or months before you have anything. I can do better. If you can pose for two minutes, I'll make a sketch. I think you'll like it."

The two ladies adjusted their coverings, and, with her pencil and sketch pad, Kathy quickly drew a picture of Amira and "Massoumeh.". She caught their expressions perfectly and in three minutes they had an excellent likeness.

Everyone hugged and made professions of eternal friendship. "Rachel" and "Teresa" promised to return soon. Amira made them promise on their next visit they would stay at her house.

As they collected their baggage and documents to continue their trek through the Mehrabad inferno, Kathy whispered to Nilufar: "There are four more of us, including our husbands. They're going through the men's side and we'll meet them at the Swissair check-in counter. We've been hiding with the Canadian ambassador for the last two months."

Nilufar told her, "I'm sure they'll make it. This place is so disorganized the Shah himself could slip through without even paying a bribe. You must not tell anyone in Washington where I am. Only Undersecretary Alan Porter knows I'm here. You can tell him if you get him alone. Otherwise you never saw me."

Cora told her, "You saved our lives. We'll protect you with ours. Good luck." She and Kathy trudged to the next stage of the gauntlet.

The next day Mehrdad spoke to Nilufar. "Nilu, you've seen the papers? They're calling the escape the 'James Bond Adventure.' Now I understand Porter's last message."

"What's happened at the ministry? Any consequences?"

"I don't think many people are upset. Everyone here hates the students and enjoys seeing them humiliated. Our minister, the ass Qotbzadeh, pretends to be angry. You know what he told ABC News? He huffed and puffed, and said, 'Canada will pay dearly for this violation of international law.' The last thing he should be talking about is international law. I can't decide if he is truly that stupid or just feigning outrage."

Mehrdad asked her, "Is everything alright at the airport?"

"So far it is. There's so much chaos they'll never figure out what happened. There will be a whitewash and they'll arrest the poor man who sweeps the floors."

Mehrdad laughed and said, "I didn't know anyone sweeps the floors. At least that's good news. In any case, it's a good time for you to move to Beheshti's office. The Constitutional Assembly has finished its work, and he needs help. I can remind him of our earlier conversation."

"I'd like a change. You know how the mollahs say, 'Every place is Karbala and every day is *Ashura*'? Well, it's like that here. For me every place is Mehrabad and every day a repeat of World War II."

PORTER

At 4:30 p.m., when what sunlight was left on a winter's day came through the windows in the undersecretary's outer office, Bill O'Donnell, the head of Diplomatic Security, and Porter sat alone. O'Donnell, a self-contained, retired US Army colonel who had joined the State Department because he had more service left in him, struggled daily to balance his natural suspicion with the need somehow to pursue American diplomacy. He participated in most meetings about the hostages, but he had not come today to celebrate the recent escape of the six Americans given shelter by the brave Canadian ambassador and his staff.

"Sir, do you know what has happened to Ms. Nilufar Hartman? Did she ever get to Iran? I am embarrassed to say we've lost track of her. She was supposed to land in Tehran after midnight on November 4. My first thought was she was caught at the embassy the next day, but her name isn't anywhere on our lists of captives. If she wasn't in Iran, by now she should have let us know where she is." O'Donnell was too smart to mention that Nilufar had gone to Iran over his objections and at Porter's insistence.

"How accurate are your captive lists, Bill?"

"They're accurate. She's the only one we can't account for. When the Iranians released the thirteen women and black employees in November, they kept only two women officers –

63

Swift and Koob – and one communicator. Hartman wasn't released then and apparently isn't there now. We're 99 percent certain we've identified everyone. There are fifty Americans, including two private citizens, at the embassy, and three camped out at the Iranian Foreign Ministry."

"Bill, I'm going to tell you some things you cannot share. With anyone. Nilufar did arrive in Tehran that morning, November 4. Her Iranian relatives met her at the airport. I am guessing the message about her arrival never reached Tehran or was overlooked in the mayhem. No one was there to meet her. So as far as we know there was no record of her at the embassy.

"That night she stayed with her relatives. The morning of the fourth she did not speak to anyone at the embassy and was not there when it was attacked. She called me several times those first days. I still have infrequent and indirect contact with her. I know that, as of two days ago, she was safe. Her parents and the leadership above me knows she's there and not captive, but no one else does. For obvious reasons we cannot talk about her."

"Shouldn't we have brought her out with the Canadian six?"

"We thought about that," Porter lied. "But getting her a fake Canadian identity turned out to be too complicated. We could have blown the whole operation." He did not mention Nilufar's role at the airport.

"What about her parents?"

"David and Farzaneh Hartman are both smart people. I've spoken to them and I'm sure they will do nothing to endanger their daughter."

"And what now? We know at least where fifty-three hostages are. But what am I supposed to do about another American diplomat hiding in Tehran?"

"Do nothing, Bill. That's what I'm telling you. She doesn't exist. Please don't ask me anything more."

"Fine. I've never heard of her. But let me tell you that we're also hearing crazy things from different sources. Things that might be related to her. First, there are stories that unidentified Iranians in Tehran gave our six "Canadians" inside help when they escaped. Second, and more worrying for me, are reports of an Iranian penetration of the department by some unknown group. It could be allies of the embassy students or leftists from the opposition. Whoever they are, they are dangerous if they find out there's a free American diplomat left in Tehran – that someone else got away on November 4 and is still there."

"Is there any sign these people – whoever they are – know about Nilufar?"

"There's nothing specific. No names or other identities. But it smells to me like someone knows or guesses something. The trouble is we have only rumors to work with."

"I agree it's bad. It's dangerous for her and dangerous for all if the Iranians can penetrate the department. Keep a close eye on this and keep me informed."

A month earlier, State Department personnel officer Edward Parsons was having lunch alone at the crowded Magic Gourd Chinese Restaurant on Twenty-Third Street near the department. As he sat waiting for his food, a striking woman, about twenty-five years old with long black hair and large dark eyes, asked if she could share his table. Parsons heard a foreign accent he could not identify. She introduced herself as Sherry, and told him she had just arrived from Greece to start a graduate program in journalism at nearby George Washington University.

She asked him about living in Washington. Where were the best and cheapest restaurants? Where were the good and bad neighborhoods? Did he have any special places he liked in Georgetown? She listened carefully to his answers and steered the conversation to his personal life. Parsons was forty years old, recently divorced, and lived alone in a bachelor apartment on Massachusetts Avenue. He couldn't remember the last time he had spoken with an attractive young woman.

She told him she was staying with a friend on Q Street Northwest near DuPont Circle, but that she needed to find her own apartment. She had been looking at places in Foggy Bottom near the restaurant, but had not found anything she liked. Parsons by this time was very much taken by Sherry and offered to help her find housing.

"That would be very kind of you," she said. It's hard being here alone and not knowing anyone. I need to get settled before classes start."

Soon he was showing her Washington neighborhoods, and taking her to dinners and movies. In a week, with his help, she found an attractive apartment in the West End near the university. A week later they were sleeping together. Parsons could not believe his good fortune. He was besotted with the exotic and enthusiastic "Sherry." He never suspected that her real name was Shahrzad, that she was Iranian, and a member of a *Mojahedin-e-Khalq* Organization (MEK) cell in the Washington area.

The MEK had spotted Parsons and, after some phone calls, discovered he worked in the Personnel Bureau of the State Department. Shahrzad's mission was to get information about the Americans at the Tehran Embassy – names, jobs, and who might be at large. After the escape of the Canadian six, there were rumors of other American diplomats hiding in Tehran.

During the uprisings of 1978, the MEK had joined Khomeini's campaign against the Shah. But Khomeini despised the group for its mixture of leftist and Islamic ideas. The group's ideology also included feminism and anti-clericalism, both anathema to the orthodox. The MEK leaders knew that, despite their part in the revolution, their political future in Iran was precarious. They were convinced the Islamists would turn on them soon.

Their plan was to infiltrate and take control of the embassy occupation. From that base, and armed with intelligence about the Americans inside and outside the embassy, they would strengthen their claim to be Iran's only true revolutionaries and anti-Americans. The current occupiers – mostly twenty-two-year-old engineering students – knew nothing about intelligence gathering and interrogation. The MEK leaders calculated that if they ran the embassy compound they could expose the whole network of American espionage in

Iran. Such a coup would make them popular heroes and immune from Islamist attacks. Even Ayatollah Khomeini would hesitate to act against them.

Shahrzad's honey trap mission was a key part of the MEK plan. On a Saturday afternoon at her new apartment, after a day of shopping, wine, and energetic sex, she asked a drowsy Parsons, "Edward dear, can you help me with a class project? We are looking at the American media and the Iran hostage crisis; but we're having trouble getting even basic information. We can't be certain how many captives there are and their names. I'm not sure where to look."

A yawning Parsons answered, "I thought all that was in the papers."

"It has been, but each account gives different numbers and different names. Nothing confirmed and nothing definite. What we need is something official we can use to reconcile conflicting stories. I thought it would be simple."

"Let me see what I can find for you. Have you asked the State Department's public affairs office?"

"Yes, and it refers us to press accounts."

"I'll get you something next week. It should be easy enough. But right now my thoughts are elsewhere."

"I don't care about your thoughts. Are other parts in working order?"

It was unthinkable for an infatuated Parsons to deny "Sherry's" request or have any doubts about her story. If alarms were ringing, he did not want to hear them. He did not know where their relationship was going and did not care. He was going to enjoy it, and do nothing to threaten his happiness.

The following Wednesday the two dined together at the West End Café. "Sherry, it's more difficult than I thought. The personnel files for Tehran are incomplete, out-of-date, or just missing. No one knows anything. I may be able to reconstruct something for you, but it will take a while. It may not be everything."

They went back to her apartment, but she seemed distant, even during sex. When he asked her why, she said, "I'm sorry. I'm worried about this damn class project. I need something next week if we're going to produce anything. It's a big part of our course grade."

Parsons didn't want anything to upset his romantic idyll, so he promised to find the records, which must exist somewhere.

A few days after their non-conversation about Nilufar, O'Donnell and Porter – with aides this time – met again. "Sir, we've had a break on those reports of an Iranian penetration. An officer named Parsons in the Personnel Bureau keeps asking about American employees in Tehran. When he can't find the files, he keeps searching. He's looking for an official list of who's there."

"Have you asked him what he's doing?"

"Not yet. We don't want to scare him. We've told our people to make promises and excuses, and to see if he persists. We've also done some checking, and we've come up with something very interesting.

"It turns out he is recently divorced, lives alone, and a few weeks ago began a relationship with a young woman named "Sherry Vassilios," who claims to be a Greek journalism student at GW. They've been spending a lot of time together at her apartment."

"Has anyone in Diplomatic Security spoken to the FBI?"

"Too soon. Right now we don't have much. They will either laugh at our suspicions or go in guns blazing and then call a press conference. Subtlety is not their style."

"At some point we'll have to tell them. They'll want to know more about this "Sherry" and if we're dealing with an Iranian spy operation."

The aides left the room and the two men spoke privately. "Bill, remember the main thing is keeping Nilufar safe. Does this Parsons have anything that could compromise her?"

"We have purged the Tehran personnel files so there's nothing for him to find. What puzzles me is who's behind him and for what purpose.

"And one more thing, sir. We checked with GW and there's no one registered anywhere called 'Sherry Vassilios.'"

"Maybe it is time we called in the FBI. Can we persuade them to step carefully and not spook either Parsons or the woman – whoever she is?"

"We can if you – and the secretary – are involved. Especially if it turns out this Sherry is Iranian or working for them. Then it becomes a counterintelligence matter."

Later that day one of Porter's staff assistants, an officer named George Arney, made a call from a pay telephone on Twenty-First Street to a prearranged number. His message was brief: Parsons is blown.

The thirty-one-year-old Arney had recently entered the Foreign Service after an eight-year career in a large Los Angeles law firm. He decided he had enough of other peoples' quarrels and took the Foreign Service examination looking for a change. Also after eight years, the gay scene in LA had become tedious. Film industry people were too flagrant for his situation at a stuffy law firm. If he were to join the Foreign Service, he had to be discreet.

Southern California had a large Iranian community and, out of curiosity, Arney went to its meetings and conferences. He enjoyed the sweets, the socializing, and the lively debates, but found he had little in common with the royalists who seemed trapped in their memories – usually fueled by opium – of betrayal and lost wealth and power. The Islamists' puritanism repelled him for obvious reasons. In Iran they were killing people like him. The nationalists struck him as hopeless intellectuals who could only write long articles and squabble among themselves over who was responsible for their country's troubles. They blamed Carter, the BBC, the Israelis, the CIA – everyone but themselves.

With the MEK he discovered a spiritual home. He found its members intelligent, well educated, and with a coherent message that combined progressive Western and Islamic thought. They were well organized, had good information about Iran's internal situation and, in his view, offered the best alternative to the clerics' religious-fascist ideology. They also believed in action.

When the State Department offered him a place in a new officer class, he immediately accepted. He concealed his homosexuality from the department's security investigators. In Washington he stayed in contact with the MEK. His first assignment after training was to Porter's office, where his energy, friendly manner, natural intelligence, and legal background made him a valued and popular colleague. He was a skilled writer and handled assignments efficiently without needing detailed guidance. As a bachelor, living on Sixteenth Street Northwest, he was always ready to put in long hours at the office.

His MEK contacts asked for reports from Porter's office, particularly on Iran and the hostages. It was never stated, but there was always the implied threat they would expose his orientation, still not accepted by the system and grounds for dismissal. He assumed the MEK had photos of him at "The Penguin" and other gay meeting places on Capitol Hill.

Porter was meticulous about security, and Arney had to be careful. By chance he learned that Porter and the diplomatic security officers had discovered Parsons' interest in the Tehran personnel files. In a breach of good tradecraft but as a sign he took as a compliment, his MEK handler had him "read-in" on "Sherry's" operation. If she were arrested and her real identity discovered, it would be disastrous for him and the organization.

Two days later, when Parsons called Sherry's apartment he heard a "line disconnected" message. Alarmed, he visited after work and saw the place was deserted. The neighbors had not seen her since the day before. Someone had seen her load her suitcases into a private car. The real estate agent said she had paid cash to break the lease and left no forwarding address. A call to the university revealed that no "Sherry Vassilios" had registered there.

The following day when Parsons came to work he found three unsympathetic diplomatic security agents waiting for him. His love affair, his career, and his whole life, were about to collapse.

TEHRAN AND WASHINGTON
FEBRUARY-MARCH 1980

The weeks dragged on. Washington remained mired in frustration. Adding to the misery was an eighteen-inch snowfall followed by temperatures in the teens. Most of the federal government shut down while an unprepared and bankrupt city left the streets unplowed for days.

In Tehran the Iranians rejected all attempts at mediation. Ayatollah Khomeini relished lecturing envoys from the UN, the Vatican, the Islamic Conference, and the Non-Aligned Movement that they should focus their efforts on persuading Washington to turn over the fugitive Shah. Never mind that he had long ago left the United States for refuge in Panama.

Porter had sent Nilufar a note of thanks when he learned how she helped Cora Lijek and Kathy Stafford escape through Mehrabad. In mid-February Porter received a message from Tehran.

> For the Undersecretary,

> Next week will begin duties in Beheshti's IRP/parliament office. His star is rising and he is now, *de facto*, the second most powerful man in Iran thanks to his control of the IRP faction in the parliament and his network of clerical allies. He is remaking Iran into a one-party state under his control.

> Beheshti is ruthless, efficient, and decisive. He closed down Iran's independent bar association and has made religious judges all-powerful. Rumors tell of his imminent appointment as chief of Iran's judiciary and chief justice of the Supreme Court. If true, he will control both the legislative and judicial branches. He overshadows the newly elected president, Abu'l-Hassan Bani Sadr, whom Beheshti has made into a figurehead. The president's chief duty now is attending sporting events.

> The atmosphere here is one of pervasive fear and intimidation. Arrests are frequent and arbitrary.

Beheshti and his allies continue to target the nationalists through the embassy students' periodic "Revelations." No one knows who will be next on their denunciation list. Iranian media give thorough coverage to every revelation and continue their vitriolic attacks against "moderates" (*miyaneh-roha*) and "liberals" (*liberalha*).

Targets include several elected MPs who have been barred from taking their seats. The crackdown has silenced almost all officials of the former provisional government, who consider themselves fortunate to avoid arrest. If Beheshti becomes head of Iran's judiciary, the repression will increase.

Groups on the left – the Tudeh, the MEK, and others – are screaming "me too," joining the denunciation of moderates, and calling for more purges, confiscations, and executions. They march in front of the US Embassy shouting, "Student followers of the Imam: Expose! Expose!" They are also demanding immediate trials and executions for the hostages.

By so doing, the leftists, particularly the MEK, are seeking both to ingratiate themselves with and outflank IRP extremists. Most observers estimate that Beheshti is cynically using these leftist groups and will turn against them when he is ready. First, however, he will use the leftists to destroy the moderates.

On personal level, all is well and identity remains secure. Look forward to your next message.

Best wishes, Miriam.

In early March, Iranians begin preparations for their New Year (*Nowruz*) celebrations, welcoming the first day of spring. It once was a time of family gatherings, picnics, travel, school holidays, new clothes, and gifts for children. In 1980, however, it was a time of fear, arrests, executions, and simmering unrest. Hope had vanished that Iranians would see normal life return after the revolution, now over a year old.

On Thursday evenings, the Rastbin family continued its custom of gathering at Ahmad and Minu's apartment. Even with *Nowruz* approaching, there was little to celebrate. Moods were dark. Everyone reported purge committees meeting at their schools and workplaces; everyone waited for the next axe to fall. They told stories of friends and neighbors leaving for Europe or the US without telling anyone. Students and teachers reported clashes between leftists and Islamists in high schools, and authorities announced plans to close the universities and carry out a "cultural revolution" to cleanse them of pernicious (i.e., leftist and Western) ideas. All expected parliamentary elections in March to cement IRP control.

With the nationalists losing their last footholds, Nilufar's younger relatives, including her cousins Babak, Iraj, and Sima, spoke favorably about the MEK. Their talk angered Minu, who warned them, "You children stay away from those people. They're dangerous. Don't trust them."

Iraj answered, "At least they're fighting the *akhunds*," using a pejorative term for clerics. "Who else is doing that? The National Front is finished. The Freedom Movement is finished. Should I join their pitiful rallies so Hezbollah thugs can beat me up? Or should I grow a beard, finger my beads, and become a thug myself? Should I go into the street with a club and bash women while shouting 'Hezbollah is the only party; Khomeini is the only leader?'"

Ahmad told the young people, "Minu is right. The clerics and the IRP may be scum, but Rajavi and his MEK are worse. Do you seriously think things would be any better if those crazies were in charge? Now the clerics execute ten or twenty at a time. The MEK would execute thousands. All of us here would be dead or starving in some gulag."

Iraj was not convinced. "How bad can they be? I'll support anyone who promises to hang the clerics with their own turbans."

A gloomy Mehrdad took Nilufar aside for a private talk. "Look at our young people," he told her. "Look what they're driven to. In one way they're right. If they care about freedom, democracy, and justice, what choices do they have? It's especially nasty for women. How can they support a system that takes away all their rights?

"I've spoken to Beheshti's office. They're expecting Massoumeh Rastbin there on Sunday. I imagine you'll be happy to leave Mehrabad."

"I will be, but sad too. I've become fond of the women working there. You cannot imagine what they put up with and how strong they are. Don't look at our lives. Theirs are completely different. It's hard to listen to their stories without crying. Theirs is the Tehran of the slums of *Meidan-e-Shoosh*. Ours is the Tehran of comfortable villas in Yousefabad. We live on different planets. And with all their problems, they somehow keep their dignity and integrity. This has been their revolution, but it's hard to see that it's made their lives better."

"Nilufar, you need to get out of the airport. Someone will start asking questions about how the six Americans escaped. They'll be looking for scapegoats. I'll pick you up next Sunday morning and take you to Beheshti's headquarters."

WASHINGTON

In Washington Bill O'Donnell was briefing the deputy secretary of state and senior department staff about Parsons and the Tehran personnel files. He told them, "As far as we can tell, Parsons was just a lovesick fool who fell into a honey trap. He says he never suspected anything, and believed, or wanted to believe, her story about being a Greek journalism student. He could no more say 'no' to her than he could fly to the moon."

The undersecretary for administration asked, "So who was she? What do we know about her?"

"That's the frustrating part, sir. We don't know. She signed a lease for her apartment in the name of 'Sherry Vassilios' and paid cash. The utilities were all with the landlord. We cannot find any other record or document with that name. Not a bank account, not a credit card, not a driver's license, not a passport. Nothing. We don't even have a picture. Parsons never took a picture of her and there are no pictures of the two of them together."

"So is she Iranian?"

"We strongly suspect so, but we don't know for certain. Before she disappeared we hoped to find out who she was working for. Somehow she smelled trouble and vanished."

Porter asked, "So how did she know to disappear? We hadn't said anything to Parsons. He insists he didn't suspect anything. If he didn't tell her, who did?"

"That's exactly the problem. I believe Parsons when he says he didn't know we were on to him. Someone else in the building must have warned her and told him nothing."

"Who knew we were investigating him?"

"Not many people. There was a small task force in DS (Diplomatic Security), this group, and the secretary. The director general and one or two people in personnel as well."

The deputy secretary told the group, "We have someone inside who is hostile who could learn about a confidential investigation and warn the target. Now we don't know who 'Sherry' is, why she wanted the files, and who she is working for. Bill, this must be highest priority. We have to stop this penetration. Have you spoken to the FBI?"

"I've asked for their help in identifying 'Sherry.' The trouble is, we have almost nothing to give them beside descriptions from Parsons and others who saw her. 'A striking young woman of Middle Eastern or Mediterranean appearance with this alias' doesn't narrow the search. By now she could be a blonde Finn."

As the meeting broke up, Porter pulled O'Donnell aside and asked, "Is there any possibility they're looking for Nilufar? Could they find out about her?" I assume her name isn't in the files. If this is an Iranian penetration and they learn about her, she will be in deep trouble."

"Sir, I think we should bring her out now. Someone knows something. Some group has spies in the department, and as long as we cannot figure out who they are or what they know, it's too dangerous for her to stay."

"Bill, I take your point. Let's wait. In Tehran she'll be working next to someone with the power to keep the hostages alive and eventually set them free. I don't want to lose that advantage unless we have to. Without her, we're totally blind. We need her there and we'll have to take the risk."

Before O'Donnell could object, Porter asked him, "I need an honest answer. Do we have any evidence that whoever is working against us here is searching for Nilufar?"

O'Donnell knew Porter had made his decision: Nilufar would stay in Tehran. "We do not. We've done everything possible to protect her. We've been working with the personnel bureau to make sure no one has access to the Tehran records. I made sure her name was not in the files."

O'Donnell asked, "Other than the two of us, sir, who else knows about her?"

"Only you and I know who and where she is. The secretary, the deputy secretary, and the other senior members of the NSC know only that we have a well-placed source called 'Miriam' in Tehran. They're addicted to her reports. That's what they know. Even the president hasn't asked who Miriam is. I'm sure he's dying to know."

To Miriam,

Congratulations again on your superb work with the escape of the Canadian six. Your quick thinking prevented catastrophe. The success provided a much-needed boost to sagging spirits here.

Your reports have a devoted following in Washington. There is endless demand and very little supply of reliable information. We look forward to knowing what you learn in Beheshti's office, particularly what relates to the fate of our hostages.

The hostages dominate the news here to the point of hysteria. There have been ugly anti-Iranian incidents. You should know that the president has sent repeated messages to the Iranians warning them of serious consequences if they put any hostages on trial. Can you learn how his messages are received?

Are there any signs that revolutionary hysteria is dying down? Is there any easing of repression against the press, political parties, and women? What is the status of the revolutionary courts and the summary executions?

Also of great interest are the authorities' plans, if any, to crack down on leftist groups, particularly the MEK. We understand that while the MEK refrains from criticizing Khomeini, it is increasingly critical of the IRP and Beheshti. We would appreciate your view of the power struggle and its likely outcome. From press reporting it appears that the MEK can mobilize large numbers of supporters for its anti-IRP rallies.

We are also witnessing a growing war of words between Saddam and Khomeini. How far is Iran prepared to take its disputes with Iraq?

We are doing everything possible here to protect your identity. You should watch for any signs you have been compromised.

With best wishes, Porter.

4

BEHESHTI

TEHRAN AND WASHINGTON
FEBRUARY-MARCH 1980

In March Nilufar began work in the "Foreign Relations" section of Ayatollah Mohammad Beheshti's office at the Islamic Republican Party. She dealt with correspondence to and from foreign officials and foreign political parties. She scheduled visits from delegations of "progressive" parties from Cuba, South Yemen, Bulgaria, North Korea, Algeria, Tanzania, Guinea, and Albania. There were visitors from fringe groups in Germany, France, and Italy. She arranged for these visitors to meet Beheshti or another IRP representative. A separate office worked on relations with groups in Lebanon and Palestine.

Although Beheshti spoke English, in official meetings he spoke Persian. Nilufar interpreted and took notes. Beheshti was a good listener and an articulate speaker. He was especially interested in learning from the experiences of one-party states: how these parties achieved power; how they kept it; how they maintained internal discipline; and how they dealt with opposition.

Beheshti quickly recognized Nilufar's talents. He was always polite, correct, and solicitous of her family. In informal settings he addressed her as "*dokhtaram* (my daughter)." He asked about her experiences at Mehrabad, and she told him, "Sir, I need to thank you. It was amazing working there. I learned so much. I understand now how much we needed revolution and how much remains to be done. Rebuilding our society will not be easy."

"Yes, the Pahlavis' repression and corruption did enormous damage. They cut ancient links between education and religion, especially for women. We are a well-educated people, but now we don't have nearly enough educated and believing young women to serve the country as you are doing. Too many young people are brainwashed. They call us 'reactionaries' and believe it is possible to unite Marxism and Islam under slogans of social justice. What nonsense! Islam already advocates the purest form of social justice."

Nilufar understood Beheshti's goal: to prevent foreign parties from backing Iranian leftists in the ongoing power struggle. He needed to refute the accusation that the IRP was reactionary. To foreign visitors he praised the anti-colonialist struggles of Cuban, Algerian, or Guinean "brothers" and stressed his party's progressive credentials. He carefully avoided using the Persian *rafiq* (friend), which Iranian leftists had adopted to mean "comrade."

Beheshti knew his history and was sure that foreign Marxists would in the end sell out their Iranian comrades if doing so served a larger national interest. That is what Stalin had done in 1946, sacrificing Iranian Azeris to gain an oil concession for the USSR.

Nilufar's reports to Porter had a small but devoted readership in Washington. Fewer than ten people, including the president, saw the full text of her messages. Others read redacted versions without details that might reveal her identity or location.

Porter met weekly with a group of senior officials who read her messages. At one of these meetings, the national security advisor reported that the president had asked him to pursue the idea of helping Beheshti's anti-leftist campaign. "He told me he is concerned that the MEK and others are continuing to gain support while hiding their real identity behind a religious façade. He's also worried they will make a grab for control of the hostages."

"We should be careful," the secretary of state told the group. "The leftists already accuse Beheshti and the IRP of being American and Zionist agents. It's farfetched, but in Tehran today nothing is too crazy. If anyone gets a whiff of our involvement, the leftists will end up stronger than ever."

The CIA director supported the president's idea. "I've spoken to my best operations people. They suggest that Miriam pass Beheshti intel on the MEK in a way that conceals the American source. We can help him eliminate a Soviet-sponsored group and consolidate his power. The sooner he does both, the sooner we'll see the hostages freed. Once Beheshti eliminates his rivals, he has no reason to hold our people."

Thinking of Nilufar's cousin Mehrdad at the Iranian Foreign Ministry, Porter said, "I think we could do that. If we do proceed, I will ask Miriam about creating a channel to Beheshti. If he suspects this information comes from Washington, that's not necessarily bad. But we should expect no thanks or immediate payback. He still distrusts us and is convinced we are plotting to topple the Islamic Republic. He will assume we are helping him for our own malign purposes."

Turning to the CIA director, he asked, "Sir, how good is our intel on the MEK? Will it help Beheshti?"

"It's pretty damn good. We have telephone intercepts that include plans, locations, and personnel. Until now we haven't shared anything with the Iranians under a 'plague on both your houses' policy. Alan, once Miriam gives us the OK from Tehran, we can put the information in a form to pass on."

The plan was too sensitive to trust to the friendly embassy's transmission service. Instead, Porter asked Arash to meet him at the Zebra Room.

Porter recognized the signs of stress. Arash hadn't slept well for weeks; he smoked continuously; and his chin stubble and Islamic fashion added to his skid row appearance.

"It's getting harder to do this. At the embassy everyone is watching everyone. Some employees have orders to return to Tehran and can't decide whether to go or stay. If they stay, what do they do? Drive a taxi? Open a sandwich shop? If they go, will they be jailed or worse? I'm not sure why we are still here and why you Americans haven't just kicked us out."

Porter described the plan to pass intelligence on the MEK to Beheshti through Nilufar. "We cannot ask her directly. Can you use contacts in Tehran? She can respond 'yes' or 'no' through our regular channel without providing details."

A few days later, at the Rastbins' regular Thursday gathering, Mehrdad told Nilufar. "Beheshti is very pleased with your work. Of course, I knew he would be."

"He's incredibly cynical and his views are appalling, but you have to admire his political skill. With the foreign visitors, for example, he tones down religion and talks about how the Islamic Republic is so progressive and anti-imperialist. I wouldn't want to be his enemy."

Mehrdad described Porter's request.

"How can I do this? If I'm directly involved, it won't look right."

"I agree. Why would the innocent Ms. Massoumeh be doing this? Who is she working for? If Porter sends you the material, you can translate it. I'll arrange the delivery."

Mehrdad said, "But if I start meeting Beheshti regularly, it will look suspicious. There's a young man, Hossein Niku, in his office who was at the Hamburg Center with Beheshti when I was there in the consulate. I did him some favors. Give me the translated messages when we meet here at Ahmad's. I'll get the messages to Beheshti through Niku. Then you are less exposed. All you will have done is translate."

"Yes. Even better that I have no contact with this Niku. Will Beheshti know the source of his information?"

"He'll suspect. I think Porter wants him to. Never underestimate Beheshti. He may realize you and I are involved somehow. I just hope what the Americans send is good enough. If they feed him junk, the whole plan will collapse, and you and I will be in serious trouble."

TEHRAN AND WASHINGTON
SPRING-SUMMER 1980

Nilufar did not receive her first message for Beheshti until mid-April. By that time Tehran and Washington were close to war.

A complicated US/UN/Qotbzadeh plan to release the hostages had collapsed in March. In early April the State Department notified the Iranian *chargé d'affaires* in Washington that the US was breaking diplomatic relations and that he and his colleagues should close the embassy and leave the country. In response, angry demonstrators flooded Tehran streets near the US embassy. Loud MEK rallies celebrated both Foreign Minister Qotbzadeh's failure and the break in relations and claimed vindication for their organization's uncompromising anti-American stand.

Nilufar gave the first translated message to Mehrdad, who passed it to Niku. She did not know the message had been the center of a bureaucratic battle in Washington. The CIA's first version was nothing but outdated generalities about the MEK and other leftist groups both in Iran and the US. As operational intelligence, it would have no value to Beheshti.

Porter knew that to justify the danger to Nilufar, the information had to be valuable enough for Beheshti to maintain the channel. With the backing of the secretary, he refused to send the first version, telling Armin Foster, his CIA counterpart, that he would close the channel before endangering Miriam. "Why do you assume Iranians are stupid? What is the point of insulting Beheshti's intelligence? He is in a fight to the death with the MEK. Whatever we send will be useless unless it helps him win that fight."

Foster mumbled something about "testing Beheshti's intentions in a first message" and "having alternatives in Iran." Porter blew up. "We're long past that point. If you still have any hope for the monarchists or the nationalists, forget them. This is not a test of Beheshti. He's the second most powerful person in Iran and the man who gives orders to the students at the embassy. Remember too, Beheshti is young, still in his fifties. When Khomeini dies, this man will probably replace him.

"If Beheshti, for some reason we don't understand, can't or won't use our material, so be it. But if we believe Miriam, he is ready to begin full-scale war against the MEK, whom he sees as a direct threat to him and the Islamic Republic. If your material is as good as the director says it is, let's use it."

Porter rejected second and third versions of CIA messages. Finally, he and the secretary convinced the president that, with other possibilities for the hostages' freedom blocked (and with US presidential elections seven months away), the administration had to take the risk of supporting Beheshti against his enemies. The fourth version of the message finally reached the Villa Avenue pastry shop.

Just after the message for Beheshti left Washington, Porter and Arash met again at the Zebra Room. Arash looked worse than the last time. He told Porter, "Well, at the embassy we were wondering what took you so long to break relations. You could talk all you want to our Foreign Ministry and nothing would happen. The embassy here was just decoration."

"What about you and your family?"

"Alan, you will have noticed that we Rastbins are survivors. I was never associated with the monarchy, so for the moment I should be fine. Our cousin Mehrdad has used his connections with Beheshti very well. I have orders to transfer to our UN Mission in Geneva."

"After you get there, let's stay in contact. I'll find an excuse to come to Geneva."

"That should work, but let's be careful. Give me time to learn my way around the mission."

"Of course. What news of Nilufar?"

"All I hear is good. I don't know if she has fooled Beheshti with her 'pious Massoumeh' act, but she seems to have convinced everyone else. Even our relatives don't know what to make of her transformation. With Beheshti, though, you never know what deep game he is playing. Nilufar reminds me more and more of her mother, my sister. She's smart, shrewd, tough, and adaptable. Iranian women have special sets of genes that make them so strong."

For the Undersecretary,

Message passed to Beheshti. His campaign against the MEK is gaining speed and a showdown is near.

The MEK attacks him and the IRP, but still refers to Khomeini as "dear father."

Khomeini himself, however, is openly criticizing the group. He likens them to the Qur'anic *monaafeqin* or "hypocrites," the seventh-century Medinans who stabbed the prophet Mohammad in the back while pretending to be his followers.

Beheshti will move carefully. He has no illusions about his own popularity and understands he faces deep reservoirs of opposition to his vision of the Islamic Republic. MEK rallies, despite harassment, attract large crowds and the group's newspaper *Mojaahed* has a much larger circulation that the IRP organ *Jumhuri-ye-Islami*. But the MEK leadership sees what is coming and is moving its publications and its university cells underground.

The divided left plays into Beheshti's hands. The traditional Communists (Tudeh) and the "majority faction" of the Maoist *Fedayan-e-Khalq* organization (FKO) have supported the IRP and its policies. In return Beheshti has left them alone. In private, however, he hints of turning on them as soon as he has dealt with the MEK.

When the showdown with the MEK comes, it will be very violent. No one is in a mood to compromise.

As for the hostages, Beheshti privately expresses frustration and disgust with the embassy students, whom he calls "naïve zealots". He resents the fact they have pushed him and Khomeini into a corner and left them with no choice but to support their action.

Whatever his personal views of the students, he still uses them to solidify his power and crush opposition to the IRP. For example, he was very pleased when the students humiliated Foreign Minister Qotbzadeh over the aborted UN mission. Although he remained silent on the mission, Beheshti encouraged the hostility between Qotbzadeh and the students.

We are unlikely to see any movement toward freeing the hostages until Beheshti and his allies gain total control of the Iranian state and feel secure in their position. Until then the hostages are too useful to be let go.

With respect, Miriam

A few days later, headlines reported eight American servicemen had died in the Iranian desert during a failed attempt to rescue the hostages. Arash interrupted his packing to call Porter for an urgent meeting where he told him, "Beheshti is furious. Not at the Americans for staging the mission – he can understand that – but at the embassy students for bringing our two countries close to war.

"There is a good side to all this misery. Whatever he says in public, Khomeini understands the danger and is seeking a way out of the crisis. It may take him a few months, but he'll act as soon as he has a pretext to start settlement talks. As for Nilufar, Arash tells me she was very depressed at the news. She feels simultaneously relieved and guilty that you did not ask her to do anything to support the mission. There was an appalling scene at the crash site when that madman Khalkhali exposed the burnt American bodies and then spat on the remains. Nilufar can't get that out of her mind. Neither can I. What a disgrace!"

TEHRAN
SUMMER 1980

"Miriam's" predictions were accurate. Over the following months, Beheshti moved ahead on two fronts. The flood of "Revelations from the Nest of Espionage" continued to target Iranian nationalists, whom the students and their allies condemned as "accommodating liberals." These exposures hung over the head of anyone who might have had any contact – however innocuous – with the American Embassy in the previous twenty years.

On his left flank, Beheshti mobilized a network of Friday prayer leaders, Imam's representatives, and other senior clerics to denounce the MEK. When words were not enough, street gangs under control of the clerics did the direct work of bashing and crashing.

On Tuesday evenings Nilufar attended meetings of the Amirieh "Sisters of Zeinab," a pro-IRP women's Islamic association in her neighborhood. When she invited Beheshti to address the group on the anniversary of the death of the Eighth Imam, thousands of women filled the hall and the surrounding streets. Loudspeakers carried his remarks to those unable to find places inside.

Beheshti was spellbinding. "In the name of God, the compassionate, the merciful. Dear believing and revolutionary sisters. Sisters of the blessed Zeinab, peace be upon her. On behalf of Imam Khomeini, leader of the revolution and hope of the dispossessed of the world, I salute you. You have made this revolution in the name of Islam, in the name of justice, and in the names of Ali and Fatemeh, the blessed daughter and son-in-law of the prophet, peace and blessings upon him and his family.

"Tonight we mourn the martyred Imam Reza, the eighth imam, and his family. We remember his sister the blessed Massoumeh, peace upon her, and his martyred brothers, Ahmad, Mohammad, and Hossein, all buried in Shiraz. May God have mercy on them all and illuminate their blessed shrines.

"But we do more than weep. I quote our leader, our imam: 'People call us a nation of tears. But with those tears we have overthrown an empire.' From your tears – the symbols of our unity and faith – came the strength to resist the infidel Shah, his secret police, and his army, all backed by the great powers of the world.

"Today our tears and our mourning give us the strength to resist those enemies who would destroy our revolution and insult the memories of thousands of martyrs. These tears give us the strength to confront the plots of America, Russia, Britain, and Israel."

Someone in the crowd shouted, "*Marg bar Amrika, marg bar Showravi!* (Death to America, death to the USSR!)" The crowd took up the cry.

"Our enemies call us reactionaries. Our enemies say we oppress women. They say we will take you back to the dark ages. Dear sisters, you know better. Where does Islam say women should be ignorant and exploited? You know Islam takes us on the path of enlightenment. It gives you rights as perfect human beings. Islam says you should be educated and contribute to society both as mothers of our children and more. I ask all of you here: go and study in schools that safeguard Islamic values. We are cleaning the old, corrupt schools and are making them safe for believers like you and your daughters. Become teachers, scholars, scientists, engineers, and doctors. If you need to study abroad, go. Did not our wise prophet himself say, 'Seek knowledge, even if you must go to China to find it?'

"You, my dear sisters, are the true heroes of Islam and the revolution. You marched shoulder-to-shoulder with your brothers until the Shah's army, with all its sophisticated American equipment, turned against its commanders. You put on Islamic clothing and observed Islamic modesty as a protest against the Shah's attempt to turn you into copies of the corrupt and decadent West, where women are no more than debased objects putting their bodies on display. Your message was clear: 'You will not turn us into dolls and playthings.'"

There was another shout from the crowd, "*Marg bar bihejabha* (Death to uncovered women)."

"Today America, Britain, Russia, and Israel are all our enemies. Their leaders are like the cursed caliph Yazid, whose men slaughtered Imam Hossein, the master of martyrs, and his followers at Karbala. We oppose them all. We are confronting them directly and also helping our Moslem brothers defy them in Lebanon, Palestine, Eritrea, and Afghanistan. May God give victory to our just struggle against world oppression and arrogance."

There were shouts of "*Aamin.*"

"But we face even more dangerous enemies among ourselves. Our blessed prophet, peace and blessings upon him and his family, could easily defeat the ignorant, greedy pagans of Mecca and their false idols of wood and clay. More threatening to his holy mission were the hypocrites of Medina. They pretended to accept his message all the while conspiring to stab him in the back."

Beheshti paused and told the crowd, "We will not allow the descendants of those hypocrites to destroy our revolution. Our patience has ended. How much forbearance? How much tolerance?

"I am announcing today a cultural revolution. Our universities will remain closed from this next fall term until we can convert them from centers of Western and Marxist deviance into centers of true Islamic scholarship. We need to educate our young men and women in the correct path of Islam. We will root out the Marxists and hypocrites who have built vipers' nests in our centers of learning."

The crowd shouted, "*Marg bar monaafeqin; dorud bar Khomeini* (Death to the hypocrites; long live Khomeini)."

"We will do more. We will have no patience with those mini-groups who under various disguises wage war against us. We will no longer tolerate those who pollute pure Islam with godless atheism and bankrupt Marxism. We will no longer tolerate those who threaten, insult, and even assassinate our pious clerics. We will close their centers; we will shut down their papers; and we will stop their marches and demonstrations.

"Islam always counsels mercy. It seeks to convince by peaceful means, and shows others the true path. Those who renounce their false beliefs, we welcome back to Islam with open arms. But to those who persist in error we will show no mercy. By God, I will denounce even my own children if I find them among the hypocrites. They are worse than the agents of the Americans and worse than those who plot to bring back the Shah. They are snakes and wherever we find them we will strike off their heads."

Again the crowd shouted, "*Marg bar monaafeqin. Dorud bar Khomeini.*"

"So, dear sisters, continue your struggle. Continue it with tears, with demonstrations, with marches, and by all your efforts to ensure the victory of our revolution and of all the oppressed peoples of the world – in Palestine, Afghanistan, or wherever they are. May the peace and the blessings of God be upon you."

TEHRAN
SUMMER 1980

Beheshti's speech signaled a brutal campaign against the MEK. Using CIA-supplied intelligence, squads of heavily armed revolutionary guards raided safe houses, arms depots, and clandestine printing plants. The authorities identified key MEK operatives and turned them into informers. Those arrested were interrogated and revealed plans and betrayed comrades. Some, showing obvious signs of torture, confessed on state television to plotting sabotage and assassinations. Others confessed to being agents of this or that foreign country. The revolutionary courts oversaw rapid trials and even more rapid sentences. Tehran's Evin prison was overflowing. Those who would not repent were executed.

Beheshti never said anything to Nilufar or Mehrdad about his flow of new intelligence. But it was obvious he was making good use of it. In a few weeks the campaign had driven the MEK to the margins and made its leaders hunted fugitives.

The same evening Beheshti spoke in Amirieh, a soft-spoken, bespectacled officer from the Revolutionary Guards' intelligence service visited Sarhaddi and Nazanin at the Mehrabad Airport *komiteh*. He told them, "We're investigating one of your former employees. But you must both keep this quiet. We're curious about a certain Massoumeh Rastbin, who worked here for a few months last winter. She was here when the six Americans escaped using false Canadian documents. What can you tell me about her?"

Sarhaddi sensed trouble and answered cautiously, "Not much. She came with an introduction from Ayatollah Beheshti. She worked at the women's checkpoint for a few months and then transferred to his office. Ms. Dowlatabadi here is head of the women's section and was her supervisor."

Nazanin said, "She was a good worker, although it was clear from the beginning she wouldn't stay long and would be taking on other responsibilities. She is well educated, from a good family, and extremely pious. She was skilled at defusing confrontations and was very effective both with the passengers and her coworkers, who respected her. You can talk with them. Some are still here. They worked closely with her."

"Perhaps later," the officer answered. "For the moment please keep this matter to yourselves."

Sarhaddi asked, "What can you say about the investigation?"

"We have found inconsistencies about Ms. Rastbin. Her identity card says she is a daughter of the late Yousef Rastbin, son of Zahra and her late husband Mehdi. But we have no evidence that confirms Yousef had such a daughter. Yousef's other children are scattered abroad and in Iran, and we haven't spoken to them. We also found that about six months ago someone reported to the *komiteh* in Yousefabad that a 'foreign woman' was living at Minu Rastbin's apartment. When the guards investigated, they were told the woman was the same Massoumeh Rastbin, recently returned from study abroad."

Sarhaddi now sensed opportunity. Still carrying a grudge from his rejected proposal to Nilufar and always ready to ingratiate himself with authority, he judged it time to pile on. He told the officer, "I always thought there was something wrong. She was too perfect. Too religious. She must have been up to something. I always asked myself, 'Why would someone with her education and background want to work here?'"

Nazanin said nothing, but thought, "What a piece of devious scum! He'd rat out his grandmother if there were profit in it. Was my husband tortured to death so filth like him could throw his weight around?"

Nazanin knew what she had to do. The next day she went to Nilufar's Amirieh apartment and told her about the officer's visit. "You know, Massoumeh, this has nothing to do with security. Our men here are insanely jealous of any smart, educated, and successful woman. They'll grind us down any way they can.

"Most of them can't help it. They were brought up that way. If they can't blacken our morals and our character, they'll hurt us in other ways. My husband, may God have mercy on his soul, was one in a million in that way. He always supported me even when his backward relatives criticized him. I am doing my best to teach our son Amir to follow his path. I hope your husband is half as good."

"As far as I know he is. Otherwise I never would have said 'yes' when he proposed. What do you think is going on?"

"Massoumeh, people are jealous of you, your family, your education, and your connection to Beheshti. I regret this revolution hasn't always brought out the best in us. That snake Sarhaddi is not only jealous, he's still fuming that you turned down his marriage proposal. It didn't matter to him that you had already signed your marriage contract. His precious manly pride is damaged because someone rejected such a gift to women. All that makes him dangerous.

"You know he got his job only because he's a nephew of Ayatollah Abd al-Hossein Sarhaddi, the Friday prayer leader of Shiraz. Most of the Sarhaddis are well-educated, enlightened people, but the ayatollah and his nephew are exceptions – fanatic, self-righteous, and full of resentment against their better-educated relatives. The story is that the ayatollah is the son of a temporary wife and full of resentment against the rest of the family."

"What should I do?"

Nazanin quoted a proverb, "Let those who cannot bear seeing this go blind. You are better than them. Just keep being better. On the other hand, rumors and innuendo can be deadly. You might need to have Beheshti intervene. He can put a stop to the whole thing."

"Nazanin, dear. I don't know how to thank you. May God bless you and the soul of your late husband. May God preserve you for your dear son Amir. I saw him when you brought him to work. *Ma'sha'allah*, he's a beautiful boy! He'll have the strength and brains of his wonderful parents."

"Don't thank me, Massoumeh. I'm doing this as much for myself as for you. If we don't stop people like Sarhaddi, what was the point of the revolution? Why did I spend all that time in prison? If they can do what they want, then all our sacrifices will have been a waste. I for one will not let that happen. I can take care of myself, but I will not let them treat you or any believing Moslem woman like an ignorant maid."

At the next Thursday night family gathering, Nilufar told Mehrdad about her conversation with Nazanin. He frowned and said, "It could be nothing, but we can't ignore it. We need Beheshti to stop it. Let me take care of that. You should tell Porter as well. He needs to know if anything threatens your safety."

She asked him, "What is happening with the MEK material?"

"You've seen how Beheshti's campaign is moving ahead. As soon as they set up a safe house somewhere, the Revolutionary Guards are on them. It doesn't take long for our people to get the information they need from those they capture. These interrogators are good at their jobs."

"Does Beheshti know the source of his intelligence?"

"He almost certainly does. More reason to stop the investigation against you. The intelligence is too valuable. He knows the US expects some reciprocal gesture even if his campaign also serves US interests. What he'll do and when I don't know, but I wouldn't be surprised if it involved the hostages."

A few days later Nazanin and Nilufar met at a women's religious event. Nazanin, who was usually all business, had a big smile as she told Massoumeh that Sarhaddi was terrified after the Guards' intelligence officer visited again. "In front of me, he told Sarhaddi that Rastbin investigation was closed and that under no circumstances should he express any opinions on the subject. He should keep his nose out of security matters that did not concern him. The snake later begged me to forget what he had originally said against you."

TEHRAN
SUMMER 1980

Beheshti's successful and brutal campaign against the MEK convinced Washington to increase the flow of intelligence. Throughout the summer the Revolutionary Guards inflicted serious damage on the organization. Armed squads raided safe houses and weapons caches. They hunted down members at their homes, schools, and workplaces. Pro-IRP gangs attacked MEK marches and demonstrations. With universities closed, cells there collapsed. Other gangs attacked clandestine printing presses and wrecked newsstands that sold the newspaper *Mojaahed*. In sermons, rallies, and speeches, clerics continued to denounce the MEK as infidels, hypocrites, atheists, and foreign agents.

In desperation the MEK struck back with assassinations and bombings, many of them suicide missions. It placed bombs in *komiteh* offices, Revolutionary Guard posts, and offices of the security services. It assassinated senior clerics, such as powerful Friday prayer leaders in the major provincial towns, including Sarhaddi's uncle in Shiraz. The authorities retaliated with fury, and the numbers of those arrested rose into the thousands. When family members came to collect the bodies of the executed, prison officials presented bills for the bullets.

From friends and relatives, Nilufar heard alarming reports of random arrests, torture, and mass executions. Even distributing leaflets could be fatal. The most graphic stories were of teenage girl prisoners forcibly married to guards, so they could be raped before execution. In that way, officials evaded a prohibition against killing virgins. Although no one could confirm this story, it spread widely.

She was terrified for her cousins and warned them, "Please be careful. These clerics are not joking. They see the MEK as a mortal enemy and have no pity, not even for their own relatives. They've abandoned any pretense of restraint or human decency. Just last week the chief prosecutor in Yazd signed the death sentence of his own son. There's no mercy for women or children. You've heard the stories of what happens to girls in prison before they're killed. Anyone arrested gets a quick choice: either confess, repent, and denounce, or execution. You've seen the confessions on television. Look at the faces. You can imagine what was done to those people."

Mehrdad, Minu, and Ahmad repeated her warnings to the young people but, as she feared, the worst happened. Her outspoken cousin Iraj was arrested at his home and no one knew his fate. His frantic parents described an early morning raid on their apartment, where armed Revolutionary Guards broke in and took him away after smashing furniture and confiscating books and papers as "evidence."

They were desperate. "No one will tell us anything. What can we do? We go from office to office, prison to prison, and no one will talk to us. We've spoken to everyone we know, but he's vanished from the earth."

Nilufar and her relatives were devastated. After some inquiries, it was clear that the usual Iranian network of connections would not work in these cases. It was total war, and the young and naïve would pay its price. So would their families.

Still the flow of American intelligence to Beheshti continued, and it fueled his deadly strikes. Nilufar now felt trapped. She was partly responsible for the regime's excesses, and even for the fate of her cousin. In the name of American policy, she was helping those murdering her own compatriots and relatives. She cursed her naiveté and asked herself, "What did I think would happen? What did I think he would do with what we gave him? How can I justify what I've done?"

In her despair she wrote to Porter.

For the Undersecretary,

Beheshti is out of control. He has taken his campaign against the MEK beyond all restraint and launched a reign of terror.

A climate of violence and fear pervades Tehran and the provinces. Truckloads of Revolutionary Guards make raids on suspected MEK hideouts and kill anyone they find. The dead are the lucky ones. No one dares to speak out against the brutality of a regime that has declared war on its own people.

Violence is breeding more violence in a bloody cycle of retaliation. The government's campaign has provoked assassinations of high-ranking clerics in the capital and provincial cities. The authorities' response is more repression, arrests, and executions.

We should no longer be complicit. We should
stop our intelligence sharing with Beheshti until he
ends the indiscriminate violence and bloodshed he
and his allies have unleashed.

With respect, Miriam

In forty-eight hours, she had a brief reply. "Understand
your concerns. We should meet as soon as possible. When can
you get to Dubai?"

DUBAI TEHRAN AND WASHINGTON
SUMMER 1980

The blue and white Iran Air Boeing 727 taxied to the spiral
ramp of Dubai International Airport. In the heat and humidity
of a Persian Gulf summer, a veiled and sweating Nilufar joined
a crowd of Iranian merchants, spies, assassins, smugglers, and
shoppers in the passport lines. She guessed from the passport
officer's name badge that he was of Iranian origin but, in the
day's tense political atmosphere, he would never reveal it by
trading remarks in Persian.

A Keralan taxi driver dropped her at the once-fashionable
and blessedly air-conditioned Ambassador Hotel on the Dubai
side of the Creek. In her room she changed into Western
clothes. A private car with regular Dubai plates met her at a
side entrance and took her to a drab villa on the Jumeirah
Beach Road.

Porter was waiting for her and was shocked to see the
signs of tension in her red eyes and thin face. She looked nothing like the radiant and cheerful Nilufar he remembered seeing
in Washington less than a year before.

She skipped the usual courtesies and addressed him in a
flat voice. "Sir, you wanted to see me. You know I'm taking an
enormous risk by coming here. I'm listening."

He was shaken by her blunt tone. Junior Foreign Service
Officers never spoke to him that way. He spoke softly and
carefully. "Nilufar, I have put you in a terrible position and I

apologize. When we began the exchanges with Beheshti, we knew we were taking a chance. We did not foresee he would use the information the way he has. Believe me, if I had known, I never would have started the exchange."

She abandoned all pretense of courtesy. "What did you think he would do? Did I not tell you who he is and what he is capable of? Mr. Ambassador, this is the Islamic Republic. It's murder or be murdered. Torture or be tortured. Look at what Beheshti did to the democrats and the nationalists. They were crushed because they were not brutal enough. They wrote penetrating articles full of insights. But in the end, none of that mattered. What they could not do was organize street mobs, beat up journalists, and throw acid in the faces of unveiled women. Whoever could do all that has come out the winner."

Porter felt her bitterness like a hot wind from the desert. "Nilufar, we've misread events in Iran for a very long time. That's why we need you there so badly. Your reporting is brilliant and there's no one else."

"Thank you, sir, but I can't live with myself any longer. I've become part of a criminal regime. I have blood on my hands. I'm working with monsters. Can I ever tell my parents I'm helping murderers? Whatever the victims have done, they don't deserve to be brutalized the way they have been." She stopped and started to sob. "I don't think I can take any more. The stories are just horrible."

Porter remained silent for a long time. Finally, he said, "Nilufar, who knew where events would lead? When I first asked you to go to Tehran I thought you would be helping our consular section for three or four months. We couldn't imagine the embassy attack or believe that a student sit-in would go on for months and turn into international melodrama. I certainly didn't foresee keeping you there and making you risk your life every day.

"I won't mince words. We're desperate and out of options. Look at the hostage rescue attempt last April. What came back were eight coffins and no hostages. Events have spun out of control and we're holding on by our fingernails. I'm terrified to turn on the news or read the morning papers. I have nightmares about trials and executions of you and of our friends at the embassy. Not just me – the president too."

"Sir, I'm not naïve. I signed up to serve the United States. But you can't expect me to lock my conscience in some sweets box and pretend I have no responsibility for today's horrors. I even feel guilty about those eight men burned alive in the desert."

"Nilufar, I wish there were some other way. There isn't. We have no choice but to help Beheshti. The president and the whole country are obsessed with the fate of the hostages. At every meeting, he asks, 'What news from Iran? What news of our people?' Despite our reassuring public statements, their survival hangs by a thread. The longer they stay, the greater the chance something will go wrong. If even one is put on trial, executed, shot by accident, or commits suicide, I can't imagine the consequences."

"What about Beheshti's reassurances? I heard him pledge to keep them safe."

"He did. But even he, with all his power, doesn't control everything. Despite our best efforts and his, we know the MEK remains powerful. They even penetrated the State Department and were looking for embassy personnel records. Their goal is to take control of the occupation. I'm terrified of what that would mean. Their first step will to be to embarrass Beheshti. They'll make an example of a hostage and show him to be powerless. An armed confrontation with the US would suit them just fine.

"I am making a personal request. Hold on a little longer. We think we're close to a resolution with the hostages. The Shah is dying in Egypt. When he dies, new doors will open. If we cut off Beheshti now, he will think we've turned against him. At the same time, ending this relationship could put you and your family in mortal danger. Why do you think he squashed the security investigation against you? It seems obvious. He didn't want to threaten his source of intelligence on the MEK."

Porter did not mention the president's concern about Iranian Communists or tell Nilufar that the president had tied his chances in the 1980 election – now just a few months away – to the fate of the hostages. He needed them free if he was to have any chance of winning. His rivals, both within the party and among the opposition, were already criticizing his inability to resolve the crisis and his "mishandling" of the entire Iran dossier. But Porter was not about to tell her that he was asking her to send Iranians to the gallows in a cold war move or to help the president's reelection.

"I know no one should have to carry this load. Let's look at the whole Beheshti channel again in a month. Can you come to Dubai again?"

"I don't think so. Not soon. I'm taking a risk as it is. This town is full of Iranian agents. I could see them on the flight here. Everyone spies on everyone. We'll communicate either through the sweetshop or perhaps via Mehrdad in Tehran and Arash in Geneva. Have you seen him?"

"I haven't. I am waiting for his signal that it's safe to meet."

"When you do, please give him my best. And say hello to my parents. Tell them not to worry. Please don't tell my mother you saw me like this. Tell her I'm still their cheerful daughter. She won't believe you of course, but she still needs to hear it."

TEHRAN AND WASHINGTON
SUMMER 1980

Back in Tehran, her cousin Iraj was out of prison. The family had pulled every string and paid a huge bribe. In prison a terrified Iraj had renounced his pro-MEK views, and, since he had no association with violence, was let out with a warning and a fine. He was one of the few lucky ones.

In late August, just a month after the Shah's death in Egypt, Beheshti asked Nilufar to arrange an urgent meeting with Gerhard Ritzel, the German ambassador in Tehran. "I'd like you to interpret. Also Doctor Sadeq Tabataba'i will join us. His wife is the sister of Khomeini's son Ahmad. He knows the ambassador quite well. It will be just the four of us. We don't need a note taker."

A day later, Ritzel and Tabataba'i came to Beheshti's office. Although Beheshti's German was fluent, he insisted on using Persian. With Nilufar interpreting, Beheshti told Ritzel, "The Imam has decided it is time to end the matter of the American hostages. He has instructed me to make the arrangements. I am asking you to take a message to the Americans that we are ready to settle based on four points: unfreeze Iranian funds; return the Shah's assets to Iran; a pledge of noninterference in Iran's internal affairs; and an apology for past actions against Iran."

Ritzel thought for a minute before replying. "Sir, of course my government is ready to do anything that will help resolve this problem. I will inform my counterpart in Washington to speak to the Americans. In my view, the last demand – an apology – will be difficult for them."

"So be it. We can waive the apology at the end. It is the Imam's opinion that this crisis has gone on too long and is distracting us from important work of building our new Islamic Republic. Doctor Sadeq here – at the direct request of the Imam – has full power to represent our government in any talks with American officials to work out arrangements. You know him well and he has my authorization to meet with you as necessary."

Nilufar said to herself, "These *akhund*s are amazing. Shameless hypocrites. First, they create a crisis. Then they prolong it and use it to solidify their power. Now that they're in control, they say that it has gone on too long and they want to end it. Only ten months ago Khomeini forbade Iranian officials from even meeting Americans."

Ritzel told Beheshti, "I will send your message to our ambassador in Washington. I will let you know as soon as I have an answer."

"Please work through Dr. Sadeq," Beheshti said. "The Americans will of course be suspicious. You can tell them they will have confirmation we are serious. They should listen to the Imam's sermon, not this Friday but the one after. He will state the same conditions. They should have no doubt this approach comes directly from the Imam."

Nilufar's report reached Washington only a few hours behind that of the German ambassador. It thus came as no surprise when the German ambassador in Washington asked for an urgent meeting with the secretary. After telling him, his deputy, and Porter about Ritzel's meeting with Beheshti and the Iranian conditions, the ambassador added, "I know Ritzel. He's been in Iran since before the revolution. He gets along well with the new government and they obviously trust him to deliver their message. This sounds serious."

The secretary answered carefully, "Mr. Ambassador, we are grateful for your government's efforts and in particular for those of your colleague in Tehran. We have been seeking a viable channel to Khomeini and his people for months.

"Please ask your colleague in Tehran to tell the Iranians we are seriously studying their conditions. Of course, we will want to hear the confirmation he describes. Please tell him also that even before we do, we are ready at any time to send the deputy secretary to meet with Khomeini's representative."

Porter asked, "Mr. Ambassador, does your colleague say anything about why the Iranians are now ready to settle?"

"He mentions several reasons. He thinks Beheshti had a lot to do with convincing Khomeini. Beheshti is now confident that he and his allies control all centers of power in Iran. They have made the president into a figurehead. They have defeated challengers on both left and right flanks. Beheshti's campaign against the MEK has been vicious, but effective. From this position of strength, holding the hostages no longer serves any purpose. The death of the Shah in Egypt didn't hurt either."

After the ambassador left, Porter and the deputy secretary stayed with the secretary. Ever since Porter had briefed them on Nilufar's situation, the two men remained concerned for her safety. The secretary said, "Gentlemen, it's perhaps too early to open the champagne, but I think we're finally on a good track. Alan, we owe a lot to you and to Ms. Hartman. You urged us to keep her there and you were right. We'll probably never know for sure, but it seems to me our helping Beheshti went a long way in his persuading Khomeini to settle."

The secretary continued, "And what about Ms. Hartman? She's a very brave young woman and very few people will ever know what she did and at what risk. Should we bring her home? When she comes back, I hope she stays in the Foreign Service, although I don't know what job can match what she's doing now."

Porter told his bosses, "If she wants to come out, of course we will agree. But if she does, we'll have to keep her out of sight for a while. If she surfaces somewhere else as an American diplomat, the Iranians will realize they've been duped and at the least will take revenge on her family.

"I prefer she stays, at least through the hostage negotiations which I predict will be long and difficult. Just because the Iranians have finally set out conditions we find reasonable doesn't mean there won't be hard bargaining ahead. They will squeeze out any advantage they can. Once our people are free, they've lost their leverage."

No one in the room stated the obvious – that with American elections only two months away, the president needed a success. For the secretary and his deputy, their jobs depended on the president's winning a second term in November.

WASHINGTON

Two hours later Porter spoke with Bill O'Donnell about the effort to get to the Tehran files.

"Bill, do we know any more?"

"A little. We know Parsons' girlfriend, 'Sherry Vassilios,' is Shahrzad Mehrparvar, an Iranian MEK operative. We've shown sketches to Iranians here and in other cities, and different people made the same identification. No one has seen her since she left her Washington apartment, and we don't even know if she's still in the country. We and the FBI are searching records, but it's a slow process and, so far, nothing.

"Here's the bad news. Someone tipped her off we were watching Parsons. And we've nothing on that front. Since she left, we've not seen any new efforts to get into the Tehran files."

"That doesn't reassure me. But why the MEK? What's their interest here?"

"Until we can question her and her controllers, we won't know. Our Iran people think the MEK still has members among the hostage-takers and wanted this information to strengthen their position. With the organization on the ropes, they are focusing on survival."

"It still bothers me we cannot find out who warned her. If we can't, Nilufar's not safe."

George Arney had acted just in time. If Shahrzad had not fled when she did, the investigation would have exposed him. Now the MEK in the US was getting desperate messages from its members in Iran: Beheshti's strikes against them were deadly and efficient.

The MEK leadership suspected betrayal at the highest level. Beheshti's intelligence was too good. The authorities were able to identify the MEK's most secure locations and arrest even agents who had operated safely for months inside the IRP. He had to have outside help, and logic pointed to the Americans. There were rumors of secret contacts and an understanding between Beheshti's office and Washington. While Beheshti waged his war against them, no hostage had gone on trial despite clear evidence of espionage at the embassy.

Arney knew he was taking an enormous risk by trying to learn about Porter's work on Iran. His Iranian contacts were insistent. "There has to be a connection. Find it. We need it to unmask Beheshti and his filthy dealings with the Americans." There was no need to threaten to expose Arney's homosexuality.

Arney could find nothing conclusive, but he gathered enough circumstantial evidence to convince the MEK that a Porter-Beheshti channel against them existed. Washington, they reasoned, was obsessed with suppressing the Iranian left and had not forgotten how the MEK had assassinated Americans before the revolution. How else to explain both these contacts and the effectiveness of Beheshti's campaign against them?

Arney did not know that the MEK had decided to retaliate. Their Washington leadership called a meeting at Pierce Mill in Rock Creek Park. While pretending to have a family picnic, they decided to assassinate Porter and claim credit, sending a message into the heart of the American government. It turned out to be easy to find volunteers among the MEK faithful in the area, including three with military backgrounds. Thanks to America's lax gun laws, many had weapons available at home.

Over three weeks of secret meetings at places like the Marsden Tract on the C and O Canal or parading in plain sight with the throngs at Tyson's Corner shopping mall on Saturday afternoons, the MEK hit squad devised plans to ambush Porter's car as he travelled from his Spring Valley home to the State Department. Like many Foreign Service Officers of his generation, Porter had used the money he had saved on his first tour in a "hardship post" to buy a solid, modestly large, brick home in Northwest DC – a home he could never have afforded today.

Washington might have seemed immune to political murders on the street. It was not. Agents of Chilean military dictator Augusto Pinochet had four years earlier assassinated Orlando Letelier and his colleague Ronni Moffitt near Sheridan Circle.

The MEK squad planned to use two cars to block Porter's car as it travelled the narrow streets of his residential neighborhood toward an intersection at Loughborough Road. Armed men would shoot him, his driver, and his bodyguard. His predecessors as undersecretary had been routinely denied what administrators called for some mysterious reason "port-to-port" transportation. But Porter's length of service and the continuing threats to him from nasty groups around the world and at home gave the national security advisor enough room to make an exception. But the bureaucrats were damned if they were going to provide an armored car, so Porter was driven by a DS officer, with another armed DS agent in the "shotgun" seat, in a Chrysler K car which the government had purchased by the thousands for its motor pools to save the American auto company from bankruptcy.

Porter and his DS bodyguards took his security seriously. As the MEK agents discovered doing their surveillance, Porter changed the times he left his home and varied his routes to work, complicating their planning.

Leaving his driveway, the driver might turn left or right with no pattern. The assassins planned to station one car at the right intersection, the other at the left. One would block him from the front, the other from the back. After he was killed, the organization would issue a statement saying he had been "executed" in revenge for causing the deaths of thousands of MEK martyrs. They chose a Thursday morning to act.

Because Porter's days were so crammed with meetings, congressional testimony, telephone calls, and public and internal State Department appearances, he often asked one of his special assistants to meet his car at State at 6:30 in the morning, ride with the DS bodyguards and then, during the twenty-minute ride back to the State Department's basement parking area, brief Porter on what he faced during the day. This coveted assignment was assigned by lottery. This Thursday morning found Arney on his way to Spring Valley.

A few minutes before seven a.m., the official car reached Porter's home on Rockwood Parkway near the South Korean ambassador's residence. The DS bodyguard got out of the car and rang the bell. The DS officer escorted Porter to the right rear of the car and opened the door, reminding Porter to watch his head.

"Good morning, George. What opportunities await us today?"

"It's a 'dentist's office day' sir. Three foreign ambassadors, two meetings with senators on the Hill, one session of the Small Group at the White House, and the swearing-in of our new ambassador to Poland. Then dinner at the Thai ambassador's in honor of their visiting minister of defense."

The DS officer in the front right seat put the loaded Uzi in his lap as the car started to move. He and the driver, also armed with a holstered pistol, saw the two cars at the same time. From their training they knew they were in an ambush. The driver hit the "attack button" which was connected to the DS command center at State, alerting the watch officer there was trouble. Knowing Porter's address and considering the time, the watch officer guessed they were still near Porter's home and immediately called the Washington, DC, police for help.

"Get down, both of you," shouted the bodyguard, raising his Uzi. The driver, taking his pistol out of the holster, slammed on the brakes, and as he had practiced a hundred times at "crash and bang school" at a racetrack in West Virginia, accelerated and aimed the front of his car to hit the lighter, rear side of the blocking MEK vehicle.

Porter and Arney were rocked by the impact. The driver fired into the blocking car while he drove. The bodyguard shot at the other vehicle now moving toward them.

The three attackers in the rammed car were momentarily disoriented by the impact but quickly regained their balance. Two of the three got out of the car, spraying automatic fire toward the K car. Porter's DS driver was hit in the head and died instantly. The killers moved closer to the car.

George Arney knew then what he had to do. Nothing would ever make right his betrayal of the United States, but he would not help the MEK murder his boss. Arney looked at Porter.

"I am sorry, sir."

"What are you talking about? Get a grip."

Arney grabbed Porter's rain coat from the seat between them, pushed the left door open and moved to get out. He kicked Porter away when Porter reached to hold him in the car.

"I am sorry, sir."

Arney got out of the car, covered his head with the rain coat and shouted as loudly as he could, "I am Porter. I am Porter. I am Porter." He was killed by a mass of MEK rounds and fell on Rockwood Parkway in a pool of his own blood.

The diversion gave Porter's bodyguard just enough time to shoot and kill the two attackers. He was able to disable the driver by shattering the windshield with bullets from the Uzi.

He turned to the second car. At that moment, two DC squad cars arrived and, as the after-action report would blandly say, the officers "eliminated the threat" in a hail of gunfire.

It was over. Thanks to the bravery of the DS officers, the timely arrival of the police, and the mysterious self-sacrifice of George Arney, Porter was alive. There would be many questions to ask and much relief and gratitude to share with the living. But, for now, all Porter could do was focus on his Foreign Service life: two more names for the plaques at State's C Street entrance that honor the Foreign Service professionals who have died in service to their country.

The next day, an armored car appeared at 6:30 a.m.

TEHRAN
FALL-WINTER 1980–81

From the Undersecretary to Miriam,

I know this remains hard for you, but Beheshti's success against the MEK has brought us two wins. It has reduced the threat of a leftist takeover and an expansion of Soviet influence and has brought a long-sought breakthrough with the hostages. I cannot overstate the importance of your efforts. The secretary and the president send their personal thanks.

We are not yet out of the woods with the hostages. The war with Iraq complicates matters but our best analysis is that the Iranians, with their advantages of size, population, and motivation will stop the Iraqi advance. Add Iraqi incompetence to the mix, and we predict the war will become a stalemate, for which Saddam has no stomach.

Of course, we are still working for an early release of the hostages. We need your insight about Iranian intentions. Also, whatever you can say about the impact of the war on society and politics will be greatly appreciated. As always, our sources are few and we rely on you.

With Regards, Porter

Porter's predictions about the war were correct. After the original surprise and advances, the Iraqi forces bogged down. For the new Islamic government, the war was a gift. As they did during the hostage crisis, Iran's rulers mobilized public opinion behind a popular cause and branded their domestic enemies as traitors. There were new waves of repression against political opponents and new social restrictions. Women who dressed or acted immodestly were now accused of "insulting the martyrs."

In Beheshti's office, Nilufar would interpret for visiting dignitaries seeking to mediate the conflict with Iraq. After meeting with the implacable Khomeini, delegations from UN, the Non-Aligned Movement, the Organization of the Islamic Conference, the Arab League, and from individual nations would call on Beheshti in the hope of hearing a more accommodating stance.

All were disappointed. He told the would-be mediators, "For us, this is not a war between Iran and Iraq. We have no enmity toward our Iraqi brothers – neither Shia nor Sunni – who have already suffered so much. It is an imposed war, and a battle between Islam and unbelief, between right and wrong. How can you mediate between the two? I suggest you refocus your efforts. Investigate who is right and who is wrong. Find out who is the aggressor and who is the victim. That would be a true mediation based on the wise principles of our religion."

Beheshti was too smart to distance himself from Khomeini.

At a family gathering, Nilufar expressed her dissatisfaction to Mehrdad. "There's nothing new out of Beheshti's office. He's winning against the MEK and is taking control of the state; about the war he just repeats what Khomeini says; about the hostages he tells everyone the same thing: 'We are ready to settle but we need to secure our rights.' For some reason he's cut out the Germans and prefers the Algerians as mediators."

Mehrdad told her, "You shouldn't stay with Beheshti much longer. It's dangerous for you. You heard about the MEK's assassination plot against Porter in Washington. They almost succeeded. They must have suspected he was the source of Beheshti's intelligence. They had to strike back. Remember how the poet Sa'adi warns us about the cornered cat. 'With its tiny claws it can tear out the eyes of a leopard.' The MEK may be cornered but they still have infiltrators and people ready for suicide missions.

"You need to get out of there while we keep the flow of intelligence going. If it suddenly stops when you leave, even Beheshti won't be able to ignore the obvious. If there's another investigation, he may not be able to protect you.

"Nilufar, your cousin Iraj was lucky to get out alive. If they arrested him today, things would be much worse for him. In the prisons they have given up any pretext of "Islamic" behavior. It's back to the bad old days with cables, electric shock, and rape."

"Yes, we're terrified they'll come and arrest him again. It's happened to others. Right now, he's hiding with friends and relatives, never staying long in one place. His parents are dealing with smugglers to get him over the Turkish border. They'll have to sell everything and go into debt. He needs to leave, but then he'll be one of those miserable Iranian refugees in Ankara or Istanbul. They can't work legally and live hand to mouth. The Western embassies turn them away, and the Turks harass and exploit them with threats of returning them to Iran. The Iranian embassy watches them and has even kidnapped some. They pay off Turkish officials to look the other way. They stuff their captives in the trunks of cars with diplomatic plates and send them back to Iran."

"You're right, *Nilu jun*. Turkey will be dangerous for Iraj. The MEK has been recruiting there and he could fall into their trap. They watch foreign embassies and find young men who can't get onward visas. They promise them papers, asylum in Sweden or Holland, a job, even a wife. They put them on the phone with a prospective bride who pretends she's in Stockholm or Amsterdam. These gullible kids are stuck and destitute in Turkey, so they fall for the act. The MEK tells them, 'We'll help you, but it will take a few months to arrange your documents. You can't stay in Turkey. We'll take you to a safe place where you can wait until your papers are ready.'

"They smuggle their victim to the MEK camp in Iraq and take away his passport. Now he's truly stuck. No Sweden, no asylum, no job, and certainly no wife. Just a camp in the desert, military drills, cult indoctrination, forced celibacy, and self-criticism sessions. Whoever makes a fuss they beat up and turn over to the Iraqis who throw him in jail for entering the country illegally."

Nilufar called Nazanin and the two met at another "Sisters of Zeinab" event in Amirieh. Nilufar explained she had decided to leave her job in Beheshti's office. "It bothers my conscience. It doesn't feel right sitting there comfortably when so many at the front are making sacrifices."

Nazanin told her, "I'm sure you don't want to come back to the airport. As a matter of fact, I'm leaving there soon. The women are all under stress and the war has made things worse. Amira's husband volunteered for the Guards. He went to the front three months ago and she's had no word from him. She's frantic for her children."

"Is she still working?"

"She is. She needs the money, but the schedule is very hard on her. We all want to help, but everyone has problems. The men at the *komiteh* have gotten worse. The best ones have gone to war and the shits have stayed. Sarhaddi is still there and he's the worst. I don't know how he avoids military service, but he does. He nurses a thousand grudges and keeps braying about his 'dear martyred uncle,' the assassinated Friday prayer leader of Shiraz.

"They have no shame or conscience. They see a widow, or a divorced woman and they start bothering her. It's sickening. A few, who don't know any better, have even come after me. But they never do that twice."

"Nazanin dear, would you want to remarry at some time? You're still young."

"I've nothing against it. But first, after things settle down, I need to finish my education. Can I do that with a husband and perhaps more children? And who could compare to Farid, my late husband? We weren't together long, but he spoiled me for other men. And what about my son? I can't bring just any *nar-e-khar* (jackass) into the house as his stepfather."

"Nazanin, you were so lucky to have found such a husband. And he was lucky to have found you. As for me, I shouldn't stay in Beheshti's office, but I certainly can't go back to the airport. It's a terrible place for a woman to work. What are you planning to do when you leave?"

"Massoumeh, in a few weeks I am joining the Tehran *gasht*, the women's morality patrols. Why don't you join too? We could work together. We'd be under the section of the Revolutionary Guards Corps called *monkeraat*, which enforces Islamic behavior in public. It's important work, especially with the war on.

"They need special women's groups. There've been a lot of problems with the men's patrols. You know most of our men don't know how to act with women. They either bully them or are completely intimidated. When confronted, the women make a scene. They'll scream, 'He touched me! He insulted me! Don't you have a mother and sisters?' An angry crowd gathers, things get ugly fast, and we have a full-scale riot on our hands."

"Are the women armed?"

"Not usually. They're not dealing with terrorists. The patrols all have vehicles and two-way radios. If things get difficult, they call on an armed men's unit for support. They claim they want to advise ordinary citizens on proper dress and behavior. They call it *ershaad* (guidance). They get to work autonomously without the men ogling them or ordering them around. I know you'll appreciate that."

"Sounds interesting. I'll let you know. I need a change from desks and papers. If I decide to join, can you help me get accepted?"

For the Undersecretary,

In a recent meeting with Algerian mediators, Beheshti said he was optimistic about freeing the hostages. He assured them Iran would follow the instructions of the Imam to reach an agreement but would insist on maintaining its rights and recovering its blocked property.

He told the mediators to convey to the Americans the need to remain at the bargaining table. He said American resistance to the Iranian demand for protection against subsequent lawsuits was prolonging the negotiation. He told them, "We have been waiting a long time for justice. We can wait a little longer."

Beheshti continues to tighten his hold on power. His ferocious campaign against the MEK continues. In a recent meeting with a Soviet delegation, the visitors said nothing about easing the pressure. The consensus here is that the Soviets will sacrifice their MEK protégés for the sake of some deeper game with the Islamic Republic.

Beheshti's next targets are Foreign Minister Qotbzadeh and President Bani Sadr, whom he has already made into a joke. Bani Sadr can only rant and rave against Beheshti in rambling speeches and incoherent editorials in his paper *Enqelaab-e-Islami*.

Two things are clear: first, Beheshti intends to force Bani Sadr to ally himself with the MEK and thus become an outlaw; second, although the leader will not take sides openly, Khomeini has already chosen Beheshti over the president. In the leader's eyes it is an easy choice. Thanks to the new constitution and the hybrid state, Beheshti has made Khomeini's vision of an Islamic government a reality. President Bani Sadr, who grows more erratic by the day, can never match his rival's accomplishments. Even the president's allies see how the political winds are blowing.

The war is bringing hardships, particularly to the lower and lower-middle classes who are the backbone of support for the Islamic Republic. Casualties at the front have been heavy and there are many wounded and missing. There are memorials and pictures of martyrs on every street, particularly in the poorer quarters. The losses have created thousands of widows and women whose husbands, sons, brothers, and fathers return from the front maimed from bullets, gas, mines, and disease. Shortages of cooking oil, gasoline, soap, bottled gas, sugar, tea, and other basic goods are common.

The ration system works reasonably well, so there are few reports of starvation. For those with money, the black-market flourishes.

Despite these deprivations, morale on the home front remains high. All Iranians despise Saddam and, whether driven by religious or patriotic fervor, are determined to defend the homeland. There is no shortage of volunteers for Revolutionary Guard units to supplement the regular armed forces. These units have put up the most effective resistance against the Iraqis.

I will leave Beheshti's office within the next few months on the pretext of wanting to serve the revolution more directly. My plan is to join the Tehran women's *gasht*, the morality patrols that enforce Islamic behavior and dress. The war has given new momentum to imposing strict religious norms in the society, and there is a need for separate women's units. Such work will fit perfectly with my "pious Massoumeh" persona.

Finally, I was relieved to hear about the failure of the assassination plot against you. It appears someone has made the connection between you and Beheshti's anti-MEK campaign. I will end by saying what you always say to me: Stay safe.

With Respect, Miriam

TEHRAN
JANUARY 1981

On the morning of January 19, Beheshti called Nilufar into his office. "Ms. Rastbin, I need your help with a very sensitive matter. You've certainly been following the news about the American hostages. Tonight, an Algerian medical team will visit them, and tomorrow evening, God willing, they will leave and we will be rid of them."

Nilufar knew another order was coming, this time not even disguised as a request. "Sir, how can I help?"

"The release has to go smoothly. The Algerian mediators will be visiting me this afternoon, and I want you to interpret at our meeting. We need to reassure them there will be no last-minute incidents and that they and the Americans will leave safely tomorrow. Between you and me, I will breathe a huge sigh of relief once those Air Algérie planes have cleared Iranian airspace.

"We've done all we can to ensure things will go well at the airport. But you never know. Something can always go wrong. Those damn students are unpredictable. One or two of them could do something stupid and foul up the whole process."

Nilufar said nothing. She knew that for over a year Beheshti had been the controlling power behind the students. They had served his purpose, and tomorrow he would be finished with them.

"Tomorrow evening I need you to be my eyes and ears at Mehrabad. The Imam usually doesn't give direct orders, but he's made himself perfectly clear: all the hostages are to fly out tomorrow and nothing can interfere with their leaving."

"Of course. I'll be there, sir. Do you have any hints something might go wrong?"

"I don't, but I'm not reassured. I worry about some hot-headed student getting into a fight with an angry hostage. I also worry about deliberate sabotage from some agent of the hypocrites who would love to embarrass us in front of the world press. Their dream is a riot at the airport, some hostage getting shot, and the whole deal collapsing. They have been railing against the release agreement and are accusing us of surrendering to the 'Great Satan.' They're calling us traitors."

She had never seen the masterful Beheshti so worried. He told her, "Tomorrow night you will be at the airport. Be there by seven. I will have a car with a phone for you and a pass for the special secured area. I don't want to show myself for obvious reasons, but I will if I have to." With a smile, he added, "I have heard you are a master of defusing airport confrontations. Tell me what is happening, and if you see anything going wrong, call me immediately. I won't be far away.

"One more thing. You can talk to a student named Asgharzadeh. He's one of the few sensible ones. With him you can use my name."

Not wanting to mention Sarhaddi by name, she asked, "What about the airport *komiteh* people? Will they be there?"

"They should not be. This operation is far above them and they'll just make things more complicated. You already know Sarhaddi. If he or any of his men show up, tell them to get lost. If they give you trouble, call me."

Beheshti's meeting with the Algerians was brief. They repeated their concern that nothing would interfere with a smooth hostage release, and he assured them he had taken all possible measures. He told them the Iranian Air Force would escort the Algerian planes as far as the Turkish frontier.

The next day Nilufar stayed in the office until after sunset. About six p.m. she got into Beheshti's car and found an armed security guard – a young man about 5' 8" and powerfully built – in the front seat. He introduced himself as Hossein Niku, who, Nilufar remembered, was an acquaintance of Mehrdad's from Hamburg and his channel for Porter's intelligence on the MEK.

They traveled west along Enqelaab Avenue toward Mehrabad Airport. Because of curfews, blackouts, gasoline shortages, and Iraqi air raids, the normally choked streets were almost deserted.

Her driver took her through a series of checkpoints to the VIP area. He stopped about fifty yards from the VIP lounge and about a hundred yards from where three Air Algérie 727s stood ready, their rear steps down and their engines running. Armed Algerian security men formed cordons around the aircraft. Outside it was about 15°F and a bitter wind blew from the mountains to the north. She sat in the car and called the number Beheshti had given her, telling him that everything seemed normal, and that there were dozens of shivering journalists on the tarmac.

She left the car and stood in the cold. As she waited she recognized Sarhaddi walking toward her from the main terminal. Even in the darkness there was no mistaking his slouch and his self-importance. With no effort to be polite, he said, "Ms. Massoumeh, what a surprise. What are you doing here? I thought you had left us for more important work. Can I see your airport pass?"

Nilufar made a head motion to her bodyguard. "Mr. Niku, please escort the gentleman out of this area. He has no business here." The guard took Sarhaddi's arm and none too gently led him away in full view of the national and international press. He told the *komiteh* man, "You heard the honorable lady. She is here on Dr. Beheshti's orders and you are not. *Gur-e-to gom kon, mardikeh bi-sho'ur*! (Get yourself out of here, you little fool!)"

About fifteen minutes later a group walked from the lounge and boarded one of the planes. She recognized the Algerian mediators, the Arlgerian ambassador Abdelkarim Ghraieb, the Swiss ambassador Erik Lang, and his deputy Flavio Maroni.

At about 7:20 three busses arrived and stopped between her and the planes. About seventy-five student hostage-takers left the busses and milled around attempting to look fierce with their weapons and revolutionary outfits. Most of the journalists, ignored the students, knowing they would soon be yesterday's news.

The TV and film crews, by some prearranged signal, turned on their lights and began to move as a herd toward a spot between the students and the airport gate. Maroni and Lang also ignored the students and waited with clipboards in the door at the top of the airplane steps.

Two of the students – one a few years older than the others and the other a heavily veiled woman a few years younger than Nilufar – walked to where Nilufar was waiting. "I'm Asgharzadeh. This is Ms. Ebtekar. You must be Massoumeh. His Excellency Dr. Beheshti told us you would be here."

Nilufar answered, "Yes. He needs to be sure there are no difficulties here tonight. Are you confident there won't be?"

"The woman answered with irritation, "We've taken care of everything. You really didn't need to come. You can go home. If you speak to Dr. Beheshti, tell him that he needn't worry."

Nilufar ignored the insult and said simply, "He'll be happy to hear that."

At 7:30 two more busses arrived and parked about seventy-five yards from the planes. Journalists and students moved to an area between the busses and the aircraft. The Algerian security men kept them from getting closer than twenty yards from the plane.

The bus doors opened, a few student guards got off. When the Americans appeared, Nilufar gasped at their appearance: thin, haggard, bearded, and dazed. They wore odds and ends of ill-fitting clothes unsuited for the wind and cold. As they stepped off the bus, they appeared confused by the noise, the lights, and the crowds of students and journalists. A few had to be directed to walk toward the aircraft.

As they began to walk, the students, performing for the cameras, began shouting slogans. Nilufar thought, "What a chickenshit group! They can't even do a departure with any style."

One of the students started pushing a hostage, an army medic, who wasn't moving fast enough for him. The medic turned on him and shouted in English, "Don't push me, you piece of shit." The student pushed harder, and the hostage grabbed his arm. A second hostage put himself inches from the student's face and started berating him in fluent street Persian. "Take your hands off him, you son of a whore. When he leaves, you can go back to buggering little boys."

Students and hostages were now shoving and trading curses. Hostages were pushing guards aside to get off the busses. Nilufar noticed a few students shouting and encouraging others to join the melee. She saw Asgharzadeh and Ebtekar, despite their earlier assurances, standing around doing nothing as the scene descended into chaos in full view of television cameras. Lang, Maroni, and the Algerians watched helplessly from the airplane door.

Nilufar immediately dialed Beheshti and reported the trouble to him. He barked, "Get me Asgharzadeh on the line. Now."

She pointed out Asgharzadeh to the bodyguard, who dragged him to the car. Nilufar could hear Beheshti screaming over the phone. Asgharzadeh handed the phone to Nilufar and ran toward the commotion that was turning into a brawl. Beheshti told her, "Keep this line open. Make sure he gets those idiots to stop."

Nilufar put down the phone and ran after Asgharzadeh. While he worked to calm the students, she pulled aside the Persian-speaking American and told him quietly in English, "Just get out of here. Get on the plane. Some people are trying to provoke a riot and ruin everything. Don't play into their hands. Go now."

He nodded in understanding, backed away from the students, and walked toward the airplane. Restrained by Asgharzadeh, the other students kept their distance. As he left, Nilufar whispered to the American, "By the way, I really like your Persian. You must have had a great teacher."

He smiled and replied, "Yes, I did. She was great."

The remaining hostages boarded without incident, and the students seemed to lose their appetite for shouting. Lang and Maroni verified their lists and, with Ghraieb, left the aircraft. The steps retracted and the rear door closed. The runway lights, normally extinguished at night because of Iraqi air raids, came on, and the plane began its taxi. The students, much quieter now, gathered near their busses and the journalists milled around waiting for takeoff.

The plane sat at the end of the runway for almost ten minutes. Nilufar checked her watch. It was a few minutes past 8:30 p.m. Tehran time, just after 12 noon in Washington on inauguration day, when the plane began to roll. She asked herself, "Why the delay? There's no other air traffic. What were they waiting for?"

As the car left the airport, she thanked both the driver and Niku, the bodyguard. The latter told her, "I got to know Dr. Beheshti when I was a student in Hamburg. I've been with him since before the revolution. He's a great man. He was worried about tonight's release and told me to do everything I could to help you."

She noticed he spoke Persian with a slight Turkish accent and asked him, "Mr. Niku, where are you from originally?"

"From Qazvin. I speak Persian and Azeri, but like most Qazvinis, I have an accent in both."

As she composed in her head her message to Porter, she telephoned her final report to Beheshti, not neglecting to praise the driver and Niku for their good work. "Thank you, my daughter. I'm glad you were there to help. I knew those students would screw things up in the end. Tomorrow I'll send them all to the war and make sure they're in the front lines."

5

IN PLAIN SIGHT

TEHRAN
FALL-WINTER 1980–81

Aunt Minu was furious when she learned Nilufar was joining the morality patrols. Leaving her tea untouched on the kitchen table, she shouted, "Don't do it! Why should you do this regime's dirty work? You'll be up to your neck in their shit. You're overdoing the 'devout Massoumeh' act. You're becoming the fanatic you pretend to be. Why should you help those sadists who harass ordinary people? Times are hard, and people need a little color, music, and joy in their lives. It's their right. Now you'd take away all that."

"I wish things were different. But I have to protect myself and the family. The longer I stay in Beheshti's office, the more dangerous it is for everyone. People are jealous of my position. Jealous people are dangerous. They're suspicious. They spread rumors and ask questions. 'Who is she? Where does she come from? Why does she speak English so well? Who does she really work for?' There was already one investigation and Beheshti himself had to intervene to stop it."

"Nilu *jun*, I understand that. We Iranians are jealous by nature. We can't abide seeing even our best friend succeed. Look at that damn neighbor who informed on you when you first arrived. These people are like dogs with a bone. They won't let go."

Minu continued, "I see and hear terrible things about the patrols. Yesterday they stopped my friend Sa'ideh near her office and said her clothes were too tight and she was walking provocatively. She was furious, but she bit her tongue, thanked them for the reminder, and apologized. At least they were pacified when she groveled like a dog. They aren't always satisfied so easily. Sa'ideh herself is a wreck. She's afraid to leave the house."

Nilufar hugged her aunt and said only, "You're right of course. And I'm afraid it's only going to get worse."

"Listen, Nilu dear, I'm begging you. Don't do this. There must be somewhere else you can work? You can teach. Schools and institutes are always looking for language teachers. You'd be good at it."

"Too dangerous. Even at private schools, students and teachers have to fill out long questionnaires to prove their ideological purity. My friend's university has closed, and before she can go back she has to answer dozens of questions. 'What's your family background? What political groups have your joined? Do you fast? Do you pray regularly?' They talk to neighbors. My 'Massoumeh' identity won't stand up to that kind of checking.

"They've declared war on education. Thousands of students are in prison. Hundreds of the best teachers have been fired. Look what they did to the former minister of education."

Minu knew exactly how vengeful the new rulers could be. They had tracked down the former minister, a sixty-eight-year-old retiree, and gave her a five-minute trial. Then they put her in a sack and shot her for creating a 'culture of social corruption' in the schools.

"Won't they investigate you if you join the patrols?"

"Not really. It all works by *parti-bazi* (connections). Even the *akhund*s can't change that part of our culture. I got the job with Beheshti because cousin Mehrdad knew him from Germany and had helped him there. Now I can work with the *gasht* thanks to my friend Nazanin from the airport. She's a certified hero of the revolution, a true believer. No one says 'no' to her."

A resigned Minu sighed, and said, "Well, Nilu, do what you must. You remind me of my sister. But please go easy on people. Everyone's nerves are in shreds from the bombings, the blackouts, the restrictions, and the shortages. There are lines everywhere. Look how angry people are. They fight over a kilo of rice or a bar of soap. Don't make things worse for them."

Nilufar spent two weeks training for her new job. Her squad practiced teamwork, emergency driving in a Nissan "Patrol" 4x4, radio communications, and dealing with public and private offenses, such as drinking alcohol, immodest dress, improper contact between men and women, pornography, music, and dancing. They learned to decide when to resolve a case on the spot and when to deliver offenders to higher authorities.

Their instructor, an obese forty-five-year-old woman with a hairy chin, looked like a crow in her black chador. She told them, "My revolutionary sisters. Never forget that this country is at war and that our dear sons, husbands, and brothers are dying at the front. Those who violate Islamic rules in any way are aiding the enemy. They are counterrevolutionaries. They insult the memory of our martyrs and undermine the holy mission of our fighters. Show them no mercy."

Nazanin pulled strings so she and Nilufar were assigned together to a fashionable district near Takht-e-Taavous (now Motahhari) Avenue in North Tehran. The patrols had a shortage of women drivers, so Nilufar was assigned to drive her group's Nissan. The group had previously used a male driver, and the women complained that he, like most of the men, spent his time ogling the women in the patrol.

Nilufar's squad inspected shops, markets, and cafés. They scolded women wearing Hermes knock-off head scarfs pushed back to reveal a few inches of (teased) hair. They reprimanded women with topcoats too stylish and stockings too sheer. One afternoon they burst into a beauty salon to check reports of immorality – that a male stylist was touching women's hair despite clear orders that only women should work in such places. No man was present when they arrived, but they did find a man's overcoat hanging in the closet. They questioned the owner, who told them, "That belongs to my husband. It was ripped and I just brought it from the tailor."

When they entered cafés, the women customers quickly adjusted their scarves and the men distanced themselves from their female companions. They asked young men and women, "Why are you together? What's your relationship? Are you married? Are you brother and sister?" Many of the couples produced documents – real or forged – showing they were married or siblings.

The next Thursday evening, Nilufar related her adventures to her family. Her twenty-three-year-old cousin Babak told her, "Dozens of places will sell you those documents. Forgers are getting rich. There's an operation just two blocks from here masquerading as a flower shop. You ask the owner for a 'special bouquet of your best *gol-e-mikhak* (carnations).' Then he asks you, 'Are these for Ahmad?' and you say, 'No, they're for Mahmoud.' At this shop the forgers do high-end work, so nothing comes cheap. Passports, ID cards, and military discharges are the most expensive. School documents, marriage certificates, property titles, cost less. A good Iranian passport with the right stamps will cost you the equivalent of at least a thousand dollars. A foreign passport costs more."

"That's a lot of money for most people."

"It is, but people are paying."

A few days later, after a tip-off, Nilufar's squad joined other units to raid an apartment off Mir-Daamaad Avenue. Three carloads of men carrying G-3 rifles and two carloads of women, along with empty vans, barricaded the streets outside a chic five-story apartment block on Yazdani Alley. Nazanin told one of men drivers, "Watch our car, brother. Massoumeh, you're coming inside with me. We're going to need you."

When they reached the target apartment on the third floor, they heard Western music and low voices. Entering the apartment they found young women hastily covering their short skirts and sleeveless blouses. Most of the men had long hair and T-shirts printed with the pictures of Abba, the Police, and UB-40. The song "Red, Red Wine" blared from an expensive stereo system. In another room, six male guards watched wide-eyed and openmouthed while a VCR in the corner played an uncensored, pirated copy of "The Blue Lagoon." When the women guards entered the room, the men blushed and pretended to be searching for alcohol.

Hassan, the chief of the guards, yelled at his men, "*Yallah*, get busy. You're not here to watch sexy movies. Put the men in one room and the women in another. Make sure no one's hiding in a closet or somewhere else. Put them in separate vans and then search the apartment. For the moment don't touch those open bottles. Also, don't touch anything that might be drugs. Put magazines and videos in plastic bags. They're evidence."

Nilufar watched the guards ostentatiously rifling drawers and cabinets while they slipped videos and magazines under their jackets. She guessed they would first enjoy their loot and then sell it on Tehran's flourishing black market for the forbidden.

She, Nazanin, and the other women herded the female partiers – now properly covered – into a rear bedroom. The young women, showing considerable dramatic talent, screamed, sobbed, and pleaded with their guards. One said, "I didn't want to come to this place. I've never done anything like this before. By God, my friend dragged me here. She told me it was a prayer meeting." Another said, "For God's sake, don't take me to jail. My mother is ill and she'll die when she finds out." Another, braver than the rest, shouted, "Why are you doing this? What kind of Islam says you harass people in their homes? We're not hurting anyone. We just want to enjoy ourselves. Is that a sin? You should be arresting thieves and murderers."

The men were more docile. Hassan and his squads put them in a van under armed guard. The women, still pleading and protesting, were led to a separate van. The guards searched the apartment and confiscated musical instruments, playing cards, backgammon sets, European fashion and movie magazines, video and music cassettes, and bottles of suspicious liquids that might be whiskey or vodka.

After the vans full of partygoers drove off to the local morals office (*monkeraat*), Nilufar asked Nazanin, "What will happen to them?"

"Probably not much. In theory, they could be whipped and spend months or years in jail. The judge will scare them, but he'll let them go if their parents pay a fine. At worst they'll spend one or two nights in a cell. We haven't found any drugs. In that case, things would be too serious for fines. They sometimes shave the heads of the boys. For the girls, the judge can order virginity tests, but he usually doesn't unless he's a real hard case. It's a scary prospect. If an unmarried girl fails the test they can force her to marry or even charge her with prostitution. In theory that carries the death penalty."

TEHRAN
SPRING 1981

For the Undersecretary,

With the hostage-taking over, the regime has made the war with Iraq its mobilizing cause. The war is a pretext for imposing the harshest social restrictions and for violent suppression of all dissent. Veiling is now compulsory everywhere. The regime is exploiting the religiosity of most Iranians both to continue the war and to label its domestic opponents as enemies of God, the prophet, and his family.

For the past three months I have been part of a cat and mouse game between hedonistic citizens and their puritanical rulers. What impresses me is the determination of both sides. There is no accommodation, no compromise. The authorities are resolved, at any cost, to suppress all immoral acts (as they define them) and impose, by force if necessary, their rigid, austere version of Islam. They seem fixated on details of personal behavior, especially the dress and actions of women.

On the other side, love of music, wine, poetry, and dance remain woven into the fabric of this culture. For centuries, Iran's poets have sung the praises of forbidden pleasures. Every neighborhood in every town has its bootlegger. Every town has dealers in banned videotapes. Every town has an underground party and music scene. Every town has its pimps and whores.

Excess breeds excess: the greater the suppression, the greater the debauchery. Our patrols have raided gatherings that were in fact orgies fueled by music, drugs, pornography, and alcohol. Those arrested explain their actions by saying, "When you outlaw our simplest pleasures, we will observe no limits."

Khomeini himself recognizes the extreme pleasure-loving streak in his countrymen. In a recent meeting with morality squad leaders, he said, "You cannot allow even the most minor infraction. Our people are weak. Give them the smallest opening to violate the rules, and they will lose control. They will have no restraint, and, given the opportunity, will dance naked and drunk in the streets."

With respect, Miriam

By *Nowruz*, the spring celebration of the New Year, the Thursday dinners at Minu and Ahmad's apartment had become gatherings of the grim. Relatives traded horror stories – friends arrested, neighbors fled abroad, and schoolmates killed, missing, or maimed at the front. They shared secrets on where to find black market tea, sugar, butter, and other scarce items. Even Nilufar's stories of ingenious citizens outwitting the morality police failed to raise spirits.

Her cousin Iraj's parents were frantic. They were hearing reports the regime was rearresting those released and executing those already serving prison terms. Iraj was in hiding and scheduled to leave for the Turkish border with well-paid smugglers. Heavy snow in the Northwest had delayed his travel.

Nilufar found a moment to talk privately with Ahmad's son Babak. "I have an urgent message for you. The patrols are going to raid your friend Kambiz Nikpour's apartment off the Old Shemiran Road. They know Kambiz is hosting a party on Tuesday night. He thinks that since he's bribed the local *komiteh* no one will bother them. But he forgot to bribe a neighboring *komiteh* and they have passed word to the patrols. Please warn him we have orders for both men and women's units to raid his place that night. My squad will be in the operation."

"Should Kambiz cancel the party?"

"He could, but if he does, he needs to make sure everyone gets the word. If the patrols show up and find even one unrelated couple, there'll be problems. Even if no one's there, they could get suspicious and make trouble. My colleagues are in an ugly mood. People are getting better at outwitting them, and they hate looking stupid. They're beating up young boys and girls, just kids, on the smallest pretext. Now it's harder to get off with just a fine. Judges are cracking down. When they find alcohol, someone gets whipped." If they do accept a fine, it's a minimum of $2000 in hard currency.

Babak laughed. "Hard currency? I thought only Tehran whores demanded that. I will warn Kambiz. Of course I won't tell him my source."

About 10:30 on Tuesday night, Nilufar drove her squad's Nissan up a deserted Old Shemiran Road. There she met two other women's patrols and three men's. The six cars, followed by four empty vans, entered a side street and stopped at number sixteen, a modern four-story apartment building. Armed male guards took up positions outside the building and at the two ends of the narrow lane. With a men's squad in the lead, Nazanin took her group, including Nilufar, close behind to the Nikpour apartment on the second floor. The whole building was quiet except for the low sounds of a television from a first-floor apartment. If there was a party going on, it was a silent one behind blackout curtains. Three guards took up positions on the landing leading to the third floor so that no one could escape to another apartment or the roof.

Hamid, the operation's commander, banged on the door and shouted, "Open the door. Immediately!" Two young men in dark, long-sleeve shirts, fatigue jackets, and three days of chin stubble opened the door. They looked at the guards and said, "Brothers and sisters, what is your command?" Without answering, Hamid and his men pushed past the two young men into the apartment's foyer. Nazanin, Nilufar, and their group followed, ready to make arrests. They saw three dozen pairs of shoes and boots lining one wall.

Hamid barked, "Where is Kambiz Nikpour?"

A bearded young man of about twenty-five, wearing revolutionary garb, answered, "That's me. At your service, sir. You are welcome. You have arrived at just the right time."

Hamid growled sarcastically, "I'm sure we have."

Very politely, Nikpour told him, "As I said, you and your brothers and sisters came just in time. We are about to begin a modest religious program this evening and will be highly honored if you would join us."

Hamid, who was used to bullying his victims, stood confused and speechless. After a few seconds, he sputtered, "What are you saying? A religious program? Here? Tonight?"

He whispered to one of the guards, "Have we come to the wrong place?" The other checked some papers and shook his head emphatically.

"Of course. Please follow me." Kambiz opened the door to a spacious salon. Inside someone had replaced the ornate sofas and armchairs with ten rows of metal folding chairs with an aisle down the middle. An eight-foot-high, heavy black curtain divided the room in half. On one side sat about twenty young men, dressed in varieties of revolutionary outfits – camouflage pants and jackets, long-sleeved dark shirts with buttoned collars, and bandanas. On the other side sat about fifteen young women, heavily veiled. At the arrival of male guards, the women drew their veils closer, revealing only one eye and a nose.

Kambiz indicated a forty-year-old man dressed in an immaculate clerical robe and green turban. He was tall and strikingly handsome, with olive skin, medium length jet-black hair, and a neatly trimmed beard. "Brother, allow me to introduce the learned teacher Sheikh Haj Seyyed Reza Torbati. You must have heard of him. He is one of our district's outstanding young Islamic scholars and is well known for both wisdom and eloquence. He has many followers among young people in this neighborhood. We invited him to address us tonight and, despite the many demands on his time, he did us the honor of accepting. You have arrived just as he was to begin speaking."

A confused Hamid shook the cleric's hand and mumbled, "An honor to meet you, haji agha."

Kambiz motioned to the two sides of the curtain. "We have plenty of room. We will bring more chairs. The brothers can sit on the men's side. The sister guards can sit with the ladies." He called out, "Reza, Soheila. Bring fresh tea for our guests." Trays appeared with a dozen small glasses of strong tea. Hamid said to an underling, "Tell the guards outside to stand down. Radio headquarters that there's no problem here. We'll stay unless there's another assignment for us. Post two guards outside so no one disturbs his excellency the sheikh."

Nilufar could barely contain herself. Nazanin asked her, "Massoumeh, I'd like to stay and listen to the sheikh. What about you? Somehow he looks familiar to me. Does he have one of those religious advice programs on television? Do you know who he is?"

Nilufar did not say she thought she too recognized "Sheikh Torbati" behind his beard and robe – and not from any religious television program. She could answer only, "No. He's new to me. But he obviously has a following among these young people. Let's hear what he has to say. It looks like tonight's anti-sin operation is cancelled."

The male guards removed their boots, the women their shoes, left their weapons in the hall, and made their way to vacant chairs in the salon. The sheikh began speaking in a deep, well-modulated voice. "In the name of God, the merciful, the compassionate," followed by some incomprehensible phrases in Arabic. He continued, "Praises be to the prophet of God and to the immaculate imams of his family. Praises be to the living imam of the ages, may God hasten his return. Praises be to our brave warriors and martyrs at the front who defend our homeland and our faith."

He waited, looked over the crowd, and when he had everyone's attention, he cleared his throat, and continued. "First, allow me to welcome all brothers and sisters here tonight. I welcome especially our brave brother and sister guards who have undertaken the sacred mission of safeguarding the gains of our revolution and of guiding our people on the true path of Islam."

After that introduction, he said, "Tonight, brothers and sisters, with your permission, I plan to talk about marriage and about relations between young men and young women." He paused, smiled, and said, "I do not want to bore you. I hope this subject interests all of you here tonight. It is natural that it should." He paused again as the room fell silent.

"Thanks to God and our great revolution, in the sensitive matter of relations between men and women, our society has embarked on a corrected path. We have abandoned the ways of sin and vice that the former evil regime and its foreign supporters hoped to force on us. No longer do our televisions, our cinemas, and our magazines display lurid images of half-naked ladies. No longer does our regime, encouraged by its foreign masters, distract our young people by the temptations of corruption and immorality.

"Make no mistake, brothers and sisters. The decadence we witnessed in our country for so long was no accident. It was a plan devised in Washington and London, and spread in our cities by the godless, puppet regime at the instruction of its foreign masters. Foreign experts with doctorates in psychology and sociology created a systematic plan to tempt you – the young people of our great nation – into following a culture without values, without justice, and – most important – without religion."

He paused again and looked at his rapt audience. "But they were wrong. Their evil plans collapsed because you held firm to the principles of pure and revolutionary Islam. You told them in one voice: 'No. We reject your degenerate values. We reject your materialism. We reject your erotic music and half-naked women.' With your raised fists you told them, 'No. We choose instead an authentic Iranian and Islamic identity. Under the leadership of Imam Khomeini, we choose purity, and a dynamic, revolutionary Islam that is worth more than a thousand of your false idols.'"

He spoke directly to the young men and women. "By being here tonight you have chosen the straight path and have rejected the foreigners' materialism and pornography.

"What do the foreigners and their corrupt Iranian agents plan to do? They plan to exploit your natural desires and lead you on the sinful path they made for you. They know that young people have powerful urges they need to fulfill. If they can persuade you to fulfill them by casual sex, drugs, dancing, drinking, and pornography, then you will never question the existing system. You will never revolt, and the tyrant will sit securely on his throne. You will be too distracted, too stupefied to ask why the foreigners and their debased Iranian friends are stealing our country's wealth; why our noble religion and the clergy are ridiculed; why our schools have become centers of moral corruption; and why the Shah tortures and murders his own people."

He paused again, lowered his voice, and said, "Of course your desires are natural, a divine gift. God has created men and women to produce children and give each other pleasure through marriage and sex. Make no mistake. The sexual urge is a gift from God. A group of companions of our beloved sixth imam, Jafar al-Sadeq, peace be upon him, reported that the imam asked them: 'What is the most pleasurable thing?' They said: 'There are many pleasurable things.' The imam said: 'The most pleasurable thing is making love with your spouses.'"

"God wants you to control your urges, but he also wants each of you to marry and have pleasure. My dear young friends, do not wait too long to marry. If you do, God forbid, those same blessed urges of your body can lead you into grievous sin.

"Don't make things difficult for yourselves. Dear sisters, why should you look for rich husbands? You need believing and virtuous ones. Don't criticize your suitors, saying, 'This one is bald; that one is fat; this one's car is too old; this one's house is too small.'

"Brothers, you too should not demand too much. Do not say, 'She is too dark; she is too skinny; her eyes are crossed; her mother has a limp.' By all that is holy, such things do not matter. Find a believing girl from a good, religious family. Even better, find a war widow, and provide for her and her children."

The audience was silent. The women pulled their veils tighter and suppressed giggles. Nilufar covered her face so no one could see her hiding her laughter. She could not read Nazanin's expression. She looked at the other women guards and saw they were almost swooning at the handsome sheikh and his hypnotic voice.

He continued, "Brothers and sisters, when you find such a virtuous person, marry soon, and then enjoy yourselves as God, his prophet (blessings and peace upon him and his family), and imams (peace upon them all) have taught us."

Again he waited for the audience to absorb his message. "Now, dear listeners, I have been speaking in generalities. Let me now talk specifics. When you have followed the instructions of our blessed prophet and imams and have found yourself a pious husband or wife, what should you do next? What are your duties?

"First, I speak to our dear brothers. Remember that satisfying your wife is a vital matter in Islam. All scholars agree it is your obligation. Indeed, a wife's lack of satisfaction over the long term can lead to frigidity and resentment toward the husband. In the sexual act you must take your time. It is narrated that Imam Ali, peace be upon him, said, 'When any of you wants to sleep with his wife, he must not rush her, for indeed women have needs too.' Remember that you can be quickly aroused and satisfied. But a woman's sexual desire is slower to manifest itself, but once provoked, is very powerful."

With a smile, Nazanin whispered to Nilufar, "Do you think any of these jackasses are listening? I can imagine how badly they perform. One-two-three and it's over. But dear, modest Massoumeh, I must be embarrassing you. I apologize."

"The traditions of our prophet and imams all stress the importance of foreplay. It is narrated from the Prophet, peace and blessings upon him and his family, 'Do not engage in sexual intercourse with your wife like an animal; rather, begin foreplay with your wife and flirt with her; then make love to her.' It is also narrated from the Prophet: 'All play and games are idleness except for three: horse riding, archery, and foreplay with your wife.' It is narrated from Imam Ali: 'Whoever wants to get close to his wife must not be hasty, because women must be caressed gently until they are prepared for the act of love.'"

The sheikh let his audience absorb these details. He told them, "Dear brothers. In the interest of modesty I will not go into more detail. If any of you require more guidance in this area, we can meet privately."

He then turned to the women. "Dear sisters. I must say important things to you. Your role is vital in ensuring the success of a marriage. You must do all you can to maintain your husband's interest in healthy and frequent marital relations. Of course in the first few months of marriage, that will be easy. Both your fires will be hot.

"But the white heat of those first weeks and months will cool. Now your duty begins. You must ensure that you maintain his excitement and that his desire for relations with you does not cool. You must do all you can so he does not become indifferent or, God forbid, seek variety and fulfill his needs elsewhere.

"You must dress and behave at home in a way that keeps him aroused and prepared for sexual relations. At the same time, you must not overdo it. No more than two or three times a week. You should make sure that your nightclothes, your hair, and especially your underwear will arouse him. If you have light skin, you should wear dark underpants. If you have dark skin, white ones. But if you try to arouse him too often, the excitement will die and your attractions will become familiar. Tempting him twice a week should keep his interest at a high pitch. If his fire is exceptionally hot, then make it three times. But twice is safer."

Some women were taking notes. The room was absolutely silent. Nilufar could barely contain her laughter. The sheikh turned to the whole audience and, in a conversational tone, said, "Dear friends. I have gone on too long. I'm afraid I have bored you with all these things. Please pardon me for doing so, but I consider happy marriage to be the base of our society. Just remember this advice: control your sexual urges until you marry, marry soon, and follow the advice of our scholars and imams by enjoying yourselves."

He took a deep breath and concluded, "When you follow the true path of Islam, especially in the matters we discussed tonight, the blessed angels will rejoice. Peace upon you, and the blessings and mercy of God."

For fifteen seconds no one moved or spoke. Then the meeting broke up and Kambiz's guests and the guards exchanged embraces and pledges of eternal friendship. Before the guards left the apartment, they asked the sheikh, "How can we hear you again? Where and when will you speak next?" Others whispered to him, "Can we arrange a private meeting? I need your advice about personal matters. The matters you discussed in your speech." The sheikh told them, "Unfortunately I will be leaving tomorrow for a few months of study with eminent Shi'ite scholars in the Arab countries. Perhaps after my return. But thank you for coming tonight. And best wishes for success in your holy mission."

Nilufar needed to leave quickly. She had not seen her cousin Babak, but still worried that someone might recognize her, even in her zealot's disguise. She took Nazanin's arm and said, "I need some fresh air. I'll meet you by the car."

Waiting outside, she overheard the other women saying, "I'll bet he has no problem satisfying his wife. *Khosh be-haalesh* (Good for her). Even if he's married, I'd be happy to be his *sigheh* (temporary wife) for just a week."

Two days later, on Thursday evening, Nilufar told her relatives what happened at Kambiz's apartment. The customary gloom lifted, and everyone roared with laughter. Ahmad found some champagne he had been hiding. "I was keeping this for a celebration. For the downfall of the *akhund*s. Since we may have to wait a while for that, I think Nilu's story is a good reason to celebrate."

Nilufar asked Babak, "So what was going on there?"

Babak grinned and said, "When I gave Kambiz your message, he and his friends decided not to cancel. That would have looked suspicious, and someone who didn't get the word might have shown up in party clothes ready to drink and dance. I'm not sure who thought up the idea of a religious lecture, but once they decided, all played their parts. Everyone liked the idea."

"And what about that Sheikh Torbati? Who is he? Where did they find him? He seemed familiar to me somehow, but I'm not sure from where. If he recognized me, he didn't show it."

"You may have seen him at other parties. Or maybe in films or TV programs before the revolution. His real name is Vartan Khachatourian. He's Armenian and is Kambiz's long-time friend and business associate. His family are big auto parts wholesalers. Very rich. He was working in the family business when, in his thirties, he decided to change careers and become an actor. He was studying at the Tehran Actors' Academy and working in TV and film when the revolution ended that plan."

Nilufar said, "Where did he get his 'sheikh' act? He was convincing and seemed very well versed in religious law. He couldn't have learned all that Islam in church or acting school."

Babak replied, "It's an interesting story. When he was at university he fell desperately in love with a Moslem girl. They wanted to marry, but he had to convert to Islam before her family – very conservative Tabrizis – would consent. He agreed, and was ready even to be circumcised." The men in the room winced.

"He made a serious study of his new religion. He took the name Abd al-Rahim and, once he started reading, he became interested in learning more. He found some excellent teachers who were more than willing to help him. He spent a year at the Haqqani Seminary in Qom learning Arabic and studying Qur'an, *hadith* (tradition), rhetoric, and jurisprudence. By all accounts he was a most diligent student."

Minu asked, "Well, what happened? After all that, did they get married?"

"No. In the end they didn't. The girl's parents would have welcomed him as a son-in-law, especially when he showed himself so serious about Islam. It didn't hurt that his family is rich. But his relatives were very unhappy and, in the end, he couldn't go against them. They were set on his marrying an Armenian girl they had already chosen. They never said anything negative to him directly, but they didn't have to. Their views were clear. If he married this girl, he would be out of the family."

WASHINGTON
SPRING AND SUMMER 1981

Washington had entered its best months of May and June when Porter met Farzaneh and David Hartman for dinner at Bistro Français on M Street in Georgetown. The new Reagan administration was steering America into misadventures in Lebanon and Central America. Iran and the hostage crisis was a painful memory and festering sore that no one wanted to touch. Iran had destroyed a Democrat's presidency and the Republicans were determined it would not happen to them.

Porter kept his post as undersecretary for political affairs. Even the new administration's ideologues admired his judgment, discretion, and mastery of complex issues. They knew he would give them honest advice and, even if they did not listen to him, would carry out policy like the professional he was. They didn't like him or agree with him, but they needed him.

Over steak-frites he told the Hartmans, "I'm sure you have your own sources about Nilufar – or Massoumeh as she is now. I can tell you that miraculously we've been able to keep her identity a secret from all but about six people in Washington. You've raised a remarkable daughter. She has done invaluable work."

Farzaneh replied, "We've always been proud of her. We're especially pleased you recognize how special she is. We can't communicate with her directly, but my sister Minu has been getting news to us. Did you hear her story about the guards' raid on her friend's party and the show with the Armenian 'sheikh'? I wish we could share it with our friends. We all need comic relief in our lives."

David asked, "Can you assure us she's safe? Are you confident? The family can't tell us much directly, but we can read between the lines. Every day the regime puts more pressure on educated, middle-class people like Farzaneh's relatives.

Porter thought for a moment and said, "David and Far-zaneh, I worry about her every minute of every day. As far as I can tell, her new identity and persona are protecting her. We have nothing to indicate anyone suspects her. We're ready to bring her out the moment she senses danger. For now, we'd like to keep her there. She's irreplaceable."

Farzaneh told him, "Ambassador Porter, it seems to me this administration has some odd ideas about Iran. Who's feeding it such nonsense? I'm sure it's not you or Nilufar. I hear that some people here have convinced themselves the Islamic Republic is on the verge of collapse and the baby Shah, with some help from his American friends, can walk in and take over. Can't you and Nilufar set them straight?"

"I wish we could and it were that simple. Tehran has its ideologues; we have ours here in Washington. They are well-connected and believe what they want to believe. Unfortunately, they can usually find someone to support their fantasies. Just because a gifted observer in Tehran like Nilufar is telling them something different doesn't mean they'll accept it. She's giving us reality, and ideologues don't like reality."

Porter drank some of his Bordeaux and changed the subject. "What do you think about her working in the morals police? Should she stay there? I know why she left Beheshti's office, and I respect her reasons. She was too close to the centers of power, and drew attention to herself. On the other hand, that very closeness made her valuable for us." Keeping his promise to Nilufar, he did not mention their difficult Dubai meeting and her feelings of guilt for the regime's bloody campaign against the MEK.

Farzaneh said, "Well, I think she left Beheshti's office at a good time. But most of my relatives cannot understand why she's doing what she's doing now. They're appalled. To them the morality patrols are the worst of the worst in the Islamic Republic. The men guards are disgusting and the women are worse – rude, uneducated, brutal, and loaded with resentments they take out on ordinary people."

Porter asked, "So why is she's doing it?"

Farzaneh smiled and said, "I know my daughter. She's a lot like me. She is testing herself. Can she do one of the vilest jobs in the country – one that goes against everything she believes? At the same time, can she mislead the authorities into thinking she's a true believer? She sees her work as the best way to build her new identity and remain above suspicion. She's hiding in plain sight. Who would expect an American spy to be a pious woman and – more than that – wallow in filth with the morals police?"

Porter's pager beeped. "Excuse me, I need to make a call." From the restaurant he spoke briefly to a senior watch officer at the state department's operations center. He returned to the table and told them. "I'm sorry, but I need to go to my office. There's news from Tehran. A bomb has gone off at the IRP headquarters and casualties are heavy. Unconfirmed reports say Beheshti is among the dead."

"Any claims of responsibility?" asked David.

"Not yet. It's still chaotic. We expect to know more in the next few hours."

Farzaneh narrowed her eyes and said, "It has to be the MEK. They have the access and the organization for such things, although until now not on this scale. They have a singular hatred for Beheshti. They consider him responsible for the bloody campaign against them. They'll do anything to destroy him.

"Now repression and the violence will get worse. Beheshti was ruthless, but he was smart and could be subtle when he needed to be. The rest of the group are thugs."

Ignoring a second signal from his pager, Porter turned to Farzaneh and said, "Actually, what just happened is forcing my hand. I need a favor. Can you contact your brother Arash in Geneva? I urgently need to meet him and talk about Nilufar and her work. I know no one wanted her to go back to Beheshti's office. But I don't know how long she should stay with the morals police. People love what she reports, but we still need information from inside the regime."

Farzaneh told him, "Well, the sooner she leaves the patrols, the happier my relatives will be. Her work there is making them miserable. I'll get a message to Arash. I can't imagine he's reassured by events at home."

GENEVA

Ten days later Porter and Arash Rastbin met for lunch at the Café de Paris, a modest restaurant near Geneva's Cornavin railroad station and famous for its medium-rare *entrecôte* in anchovy/butter sauce with *pommes frites*. Porter knew Arash detested the Islamic regime while skillfully acting the part of its representative. He wore a trimmed beard, a well-cut European suit, elegant shoes, and a silk and cotton white shirt buttoned to the throat. No necktie.

Porter told him, "Arash, I need to thank you for all your help. You know what your niece is doing is incredible. You know how she saved our colleagues at Mehrabad last year. You know how she helped us get intelligence against the MEK to Beheshti. I'm sure you know what a remarkable woman she is. Her work there has been priceless to us."

"Alan, of course I understand what she does is important to you. It's important to me too. Some of us still want to stop the fanatics from destroying what's left of our country. She's also helped us stop those MEK Stalinists from turning the country into a gulag. They're smart, violent, and well organized. They can turn out half a million for a demonstration in Tehran, and the authorities are terrified. Their only response is to kill and create martyrs."

Arash ate more of the *entrecôte* and continued, "She had to leave Beheshti's office, but I regret to say some of my relatives are very upset at what she's doing now. They just can't swallow her working with the morals police, who to them are the dregs of our society. They have all had nasty run-ins with the patrols, so it's easy to understand how they feel.

"It's good they don't know about her work with Beheshti in the anti-MEK campaign. We shouldn't fool ourselves. That was worse. Some of Beheshti's victims were children of friends and close relatives. The three of us have their blood on our hands. Fortunately no one else in the family except Ahmad and Mehrdad knows what she did. They think she was just a translator in Beheshti's office." Arash shook his head.

Porter said nothing but nodded in agreement. "By the way, you can tell the family that your cousin Iraj is now safely in school at Chapel Hill. Electrical engineering, I think. It's never easy for young Iranians but, once he got to Turkey, we were able to help him with his papers and visa. As for Nilufar, she had a serious crisis of conscience about her assignment. She is a thorough professional, but her work truly disturbed her. Matters went much farther than we thought."

"Alan, what did you think would happen? There is never going to be any outcome except one side being annihilated. You know how ruthless Beheshti is. You know what the MEK is like. You know politics in my country is a blood sport. Torture or be tortured. Kill or be killed."

"That's just what Nilufar told me. The two of you have given me in-depth lessons in Iranian reality. Do you agree it was best she left Beheshti's office?"

"Definitely. It was dangerous there for all kinds of reasons. God forbid, she could have been at IRP headquarters with Beheshti when the bomb went off. No, I have to admit that this work with the patrols, odious as it is, is perfect cover for her."

Swirling the French fries in the anchovy sauce, Porter said, "Arash, at some point she will need to get back inside the government. With Beheshti dead, I don't know who will replace him as the mover behind Khomeini, but we need Nilufar on the inside. Can you help us?"

"Let me check with Mehrdad Dashti and see what he thinks. Despite all the changes and purges, he's managed to keep his influence and stay in the Foreign Ministry legal department. Beheshti was a key patron for him, but I'm sure he has other protectors. For the moment, I think he'll advise us to wait until the dust settles from the IRP bombing. That would be my advice too. There are true horrors coming, and we don't want Nilufar – even in her Massoumeh persona – too close to them. When things are calmer, he can find a place for her."

"Agree. Let's finish with a *Coupe Dänemark* for dessert."

For the Undersecretary,

Beheshti's death has brought more repression. The gangs from the so-called "Party of God" (*Hezbollah*) are on a rampage against both political opponents and those who violate the most trivial social regulations. The wrong cassette in your car can get you condemned as a *monaafeq* (MEK supporter), *mosfed fi-l'Arz* (spreader of corruption), or *mohaareb-ba-khoda* (enemy of God), all capital crimes.

A joke captures the prevailing climate: A fox flees Iran and meets his brother foxes in Turkey. When they ask him why he left, he replies, "Things are so bad there they are castrating all foxes with only one testicle." They ask him, "So what's the problem? You clearly have two." He answers, "You Turks are so simple. You don't understand anything about the Islamic Republic. First they cut; then they count."

The patrols have become more intrusive and aggressive. They search out trouble. "Un-Islamic behavior" is whatever the guards say it is. Dress or documents that satisfy one patrol can cause serious trouble with another. They are in a surly mood and are no longer content to give warnings. Encounters now lead to fines, whippings, and prison. Women's patrols no longer operate without armed support from a men's squad. It is too dangerous.

People are both cowed and angry. They are under stress from shortages, bombings, lines, rationing, and repression. Finding essential medicine can take days. When challenged by patrols, some will grovel and some, pushed beyond endurance, shout and scream curses at the guards and the regime. They no longer care about the consequences. They say, "Go ahead and shoot me. You'll be doing me a favor."

It is still unclear who will replace Beheshti as the brains of the regime. He had been making the

IRP into the ruling party in a one-party Islamic Republic. Within weeks of his death, the party, lacking Beheshti's strong leadership, dissolved into squabbling, ineffective factions. Now it is doubtful the IRP will survive. Other powerful clerics are maneuvering for position, but so far no one has emerged as a favorite to replace Beheshti.

The war is draining the country of manpower and resources. There are rumors that senior clerics, including rivals Hashemi-Rafsanjani and Ayatollah Montazeri, are urging Khomeini to accept a settlement with Iraq through mediation. So far he has refused. The war serves his purpose.

The collapse of world crude oil prices and the regime's failure to invest in oil infrastructure has meant that all of Iran's oil income goes to buy munitions and essential foods. Nothing else. Power outages are frequent, and uncollected rubbish is littering the streets and alleys of the capital.

By all indications, despite the problems, civilian morale remains high and many Iranians are willing to set aside their dislike of the regime to fight the hated Iraqis. The singer Sadeq Aahangaraan, known as "Khomeini's Nightingale," continues to chant "*aamaadeh baash* (get ready)" and inspire young volunteers and aspiring martyrs with songs of sacrifice, mysticism, and patriotism.

Working with the morals police has provided excellent cover. Although the regime is obsessed with spies, and every day its mouthpieces trumpet some new plot uncovered, no one expects to find the enemy "hiding in plain sight" among the most hated and fanatic group of regime supporters.

With respect, Miriam

PART TWO

A TIME TO LOVE

6

RUZBEH

Nilufar had stayed too long with the morals police. After three years of this ugly work, she could take no more. Her family's tolerance had long run out. The regime had not eased its repression. The war with Iraq was going badly and the economy struggling, with the enthusiasm of the early years lost. There were no more mass demonstrations and parades. Ordinary Iranians recognized three rules: shut up, follow orders, and send more men and boys to die at the front.

The authorities blamed bad news on foreign plots and domestic opponents. They increased pressure on intellectuals, leftists, liberals, and women whose dress and behavior were not "Islamic" enough. Nilufar's morality squad was no longer there to advise. It humiliated and punished.

Mehrdad was blunt. "Nilufar, you have to leave the *gasht*. Your family has put up with this act for three years. No more. Either there will be a family split or, worse, someone will betray you. Stop before someone does something stupid."

"Dear Mehrdad, I know how awful this has been for the family, especially for Auntie Minu and your wife Pari. Everyone has been tolerant beyond all limits. Ahmad is polite, but Auntie Minu barely speaks to me. But I needed to stay in Iran to carry out the mission I have been given. This is my duty and my destiny. What do you suggest I do now?"

"Things have settled down since Beheshti was killed. Ironically, your work with the *gasht* kept you away from the violent pushing and shoving. I can get you a position in Hashemi-Rafsanjani's office. It would be much the same work you were doing for Beheshti. His title is Speaker of Parliament, but he's much more. No one can replace Beheshti, but Hashemi-Rafsanjani comes close. The two were allies and co-founders of the IRP. Your experience with Beheshti will be a great recommendation. My friend Hossein Niku is Hashemi's office director, and I can talk to him."

"Is that the same Hossein Niku from Qazvin who used to work for Beheshti? I remember him well."

"It is. I knew him in Hamburg when he was a student. Very smart and absolutely devoted to the revolution. He abandoned his studies to work under Beheshti against the Shah. He left Beheshti's office about the same time you did and volunteered to serve at the front with a Revolutionary Guards unit. Had a very distinguished war record, I understand. He was wounded near Mehran and walks with a cane. Now he's Hashemi-Rafsanjani's chief of staff."

WASHINGTON

Alan Porter chaired something called the "small group" of five American officials who knew of source Miriam's existence and activities. In addition to Porter, there were counterparts from CIA, NSA, Department of Defense, and the White House. This group received her unabridged reports, decided on their editing and distribution within the US government, and responded to her messages with instructions, questions, and comments.

Her latest message, reporting from her new position in Hashemi-Rafsanjani's office, included an emphatic "no" to the small group's latest proposal. They had decided she needed to improve her makeshift communication system via the pastry shop and the friendly embassy. This crude system could not remain safe much longer. The group proposed sending a CIA officer to Tehran to set up a secure and direct communications link.

When she read that they would send someone under a false Italian commercial identity, she exploded. "Yes, I need better communications. But sending such a person here is folly. He will get himself, me and my family killed. He will not last a day in Tehran. The security service assumes every foreigner here is a spy. He will be followed from the minute he steps off the plane. I assume I am already watched. Any contact with a foreigner will be fatal for me. Do not send him or anyone else."

George Blessey, the lanky, CIA veteran surveyed his colleagues from behind his unstylish glasses and asked, "So, gentlemen, what do we do now? Miriam's been in Hashemi-Rafsanjani's office for some months. He's not Beheshti, but he's made the office of Parliament Speaker a major power base. She's at the center of things. Her reports are excellent, especially on the war, the power struggles, and the economy. But we can't keep trusting our luck to keep her and her pastry shop channel secure. It's only one step above using invisible ink and carrier pigeons."

Porter thought for a while. "It was a makeshift arrangement when we started it, and we never foresaw using it this long. If we're going to keep her there, she needs something safe. But we also must defer to her about Tehran. She's been on the streets five years. I for one am not going to tell her, 'Look, we know better than you how to operate there.'"

Blessey shrugged. "Alan, the hard truth is that we lose her either way. We either send our officer and he and she both get caught, or we leave her with the pastry shop and she gets caught and our friendly embassy channel disappears. We can't do nothing. We have to take the risk. We either give her secure communications or I will recommend to the president that we bring her home."

"But we're asking her to take the risks." Porter paused, and asked Blessey, "Do you have anyone else? Someone she'll believe won't be wearing a sign that says, 'American Spy' and get her killed?"

"We'll need a fluent Persian speaker and someone who knows his way around Tehran. I just don't know how many of those we have. Or if we have any."

Three days later Blessey called Porter. "Alan, I think I have someone. There's an Iranian-American operations officer who is training for a post in India. Everything about him looks right. His instructors say he is very good on both the technical and operations sides."

"Send him to me tomorrow. The sooner we can make her safe, the better." If they could not provide her secure communications, Porter was ready to bring Nilufar home. They had pushed their luck beyond reasonable limits. Nilufar's parents were worried, and Porter did not want to give them assurances they would never believe. He was responsible for their daughter's life. He had sent her to Tehran five years ago and kept her there in danger for too long. He was having nightmares of Tehran radio's announcing the capture of another American spy.

He had first imagined she would be in Tehran for a few months at most until the embassy hostages were released. He and many others had misjudged events and had not foreseen their ugly and violent direction. Porter and his colleagues had come to depend on Nilufar's insights and made the danger to her life a secondary consideration.

Ruzbeh Parvizi arrived at the State Department's C Street entrance at 2:30 for his 3:00 p.m. appointment with undersecretary Porter. A young man of medium height, with fair complexion, dark hair, and dark eyes, he wore the young, aspiring Washington bureaucrat's uniform: a three-piece dark suit from Raleigh's and black Johnston and Murphy wing tip shoes.

His bosses would or could not tell him why he had been summoned by the undersecretary of state for political affairs. "Above my pay grade," each of them said. But Ruzbeh had learned, even in his short time at CIA, a truth about government service: no good deed goes unpunished. He guessed this maxim was likely to apply to his coming encounter with Porter.

Ruzbeh saw a crowd of foreign diplomats at the State Department reception desk. The flags of nations having diplomatic relations with the United States formed the colorful but uninspired decoration of the C Street lobby. Ruzbeh joined another line of businesspeople and journalists seeking access to the building. People in both lines were waiting to be escorted to meetings where they would give as little information as possible in exchange for some useful policy or operational nugget from the department's desk officers, press officers, and regional experts, who worked mostly on floors one through five. If they were lucky, they might have a conversation with someone better informed on floors six or seven.

Ruzbeh rode the elevator to the seventh floor and calculated he could make good use of this visit in preparing for his assignment to the CIA station in New Delhi. He'd been to the State Department only once before, when he was sworn in as part of a class of Foreign Service Officers. The ceremony was supposed to build his cover as a junior officer in the economic section in India. However today turned out, he could now elaborate on his story by describing the undersecretary's office and a few more scenes from "mahogany row," the part of State's seventh floor with offices for the secretary, the deputy Secretary, and Porter.

After a few minutes ruffling through out-of-date *Time* and *Newsweek* magazines on the table outside of Porter's office, a staff assistant escorted Ruzbeh into an outer office full of dark wood, American landscape paintings, and a view of the Lincoln Memorial, the Potomac, and the Pentagon.

Porter shook Ruzbeh's hand and took him through a door leading to a smaller, private office; still plenty of mahogany, but more personal. Family photos and what looked like a painting of a small house on North Carolina's Outer Banks. Almost hidden in the back, behind the blond-haired, Midwestern faces in the family display, was a group photo taken on the eighth floor of Porter and a class of junior officers. He must have just sworn them in, Ruzbeh said to himself. He was attracted to the happy-looking people in the picture and wished he had a memory like this of the class he had joined – even as an imposter – for its ceremony. Porter offered a glass of water and asked Ruzbeh about his background and how he chose the CIA as a career.

"My father was born in Iran and studied medicine there. He got his degree in radiology. At that time, there were few jobs in Iran for people in the field, so he applied for and received an offer to do postgraduate work at the University of California, Los Angeles, medical school. He arrived in LA in March 1953, expecting I suppose, like most young Iranians studying abroad at the time, to do his coursework and go home."

"As Dad describes himself at the time – he was twenty-three – he was a supporter of Prime Minister Mosaddegh. He supported the nationalization of the Iranian Oil Company. He also liked Mosaddegh's effort to bring more democracy to Iran and limit the power of both the Shah and the clerics. He did not believe the British propaganda that Mosaddegh – whom they dismissed as "Mad Mossy" – would deliver Iran to the Communists.

"The CIA-backed coup that overthrew Mosaddegh in August 1953 -- my Dad always referred to it as the 28 Mordad coup-d'état not Operation Ajax as I learned in school -- shocked him profoundly. In Iran, the CIA's role was widely known. My father resolved never to return to Iran while a Pahlavi was in power. At UCLA he also met the woman who was to become his wife and my mother. She was in the School of Education studying for a teaching certificate. As it often does, love and politics combined to make America home. I was born in 1955."

"Where did your family settle," Porter asked. "Was it important to your father that you maintained a connection to Iran?"

"My Dad made his way to Orange County, opening his radiology practice in Santa Ana. There were still orange trees everywhere. Beach Boulevard was a two-lane road to Huntington Beach. I went to Santa Ana High School. I was unique, father from Iran, mother half-French on her mother's side. I spent the summers in Nice with my maternal grandmother's family. I can get by quite well in French, although not in the local slang."

"It was important to my father that we kept some parts of Iranian culture, but we had a California mélange. I speak and read Persian well, but grew up Catholic, my mother's faith. My father insisted that I should also know the basics of Islam. I was always proud of my name and my Iranian heritage, even if most of my experiences came secondhand.

"My father would send me to Iran during summer vacations. I picked up a Tehran accent and learned my way around the country. When the Shah fell in 1979, my Dad went back, hoping to join his friends in building a democratic country after years of dictatorship. He lasted only a few months. He saw how the winds were blowing. His friends who stayed were not so lucky.

"How about college?"

"My high school debate coach had been to Stanford and she steered me there. She said I needed to get out of Southern California. I majored in history and minored in religion."

"Why CIA? You'd have made a great Foreign Service Officer."

"I suppose you or some CIA shrink will see a pattern here, but in my senior year at Stanford my thesis advisor asked if I'd like to 'meet someone from the government' and I said yes. CIA needed people with backgrounds like mine.

"I had learned something from the Iranians who had ended up in southern California after the revolution: if you don't fight for your way of life, someone is going to take it away."

"How did your Dad feel, I mean with Mosaddegh a CIA victim and all?"

"He doesn't know. Neither does my mother. They think I work for you."

And now you do, thought Porter, his concentration on Ruzbeh momentarily lost by the question of where Nilufar was at that moment. Safe, dear God, I hope safe.

Porter, who had spent his entire professional life at State and was now – in his late forties -- its highest-ranking career diplomat as undersecretary, felt uneasy with the role reversal that was coming. He needed to recruit a young CIA officer to join his scheme to protect Nilufar, and, if they were lucky, keep her vital information flowing. He had no money to offer, no future citizenship to bargain with – only a call to duty.

"Ruzbeh," Porter began, "I admire you, your family, and how you are serving our country. I need your help."

When Ruzbeh said nothing, Porter continued. "It's no secret that Iran has been a policy disaster for us. We understand almost nothing of the new reality there. We now have a key source in Tehran, and the information it provides is crucial to our interests in the region. I can't, and I won't tell you more until you agree to help us. I can say we will need you to go to Iran to help protect our source. It will be dangerous. It may also be the most important thing you do in your career and you can do it now."

With a smile, Porter added, "And, you won't have to mislead your parents. You will work for me."

Ruzbeh recognized an order when he heard one. Porter had appealed to his patriotism, his sense of adventure, and his curiosity about what had become, or was becoming, of his father's homeland. He left the office after a few more minutes' conversation.

Porter immediately called George Blessey. "He's our man. Get him ready and then let's get him there."

Over a cup of bland coffee in the State Department's first-floor cafeteria, Ruzbeh considered what Porter was asking him to do. The CIA had firmly kept him away from anything Iranian. He understood but still deeply resented the unspoken message: we are suspicious of your mixed heritage, your loyalty to America, and the fact that you might know too much.

Something had caused this unfounded, and to Ruzbeh insulting, prejudice to change, at least for now, at least in this case. Porter must be so desperate to protect his Tehran source that he had persuaded CIA to abandon its fears. Whatever the reasons, Ruzbeh had his orders. He knew working in Iran could get him killed, but he felt that, for the first time in his career, he would be doing work for which he was uniquely qualified. And he would show any doubters that he was an American patriot.

TEHRAN
DECEMBER 1984

Phillipe Tehrani, the newly appointed Iran stringer for Agence France-Presse, tried to control his breathing as he presented his

Iranian passport to the sullen and suspicious border control agent at Mehrabad Airport. As Ruzbeh Parvizi, he had practiced this entry a hundred times, his CIA and French DGSE coaches alternately criticizing and encouraging his evolving tradecraft. He carried an Iranian passport because Tehrani's story was that his father was Iranian and mother French, and the laws of Iran mandated that he could be only Iranian. Porter and his colleagues also hoped that this Iranian nationality would appease Nilufar, who had insisted that no "foreigner" could come help her.

He explained to the immigration officer, in fluent and rehearsed Persian, that he had come to cover events in Iran for the French news agency. His father was Iranian, mother French. He had learned Persian well because his father was proud of his heritage. He had grown up in Thionville, on the border with Belgium. He intended to rent an apartment in Tehran. Yes, he hoped to travel around the country and report from the front. As an Iranian and a Frenchman, he was always suspicious of the Americans. He was proud France had sheltered the Ayatollah Khomeini in 1978–79.

There was enough truth in his story to make the lies believable.

The immigration officer shrugged and waved his hand, allowing Parvizi to pass to the baggage claim area. There was nothing on him or in his bag that would identify him as anything other than a young journalist who did not have enough experience to be a correspondent, but was only a stringer paid by the piece, and then only if it was used. Indeed, Ruzbeh still did not know exactly who he was looking for, who he was supposed to support. The higher-ups at CIA and State did not want him to have even this information in case he was discovered and interrogated right away. He could not reveal what he did not know.

Phillipe Tehrani was a good "legend." The director of Central Intelligence had waived the rule against the agency using journalism as a cover story, and the French service had put in the fix at AFP. The French had even planted a few back-dated stories from what Parvizi would claim was his last assignment for AFP in Mexico City. This cover should work, Parvizi thought, and fervently hoped so.

As Ruzbeh passed through the turnstile, the man at immigration took one last look at Phillipe Tehrani's landing card and was about to put it in the drawer strewn with hundreds of other arrival forms. Then he remembered a new directive: keep foreign journalists' papers separate and hand them to a supervisor at the end of your shift.

Parvizi picked up his bag, and joined the crowd waiting for taxis. He told the driver to take him to the Sofitel downtown.

At the end of his shift, the immigration officer took Tehrani's paperwork to his boss, who, without looking at it, put it into a folder that was picked up each evening and delivered to the Revolutionary Guard office at the airport.

Parvizi and his instructors at headquarters in Langley and his DGSE handlers, agreed that he should live his AFP stringer legend for several weeks after arriving. He was told to make early contact with Arthur Harley, the BBC's stringer, who had come to Iran from an assignment in Pakistan before the revolution and had covered the tumultuous events since. Harley had made the big leap from stringer to full-time BBC reporter and was being assigned to London. Parvizi found Harley at the Foreign Ministry's weekly press briefing.

Some days later, Harley and Parvizi met at a coffee shop on Sa'adi Street, not far from the old parliament building. Harley, who had adopted the British journalist's standard persona – disheveled clothes, old shoes, and a sharp and sarcastic wit – wondered why his new bosses had made such a big deal out of his giving advice to some young pup from AFP. They were competitors, after all. But, he was headed home to work for these same people, so he did as he was asked. Besides, stringers were the lowest form of journalistic life and had to stick together.

"This is hard duty," Harley said. "The Revolutionary Guards are everywhere. People fear each other. What I've learned here is to beware of certainty from any quarter. Anyone who says he has the answer to every question is not to be trusted. On the other hand, there's never a dull moment here, and people at home print what you write."

As he was asked to do by the men at BBC's Bush House head office on the Aldwych, who he did not know were acting on behalf of the men at MI6's head office at Century House in Lambeth, Harley gave Parvizi a list of useful sources and social contacts. He told him where to get black market scotch.

He told Parvizi about an unmarked Korean restaurant hidden on a side street off Vali Asr (formerly Pahlavi then briefly Mosaddegh) Avenue. "A few years ago, the owners paid the local *komiteh* to license them as a 'rehabilitation center' for alcoholic foreign journalists. The place opens and closes according to who gets bribed and who feels the need to crack down." Giving Parvizi a card, he said, "You can call this number to see if it's open. When it is, they serve cold Dutch beer. The food isn't bad either."

After much debate in Washington, London, and Paris, they agreed that Parvizi would take Harley's apartment on Somaya (formerly Soraya) Street. The intelligence professionals calculated that the Iranian watchers would see a journalist/spy's flat passed from one to another and nothing more.

Harley departed Iran as planned, unaware that he had helped establish a CIA officer in Tehran. Parvizi started his new lives. There was just one question Parvizi could not ask and, if he had, Harley could not answer: how to identify and safely contact the agent Miriam?

Twelve hours after Parvizi's arrival as Phillipe Tehrani, a messenger carried his immigration form to a smoky room on the third floor of the Mehrabad airport's main building. The chief of the office looked at the landing card and, as instructed, sent it by courier to the counterintelligence section at the Revolutionary Guard's intelligence headquarters on Revolution (formerly Shah Reza) Avenue.

Phillipe Tehrani's card landed on the desk of Reza Akbarzadeh, head of the counterintelligence section of the Revolutionary Guards responsible for watching foreign journalists. "Another young French lover boy from AFP," Akbarzadeh called to his colleague across the metal table. We'll let him work for a few months and then see if he would like a little sex with some foreigner's wife, or maybe a husband!" He put the paper into a file folder he saved for possible mischief-making and wrote on it that he should look at it again in forty-five days. He never did.

TEHRAN
JANUARY 1985

Nilufar enjoyed working in Hashemi-Rafsanjani's parliament office. The Speaker held the religious title *Hojjat al-Islam va Moslemin*, which made him roughly a senior associate professor in the Shia scholars' hierarchy. He lacked Beheshti's intellect and broad vision, but was a skilled political operative and utterly devoted to Khomeini, his former teacher, and to the cause of Iran's revolution. He had served four terms in prison under the Shah.

Now he identified the new regime's fortunes with the Islamic Republican Party, which he and Beheshti had co-founded in February 1979, just a week after the fall of the Shah. After the loss of so many party leaders in the explosion of June 1981, the party fell on hard times. But Hashemi-Rafsanjani ensured survival of the tight network of pro-IRP clergy who – thanks to their control of intelligence, the judiciary, parliament, and the Friday pulpits in major cities – continued to dominate Iran's political life.

When Nilufar met him, she saw a forty-five-year-old cleric with a high-pitched voice: short, beardless, limited scholarly credentials, and little charisma. She did not underestimate him. His enemies called him *maahi-kuseh*, the shark, a survivor. He came from a wealthy family of pistachio merchants, and his obscure thoughts and intentions were difficult to follow.

He was neither theoretician nor intellectual. He reminded her of the mysterious *siyaaq*, a coded system of Persian writing and accounting known to very few outside the bazaars. She quickly came to realize she was working for an astute master politician who immediately turned all situations to his advantage. It was also obvious that his priorities included enriching himself and his family.

Hashemi-Rafsanjani spoke no foreign languages. He soon came to rely on the competent and discreet "Massoumeh" to interpret and take notes at his meetings with foreigners. The war and continuing political violence had increased Iran's isolation, and these days fewer foreign delegations visited Tehran.

Unlike Beheshti, the Speaker enjoyed meeting with foreign businessmen. Nilufar found most of them a dubious bunch. Representatives of respectable international companies would go nowhere near Iran. Those who showed up were shady fixers who literally "made the business fat." Their proposals involved complex transactions with obscure banks and generous commissions for themselves and their Iranian partners. Iranians knew they were being robbed, but no reputable foreign company would do business with the Islamic Republic.

In January 1985 Nilufar found herself translating in a meeting with her boss and three men she did not know. Hashemi-Rafsanjani did not introduce his visitors and told them she was "Massoumeh, his private secretary and translator in the most sensitive matters." In keeping with her persona, the closely veiled Nilufar did not shake hands or make eye contact with the men.

There was a tall, cadaverous, middle-aged Iranian cleric; a forty-year-old, obese Iranian, with a mustache and graying goatee in ill-fitting Western clothes and mismatched socks; and a fifty-year-old Arab – bald, slightly overweight, with a neatly trimmed mustache, a very expensive tailor-made suit, and shoes that could not have cost less than two thousand dollars. The Iranian spoke fluent, if ungrammatical English. The Arab spoke educated American English but no Persian. It sounded like he had spent time in an exclusive eastern boarding school. In deference to local custom, neither the Iranian nor the Arab wore neckties. They considered Nilufar, as a woman, of no importance.

Hashemi-Rafsanjani began, speaking Persian, which Nilufar translated into English for the Arab visitor's benefit. "Gentlemen, I will go straight to the point, because the matter is most urgent. It concerns the survival of our beloved Islamic Republic and the outcome of the imposed war." (Iranians' term for the war with Iraq.)

"Against our enemies' expectations, we have fought the Ba'athi invaders to a standstill and have driven them out of our land. The Imam and our people are one in their determination to continue this sacred battle until final victory. All this we have done and will do despite having to fight alone. With apologies to our Arab guest here, your sheikhs and amirs have squandered their nations' wealth to finance Saddam's campaign of murder against us. Although some naïve people here have urged us to settle with Saddam, our Imam has wisely insisted there can be no peace between right and wrong, between Islam and unbelief. For us, this is not only a battle against Saddam and his Ba'athi infidels; it is the first step on the road to Jerusalem, which, God willing, we will liberate soon."

Nilufar smiled to herself. It was common knowledge that in 1982 Hashemi-Rafsanjani had urged Khomeini to accept Saddam's offer of a cease-fire and a return to prewar borders. When Khomeini rejected the offer, Hashemi-Rafsanjani joined the chorus chanting "*Jang, jang, taa piruzi* (War, war, until victory)." The stalemate, the bombings, and the slaughter of young Iranians and Iraqis went on.

Hashemi-Rafsanjani continued. "Thanks to his foreign money, Saddam is resupplying and modernizing his military. The Iraqis have leased modern aircraft from the French and are buying several hundred new Soviet tanks. The Europeans, the South Africans, and the Brazilians talk piously about neutrality but, please excuse my vulgarity, we all know they'll sell their own sisters and daughters for Arab cash.

"Of course, we are ready to fight and win alone. But the reality is we cannot match Saddam's new weapons. Our weapons are mostly American, but we cannot resupply and the American advisors never gave us what we needed to operate them properly. Our technicians have been able to improvise, but only so far. We have warehouses full of missiles, bombs, and spare parts, but the Americans never shared the codes we need to use them. Just now we're scouring the international black markets for aircraft parts and a particular missile. I'm not sure exactly what it's called, but it sounds something like *sag-e-haar* (rabid dog)." Nilufar assumed he meant "Harpoon," an American anti-ship missile the Iranians were modifying for short-range surface-to-surface use on land.

"We get cheated in the international arms market. We pay double or triple prices to con men who disappear or deliver shoddy, obsolete equipment that doesn't work."

He paused and looked at his visitors.

"We would like you to help us. We already know how to use our American weapons. Our people are smart, and they learn fast. We need to find replacements so we can defend ourselves against what the Iraqis are buying. The most urgent need is for antiaircraft and anti-tank missiles. The first are called 'Hawk' and the second 'TOW.'

"So far the Americans have turned down our approaches. Saddam has bought them, and they are determined to destroy us. They can't forget how we held their people and humiliated them during the nest of spies episode."

The obese Iranian asked, "So how can we help defend our dear homeland?"

Nilufar almost choked at his reeking insincerity. "'Dear homeland' indeed," she thought. It was obvious the questioner cared nothing for the fate of his country. She could see the greed in his eyes and hear the real question in his voice: "How big is my cut?"

Hashemi-Rafsanjani continued, "You know the people who can help us and how to talk to them. Brother Hassan and I – pointing to the Iranian cleric – are just simple seminarians. What do we know about the international arms market, or aircraft, missiles, and other weapons? We have spent our lives studying theology and jurisprudence, not logistics and tactics. So we come to you."

Nilufar again laughed to herself. Her boss delegated very little and trusted no one. If he didn't know the arms business when he started, he would learn quickly. How different were missiles and pistachios?

The Arab responded, "Your excellency is quite correct. This American administration has not forgotten how Iran's campaign for justice humiliated the previous president. You need an indirect approach that offers something of such value to the Americans that they'll have to listen."

"So, brother Adil, what will make them pay attention? You and Brother Morteza have lived there and speak their language. You know them. What will work?"

Nilufar noted the names and filed them away.

The Arab answered, "This American administration views every problem in the world through an anti-communist lens. Every terrorist incident, including the recent assassination attempt against the Pope, and every conflict in the world, it lays at the door of Moscow. In their view, the Soviets have never abandoned their goal of ruling the world and defeating the Americans and their capitalist allies. "The one thing the Americans dislike more than your Islamic Republic is communism. They look at the map and see an aggressive neighbor to your north, which they call the 'evil empire.'"

Hashemi-Rafsanjani nodded his head. "Yes, they tried to use the Soviets to scare us in 1979 after we overthrew the Shah. It didn't work. We're not so gullible that we couldn't see their motive: prey on our fears and use a Soviet threat to restore hegemony here. We already knew what the Soviets and their Iranian agents were up to. We took care of them ourselves and foiled their plots. We took casualties, including great martyr Beheshti, in the process, but when it came to a test of strength, we crushed them."

Hashemi-Rafsanjani paused and asked, "So how can we make the Americans worry about a nonexistent threat to us? And how does all that get us the weapons we need?"

"We scare them and we tempt them," said the Arab. But you can't do it yourselves at first. They won't listen. They need to hear it from someone they trust. In this case the Israelis. Brother Morteza here and I have been talking to our Israeli contacts. They will tell the Americans that you and other Iranians have approached some Israelis on behalf of a moderate, anti-Soviet faction that is competing with leftists inside the Islamic Republic. These leftists, under cover of Islamic ideology, are gaining power and threaten to turn Iran into a Soviet satellite.

"You think the Americans will believe all that?"

The Arab continued, "They will if they hear it from the Israelis. The Israelis know influential Americans who are obsessed with the communist threat. The Israelis will feed their worries."

"How do you get your Israeli friends to do that?"

"The Israelis don't share the Americans' obsession with the communists. But they are desperate to restore some relationship with you. They don't expect the pre-1979 level, but they would be happy with even 40 percent of that. They want a strong and friendly Iran as a counterweight to their Arab enemies.

"We tell our Israeli contacts we are talking to the highest officials of the Islamic Republic. We tell them you are saying that moderates in the government are battling pro-Soviet leftists, and, with Khomeini's blessing, are seeking better relations with both Israel and the United States. We say these moderates need to show they can procure the American weapons Iran needs to fight the Iraqis. If the moderates can find the arms, so this story goes, they will be well placed to defeat their leftist rivals and establish better relations with both Tel Aviv and Washington."

Hashemi-Rafsanjani looked carefully again at his visitors. "You understand the Imam will never allow us to open relations with either country. When anyone mentions talking to the Americans, he responds, 'What does the wolf want to negotiate with the sheep? They don't want to talk to us. They want to eat us.' At the same time, he will not object to our getting American or Israeli weapons to defend ourselves against Saddam. But not at a price that will betray the revolution."

The Iranian visitor responded. "Excellency, we understand that. But we know the Americans and Israelis are, for different reasons, so eager to open contact, and they'll be ready to hear what they want to hear."

Indicating the Iranian cleric, he said, "Here is where Brother Hassan will help us. After our first approach, we will introduce him to our American and Israeli counterparts as "ayatollah" and a clerical leader of the anti-leftist moderates. He will give details about the competing factions and stress the need to support him and his allies against a leftist takeover. It helps that he's related to the head of the Foundation for the Oppressed and your deputy in the parliament. This whole story will be more believable if it comes from an Iranian ayatollah. Who can resist that? Americans have always been suckers for people in funny hats. If the story comes directly from Brother Adil and me, they'll be suspicious."

Hashemi-Rafsanjani said, "If we weren't desperate, I would never agree to all this. It's very risky and if it goes bad our opponents will tear us apart. Brother Morteza and Brother Adil, please go ahead and speak to your contacts. But cautiously please. Keep me informed. Brother Hassan, thank you for your help. Your role is going to be vital. Have you studied acting?"

Everyone smiled, and the cleric answered, "Just what everyone in a robe and turban needs these days. Don't we perform on a stage every day?"

"That's true, Brother Hassan. Even though I wear the costume, I'm still not a very good actor."

Everyone smiled politely, and Massoumeh remembered the unemployed Armenian actor playing the role of sheikh in front of the morals police. Hashemi-Rafsanjani continued. "There's another factor. The Americans may put releasing their prisoners in Lebanon on the table. If they do, I'm not sure how to handle that. But the important thing is to get the weapons. If we need to go to church to find them, I for one am ready. Ms. Massoumeh, please write up a summary for me. There should be no copies. I will brief the Imam that we are procuring the weapons to fight Saddam. That will please him, and he's unlikely to ask many questions. Let me know when we should meet again."

DUBAI
WINTER 1985

Nilufar immediately sent a message to Porter asking for an urgent meeting in Dubai. She told her employer that she needed a few days off to see her mythical husband.

A week later she and Porter were drinking tea in the featureless living room of a safe house on the Iranian Hospital Road. Nilufar repeated all she could remember from the meeting, including the names and descriptions of the three visitors. "Hashemi-Rafsanjani called the cleric, 'Brother Hassan,' and the other Iranian said he was a relative of the deputy parliament speaker and head of the Foundation for the Oppressed. That would be Ayatollah Mehdi Karroubi, definitely a big shot and regime insider."

"And the others?" Porter asked.

"He called the Iranian 'Morteza' and the Arab 'Adil.' There were no last names, and I can't be sure those names were real." She described the two as best she could. "Both spoke English. The Arab was smooth. He had the look of a wealthy Saudi, Kuwaiti, or Emirati. Expensive clothes, jewelry, haircut. The Iranian was anything but smooth. He looked one step up from a *bazaari*. He wore expensive jewelry, but his suit looked like he bought it from Syms and skipped the alterations. I could almost hear the calculator going as he counted his commissions. The Arab's mental calculator was working as well, but it was a more sophisticated, silent model."

Porter made notes and said, "It sounds like those two will be known in Washington. They obviously get around. Did they name any of their contacts?"

"No. But they hinted at high-level ones among both Israelis and Americans. I expected them to drop names, but they didn't. Hashemi-Rafsanjani desperately wants the weapons and doesn't care who supplies them."

"Was he going along with this scheme?" Porter asked.

"More than that, sir. He seemed right in the middle of it. He encouraged the so-called "ayatollah" to perfect his story. He pretended to be reluctant and to agree only because Iran needs the American weapons so desperately. I don't believe that for a moment. I haven't been in his office very long, but this kind of scheme is his specialty. He has no objection to dealing with Americans and Israelis if it's to his advantage. I don't know if he'll make a personal profit from this deal, but I wouldn't be surprised if he's already been promised a share."

"Nilufar, you did well to ask for this meeting. What you heard was much too sensitive to send in the usual channel. I'll get this all back to Washington as soon as possible."

"What are you going to do with it, sir? I assume you can warn people and stop these con artists."

"It may not be so simple, especially since the Israelis are involved. There are freelance operators all over Washington. They're crusaders in two holy causes: enriching themselves and stopping the communists everywhere by any means. At the same time, they're ready to believe anyone with a briefcase, an accent, and a story. The worst are those who claim they want nothing for themselves but are doing it only out of their love for America. When I hear that I run away as fast and as far as possible."

"Well, if you met those I saw in Tehran – Adil, Morteza, and Hassan – you would definitely run. I kept asking myself, "Where are the other thirty-seven thieves?""

"I'll remember that. In Washington there are rumors of secret meetings, shady deals, big profits, and money and arms transfers. Some of them are probably true. Our people in the Middle East are hearing bizarre stories about American weapons going to Iran. Some of the rumors even mention the contras in Nicaragua. Whatever is going on, state, defense, and CIA are cut out of it."

"So this story doesn't come as a complete surprise."

"Yes and no. I've never heard anything this specific. All I've heard until now are fragments and rumors. But Arab diplomats keep asking us, 'Why are you letting the Israelis send American weapons to Iran?' We had written off this talk as Middle Eastern *conspiratoria*, but after your story I'm not sure."

The two of them took a break for lunch. The trusted keeper of the safe house had bought roasted Lebanese chicken from the Satwa district, and *za'atar*, pita bread toasted with olive oil, sumac, and thyme, eaten with the strained yoghurt called *labnah*. The combination was among the world's greatest fast food. While they ate they talked Washington gossip and family.

After lunch, Porter and Nilufar went over her story. He asked for as much detail as possible about Hassan the cleric and the two middlemen. She appreciated his systematic questions and the way he sought her opinions, asking "Are they serious people? What do other Iranians know about this plan and this meeting? What does Khomeini know?" He wanted to know more about Hashemi-Rafsanjani's statement that Iran was desperate to get weapons to match what Saddam was buying. "What did he say about the military situation?" He asked about the rivalry between Nilufar's boss and the relatives of Ayatollah Hossein Ali Montazeri, the designated successor to Khomeini as supreme leader. He asked about Hashemi-Rafsanjani's reference to American prisoners in Lebanon.

"He didn't say much there. Only that the Americans might raise the subject. There wasn't any discussion."

"He's right. The president is determined to free those prisoners. He has met their families and the situation affects him personally. He's determined to avoid comparison with Jimmy Carter and the embassy hostages. But if it ever came out that the United States was exchanging weapons for hostages...I can't imagine the repercussions. It could cost him the presidency."

When they finished reviewing Nilufar's report, Porter said, "Nilufar, before you leave I have something else to tell you. I am worried about your communications. You need a better system. What you have now you were supposed to use for just a few months. Now you're a victim of your own success. Your reports are so important to us that no one wants you to leave. I have to remind everyone in Washington at least once a day just how dangerous your situation is."

"Some days I'm terrified, sir, but most of the time I'm too caught up in my job. To be frank, it's fascinating. I joined the Foreign Service for this. What could match it?"

"Nothing like my first tour in the Foreign Service, getting drunk and disorderly Americans out of Turkish jails.

"But here's what you need to know. We have sent a CIA officer to Tehran to help you set up secure communications. When that happens, I for one will sleep much better at night."

Nilufar looked surprised. "I thought we had been over this. I cannot and will not have any contact with such a person. Last year you wanted to send someone with an Italian passport. That plan would have gotten us both killed. Has something changed?"

Porter smiled and said, "You made your views perfectly clear, Nilufar. You were right. I argued that we had to defer to you. You were on the ground. We were not."

Nilufar asked, "What changed your mind?   You don't trust my judgment anymore?"

"I do. That's why I insisted then we had to accept your refusal, although some people at CIA thought they knew better. But using the system with the sweetshop has pushed your luck beyond all limits. It can't last.

"The CIA has found an Iranian-American officer. I've met him. He is in Tehran now. He speaks fluent Persian. I can't say more, except that, like you, he's half Iranian, but on his father's side. He's like you in other ways. A tough, very patriotic streak under a cultured, soft-spoken exterior. He is already building a cover story that will allow him to live and work in Iran without arousing suspicion. For your sake, it's important you make contact soon, but not before he can make sure his cover is strong."

Nilufar remained silent and then answered, "Iranians like to say that we 'cut off heads with cotton.' That's what you're doing to me now. But it does sound better than the Italian plan. Does he understand the risks? This regime is obsessed with spies and foreign agents. Every day the government claims it's uncovered some new espionage network. They trot out miserable prisoners on television who make absurd confessions about working for the Americans, the British, the Israelis, and the Ba'athists. Sometimes they throw in the Freemasons and the Baha'is. It's clear from their voices and faces they've been coerced into making these statements with promises of release, a lighter sentence, or just stopping the torture."

"That's exactly why we need our man there to help you. Nilufar, you're in the eye of the storm, but it's still a storm. Tomorrow, God forbid, you could be one of those people on TV. What do I tell your parents then? What do I tell myself? I'll do everything I can so that doesn't happen."

"You're not leaving me much choice. Can you give me a name? How is he going to find me without exposing us both?"

"I can't give you a name yet and I can't give details about contact. He'll need to spend some time in Iran before he approaches you. He'll figure out the safest way. I can tell you this. He won't make any contact with you unless you tell me now you agree. But if you don't, we're out of options. You'll have to leave Iran. If you said no, and if we didn't need to protect your family, I'd put you on a plane for Washington tonight."

Nilufar laughed and said, "That's really no choice. You're offering me Tehran with your mysterious CIA man or the visa line in Tijuana. For his sake and mine, I'm appealing to you to make sure of two things: first, that he knows what he's getting into; second, that he knows what he's doing there. I know you want us making contact soon. But we don't want someone there who makes stupid mistakes and gets us both killed. Don't underestimate this gang in Tehran. They'll do anything to keep power. Most of them are brutes, but some are smart. And they're getting smarter."

"I'll see to it personally. I'm flying back to Washington tomorrow. I'll make sure the CIA people hear what you've said. My reading is that you'll be dealing with someone very clever, skilled, and cautious. I've met him, and I agreed only because he will help you.

"I'll also follow up on your report about this strange meeting in Tehran. We should be able to identify the two middlemen and perhaps the Iranian cleric. My first job will be to make people believe such a crazy story. Their reaction will be, 'You must be kidding!'"

TEHRAN
WINTER 1985

As the Iran Air flight from Dubai began its final approach to Tehran, the usual announcement proclaimed that, "female visitors to the Islamic Republic should ensure they observe the rules of proper dress." Nilufar had changed into her Massoumeh costume before leaving the Ambassador Hotel. In Dubai it identified her as Iranian, and brought curious looks from some, hostile glares from others, and whispers of support from those who – out of sight of the UAE authorities – assured her of their love for Khomeini and the Islamic Revolution.

Tehran was gray, smoggy, and cold. Snow had fallen ten days before. All that remained were grimy piles of slush and some icy spots to trap unwary motorists and cripple pedestrians. From the airplane Nilufar could see where Iraqi bombs had damaged the airport. On the military side of the airfield, Iranian F-4s, F-5s, and C-130s came and went frequently. She told herself, "Once they cursed the Shah for splurging on expensive American weapons. They are singing a different tune now. If Iran hadn't cut off the US resupply and if we hadn't executed our best pilots, we wouldn't be dealing now with international con men to defend ourselves."

She joined a line of silent, shuffling fellow passengers resigned to the ordeal of entering the new religious paradise. Some were merchants who specialized in evading international sanctions to provide vital goods – at high prices – to Iranians. Others were older couples who had gone to Dubai seeking American visas. A couple in their sixties told her how they wanted to visit their son, daughter-in-law, and grandchildren living somewhere near Omaha. They had both wept when they told the consul in Dubai they had not seen their son in ten years and had never met their daughter-in-law and grandchildren. Even the consul started crying. "You know," they told Nilufar, "she was a good-hearted lady. I was expecting her to yell at us, but she listened, cried, and gave us the visa. After what those crazy students did to their diplomats, I was surprised."

Pictures of martyred young men covered the water-stained walls of the arrival area. Surly officials pawed through passengers' luggage looking for alcohol, forbidden books and magazines, video- and audiotapes, and un-Islamic clothing. Nilufar had left her western outfits in Dubai and had brought back only a few modest gifts for friends and family: some cheap Chinese clothes and shoes for the children, a few boxes of chocolate, and, for Auntie Zahra, a length of black *chador* material purchased from an Indian textile shop near her hotel on the Dubai side of the Creek. The inspector fingered the delicate cloth enviously. Cloth was now rationed in Iran, where shops sold only low-quality synthetics.

When Nilufar entered the arrival hall, she heard "Massoumeh, Massoumeh. *Biya inja bebinamet* (Come here and let me see you)." She saw Amira with a five-year-old girl hugging a doll. The women embraced. "Amira! What a wonderful surprise! You're still working here?"

"Yes, and as you see today I brought my daughter Somaya. The older ones are alone at home and I don't trust them to take care of her. She's very good, and she doesn't bother anyone while I work here. The other ladies help me with her."

Nilufar bent down and kissed the child. "Somaya dear, I know you're a very good girl and help your mother."

"Massoumeh, I can't talk now. I must get back to my post. But I have a problem and I've asked Nazanin to tell you about it. I need help. Things are very hard."

"I'll do what I can. Do you need any immediate help?" Nilufar would never use the word "money" with her friend.

Amira, her pride intact, answered, "Not that kind. Nazanin will explain."

She took some bills from her purse and gave them to Amira. Please, buy a toy or a dress for beautiful Somaya. Something from her Auntie Massoumeh."

Amira insisted she would not take the money, but after the ritual refusals and insistence, she took the bills, saying,

"You've made her very happy. Please come and visit us soon. Come for dinner tonight."

The two women observed the rules of *ta'aarof*, the elaborate Iranian system of courtesy that governed almost all interactions. After the correct amounts of insistence and refusal, Amira said, "Well, if you can't come tonight, promise me you'll visit soon. It's your house."

The next day Nazanin called and asked if she could visit the coming Friday when she could leave her son with her late husband's family. She arrived around four in the afternoon as the streets were beginning to grow dark. After sweets, fruit, and glasses of strong tea, Nazanin told her, "Massoumeh, I'm here with a request for Amira. She needs urgent help. I understand you saw her at the airport. She's still working there, and it's taken a toll on her. She has three young children and depends on that income."

"What happened to her husband at the front? Any news about him?"

"Unfortunately, yes. He went missing over a year ago. They never found his body, but witnesses confirmed he died near Shalamcheh on the border. Some of the worst fighting was there."

"That's terrible. She looked worn out at the airport." Nazanin's face clouded. "As the widow of a martyr and the mother of war orphans, she's entitled to benefits. They would help her a lot if she could get them. Every time she applies, they give her the runaround. They make her go from office to office, and whatever she brings, they find something wrong and ask for something more. When she has a document, they tell her it needs more stamps or another signature.

"Some of them suggest she leave her children with her husband's family and then they will marry her. Of course, they would then have a beautiful, young wife and a share of her widow's pension."

"*Kesaafatand*! (They are filth!)"

"It gets worse. A certain Haji Orgaani approached her about a partnership. He officially works for the Martyrs' Foundation, but they've named him *Orgaani* for his connections to state organs. He persuades war widows to become madams. They live in one room and turn their homes into brothels for use by officials and high-ranking clergy who are supposed to be foundation people visiting from the provinces. He takes most of the profits and pays the widows with food, clothes, and cash. They recruit other, destitute widows, orphans, and young girls from prisons to be prostitutes and bribe the local authorities with cash and services. When they get caught, it's the women who suffer. The judges are in league with Haji Orgaani and his friends."

Nazanin handed Nilufar a folder. "Can you help her? Here are her documents, including her husband's death certificate."

She looked at the papers, and told her friend, "I'll do what I can. She deserves better." Then she changed the subject and asked, "Nazanin, what about you? Are you still with the patrols?"

"God forbid. I've had enough of playing holier-than-thou with those hypocrites. I thought we would be doing something for the revolution, but for most of them it was a chance to feel important, torment people, and steal. Massoumeh, you've lived abroad. Tell me. Is it the same there? Do Americans become tyrants as soon as they have a little power?"

Nilufar answered carefully. "I was a student there, so I didn't see much of the larger society. I suspect people are pretty much the same mix of bad and good everywhere. Our people here were beaten down, bullied, and humiliated for so long. It's what they're used to. Now all they can think of is revenge. It's ugly, but what else do they know? What can we expect? It will take years to teach people better ways."

Nazanin continued, "In any case, I've decided to go back to the university and finish my studies. There are rumors the faculties will reopen soon, starting with medicine and engineering. There's been plenty of time to root out leftists, and we can't keep them closed forever. I've been reviewing my books and notes with a few classmates from those days. Who knows? Maybe I'll even be able to go abroad like I was supposed to before the revolution."

Nilufar looked at her friend and said, "Good for you, Nazanin. This country needs educated and smart people like you. I hope you don't have to wait too long."

Nazanin sipped her tea and sat silently for a few minutes. The sound of the call to prayer echoed from a nearby mosque.

"It's late. I need to go and get Amir from my in-laws. Before I go, there's one other thing. Massoumeh, I'll say this because I think you are different. I knew it from the first day we met at the airport.

"I have a group of friends who are very unhappy with the current course of events. We are all educated people and believers. We all believed in the revolution and fought for it. I spent years in prison and had to listen to my husband's screams while they tortured him to death. His torturers would tell me in detail what they had done to him. They even played tape recordings for me."

Nilufar gasped and said, "May God have mercy on his soul and keep you safe for your son. May you always be there for him."

"I don't talk much about those times. We believed in what we were doing. We believed in sacrifice. We believed Khomeini was leading a movement that would overthrow the Shah and bring us back to who we really are as Iranians and Muslims. You've read the late Dr. Shariati's essay called 'Returning to the Self?'"

"Of course. He said that we Iranians should find our identity in a progressive, purified, and dynamic Shia faith. He said we were chasing mirages if we identified either with Western materialism or with an imaginary pre-Islamic past. He told us enlightened, activist Shi'a Islam alone offered us something authentic."

"Well, Massoumeh, many of us still believe that. But what would Shariati say about this Islamic Republic we've created? What kind of 'self' has it made for us? You know he was a provincial teacher, then a doctor of sociology, and he understood our society very well. Before we could free ourselves, we needed to choose the correct self to set free."

Nilufar said nothing, and Nazanin continued, "This group I mentioned meets every Thursday evening. We discuss Dr. Shariati's works. We read and discuss essays by other thinkers who share his vision of a renewed and open-minded Islam that follows our best traditions as Iranians. For example, the philosopher Dr. Abd al-Karim Soroush has written some provocative studies on the relationship between religion and science. They appeal to those who have studied in the technical faculties."

Nilufar remained silent. She knew Nazanin was on dangerous ground. The young religious intellectual Soroush – who had studied chemistry in England – had been among those directing Iran's cultural revolution to Islamize the teaching of science at universities. He had recently fallen afoul of powerful clerics and had given up his post.

Nazanin continued, "Look at our leaders today. What's the difference between them and the Shah's corrupt gang? In those days, there were at least some with skills, integrity, and education who worked to improve the country. Our officials now have moved into luxury villas and apartments, taken the chauffeured cars, and sent their children abroad to evade military service. You see the problems Amira faces just to survive. Multiply that by millions and you have a picture of Iran today. Where's the justice in all that?"

"Nazanin, this is dangerous talk. Where are you going with it?"

"For the moment we just discuss. We also write and speak to those who will listen. We are looking for answers to Lenin's famous question, 'What is to be done?' We know there is a better path and that our religion has shown it to us."

"I beg you, please be careful. You've already been in jail. For Amir's sake, don't end up there again. This time you might not survive. They are hanging people for much less."

"Massoumeh dear, you know I'm not afraid of them. I want Amir to be proud of his parents. If they kill me, so what? I'm telling you all this because I want to ask you something."

"Nazanin, please don't ask me to join your group. I was not here during the revolution. I did what I could when I was abroad, but nothing like you and your friends. I don't follow all these arguments. They are far above me. Things are not perfect, but we still need to work for our country and our religion."

"Don't worry. That's not what I'm asking. That was all just a long introduction to my real subject. Massoumeh, please tell me who you really are and what you are doing. I am sure you are not the pious, simple, modest girl you appear to be. I think you are hiding something. As we say, you are like water hidden under straw.

"You tried hard, but you didn't fit in at the airport and you certainly didn't fit in with the morality patrols. Why did you do such work? You worked with Beheshti and now you're with Hashemi-Rafsanjani. One was the second most powerful man in the Islamic Republic, and Hashemi-Rafsanjani is not much less. Have you been spying for them? Or spying on them for someone? Or is something else going on? Tell me."

Nilufar's mouth went dry and her stomach curdled. Nausea and fear gripped her whole body. What was happening? Was her world about to fall apart? Were her next stops a cell, a torture chamber, and the gallows? She had worked so hard to create a new identity, and Nazanin had seen her for the sham she was. Now what was she going to do and say? She knew she must not treat her friend as stupid. She had underestimated Nazanin, and she had to do something to save herself. Her survival hung by a thread.

But what to say? At first, she temporized. "I can ask you the same question, Nazanin. You're a brilliant young woman. Top of your class at the university. Why were you working where you were? I can't believe you couldn't have done something better. If I didn't fit in, what about you?"

"Don't change the subject, dear. We're not talking about me. I don't have a foreign university degree like you. I don't have any university degree. I'm a widow raising a son alone in the Islamic Republic. We're not in the same league. Your story about 'wanting to serve the revolution on the ground' never made sense. Look, you can trust me. I haven't told anyone what I suspect. I have no wish to make trouble for you. Just tell me the truth."

"Nazanin, I'm not going to lie. I have too much respect for you. But you'll have to accept for your own safety that there are things I can't tell you. Here's what I can say. Like you, I am working for a better Iran. One that our people deserve, not one ruled by corrupt, ignorant hypocrites. You and your friends are doing your part. I'm flattered you confided in me about your group. For your own protection, I can't tell you more. Please don't ask. Can you tell me if anyone else is suspicious?"

"Not that I know of. A few years ago that hideous Sarhaddi at the airport was making noises about suspecting you. He didn't know anything. He was saying all that just because he was jealous of your education and your being close to Beheshti. You also hurt his manly pride when you rejected his marriage proposal. I want to throw up just thinking about him."

"I still owe you for warning me about him and about the investigation after the Americans escaped. Is Sarhaddi still at the airport? The other day when I came back from Dubai I was terrified I might see him there."

"He's not there anymore. Not long after you left, something happened to him. He was absent a lot, but when he was around he was worse than ever. Screamed at everyone. People said they saw him drunk. I heard that on the night the American hostages left, someone from Beheshti's office publicly humiliated him at the airport. Whatever happened, it left him shaken.

"But he hasn't disappeared. When the pot boils, the scum also rises. He used his connections to important Sarhaddis in Shiraz to stay away from the front. Last I heard he joined the domestic intelligence service of the Revolutionary Guard Corps. He'll go far there. He can bribe or intimidate people to inform on their friends, relatives, and neighbors. The perfect job for him!"

Nilufar had known that eventually someone would see through her. She had been living a lie for so long she had convinced herself everyone believed it. If she had been thinking clearly she would have faced the prospect of a midnight knock on the door and the terrifying dungeons of Evin Prison. Rather than admit the unthinkable, she burrowed deeper into her false persona and pretended the dangers did not exist. She also knew that Sarhaddi, wherever he was, would not forget what had happened to him four years earlier.

"Massoumeh, if that's your real name, tell me something else. That religious meeting in the apartment with 'Sheikh Torbati' and his lecture about sex and marriage. Was that for real or was that something you set up? Tell me the truth. If it was arranged and you had a hand in it, I will be your friend forever. It was so brilliant, there's no way I could ever give you away. I still laugh remembering the faces of those drooling donkeys while he lectured them on foreplay!"

The tension eased. "Nazanin, what can I say? I'm glad you liked him."

"Who was he? If all our sheikhs looked and talked like him, Islam would flower everywhere. The Islamic Republic would be a paradise instead of a hellhole."

"As you can probably guess, he was a TV and movie actor before the revolution. He also is quite well versed in religion. He studied in Qom under our most eminent scholars." She omitted the fact he was a Christian. That revelation might be too much, even for the open-minded Nazanin.

"Look, Massoumeh. I've had my doubts about you for too long and they were eating at me. It turns out you and I are working for the same goals. I will ask you no more questions and you don't have to tell me anything you don't want to. I admire you for whatever you are doing. Your secrets are safe. From now on consider me not only a friend but an unconditional ally. Now I have to go and pick up Amir. It's late."

The two embraced, and when Nazanin left, Nilufar collapsed in a chair and took a deep breath. She desperately needed a large glass of Ahmad's contraband whiskey. What now? Could she trust her friend to protect her? Was Nazanin truly part of an opposition group or was she a provocateur playing a double game to expose the real Massoumeh? Should she go into hiding? Should she send a prearranged signal to Porter and flee Iran as soon as possible? If she did, could she travel openly as "Massoumeh" or, with her cover blown, would she have to follow so many others through the mountain passes into Turkey? Finally, what should she do with this new information? Everything had changed for her. She just wasn't sure how.

TEHRAN
MARCH 1985

Parvizi, as Tehrani, did his cover work well. AFP regularly printed his dispatches from Tehran and from short visits to Isfahan and Tabriz. He was good at reporting, liked the unofficial Iranians he met, and his Persian was becoming more up-to-date by the week. He was careful not to cross the ever-shifting red lines that all journalists in Iran had to observe.

He had made a few friends in the small expatriate community; he preferred the business people to the self-absorbed diplomats with their talk of allowances, the size of their apartments, and how the public back home ignored their important work. At least with the business people it was about how quickly they could make a profit and leave Iran. No one seemed overly interested in him, although he knew the Revolutionary Guard kept a close eye on foreign reporters.

Almost all his father's relations had left Iran, and the few distant cousins who had stayed would probably not know him. Still he was careful to avoid any gathering where he might encounter a relative.

By March, he was feeling confident enough to contact CIA headquarters through the French DGSE liaison and begin the effort to connect with Miriam. He found a phone box outside his immediate neighborhood, but not so far away to be out of the ordinary. He often called AFP in Paris, both to keep up his cover and to make the day he had to make this call seem normal.

He dialed the number he had memorized in a training session in what seemed another century. He left the message he had learned by heart. "This is Phillipe Tehrani calling for Doctor Fabrice on extension 2543. I wanted to report that the medicine he prescribed before I left has worked well and I will see him again when I am next in France."

The DGSE operator in Paris quickly looked up code number 2543 and alerted the Iran section on the fourth floor. Understanding from the message that Tehrani was ready for a face-to-face meeting, DGSE-Iran Section sent an immediate instruction to the covert station housed in the French Embassy in Tehran where preparations began for an encounter.

From the phone message to the nonexistent Dr. Fabrice, the French officers with a need to know understood that Parvizi was to meet his DGSE liaison at 3:00 p.m., two days after he called.

"You can call me Alain," the DGSE officer said as he sipped a cup of strong coffee in the café set long ago for the first meeting.

Ruzbeh thought Alain, or whoever he was, was oddly dressed for a discrete meeting: a too loud plaid sport jacket of the style favored by French TV news anchors. He took out his reporter's notebook so things looked as much like an interview with an AFP source as possible. In French, he told his contact, "Whatever you say. You can call me Phillipe."

"*Alors*, Phillipe. The person you are looking for is a woman – code name Miriam – who works in the office of parliament speaker Hashemi-Rafsanjani. Of course, you can't just walk in and ask for the secret agent you are sworn to protect. I suggest you observe the office, comings and goings, and then find a way to pass her a message. But you will know best how to do this with all your so modern American 'tradecraft.' That is what you call it, no? We have safe houses that you can use for a first meeting and then we can decide how to manage after that. Here is her picture. Very charming. But it won't be easy to spot her in all that religious catastrophe they have to wear, but that is not my problem."

"No, it's not," said Ruzbeh Parvizi aka Phillipe Tehrani as he looked at the face and eyes of a woman he was certain he had seen before. But where? He was sure she was in the picture in Alan Porter's private office of newly sworn-in Foreign Service Officers.

TEHRAN
APRIL 1985

Using a different disguise for each observation, Ruzbeh watched people come and go from Hashemi-Rafsanjani's office for six days.

He began to see patterns. Female employees dressed to pass Guardians of Virtue inspection, but engaged with one another, talking, some laughing, as they passed in and out of the entrances and exits. Male bureaucrats came and went as they pleased, smoking, drinking tea, and spending as little time as possible behind their desks.

Others were there to plead for a loved one in Evin or another of the prisons the Revolutionary Guards ran in a way their SAVAK predecessors would have recognized and approved. They were shabby and haggard from their daily ordeal of worry and begging for mercy. He had yet to identify Miriam.

On the seventh day, he gathered Philippe Tehrani's journalist's credentials and entered the building. He went to the security checkpoint and asked how he would seek an interview for the AFP with Mr. Hashemi-Rafsanjani. One layer gave way to the next and he found himself in what passed for a press office. He explained his interest in meeting the speaker and told the press officer he hoped his interview and reporting would convey the great man, and the revolution of course, in a favorable light to his readers in France and around the world.

"Come back next Tuesday. We will see what is possible."

Ruzbeh left the building for the day but continued his so far unproductive surveillance for the intervening days.

Tuesday arrived, and Philippe Tehrani again made his way back through the layers to Rafsanjani's headquarters. In the mysterious, unexplainable way of Iran, he was told he would meet Rafsanjani "in a few minutes." He knew better and settled in for a long wait.

After an hour, he asked if he could use the toilet, using his physical need to look around the office.

"It's over there."

Ruzbeh made a slow circle, heading vaguely in the direction to which he had been motioned, looking carefully at the people in Rafsanjani's inner office. He was between desks on his way to the toilet when he saw her: Miriam. Porter's brave and resourceful source of priceless intelligence.

He made no attempt to speak to her. That was for another place and time. He tried to memorize anything about her clothing that might be unique or stand out. He quickly understood that she was much too smart for that, so he imagined what she would look like on the street wearing the revolution's required costume. He hoped he would recognize her among the flocks of women forced to wear the same clothes.

He went to the toilet, returned to his wait, and began to form a plan for contacting Miriam.

His session with Hashemi-Rafsanjani produced no news, but he dutifully wrote his 800 words and filed it with Paris. His story ran the next day. He hoped Hashemi-Rafsanjani would think it just sympathetic enough to get him invited back.

For three more days Ruzbeh disguised himself and watched the comings and goings from the Rafsanjani collective. At the end of the day on the third day, he saw her: a gust of wind had momentarily blown her head covering back a few inches and there she was.

He followed at a professionally trained and practiced distance, hoping he was better at trailing his target than she was at detecting him. Nilufar walked quickly for several blocks and then turned into a residential area and slowed her pace. She seemed more comfortable with the surroundings and maybe, Ruzbeh reasoned, she was nearing her home.

As she greeted the doorman, entered the passage in front of her building and loosened her chador, Ruzbeh Parvizi had his first almost full view of Miriam. He also had his contact plan.

Ruzbeh spent the next few days watching Nilufar repeat her walk home from work to her apartment in Amirieh. Was she so confident in her secret life that she did not bother to vary her times and routes? She seemed oblivious to possible surveillance. Maybe her consistency is a mind game that she is playing with the Iranians. "I have nothing to hide so I don't act like a spy. There is nothing to see here." Whatever the reason, her pattern benefited Ruzbeh and he would take advantage of it. *I'll get her to change her habits, but not now,* he thought.

He wrote and rewrote the message he would pass to her. He settled on the truth, or what passed for it under the circumstances.

P. sends his respects. He sent me here to support you. We need to meet so that we can begin our work. Acknowledge this message tomorrow evening as you come home from work by moving your handbag from your right to your left shoulder as you cross in front of the house with the green door two houses down from where you are staying. I will see you do this and I will be back in touch with a safe place to meet.

Ruzbeh typed the message onto a quarter sheet of paper using an ancient Latin-script typewriter he had purchased in the bazaar a month before and had never used for any of his AFP work, waiting for a possibility like this. Untraceable, he hoped.

The next evening, disguised as an elderly Tehrani gentleman with a cane, Ruzbeh waited on the last stage of Nilufar's journey home and anticipated her passage. She arrived on schedule. Ruzbeh moved toward her and then pretended to stumble just in front of her, almost falling to the pavement, grasping her arm for balance. He apologized profusely for having touched her. "Excuse me, my daughter. I did not see the pothole in the alley." He slipped the note into her handbag. Loudly admonishing himself for his clumsiness so that all the neighbors could hear, he moved quickly away and out of sight.

Nilufar automatically responded, "May God excuse you, father." Thinking nothing about the encounter, she let herself into the place that she had made her home so far away from home. As she removed her coverings, she thought – as she always did – about her parents and hoped they were well.

She found Ruzbeh's message while unpacking her things. She read it three times. She tore the paper into pieces and flushed it down the toilet.

Even though Porter had alerted her in Dubai, the reality of a contact came as a shock. "He has put us both in danger," she thought, finding herself embarrassed to be so furious at Porter. "And what if this message is a trap set by the Revolutionary Guards?"

She reviewed her meeting with Porter in Dubai. She had no choice if she wanted to continue her mission. She would acknowledge the message. She would agree to one meeting and tell this well-meaning fool to go home.

The next evening as she passed the green door two houses from hers, she switched her handbag from right to left shoulder.

Two evenings after his performance as an old man, Ruzbeh fitted himself out as a morals policeman, complete with bamboo swagger stick. He stood outside Hashemi-Rafsanjani's headquarters and waited for Nilufar to emerge.

He moved to intercept her, this time booming a reproach about the angle of her headscarf. "*Khaahar, khejaalat bekesh. Hejaabetro dorost kon.* (Sister be ashamed. Fix your covering.)"

"How dare you," barked Nilufar. "Get out of my way."

"Listen to me, woman, or much worse will come your way. There are rules in the Islamic Republic. You must obey them. They are written clearly on this paper. You work in an important office. Can you not read?" the agitated morals policeman shouted as he thrust a paper in Nilufar's hand.

Nilufar took the paper and stared at its contents: "Saturday. Vessaal Shirazi Street, Near Tehran University. Behnam Alley #36. Second floor. 1800."

She spit on the paper, wadded it up, threw it back at the glowering officer, and turned away, simultaneously amazed, furious, and intrigued.

TEHRAN: BEHNAM ALLEY

Two hours before their first meeting at Behnam Alley #36, Ruzbeh began the crucial but tedious effort to detect and then foil any possible surveillance. Ruzbeh remained militantly old-fashioned about "tradecraft." Successful spying was about paying attention to details. The careful way was the right way.

Plus, these days, countersurveillance was hardly a secret procedure, even if training in this obscure art form at the CIA's "Farm" was carried out behind barbed wire or practiced lurking in alleys in Baltimore.

Anyone reading John Le Carre's *Tinker, Taylor, Soldier, Spy* and *Smiley's People* got a free education into tricks of the "watchers" and the "watched.". Ruzbeh recalled both his training and the novels as he checked people's shoes or paused in front of a plate glass shop window to see who might be more interested in him than they should be.

He had tea. He jumped on and off the #25 bus. He pretended to read today's *Kayhan* newspaper sitting in the municipal park. He finally convinced himself he was alone and made his way to his first meeting with Nilufar.

Nilufar set out for the rendezvous an hour early, not because she was less committed to her safety or the mission, but because after six years of living a double, or sometimes a triple, life, she knew that her Islamic dress and her position in Hashemi-Rafsanjani's office provided some protection.

She walked and window-shopped, also using the glass windows to reflect the world back to her and arrived at Behnam #36 convinced she had not been followed.

Nilufar pushed open the door, walked up one flight and entered the apartment, which had been swept for bugs by the DGSE earlier that morning. She found herself in a large, windowless foyer of a typical two-bedroom, middle-class Tehran apartment. The foyer was also the main sitting area, with a dining table and four chairs, a sofa and cabinet with a Grundig television, a radio, and a Sharp videotape recorder. She noticed some videotapes in the cabinet, and a collection of books and magazines, mostly in Persian or French. On the floor were a couple of medium-quality, two-by-three-meter Hamedan carpets. There was a modest kitchen with a bottled gas stove, basic pots and pans, dishes, glasses, and flatware. There was a compact *Arj* refrigerator, a Siemens washing machine, and the obligatory electric samovar and Toshiba rice cooker. Later she would check the living room, which, she suspected, would get little use.

As her eyes adjusted to the dim light, she removed her veil and head covering. Ruzbeh Parvizi, aka Phillipe Tehrani aka Yousef, stood to greet Nilufar Hartman, aka Massoumeh Rastbin aka Miriam.

Ruzbeh was again struck by Nilufar's dark, almond eyes, which had more than survived the mixture of her parents' genes. She also radiated a combination of inner serenity and awareness – in Persian *safaa-ye-baaten* – traits he had come to associate with the most exceptional Iranians.

Ruzbeh knew he had spent more time in the morning than usual thinking about what he should wear for this meeting. As he dressed, he had wondered whether he wanted to avoid detection or impress this young woman. Be careful, he reminded himself. Keeping this relationship professional was the careful, old-fashioned way. The way to get them both home safely.

Speaking English, he said, "I am Ruzbeh Parvizi. I know you as Miriam. It is an honor to meet you. You have done astonishing service for our country."

Ruzbeh knew this opening had not worked. He sounded like he had memorized a page of bureaucrat's talking points. He was mad at himself for spending more time thinking about his clothes than his first lines.

"I am Iranian-American," Ruzbeh continued. My father is Iranian, my mother American. I speak Persian and French. Like you, I wanted to serve the United States. I was preparing for an assignment to India, a job under cover as second secretary in the economic section, when Undersecretary Porter asked me to come here and support you. I am glad he did."

Nilufar did not speak. She knew that silence in conversation made most men uncomfortable and the more she knew about Ruzbeh, the more prepared she would be to respond.

He continued. "I have been in Iran for four months. My cover is to work as a stringer for AFP. Until three weeks ago, I did nothing but that job. I am confident I have not been discovered. The French Service is my connection back home and keeps several safe houses like this one. My only covert mission is to support your work. I have been assigned no other tasks."

Nilufar again kept silent. She was not happy to hear that another intelligence service was involved in her life. Why did Porter make everything so complicated? But Nilufar simultaneously felt relief to be with another young American. She often thought about how profoundly she missed talking to someone in the casual conversation style Americans practiced or at least affected, and the implied background of shared experiences.

Hoping to stay professional, she tried to put out of her mind that she found Ruzbeh attractive. She had pushed her need for a loving relationship to the bottom of her consciousness these past five years. Sitting here, alone and unveiled with an unrelated man her own age for the first time since November 1979, she knew she had missed that kind of relationship many times more than the conversation which might lead to it.

She continued listening to Ruzbeh.

"I know you have been very successful so far, but you ought to pay more attention to countersurveillance. I know your sweetshop channel has been working, but it is vulnerable and slow. It is safer if you communicate through me and the DGSE. And I suggest we meet on a regular schedule so we can make the best use of your sources and reporting." As soon as he had finished speaking, he knew he had for the second time in fifteen minutes chosen the wrong approach. He had sounded patronizing to this self-possessed woman. He would have to take what he deserved and try again.

"Damn it, he's everything and exactly what I feared," Nilufar thought.

Nilufar knew that she had to work with this man. If she refused, her mission was over. But she was not going to make things easy for him. Speaking rapid, formal Persian, with a calculated chill in her voice, she told him, "Mr. Ruzbeh Parvizi, thank you for coming here. I am Nilufar Hartman, although here I live under the name of Massoumeh Rastbin.

"You are a very brave man. And I know how persuasive Undersecretary Porter can be. But unless people at home are dissatisfied with my work, I don't need or want your help. And I certainly don't need any more people involved – especially not those from a foreign intelligence service. Please finish your work for AFP and go home. Maybe that assignment will still be open in India. They owe you that much."

She stood and looked directly into his eyes. "*Farmaayeshi diger nist*? (Do you need anything else?)"

He knew he was being tested and it was no time to make a show of being clever. Using the common idiom, he told her, "*Ajab gohi khordeh-am, man*. (I have truly fucked this up.)"

Continuing in his fluent (and politer) Persian, he said, "Ms. Hartman, please don't leave." He spoke to her not with a command or even a request. It was a plea.

"I am sorry for being so presumptuous and giving you advice which you obviously do not need or want. I was wrong. No one could be anything other than grateful and astonished by what you have done here. I apologize. Will you please let me start again, if not for me then for Ambassador Porter?"

"A pretty cheap appeal to my admiration for Porter," Nilufar thought, but she nodded assent. She did like his admitting mistakes. Too few people did. She knew she had no choice but to accept his help if she was to stay in Iran. Porter had made that clear.

"As you know better than anyone, Porter is a professional but also a man of deep feelings and emotions. He needs what you produce but worries about the risk. He did not send me here to interfere with or complicate your mission. He sent me here because he wants you to be safe. My only assignment is to make your life more secure as you carry out your job. Let me do that for him and for you."

Switching to English, she told him, "I appreciate that, Ruzbeh, and I know how hard this is for Alan Porter. But how will I be safer when more people know who I am and what I am doing? What greater safety is there in coming to 'safe houses' that are supposedly made safe by people I do not know or trust?"

Noting she had warmed enough to use English and his first name, he answered in the same language, also using her first name. "Nilufar, please give me a chance. I think we can make it work. Let us meet here again in two weeks. I will signal by leaving an exact time inside the concrete planter next to the postbox at the head of your street. We can talk again then. You can give me a message to send home via the DGSE and perhaps I will have one for you from Porter. The important thing is that we come to trust each other so I can support your work in the best way."

Ruzbeh's offer hung in the air of the safe house. Nilufar knew these were complications she did not need. But she was overwhelmed by a recognition that he was offering her both better odds of staying alive and connections to home and emotions long denied. After five years of life in the shadows, she needed both.

She looked directly at him and said only, "I will look for your signal." She rose, shook his hand, left the room, covered herself carefully, and walked downstairs and out the front door into Behnam Alley.

7

THE TWO RAFSANJANIS

TEHRAN AND RAFSANJAN (SOUTHEAST IRAN)
SUMMER-AUTUMN 1985

Nazanin kept her word. Following Nilufar's revelations, there was no early morning arrest and no hooded trip to an Evin dungeon.

Nilufar did not reveal her partial confession to Porter. As soon as she could, she did tell Mehrdad Dashti. His advice was that she not panic, but continue playing her role as the pious and diligent employee of the parliament speaker. They both feared that if Porter learned what had happened, he would immediately end her mission at a time of sensitive maneuvers between Tehran and Washington. Mehrdad had heard rumors about US-Iranian contacts and weapons sales, but officials at Iran's Foreign Ministry – like those at America's State Department – knew little.

Nilufar mentioned Amira's difficulties to her boss. Hashemi-Rafsanjani made some telephone calls and, within days, the bureaucratic obstacles disappeared. Amira soon appeared at Nilufar's apartment with her daughter, flowers, and a box of sweets. "Massoumeh dear, I don't know what you did, but I kiss your hand. It's a miracle. I now have food and help with rent and electric bills. The children are in better schools, much closer to home. I can work fewer hours at the airport, and in a month I'll be able to transfer somewhere more convenient. How can I repay you?"

"Amira dear, this is what you deserve. Your husband was martyred for Islam and our country. I didn't do anything. Now you must take care of yourself and raise your beautiful children."

Nazanin reported that the engineering faculty at Tehran University would reopen in late September. The new university administration decreed that students and teachers could resume classes only after filling out lengthy ideological questionnaires and submitting to interviews with mysterious committees. The interviewers were hostile and suspicious. They excluded Baha'is, leftists, and the westernized. Even Nazanin's history and heroine-of-the-revolution status did not give her an easy pass.

She told Nilufar, "It's not clear who they are or what qualifies them to decide who studies and who does not. I doubt any of them ever finished eighth grade. Since their own backgrounds are suspicious, they assume everyone is hiding something."

In July, Nazanin took time off from preparing for classes, and traveled with her son to visit relatives in her native Rafsanjan. The family farm was in a remote, sheltered valley off the mountain road between Rafsanjan city and the isolated village of Riseh. They enjoyed the *yeilaaq*, the cool uplands favored by nomads in the region. Nilufar also took a much-needed vacation. She flew to Kerman, and joined Nazanin and her family for two weeks at the farm. She hoped the break would let her relax and sort out her feelings about Ruzbeh.

He had changed her life. In the months since their first meetings, she had let him use his channel to transmit messages to Porter. While they kept face-to-face meetings to a minimum, Nilufar often found herself hoping to see a chalk mark on a park bench or ribbon on a telephone pole that signaled a conversation. She wondered if Ruzbeh felt the same.

Nilufar knew that Ruzbeh had brought more professional and perhaps personal complications into her already tangled life. Who was he? Could she ever become close to an attractive, well-spoken, and courageous young man who chose to make a career of deception?

During their days at the farm, the two young women walked through walnut, pear, and apple orchards, and stopped at shaded teahouses beside water channels for snacks of fried eggs, raw onions, yoghurt, tomatoes, and village bread. By tacit agreement, they never spoke of politics. One Friday they attended community prayers in Rafsanjan's main mosque. They visited the therapeutic mineral spring at Hoseinabad. They made a daylong pilgrimage to the famous fifteenth-century Sufi shrine of Shah Ne'matullah Vali at Mahan, about twenty miles southeast of Kerman. The towns in the region sat on the edge of Iran's great central deserts, but the foothills reached 8,000 feet above sea level and were pleasantly cool. During the day the family sat on carpeted platforms outdoors. At night they lit fires and slept under blankets.

Nilufar was delighted to rediscover the small-town Iran she remembered from her travels before the revolution. Political upheaval had brought changes, both good and bad. Since Hashemi-Rafsanjani was a native of Bahreman, a district northwest of Rafsanjan city, the region received a generous share of public funds for new roads, schools, clinics, and water and power systems. The people of the district – like their compatriots in most of Iran's smaller towns – enthusiastically supported the new order. Many of its young men had gone to fight the Iraqis, and there were sad reminders of the war's cost in wounded veterans, death notices, ornate towers called *hejleh*, and frequent memorial services. Each tower had photos and commemorated a *javaan-e-naa-kaam*, a young man cut down in the prime of life.

In the intensity and stress of life in chaotic Tehran, Nilufar had almost forgotten that provincial towns like Rafsanjan followed distinct rhythms and provided Iranian society with much of its strength. This was Iran's Midwest, where, like in her father's native Indiana, life was slower and people nicer. Middle-class people were content to lead middle-class lives free of the crowding, noise, pollution, and fierce competition of life in the capital. Networks of kinship and friendship remained intact, often despite sharp political differences. People had time to socialize and to exchange the warm hospitality that characterizes so much of Iranians' social life.

Even the rantings of Rafsanjan's Friday prayer leader could not affect the basic good nature of its inhabitants. The congregants listened to his sermon, shouted "death to" slogans on cue, and went back to their daily lives. The people of the region respected Nazanin's family, the Dowlatabadis, and made Nilufar feel welcome. She and Nazanin had to deal politely with a flood of invitations. Everyone was curious about Massoumeh, the young, pious, well educated, and attractive Tehrani visitor. Hopeful matchmakers were disappointed when they learned about her "husband" in Dubai.

Through the long days, the two young women spoke at length about their lives. Nilufar talked about her "grandmother" Zahra and how she had taught her prayers and other rituals. She recounted their leisurely pilgrimages to remote village shrines. If Zahra learned, for example, that visiting a certain saint's distant tomb guaranteed a family good marriages, she and Nilufar immediately packed for the required three-day bus trip.

Nazanin related stories of her ancestors, including the progressive cleric Haj Mirza Yahya Dowlatabadi, who fought for the Iranian constitution in the early twentieth century and – as a member of parliament from Kerman – opposed Reza Khan's becoming Shah in 1925. Another ancestor was Sediqeh Dowlatabadi, an activist for women's rights and unveiling in the 1920s. After the 1979 revolution, zealots desecrated both Yahya and Sediqeh's graves.

Nazanin described how her enlightened and religious father encouraged his daughters to study and pursue independent paths. She occasionally spoke of her brief and happy marriage and of her hopes for her son Amir. Of her anti-Shah activities and her time in prison she said nothing.

On their last evening together, after her relatives had gone to sleep, Nazanin broke the no-politics rule. "What I'm doing with my friends in Tehran, Massoumeh, I'm doing for Amir. I owe at least that to my ancestors and my late husband, Amir's father. I want my son to live in an Iran more humane and just than this. I don't want him thinking that our beautiful religion means brutality, repression, and ignorance."

After a brief silence, she continued, "If you want to join our group you'll be welcome. You will find thoughtful, sincere people seeking a better way forward. Please don't claim that you can't understand these ideas. You understand them very well."

"Nazanin, that's very kind of you. For now I'll have to be excused. I'm usually exhausted after work. And to be frank, my being there might draw attention you don't want. In the fall, if your course load is not too heavy, we will keep seeing each other."

"It probably won't be. With all the purges, no one knows what to expect. How many students have been expelled and teachers purged? What is 'Islamic engineering'? Where do you find its textbooks? Where do you find professors to teach it? No one knows."

Nazanin changed the subject. "Massoumeh, please forgive my asking, but when are you and Mr. Reza'i finally going to celebrate your wedding? I know that officially married couples sometimes delay their weddings for years, but isn't it time you started a family? It's been hard for me living alone, but my son is a great comfort."

Nilufar laughed and replied, "Of course we'd like to start living together. But, as long as his work keeps him in Dubai and I'm in Tehran, it's very difficult. You know what the economy is like now. Our university classmates – all with good degrees – are struggling with two and three jobs. A decent apartment is impossible to find and we can't live together where I am now, with the two widowed ladies. A young, unrelated man living there would upset everything. Maybe after the war things will improve."

Nazanin grinned and Nilufar prepared for another gust of cold truth. "Sometimes, Massoumeh dear, I suspect that, God forbid, your fortunate Mr. Reza'i does not exist. Waiting this long makes no sense. Of course such a marriage is a very convenient way of keeping men from pestering you. Too convenient, perhaps. That was certainly true when we worked at the airport. But after this long? You know you can never fool me."

Nilufar had long expected this discovery from her friend, and welcomed the chance to unburden herself. Living an invented life for so many years made her desperate for a confidant. "Well, dearest friend, you're right. Mr. Reza'i does not exist. If he did, I would have to thank him for keeping me free of persistent suitors, especially that nasty Sarhaddi at the airport.

"Of course at some time I'd like to get married and have a family. But how do I find the right man in this society? It's not as though I was promised to some first cousin at age eight. Now, as soon as men know I have a good position and a graduate degree from the US, they run away as fast as they can. They're terrified of a woman who's better educated than they are.

"But since I can never hide anything from you, I'll let you in on a secret. In Tehran I recently did meet someone interesting. I can't say much, except that he's young, good-looking, and well educated. I don't know him that well yet, but he fascinates me."

Nazanin laughed. "Why is something always up with you? Why are you always hiding something? They invented the word *zirak* (devious) for you. So, tell me more about this mysterious, handsome stranger. I promise I won't be jealous or try to steal him."

"I can't say more now. I just met him and we'll have to see where things go. Please, dear, keep this to yourself. You are the only person I've told. I don't want my family to know about him. It may turn out to be nothing, and I don't want to make a fuss over something that may go nowhere. And I definitely don't want people talking and spreading stories. You know, as Iranian women, we have so many self-appointed guardians of our honor – brothers, fathers, uncles, cousins, even neighbors. Everyone 'protects' our precious reputations."

"Of course I won't say anything. But you deserve happiness, dear Massoumeh. When you do have your wedding, I promise personally to bribe our brothers and sisters in the morals police so we can sing and dance all night."

Nilufar left Rafsanjan in a taxi early the next morning to catch a flight from Kerman to the capital. On the car radio she heard the hypnotic voice of "Khomeini's Nightingale." He sang,

Ey shahidaan-e-be-khun ghaltaan-e-Khuzestaan, dorud.
Laalehhaa-ye-sorkh-e-parpar gashteh-ye-Iraan, dorud.

O, blood-soaked martyrs of Khuzestan, hail to you.
Wilted red tulips of Iran, hail to you.
Hail to Sussangerd, Khuninshahr [Khorramshahr],
and Abadan
Because of you, the plains of Khuzestan are aglow
with red.

She asked herself for the hundredth time why Iranians' magnificent music and poetry must always tell of their grief. Like the Irish, one of her professors had said.

TEHRAN
AUTUMN 1985

In Tehran Nilufar spent long hours interpreting at meetings and translating letters for the Speaker. In late November, he asked her to interpret and take notes at another meeting of the same group that had discussed arms sales the previous January.

If Porter had identified the participants, he had not shared the information with Nilufar. She had made her own nicknames: Hassan the hypocrite, Morteza the moocher, and Adil the Arab. As before, none of them paid her any attention. For them she was only a woman and an interpreting machine.

Hashemi-Rafsanjani came directly to the point. "So, gentlemen, where are the weapons we need? Are the Americans going to help us?"

Morteza began, "They are. They've already promised us their most sophisticated weapons, including high-altitude anti-aircraft missiles. They're ready to open their arsenals to us."

Hashemi-Rafsanjani remained expressionless. He nodded, and asked, "And what do they want in return?"

Adil answered, "Let's back up a minute. Last July the three of us met with a group of Israelis at the Four Seasons Hotel in Hamburg. Brother Hassan gave an excellent presentation on the current leftist threat and how Israel and the United States can guarantee a strong and independent Iran free of Soviet control."

Hashemi-Rafsanjani turned to the cleric. "Brother Hassan, what did you tell them about the Iranian leftists?"

Hassan checked his notes. "They first said the Iranian left is no longer a threat." I told them, 'No. That is not so. That's what they want you to believe. The left is still in the government, although not officially. When the Iranian communists recanted on television, it was just a show. The government wanted to convince people it was acting decisively against the leftists and their Soviet supporters. In fact, undercover Soviet agents are still infiltrating Iran. Some of them even wear clerics' robes. You Americans and Israelis risk losing Iran forever. You must act quickly and decisively.'"

"How did they react?"

Morteza answered the Speaker. "Hassan got their attention. I think they were pleased. Even if the Israelis don't care about the communists, they realized they could use his warning to play on American obsessions with our puny leftists. They were very impressed with the presentation, but they wanted further assurances. As we had agreed, we gave them a letter from Hassan that summarized the main points."

He read,

> I believe that if our friends in the West do not display dexterity, do not see that the forces supporting them are organized, and do not answer our requests positively, then after Khomeini's death, and in light of his full support of the extremists and the Left, support that even religious fanatics unwittingly become party to, and in light of the fact that Iran has a long border with Communist Russia, our country faces two options: first, to become a second Leba-

non, but on a larger scale; or second, to become a
Communist puppet state within two years.

Morteza continued, "I am confident that, thanks to the Israelis and Hassan's eloquence, the Americans are now definitely interested. I was in Washington in early October and met
with an official called 'Al-Deen,' who works at the highest lev-
els of the White House. His office is next to the president's.
The Israelis had spoken to him after our Hamburg meeting in
July. He was fascinated by our ideas, and agreed to come to
Europe to meet Ayatollah Hassan. We met in Geneva at the
end of October."

Hashemi-Rafsanjani seemed surprised and asked, "Al-
Deen? That's an odd name for an American. Who is he? Is he
Moslem? An Arab?"

Morteza continued, "I don't think so. He seems to have
good relations with the same Israelis we met. He belongs to a
powerful anti-Communist faction in Washington called 'neo-
cons' [using the English term]." Adil added, "Whoever they
are, they have influence, and brother Morteza here convinced
one of their leaders to meet our ayatollah in Europe."

Hashemi-Rafsanjani turned to Hassan. "Can this Al-Deen
deliver what we need?"

Morteza answered for the cleric, evading the question.
"Hassan was masterful. He said that while his faction was
faithful to Islam and the Islamic Republic, it was not inflexible.
It was prepared to make compromises to protect Iran's national
interests. He said that at the end of the day he and his allies
were more concerned with national goals than religious ones."

Morteza continued. "Al-Deen raised the issue of releasing
all the American prisoners in Lebanon. Hassan said that would
require delivering not only Hawk and TOW missiles but also
Sidewinder and Phoenix air-to-air missiles for our fighters, and
high-altitude surface-to-air missiles – modified Hawks – that
could shoot down Soviet spy planes. Al-Deen didn't say no.
It's clear to me that the Americans want the prisoners out and
are willing to pay full price. Hassan made it clear that Iran
would not be cheated."

Hashemi-Rafsanjani smiled. "But what will the Americans actually supply us? They always talk much and deliver little. They also overestimate our influence with those Lebanese believers who are holding the prisoners. They don't take orders from us."

He turned to Nilufar and said, "Ms. Massoumeh, please excuse us while we continue our discussions. Thank you for your help. Brother Morteza can translate for our Arab friend. Please prepare one set of notes for me as before."

Now Nilufar no longer needed to visit Dubai. She could send this urgent and especially sensitive message through Ruzbeh's "safe" channel via the French Embassy.

> For the Undersecretary,
>
> From the recent meeting of the gang of four in the Speaker's office, I learned the following:
>
> 1) Last July M and A introduced H, the dubious ayatollah, to the Israelis in Hamburg. He apparently made a convincing case for their aiding his (imaginary) "moderate faction" in resisting its (also imaginary) pro-Soviet rivals. He followed his presentation with a letter – drafted with the approval of Hashemi-Rafsanjani – making the same points – that the Iranian communists are alive, well, and dangerous.
> 2) M and the Israelis took H's ideas to Washington. They met an American they call "Al-Deen" and convinced him to meet with the "ayatollah" in Europe.
> 3) That meeting (without A) took place in Geneva at the end of October. H again made his case, asking Al-Deen for a comprehensive arms package. He demanded not only conventional Hawks and TOWs, but also air-to-air missiles and Hawks modified to shoot down high-altitude Soviet spy planes.

4)   Al-Deen asked that all American prisoners in
      Lebanon be released.

At this point I was told to leave the meeting, so
I did not hear the rest of the discussion. My best
guess is that they talked about deliveries, payments,
and possible hostage releases.

M is playing a double game, telling both sides
what they want to hear. He is telling Hashemi-
Rafsanjani the Americans are ready to supply all
the sophisticated arms Iran is asking for. At the
same time he is telling the Americans and Israelis
they will get both improved relations and freedom
for all Lebanon prisoners. He wants to keep the
process alive by any means. His commissions depend on it. It sounds like he's lying – or at best exaggerating – to both sides.

Hashemi-Rafsanjani is no fool. He seemed
skeptical about M's account of his meetings, which
to him appeared too good to be true. As a business-
man himself, he understands M's motives. HR will
press for maximum arms delivery, but knows he
will get less than M is promising. At the same time
he will not object to M's making unrealistic assurances about prisoners and relations to the Israelis
and Americans.

M. did not identify the American "Al-Deen"
beyond claiming that he has great influence in the
White House and is a powerful member of the
American "neocon" faction – a term meaningless to
the Iranians. I suspect M is exaggerating "Al-
Deen's" influence in order to inflate his own importance.

The focus of these exchanges is shifting from
improved relations and backing (nonexistent) Iranian moderates against leftists to freeing American
hostages in Lebanon. Unlike better relations or resisting leftists, for the Americans freeing hostages
is a measurable goal.

What the Americans believe or want makes little difference to Hashemi-Rafsanjani. He will use
whatever bait he must to get the weapons he needs.

> If looks like M and A are now brokering a straight
> arms-for-hostages deal with the backing of the sec-
> ond most powerful man in Iran.
>
> Respectfully, Miriam

TEHRAN
AUTUMN 1986

In November the story of the arms-for-hostages deal and the North-McFarlane secret visit broke in the Lebanese paper *Al-Shiraa*. Hashemi-Rafsanjani and his allies kept the story out of Iran's state-controlled media, and Khomeini remained silent. But the Speaker knew he could not count on the Imam's support if the chorus of denunciation grew too loud. Behind the scenes, Hashemi-Rafsanjani's enemies were circulating vicious attacks against him for working with the Americans and for enriching himself from the arms deal.

If Hashemi-Rafsanjani was shaken, he did not show it. When asked about the incident, he said, "The Americans were desperate. They showed up at Mehrabad uninvited, and no official met with them. A few low-level protocol and security people made sure they left Iran as soon as possible."

Nilufar knew the Speaker, despite his outward calm, understood he was threatened and was furious that someone had leaked the story. He charged his people with finding the leaker.

In late November Hashemi-Rafsanjani called Nilufar into his office to meet with chief of staff Niku and a tall, handsome forty-something cleric she recognized as Mohammad Khatami, minister of culture and Islamic guidance. She knew little about Khatami except that he had, like Beheshti, been director of the Hamburg Islamic Center and, later, a deputy in parliament. He had a reputation for being open-minded and a supporter of arts and culture.

Unlike most of her boss's visitors, Khatami did not pretend Nilufar was invisible. He smiled at her and inquired about her background and family. They found a connection through a

distant cousin who had married into a Yazdi family related to
Khatami. She only hoped he would not investigate too closely.

Hashemi-Rafsanjani told her, "Ms. Rastbin, we need your
help for an event next week. There is a regional theater festival
here in Tehran, and I am expected to make a brief address at
the opening. I am not fluent with words, and I need you to
write a short speech for me. Of course, the learned Seyyed
Mohammad here will give the main address, but he has gra-
ciously asked me to say a few words of welcome as well."

Khatami added, "The Honorable Speaker is too modest.
His very presence and words will be invaluable at this event."

Behind the fog of circumlocutions, compliments, and self-
deprecation, Nilufar understood her assignment. Theater, music, cinema, radio, and television were all battlefields in the Islamic Republic. Artists tested limits, and religious extremists
pushed back hard, banning Iranian classical music from the radio and strictly censoring film and television.

Khatami needed help. As minister he was quietly encouraging a revival of culture, but was meeting bitter resistance
from those who saw all artistic expression except the religious
– like the chants of Khomeini's nightingale – as decadent and
corrupt.

If this festival were to operate without harassment, it
needed Hashemi-Rafsanjani's blessing and both revolutionary
and Islamic credentials. Hashemi-Rafsanjani also had to show
the public he remained powerful, despite the recent revelations
of his dealings with the Americans.

Khatami continued, "You can appreciate how delicate this
is. We have opponents who will seize on any excuse to accuse
us of encouraging 'non-Islamic' performances. Just last week I
had to deal with an uproar over a television program. We had
worked for months to get approval from the religious authorities and to ensure there was nothing objectionable. Then what
happened? Someone noticed in the credits that a man had done
the makeup and hairstyling. The conservative newspapers
made a stink, asking, 'In his work did the stylist touch the hair
or faces of the female actors? Did he see them unveiled? If he

did, is he related to them in a way that permits him to do so? Are they his sisters? His daughters? His wives?'

"If it hadn't been for the intervention of our friend of culture here, the Honorable Speaker, I don't know what would have happened. Somehow he quieted the noisemakers and made the whole thing go away."

Hashemi-Rafsanjani spoke. "We need to stop these fanatics who will strangle our cultural life under the cover of religion. The Imam is not happy with them, but won't confront them directly. Vigilantes are running amok, shutting down private parties and events – even those with permits. They beat up musicians and smash their instruments. But people want culture, even in wartime." Turning to Nilufar, he said, "Ms. Rastbin, please write a speech for me to use at the festival opening. It should both support the art of theater and silence those who accuse it of being un-Islamic. Mr. Niku will help."

"Of course, sir."

The following week, hundreds of actors, composers, choreographers, playwrights, directors, and others assembled at Tehran's Rudaki Hall. Most had not worked in the arts for years, and eked out livings as private tutors, taxi drivers, and hawkers of black-market videos. They saw the very fact of the conference as a sign of hope they might resume their professions. Hashemi-Rafsanjani had ensured that the media covered the conference and did not give a forum to extremists who would denounce the event as a sign of decadence and foreign influence.

Nilufar, with advice from Niku, had prepared the Speaker's remarks carefully. He told the audience: "The true Moslem artist prays before the shrine of divine virtue to purify the beautiful face of art. He cleanses it from all the pollution created by those servants of tyrants and false gods who seek to use art as a tool to spread corruption and to strengthen those who wish to impose their unjust authority."

The audience breathed a collective sigh of relief. They understood they had just received blessing for their work from the second most powerful man in the Islamic Republic.

Hashemi-Rafsanjani concluded, "The art of the theater has ancient and deep roots in the religious and revolutionary culture of the Islamic people of Iran. Now that the victory of our brave warriors is near, all of you active in the field of Islamic theater must show how its beauty can exalt our fighters. All of you, God willing, must redouble your efforts to do what is needed for your art to honor their great sacrifices." He concluded, "Thank you for your attention. Peace and the blessings of God be upon you."

The audience applauded loudly and shouted, "Long live Khomeini! Long live Hashemi-Rafsanjani! Long live Khatami! Death to America!   Death to the Soviet Union! Death to Israel! Death to the hypocrites!"

Later that day, Niku told Nilufar, "Bravo to you, Ms. Massoumeh. What you wrote was brilliant. You covered all the bases: the war, the nation, culture, and Islam. The Speaker is very pleased. He always asks, 'Where can we find more educated, enlightened, and devout young people like Ms. Rastbin?'"

Nilufar allowed herself a smile and thought, "Yes, and when you find them, you'll throw them all in jail."

TEHRAN
JANUARY-FEBRUARY 1987

Adding to Tehranis' usual winter miseries, in January Saddam began launching salvos of Scud missiles, each carrying several hundred pounds of explosives, at indiscriminate targets in the capital. With no purpose beyond spreading terror, he could hardly miss hitting something in Tehran's vast urban sprawl.

There was no warning or defense. Death or survival was in God's hands. On a cold afternoon, as the AFP stringer, Philippe Tehrani, Ruzbeh visited the sites of missile hits in the eastern suburb of Narmak and the neighborhood west of Enqelaab Circle, on the road to Mehrabad Airport.

He saw rescuers tending to the injured, clearing rubble, and making quick repairs to damaged buildings. He saw   ruined homes, shops, schools, and hospitals, and dead and maimed civilians, including children. The authorities had a message for him to tell the world: Iran's humanity and Saddam's cruelty.

Ruzbeh, as the journalist Tehrani, spoke to survivors, grieving family members, and rescuers. Within earshot of the Revolutionary Guards, all recited the official line of hatred for Saddam and his allies, welcoming martyrdom, support for the Islamic Republic, and "War, war, until victory." One proudly told him that victims crushed under the rubble, with their last breaths, were gasping, "Death to America."

Away from the Guards, Ruzbeh heard a different story – one he could not put into his reporting. At a bombed area in Narmak, one of the local residents quietly said to him, "Sir, my name is Karim. I want to show you another damaged place." Pointing to his right, he said, "Meet me in twenty minutes at Alley #3, house number 7. The ground floor."

Ruzbeh picked his way through a rubble-strewn alley to number 7, a modest three-story building. The only signs of damage were the plastic sheets replacing most of the window glass. The few remaining panes were strengthened with masking tape to prevent shattering.

Ruzbeh met Karim and six others – men and women – in a small sitting room. He introduced them to Ruzbeh as relatives, friends, and neighbors. After tea and a few polite preliminaries, a fifty-five-year-old veiled women launched into a tirade. "Sir, don't believe anything those sons of whores tell you. They don't care about us. I sent two boys to the war, and they're both in the cemetery. Came back in pieces. A missile hit my granddaughters' school. One died and the other is crippled for life.

"God damn their fathers to hell. They sit in their palaces, ride in their Benzes, steal our money, and get fat on our sacrifices. I told my pimp of a husband – he's a driver – that they're not getting our last son. I warned him, 'If you let our little Reza volunteer for the Guards, I'll leave you – after I rip out your liver.'"

Ruzbeh had no doubt she would do as promised.

Other members of the group had the same message. They had sacrificed for the revolution and the country, and were now fed up. Their most polite description of the ruling clerics was *khaa'en* (traitor).

Ruzbeh, who had heard criticism from his upper-middle-class friends, was shocked at this bitterness coming from a class of Iranians he had assumed were core supporters of the regime. He asked, "Do your friends and relatives feel the same way?"

Karim answered. "They do. Of course they're all afraid to speak up, so in front of the Guards they'll just repeat the usual slogans. You saw the theater they arranged for you today."

A younger man told him, "I have friends in the local *komiteh*. From what I hear, the military is short of everything. Casualties are high and our troops don't have enough food, fuel, ammunition, or medical supplies. The wounded are left to die on the field, because someone stole the gasoline for the ambulances. There aren't enough volunteers for the Guards, and young men are fleeing and hiding to avoid the draft. Thousands – all educated young men – are selling pencils in the streets of Istanbul."

After others vented their anger, Ruzbeh told them, "I appreciate your honesty and your courage in telling me these things. I should leave now, before others get suspicious."

Ruzbeh had rarely witnessed such bitterness from people at this level of society. Now, in his visits to other damage sites, he was hearing similar views when people knew the Guards were not listening. Since he could not put these stories in his regular AFP reporting, he now had a reason to meet Nilufar and tell her what he was hearing.

Nilufar and Ruzbeh treasured their infrequent meetings as a chance to relax and speak openly, free of the hundreds of constraints on where they went, what they said, how they dressed, and to whom they spoke.

In the eighteen months since he had first met Nilufar, Ruzbeh had come out of his professional shell. Nilufar had warmed to his quiet courage, competence, patriotism, and curiosity about her history. They shifted easily between Persian and English, and seemed to know precisely when to use which language. They shared family stories and found much in common

– both amusing and sad – from the Iranian-American experience. He told her how his disillusioned father – who had opposed the monarchy for decades – believed the revolution had betrayed him. He told her of the suspicion and hostility he encountered at his American workplace. She told him stories of her religious education and of her adventures in the Tehran morals police, including the performance of "Sheikh Foreplay." She told him about Nazanin and her courage and nobility of spirit.

They were taking risks by being together – a morals crime if not a political one. It was safer to exchange written messages left in public places. But neither would forego a meeting if they could find a pretext.

Meeting at a safe house in Amirabad, Ruzbeh told her about his conversations at the bombing sites. "I don't know if all that was just the usual grumbling, or if something deeper is going on. I'm surprised morale has held up as long as it has. Do you think it's finally cracking?"

"It's possible. Hashemi-Rafsanjani realizes things can't go on as they are. He has already spoken out against the human wave tactics that are killing so many Iranian boys. A few days ago he asked me at the last minute to interpret at a meeting with a representative of the UN Secretary-General. His regular interpreter, a young man named Zarif, couldn't make it.

"It was clear he wants Iran out of the war. I've almost finished writing up that meeting for Porter. Let's do a combined message adding what you are hearing from ordinary people. He needs to hear both, but the censors here will never let you send out such negative reports."

Neither said it, but both welcomed any chance to stay together for longer than the usual fifteen minutes.

WASHINGTON
FEBRUARY-MARCH 1987

While Ruzbeh and Nilufar were stealing moments together in Tehran, at the State Department Porter hosted the "small group" to review source Miriam. The CIA's Blessey and coun-

terparts from NSA and Defense attended. The White House –
consumed by the growing scandal from the Iran-Contra
scheme, which had grown to include actors as diverse as the
Contras in Nicaragua and the Sultan of Brunei – asked to send
a GS-12 officer from the National Security Council staff. Porter and the others refused to admit him, especially when they
learned he knew nothing about the Miriam operation. For the
moment, the White House remained unrepresented. Porter and
the others knew from experience that NSC representatives at
these meetings usually played with their buzzing pagers to
show how important they were. It was a relief not to have to
deal with that irritant.

"Maybe he's the only one there who isn't talking to his
lawyer and making a plea deal with the prosecutors," joked
Blessey.

"George, that would be amusing if it weren't so true," replied Porter. "Ever since that damn Lebanese paper blew the
whistle, everyone at the White House has been running in circles."

The NSA deputy director, a tall, three-star admiral with
white hair and a uniform jacket covered with decorations,
asked, "What the hell did they expect would happen? Our intercepts, our defense attaches, our spooks, and our diplomats were
all picking up some version of the story starting at least two
years back. Hell, Miriam was in the room when the Iranians
made the plot."

Porter sighed. "She was, and she told me about it in Dubai
almost two years ago. Everything played out just as she said.
The damn story was so absurd, at first I couldn't believe it.
And when I told you about it, what was your reaction? 'Whis-
key-tango-foxtrot? (What the fuck?),' as I remember. We
couldn't get anyone here to listen. People said Miriam was de-
lusional from being in Tehran too long or the Iranians were
feeding her a story. There's a lesson to be learned in all this.
I'm just not sure what it is."

Porter turned to Blessey and said. "George, I need to congratulate you again for finding 'Yousef,' your man for Tehran.
By all accounts, he's all we hoped for. "

"Alan, I still can't believe I had to break all that CIA crockery just to employ someone with his background, let alone send him to Tehran for a mission like this. I know you had a similar problem convincing the security people to let you hire and then send Miriam to Tehran. Just last month the director had to intervene when we wouldn't hire someone who speaks near-native Azerbaijani. The examiners said his English wasn't good enough. 'Holy shit,' he said. 'We have twenty thousand employees who speak perfect English. How many do we have who speak fluent Azerbaijani?'"

As the group dispersed, Porter pulled Blessey aside and asked, "What did you think about Miriam's last message? It sounds like these arms sales revelations are hurting her boss. He's keeping up a brave front, but it's not clear he'll survive."

Blessey asked, "Should we care? Remember what he and his friends tried to pull on us."

"I think we should. We know Mehdi Hashemi leaked the story to the Lebanese paper. He is the brother of Ayatollah Montazeri's son-in-law, Hadi Hashemi. Montazeri and his supporters are barely talking to Hashemi-Rafsanjani and the old IRP crowd. It's open war between them. Each group is doing its best to destroy the other."

"Again, why do we care? On the Islamic Republic scale of zero to minus ten, Montazeri isn't that bad. He's never been comfortable with the extremists and their program. You just said that the Speaker engineered the arms-for-hostages scam that could still bring down our president. So why protect Hashemi-Rafsanjani? If we have to choose sides, why not choose Montazeri?"

"George, you're right about Montazeri himself. The ideologues don't like him. His family is the problem. His late son 'Sheikh Ringo' was crazy, and now it's Mehdi Hashemi and his allies I worry about. I don't think Montazeri can control them. Then there's Miriam. If her boss goes down, what happens to her?"

"As usual, we have a choice between worse and worser. What do you suggest?"

"Back in October, Mehdi Hashemi was arrested, not for leaking the arms deal, but for kidnapping. Hashemi-Rafsanjani still doesn't know who blew the whistle on him. Miriam says he doesn't have enough on Mehdi to keep him in jail. If he gets out, he'll continue his crusade against the Speaker.

"Miriam believes her boss is vulnerable, and it's uncertain how far Khomeini can support him as details of the arms trade come out. Can't you see the headlines? 'Dealing with the Murdering Zionists. Dealing with the Criminal Americans.' Mehdi Hashemi and his crowd smell blood. I think we should pass to Hashemi-Rafsanjani the identity of the leaker. That's his ammunition. He'll know what to do with it."

"Can Miriam do that without exposing herself? It could be very dangerous."

"I will use another channel. One I used when we helped Beheshti against the MEK."

Blessey got up to leave. As he departed he said to Porter, "Give me two days to prepare something about Mehdi Hashemi that you can pass on. I still think Hashemi-Rafsanjani can help us with the prisoners in Lebanon. In public he insists Iran has no role there. We know that's complete bullshit."

TEHRAN
AMIRABAD SAFE HOUSE

As much as they enjoyed being together, Nilufar and Ruzbeh knew they had to write their dispatch quickly and then separate. After about an hour's work, they had reduced their joint message to the essentials. Ruzbeh left first, with the text. Nilufar left just after dark, blending into the crowds as she made her way south to Amirieh. Neither said so, but both looked forward to another chance to meet.

For the Undersecretary,

We are seeing multiple signs that, after eight years of bloody, inconclusive war, Iranians' will to fight is cracking. The Iraqi Scud attacks – while lacking any military purpose – are undermining Tehranis' morale. People feel helpless and victimized, and the Islamic Republic – for all its rhetoric – can do nothing to stop the missiles, which kill at random and without warning. When Yousef, in his AFP role, speaks to people at the site of missile strikes, he first hears them repeat the official slogans of defiance. When the Revolutionary Guards are not listening, however, he hears bitter criticism and disillusionment.

Others report sagging morale in the Iranian military and shortages of everything needed to continue the fight. Ordinary Iranians have borne most of the burdens, including very high casualties, and there is no end in sight.

The ruling clerics are putting up a brave front, but Hashemi-Rafsanjani (HR) can read the public mood and is quietly shifting his position. Miriam interpreted at his recent meeting with Eduardo Ricci, the Italian representative of the UN Secretary-General. HR first repeated Iran's demand that, before it would accept the UN ceasefire resolution, there must be a commission of inquiry to identify the aggressor. In other words, the international community must publicly blame Saddam for the war.

Ricci pointed out that the US, as a permanent member of the UNSC, would not allow such a commission to be formed. He suggested, however, that the American position might change if the Iranians were seen as helpful in freeing American hostages held in Lebanon.

The important thing, Ricci noted, was having a cease-fire to stop the suffering on both sides. The two sides could deal with hostages and the commission at a later date.

HR was receptive to the idea: a cease-fire first, with promises of an inquiry and efforts to free the hostages. This position is new, and may reflect his understanding that Iran cannot absorb heavy casualties, economic hardship, and random Scud attacks for much longer.

With respect, Miriam and Yousef

GENEVA

A week later, Porter took a suburban train from Geneva's Cornavin station to Versoix, a small lakeside town about twelve miles east. The day was typical Geneva winter: gray, raw, about 35°F. From the station he took a taxi along the lake to Pont-Céard, where he met Arash at the Auberge du Vieux Port. Soon the two men were enjoying *filet de perche* in a lemon-butter sauce with a chilled Swiss *Fendant de Valais*. The restaurant was almost deserted, since tourists and Swiss frequented such places in the summer when they could sit outside and enjoy the magnificent views of Lac Léman, the vineyards on its south shore, and, on a clear day, the snow-covered summit of Mt. Blanc.

Arash still dressed elegantly, but Porter could see the signs of stress in his face, particularly in the lines around his eyes. He had visibly aged. He kept up a front of confidence and good spirits, but the last five years of war and turmoil had taken their toll.

He told Porter, "Frankly, I don't see much future for me. The Foreign Ministry was a last bastion for the reasonable, but it's falling fast. I don't know how much longer I can last or what I'll do if I'm recalled to Tehran. More and more ideologues – including some of the former 'hosts' at the US Embassy – are taking key posts in the MFA and overseas. The holdovers like me – those who haven't been purged – are either retiring or being shunted into irrelevant jobs. Our bosses are usually somebody's crony with no education and no foreign experience. They can barely speak correct Persian, and, as we say, even their souls haven't a clue about French or English. They pray a lot, but I'm sure their Arabic is bad too. I feel sorry for God, if he's listening."

Porter told him, "Arash, I am so grateful you have stayed on. Without you, we could never have kept Nilufar in place."

"Well, between me and Mehrdad Dashti in the MFA, we do what we can. Not only is she my beloved niece, but what she's doing is incredible. Who would have thought it six years ago when she went off to Tehran to issue visas?"

Porter took a manila envelope from his briefcase. "Arash, we need you to get these papers into Hashemi-Rafsanjani's hands. Our analysts think he's under serious threat after exposure of the arms-for-hostages deal. We're passing him information about the people who leaked the story and are doing everything they can to destroy him. This material should help."

"You know who leaked?"

"The main figure was Mehdi Hashemi, the brother of Hadi, the son-in-law of Ayatollah Montazeri."

Arash took a deep breath. "That explains a lot. Mehdi hates Hashemi-Rafsanjani for being too 'accommodating' and for undermining Montazeri, his brother's father-in-law. He's very dangerous. He's also impulsive. You know he was arrested for kidnapping a Syrian official in Tehran."

Porter said, "He doesn't sound very smart."

"He's not. He panicked and moved too soon when he leaked the arms deal story. Maybe he thought he needed to act before Montazeri lost any more ground. Everyone is saying that Khomeini is fed up with his criticisms and will choose a new successor.

Porter asked, "Can you get this material where it needs to go?"

"Of course. Anything to stop Mehdi and his crazies. I won't involve Nilufar. That's too dangerous. I'll work through Mehrdad. He'll know how to manage it."

"One more thing. Even if Nilufar is not involved, it won't hurt if Hashemi-Rafsanjani suspects the true source of the information against Mehdi. We need his help freeing the Lebanon hostages. Our president is obsessed with getting them out. His frustration led to this whole fiasco with the weapons in the first place."

Arash nodded and said, "Well, Alan, I wasn't going to say anything about that. But really, how stupid can they be? What were they thinking? Were they thinking at all? I assume you knew nothing about it."

Porter showed a grim smile and said, "I appreciate your being so polite. For the last few years we had been hearing reports and rumors about suspicious goings-on at the White

House with Israelis, Arabs, and Iranians. A lot of us in Washington tried to find out what was happening and stop it before it blew up in our faces. We failed. It seems some cowboys were determined to ride their horses over a cliff. Didn't Schiller say, 'Against stupidity, the gods labor in vain?'"

As he finished his lemon sorbet dessert, Arash said, "Alan, there's another thing you should know. My sister Minu tells me Nilufar is seeing a young man in Tehran. One part of me is very pleased. She's a brilliant young woman and deserves happiness and a normal life. In such matters I trust her judgment completely.

"Another part of me is worried this could hurt her cover and put her in danger. Remember, we created a fake Iranian husband in the UAE for her. He was crucial in giving her status as a married woman. Otherwise she would have had to fight off every horny male – young and old – in Tehran. If this story gets beyond the family, she will have serious problems. Either people will start investigating her 'marriage' or conclude she's cheating on her husband. Bad in either case."

Porter asked, "What do you know about her friend?" He assumed (and hoped) the young man was Ruzbeh. It would not have surprised Porter if their relationship went beyond the professional. Both were young and attractive, and Nilufar had been living like a nun in Iran for over seven years. As far as he knew, no one in Nilufar's family had uncovered Ruzbeh's mission and his CIA connections.

Arash said, "Almost nothing. Not a name. Not an occupation. Only that he's a young man, and Nilufar is seeing him. We Iranians are incredibly *fozoul* (nosy), especially about the romantic lives of our young people. If there's no story, we'll create one. But this could be tricky if it becomes known. We don't much care what people do as long as there's no public dishonor. But we may have to kill off or divorce the imaginary husband. Then Nilufar becomes a young widow. With the war dragging on, there are thousands of widows, and their lives are not easy. Most men see them as fair game. But better that than a scandal that could expose her."

The two men stood to leave the restaurant. They shook hands. "Alan, I'll make sure this message gets to Hashemi-Rafsanjani. We need to help him against Mehdi and his people. I like Ayatollah Montazeri as a person – he always opposed the hostage-taking – but he cannot control his lunatic relatives. Even Khomeini can't always stop them, even if he wants to."

Porter asked a last question. "Does Farzaneh know about Nilufar's friend?"

Arash smiled. "I'm sure she does. Even if her sister Minu hasn't said anything, she would know even before Nilufar met him! I don't know what she's told David. I'm sure she's happy for her daughter. She trusts Nilufar's judgment in all things, especially men. Unlike many Iranian mothers, she's never pressured her to get married. But please say hello to them for me."

TEHRAN
SPRING-SUMMER 1987

Arash kept his promise and Mehrdad worked his magic. He had Nilufar's identity card altered to document a separation from her Dubai husband. It was relatively easy since the marriage had never been celebrated. She was now officially a divorcee with no children.

Arash and Mehrdad made sure Porter's message about Mehdi Hashemi got to Hashemi-Rafsanjani. The Speaker, with his new ammunition, used his influential network to move carefully and decisively against his enemies. Mehrdad briefed Nilufar, but the transaction never touched her as she reported the unfolding drama from deep inside the regime.

For the Undersecretary,

In the aftermath of the arms-for-hostages revelations, the rivalry between parliament speaker Akbar Hashemi-Rafsanjani and Ayatollah Hossein Ali Montazeri, Khomeini's designated successor, has become all-out war. Allies of the jailed Mehdi Hashemi, brother of Montazeri's son-in-law, are using the revelations to attack the Speaker as "an American and Israeli agent" and "a traitor to the Imam and his revolution."

For his part, Hashemi-Rafsanjani is using his powerful web of supporters to eliminate Mehdi and limit Montazeri's influence. Hashemi-Rafsanjani and his collaborator, Minister of Intelligence Mohammad Reyshahri, are determined to crush Mehdi and, by extension, Montazeri. Interrogators have "persuaded" Mehdi, after months in prison, to confess publicly to "deviant behavior," sedition, storing weapons, forging documents, and sowing dissension among clerics and Revolutionary Guards.

The long list of charges omits Mehdi's leaking the story of the arms-for-hostages trade to *Al-Shiraa*. It is clear, however, that was his unforgiveable sin in Hashemi-Rafsanjani's eyes. Mehdi's other acts, even including a 1976 murder, would probably have been written off as youthful folly if he had not challenged the second most powerful man in the Islamic Republic.

Unless Ayatollah Montazeri can save him, Mehdi's future is grim. Ayatollah Khomeini has announced he will reconvene the special clerical court specifically to try Mehdi. Odds are that Mehdi will be dead before the end of this year.

Mehdi's fall will leave Ayatollah Montazeri – once a respected and powerful senior cleric – mortally wounded. He has been openly critical of the IRP ruling clique and is calling for "open assessment of the Islamic Republic's failures." Hashemi-Rafsanjani and his allies see that call as a personal attack and a direct challenge to their power. If Khomeini – as is probable – humiliates Montazeri by ignoring his pleas to pardon Mehdi, then Montazeri's days as successor to the Imam are numbered.

Respectfully. Miriam

TEHRAN
JANUARY 1988

This month's DGSE liaison left a chalk mark on the bus shelter bench near Ruzbeh's AFP office, alerting him to the need for a face-to-face meeting. Following the agreed protocol, Ruzbeh arrived at the safe house on Behnam Alley at 11:30 a.m. two days after he had seen the mark.

"I have something for you. We are becoming even more technological, Phillipe, just like you Americans. Very modern."

"I'm listening."

"Why are you so skeptical? This will make your hard life easier."

"I am sorry. Please, what do you have?"

"I have MRCS, the mid-range communication system. The very latest toy from Langley. Like all Americans, they have made a name from the acronym: so they call it 'MERCS.' We won't have to risk meeting in person. You can send us encrypted reports which we will then forward to your charming bosses in Washington. They move in something called 'bursts.' The bursts squeeze your report into a tiny packet of electricity. You have one node, we have the other. Small, simple, foolproof."

"These 'bursts' can't be detected by the Iranians?"

"No chance. They don't have the technology. You can use it as you are able, and we pick it up whenever you transmit. These bursts last a few seconds. Untraceable by the Revolutionary Guard, I am assured."

"But the old way is the most secure way. It works even if it is slow. Slow is safe."

"Oh, Philippe, the world that we know is changing. Satellites. Computers. Technology is now the answer to all questions. We dinosaurs are doomed unless we go along. So I will show you how this works. You should send your first report on Sunday."

PARIS
FEBRUARY 1988

Gabriel Moreau signaled his Iranian handler in the usual way: two pots of geraniums on the left side of the window sill of his third-floor apartment on rue Descartes in the sixth arrondissement meant he needed to meet, using the usual arrangements.

Moreau made his way early to a café near the Musée Rodin on rue de Varenne, in the seventh. He had coffee, an oily omelet, and a mediocre brioche, and considered his path to this place. He was now a seventeen-year DGSE veteran. He had served the nation. He had fought for France in Africa as an army officer and covertly here and there around the world.

It had been an honor to be named, in late 1978, the DGSE liaison to the Ayatollah Khomeni's retinue in France for the months the Iranian cleric lived and worked in the Paris suburb of Neauphle-le-Château. He traded information with the Ayatollah's men. He gave them tidbits about the Shah's state of mind and what the French Embassy was saying about public opinion in Iran. He facilitated travel of Khomeini's agents and the distribution of his now-famous cassette tapes.

He knew it was not strictly professional, but Moreau had become friendly with the Ayatollah's followers, some of whom were French-educated. They introduced him to the writings of the late Ali Shariati, the Iranian sociologist with a French doctorate who advocated a progressive version of Shia Islam. It all somehow seemed natural. He admired his friends' determination to return to their country and change Iran forever. He was appalled by the stories he heard about SAVAK, the Shah's cruel and violent intelligence agency.

He began to study the Qur'an. In its verses he found answers that his Catholic upbringing could not answer. His Iranian friends encouraged the emerging devotion they saw in Moreau, and then, with no second thoughts, exploited his interest and informal conversion.

Almost exactly nine years ago, he remembered, on a day as rainy and raw as this one, he was invited to see Khomeini himself. The supposedly austere cleric was surprisingly easy to talk to. He asked about Moreau's mother. He wanted to find out which parts of the Qur'an Moreau liked best. And in the end, he asked if Moreau would help him make a successful revolution in Iran.

The Ayatollah and his party returned to Iran a month later, on February 1, 1979. At first Moreau did not hear anything from his friends. In the chaos of those early years, some thrived, some fled into exile, some were executed, and some died on the Iraqi front. But after six months, the requests for information began, just a few at first but then more frequent and more challenging. He was assigned a handler from the Iranian Embassy. They developed routines for meetings. Flowerpots and dead drops. He was hooked and he knew it.

Moreau left the café and walked into the Musée Rodin, paid his fee, and went into the garden. He had chosen to meet his contact in front of Rodin's sculpture, "The Burghers of Calais." Moreau hoped that, even though he had betrayed France, he might in the end, like the burghers, be spared. But by whom?

Mehdi, his long-time Iranian handler, rose from the iron bench and approached Moreau.

"How are you, Gabriel? Well, I trust. Your mother?"

"She is also well, thank you for asking."

"Our revered leader, Ayatollah Khomeini, sends his blessings to you and your beloved mother and thanks you for your devotion to Islam and to the Iranian campaign to bring the Prophet's vision to life."

"Please thank the leader," said Moreau, knowing this greeting was nothing more than part of the polite bluster designed to keep him in the Iranians' web. And yet he admitted he enjoyed the flattery.

"I have something important, something you or your friends in Tehran need to know."

"I am listening."

"There are reports of a DGSE-controlled agent in Tehran. We don't have a name and we're not even sure it's a man. He (or she) is said to have been working in Iran for some time. His information comes from deep inside the state. People at headquarters are so excited about new equipment the agent uses to communicate that they talk too much. That is all I know."

"God bless your commitment to our cause. I will ensure this warning is acted upon. I know the leader himself will be grateful for your vigilance. We are burdened by enemies, inside the country and out. We value our friends."

With a practiced touch, the Iranian put an envelope into Moreau's hand. Faith fills the spiritual gaps, Moreau thought, cash the quotidian.

We own all of him, thought a satisfied Mehdi as they parted.

TEHRAN
FEBRUARY 1988

Gennady Mikhailovich Bonderev, a KGB communications technician at the Soviet Embassy on former Stalin Street in Tehran, took off his headphones and tried to make sense of the noise he had just heard. It was just like what he had noticed on other Sundays this month, or sometimes on Thursdays. Never at the same time, but always the same noise. It was an electronic pulse of some kind, not natural background noise. It never lasted more than a second or two.

"Maybe it is nothing," he thought to himself. But his experience and his training told him he'd better keep his ears on this.

8

BEHNAM ALLEY

TEHRAN
MARCH 1988

Nilufar first about the massacre on Tehran radio's March 16 evening newscast. In a trembling voice the announcer read, "Reports arriving from the northwestern front in the Iraqi region of Halabja indicate that the filthy Ba'athi regime has committed another and even greater crime against religion and humanity. Saddam's shameless Ba'athi forces launched an aerial chemical attack against the innocent women and children of this Kurdish area and have slaughtered at least ten thousand of them. The number of injured is unknown. It is not clear if there are any survivors of this hideous act."

"Our brave soldiers from the Fourth Mountain Division have undertaken humanitarian rescue operations. Ignoring the danger to themselves, our self-sacrificing warriors are searching for survivors and bringing aid to the injured. We are witnessing a tragedy far beyond the scale of the Ba'athis' previous black deeds of murder and destruction."

Nilufar immediately called Minu. "Auntie, have you heard this news about Halabja? It sounds horrible." Minu said, "I'll call Mehrdad. He may know more."

A few minutes later Mehrdad called. "Can we meet at Ahmad's place now?" he asked her.

"Probably not a good idea with the curfew and air raids. What can you tell me?"

"Our ministry is working with the ministry of information and the army to send a group of foreign journalists to Halabja tomorrow. The world needs to know what happened there. No foreign media has picked up the story. That is all I can say now. We will talk more tomorrow."

Nilufar put down the phone. Mehrdad had told her, in a roundabout way, that Ruzbeh, along with other foreign reporters, would be going to Halabja tomorrow. She wished she could go herself or at least talk to him before he left.

As soon as possible after his return, Ruzbeh used their signaling arrangement to set up an evening meeting at the safe house at 36 Behnam Alley. Ruzbeh looked exhausted – unshaven, hollow-eyed, still trembling. Since his return from Halabja, he had been sending nonstop reports to AFP, which wanted to get the story out before the other foreign outlets.

He began talking to Nilufar as soon as they sat down. "There were fifteen of us. We left Tehran in an air force transport about 5:00 a.m. We flew to Sanandaj and took helicopters from there to Halabja. We had to wait several hours in Sanandaj until the area was clear of Iraqi MIGs. It's only about an hour's flight, but we flew the terrain, staying as low as we could. There is still snow on the mountains, and in the valleys the fruit trees are beginning to blossom.

"We landed near the town about 10:30 a.m. Nilufar, may you never see the horror we saw. What struck us first was the silence. There were no voices, no car horns, no animal sounds, nothing. Just the sounds of a few crying children.

Then there was the smell. A faint smell of rotting apples from the lingering gas, and the smell of human and animal corpses. Fortunately, it's still cold there, so it was too soon for much decay. I'm sure by now it's much worse. Jackals were already feeding on the dead."

He pulled out an envelope. "I have some photos, but they're hard to look at."

Nilufar did not pick up the packet. "Not now," she said. "Go on."

"There was an Iranian army unit there. It was part of operation *Val-Fajr* (Dawn) 10. The commanding officer, Captain

Dezfuli, was our guide. The soldiers set up a makeshift morgue, an emergency clinic, and a shelter for survivors. For better or worse, the Iranian army has experience dealing with gas attacks in the South. But they couldn't stay there long, exposed to Iraqi bombers.

"The survivors we interviewed told us that the Iraqis had been bombing the town with conventional weapons for weeks. The people had learned to cope. Most of the families were cleaning their houses and preparing as best they could to celebrate *Nowruz,* a major holiday for the Kurds. On the morning of the sixteenth there was conventional bombing and people took shelter in their basements.

"When the bombing stopped, people came out of their shelters. In the afternoon the Iraqi planes returned. This time the bombs exploded at high altitude, and the winds carried the clouds of gas westward toward the hills. People reported smelling apples, just as I did. It's a sign of mustard gas."

Ruzbeh's voice cracked. "We saw whole families – old men and women, children, everyone – who were caught in the open as they were fleeing toward the hills. Bodies of children who had come out of their shelters and were playing in the fields and the alleys. Basements full of corpses. The soldiers estimated at least 5,000 dead. I think there are many more. All civilians. Many, many children."

"There were dead babies in their cradles. There were dead children next to mothers who tried to protect the little ones with their bodies and pieces of cloth. There were a few living babies still trying to breastfeed from their dead mothers. Three little girls in their colorful Kurdish clothes were floating face up in a river. There were families in the middle of a meal. Those who survived were lucky that the winds moved the gas around and by chance they were out of its path. One of the survivors, a woman, showed us her whole family dead in their house. She told us, 'I could not see death coming. But I could smell it.'"

Nilufar asked, "What about the survivors?"

"I'm not sure the dead aren't the lucky ones. Some who survived are OK, but most are very sick. They'll need treatment and will carry scars for the rest of their lives. The officers told us that the Iraqis had used a combination of sarin and mustard gas – agents that kill by breathing or on contact. Sarin kills quickly, but mustard gas interacts with moist areas of the body such as the eyes, and we saw dozens of people blinded. The army was organizing transport for survivors to the Iranian frontier. Perhaps in Kermanshah or Sanandaj they can get treatment."

Nilufar looked at Ruzbeh's pictures. She saw a photo of a one-year-old boy bawling next to the body of his mother. "My God! What will happen to these children? Even if they're physically cured, how will they live with this?"

"That's something I wanted to tell you. There were some surviving children, too young even to tell us their names or identify their parents. Most of their families are probably dead. We had to leave quickly, and with our escorts we brought about twenty children to Tehran on the helicopters and airplanes. We couldn't just leave them there to starve or freeze, and they probably would not have survived an overland trip. Now they're here in Tehran with social workers and nurses. Most of them are physically OK and too young to understand what happened."

"What will happen to them?"

"They'll need to find families here to take care of them. I saw a beautiful little girl, about fourteen months old. One of the Kurdish-speaking soldiers named her *Kazhal*, Kurdish for gazelle. Light brown hair; dark eyes. A gorgeous smile. If I could, I would adopt her myself."

Nilufar thought for a moment and said, "That might be hard. But why not ask Nazanin? She has a nine-year-old son, and I doubt she'll ever marry again. She'd be ideal."

"From what you've told me about her, she'd be perfect as a mother. The two of you might have enough *parti* (influence) to pull off an adoption to a single parent. Stranger things have happened, Ms. Massoumeh."

Nilufar put aside the envelope with its heartbreaking photos and poured two more glasses of tea. Ruzbeh took the tea, dipped a lump of sugar and put it in his teeth to have his *chai-*

ye-qand pahlu (tea with sugar on the side). He peeled an orange as the two sat silently. Outside the sky was darkening.

Neither wanted to end their meeting. "Ruzbeh, let's see what we have for supper. There's bread, cheese, and some eggs. We could make an omelet. Outside you're not going to find much open now. With the air raids and the missile attacks, shops close early, and no one wants to be outside."

"That sounds perfect. I'm exhausted. Let's just sit. Perhaps we can find a radio station with some real music to take our minds off all this. Radio Iraq? Radio Israel? The state 'mollavision' or 'Khomeini's nightingale's' songs of martyrdom don't appeal just now. Too many beards. Too much death."

The two of them pulled the table aside, spread a cloth on the Hamedan carpet and ate with little conversation. Neither talked about work or what Ruzbeh had seen at Halabja. Behind the comfortable silences lay the thought that their mission could end soon, either by orders or by betrayal and capture. Neither wanted to contemplate what the latter might mean.

Nilufar had made her decision. She was not going to let Ruzbeh leave. Despite the horrors they were facing, she was determined to keep this exceptional and brave young man close to her, both as colleague and friend – and soon as lover. Events in Halabja had taught her how precious and precarious their lives were. Secrecy, the dangers of meeting, and society's taboos just made her desire stronger. Eight years of enforced celibacy were enough.

When they finished eating and cleaning up, Ruzbeh rose to leave. Nilufar looked at him carefully, and said softly, "Ruzbeh, it's late. It's near curfew. You don't want to be on the streets now. There are too many checkpoints with bored guards who'd love to make trouble. Better you stay here tonight. Besides, after all you have told me about what you have just seen, I don't want to be alone."

After a pause, he told her, "What I've seen makes me think that human beings are too adaptable. At funerals we promise ourselves we'll live every day like it is our last. But two days later, we are stuck again in our routines. Will it be the same with Halabja? Will you and I do anything different even in these made-up lives we lead? You'd think, given our current circumstances, you and I would remember every hour that life is precious. But if we did, perhaps we could not live these lives."

She took his hand. "Ruzbeh, listen to me. Our lives are a gift from God. I am proud we are spending these years serving our country. But knowing you has made me want more and want it now. I'm not asking you to stay with me just to avoid the guards in the streets or to stay up and play *paasur* (casino). I want us to learn the lesson of Halabja. I want to be close to you. And I want to start our love and a better life tonight."

She tried to lighten the mood. "After all that, I hope I haven't misread you. I can't wait much longer for you to get the point. Should I draw you a picture? Does one of your aunts need to explain?"

Ruzbeh joined her switch from philosophy to an immediate connection. He pressed her hand, and said, "Well, dear Nilufar, I must confess I'm shocked. The modest Ms. Massoumeh has suddenly become very forward. Won't she be scandalized?"

"Very. But I've given her the night off. Look, there's a narrow, uncomfortable bed in the next room. Not the best place to start our love life. Let's put some quilts, sheets, and pillows here on the carpet. Iranians have been making children that way for centuries."

Using the most exaggerated formulas of Iranian *ta'aarof*, he said, "Since you insist. How I can possibly refuse such a command?"

"You want a command? Stop talking."

The two of them spread the bedding, slowly removed each other's clothing, and spent the night exploring their newly revealed bodies. Neither was inexperienced, but Tehran, where solitary meetings between unmarried men and women were strictly forbidden, had forced them into years of monastic life. The result was like a dam breaking, with intense lovemaking that surprised and exhausted both of them.

The next day, Ruzbeh left while Nilufar was still dressing. As he kissed her, he said, "Be careful when you go out today. *Rang-o-ru-yet baaz shodeh*. (You are glowing.) People will notice and know what you've been doing. Our people have sharp eyes for such things."

"You too, my dear. I promise that when I go out I'll be sufficiently gloomy. Positively funereal. I've had years of practice. This is the Islamic Republic, after all. I'll call Nazanin about the little Kurdish girl today. Do you think adoption is possible?"

"I think so. They want to place those children with families as soon as possible. You should talk to her as soon as you can."

AMIRIEH, TEHRAN
MARCH 1988

Nazanin came to Nilufar's apartment that afternoon. Nilufar usually left her office about two p.m. and Nazanin's son Amir was happy to spend a few hours after school with his aunt and cousins. Nazanin's class schedule – even six months into the school year – remained irregular, as the university struggled to reconcile technical education with the shifting, murky demands of Iran's new theocratic order.

Nazanin related how zealots were demanding stricter dress codes and putting men and women students in separate classrooms. But students and professors, with budgets and logistics as allies, were usually able to resist. There were neither enough teachers nor enough rooms for segregation to work.

When Nazanin arrived, she saw Nilufar unveiled and glowing. The first thing she said was, "My God, Massoumeh! You look different. Beautiful! What happened? If I didn't know better, I would say your relations with Mr. X have advanced to a new level. You can hide a lot, but you can't hide this. Not from me, at least."

Nilufar blushed and smiled. "I promise I'll tell you the story – or at least most of it."

"Is THAT why you wanted to meet today?   You said it was urgent. I'm honored, but if I had known I would have brought flowers and sweets. Under all that piety, your fires are hot. I hope there's going to be a wedding and a baby soon."

"Actually, there's all that, but there's something else first." Nilufar told her what Ruzbeh saw in Halabja and about the Kurdish orphans the soldiers brought to Tehran. She told her friend how the authorities were looking for families to adopt these children. "Nazanin, I've seen pictures of little Kazhal and I immediately thought of you. Look at these."

When Nazanin saw the pictures, she shook her head in admiration. "*Mashallah*, what an angel! Do you think it would be possible? I've always wanted a little girl. The poor thing will need a family. God forbid she should end up in an orphanage or with someone who mistreats her. Amir is growing up, and soon he'll be on his own. Are we sure her parents were killed in the bombing?"

"There was a lot of confusion out there. Soldiers were in the open and exposed to Iraqi bombing. They needed to pull out fast. They couldn't just leave small children there to starve, die of exposure, or be gassed and bombed when the Iraqi planes came back. They rescued as many little ones as they could. Most of them, by blind luck of the winds, were not affected by the gas. The youngest children either died or were not injured at all. The older survivors were not so lucky. Most of them will be crippled for life. Their lungs are ruined."

Nazanin thought for a few moments. She took a deep breath and said, "Massoumeh, this would be a dream for me. At some time in the future, when this little girl grows up, and, God willing, there's peace in Kurdestan, she should go back and find her surviving relatives or at least visit their graves. I promise I'll do everything possible so she can do that."

"When I heard about her I immediately thought of you. This is a good deed (*savaab*). If you agree, let's go ahead. I'll speak to Hashemi-Rafsanjani tomorrow. Since you're a single parent, it will take intervention at his level. He may want to talk to you."

"I'll do whatever I need to. The Speaker and I are *ham-shahri*, both from Rafsanjan, and our families know each other. That should help. Amir will be overjoyed to have a little sister he can play with, take care of, and whose honor – as a good Iranian older brother – he can protect when some man looks at her the wrong way! Now tell me the rest of your story. What's the connection between Halabja and all that new color in your face?"

Nilufar had already decided she was going to share every-thing with her friend. She had lived too long with lies, mistrust, and hiding the truth. Now there was little point in holding back. Nazanin already knew enough to send her to Evin Prison for a very unpleasant stay. If Nazanin were ever questioned, what she already knew would get them both into serious trouble.

Nilufar knew that if she were caught, she had no hope of clemency. Vengeance was now the order of the day. Khomeini had ordered a secret court organized to deliver summary justice to thousands of leftist prisoners already serving sentences. He had decided he would not let imprisoned Marxists go free, and would execute those unwilling to renounce their beliefs, inform on their comrades, and make full repentance.

"Nazanin dear, before I start talking, I should warn you. What I'm going to say will get me killed if it becomes known. And I don't mean killed for some improper relations with a man. But if you know my secrets, they will get you killed as well if you're ever caught."

"*Bachcheh nashow* (Don't be a child), Massoumeh. I un-derstand all that. I made my choice years ago when Farid and I worked against the Shah. If they catch me, so what? As we say, 'there's no color beyond black.'"

Nilufar told her everything. She told her friend her real name and history; her real profession; her work over the past eight years; and her relationship with Ruzbeh, including se-lected details of their encounter the previous night.

Out of consideration for Ruzbeh's safety, she used his cover name and occupation. As far as Nazanin knew, Nilufar had fallen in love with an Iranian-French AFP reporter named Phillipe Tehrani. When Nazanin pressed for details of their lovemaking, Nilufar told her, "Well, without shocking you, I can say for certain that the learned Sheikh Torbati, the 'expert' who advised us on sex and marriage, would have been very pleased. We followed his advice and the divinely inspired instructions of our holy saints."

When she finished, Nazanin took a breath and said, "Bravo, my brave sister. Among ourselves, can I now call you Nilufar? I like it much better than Massoumeh. It suits you. Now I understand so many things. You are a very courageous woman. I salute you."

Nazanin embraced and kissed her friend and continued, "You've burrowed into the core of this sewer of a regime and have fooled everyone. You spent those years in the morals police pretending to be a fanatic, and berating people for showing too much hair or listening to the wrong music. How did you do it? How could you stand it? Under that kind and gentle exterior you are made of steel. In the future I'd like to meet your family, especially your Iranian mother. She must be very special to have a daughter like you."

"You embarrass me, Nazanin. I could never have done it without you. Look how you saved me from that airport investigation years ago. In comparison with you, I've done very little. I just listen, watch, and report what I see. Look at what you have suffered for your ideals. I can't imagine what your time in prison was like."

"My dear, that's all in the past. Now I want to meet this man in your life, this Phillipe. He'd better be as great as you say, and more. If I suspect he's just using you or playing with your feelings, I'll tear his eyes out. I'll know right away if he's worthy of you. I doubt he is, but sometimes we Iranian women have to settle for less than perfection."

As Nazanin left, she told Nilufar, "By the way, Tehran University classes are still chaotic. I've taken a part-time job back at the airport with the women's security service. Maybe the university will get organized soon, but for now I have the time and I can use the extra money. Amir's in school most of the day, and when he's not he loves to spend time with his aunts and cousins. Best of all, that creep Sarhaddi isn't at the airport anymore. From what you've told me, one day you may need help there."

Meeting in the White House situation room, Porter asked other members of the small group, "Has everyone read Miriam's and Yousef's joint report on Halabja?" They nodded. Blessey, the CIA representative, said, "We haven't had anyone in that area for years. The Iraqis sealed it off while they ran their *anfaal* campaign against the Kurds. That was a euphemism for loot, expel, and murder. All our reporting was secondhand. Saddam was running a genocide, but no one wanted to see it."

After a brief pause, Porter continued. "I have argued for years that we take a stand against Iraq's using poison gas. We waffle and now we see the results. If we're going to have a shred of credibility, we need to send Saddam a clear message: 'We know what you did. You used chemical weapons on civilians and killed at least 5,000. We will accept no more.'"

The National Security Council and Department of Defense representatives exchanged looks. The latter, Martin McDermott, a stocky, balding sixty-three-year-old civil service veteran, told the group, "It may not be so straightforward. You will have trouble getting Defense to agree to a clear condemnation. Our Defense Intelligence Agency (DIA) people in Iraq – at White House direction – have been working closely with the Iraqis to prevent Iranian breakthroughs, both in the south near Basra and in the north, in Kurdestan. Now they have excellent working relations with the Iraqi military and are providing them intelligence and targeting information, particularly against the Iranian air force. We don't want to jeopardize that relationship."

Tom Verranzo, the forty-two-year-old White House representative, who had a master's in international relations from the Johns Hopkins School for Advanced International Studies and who had spent ten years at the American Enterprise Institute before joining the NSC as Middle East director, told the group, "The president has made his views clear. Whatever else happens, the Iranians must not break through Iraqi lines. The Iranians cannot be allowed to win. He detests them. They made him look like a fool during Iran-Contra and almost destroyed his presidency. If we condemn the Iraqis for Halabja, we lose all the progress we've made in getting close to Saddam. And the Iranians are never going to thank us. We're done trying to please them."

Porter said nothing for twenty seconds and appeared to weigh what he had heard. "Gentlemen, tell me just one thing. How much is military cooperation with the Iraqis worth to us? What's its price? If the Iraqis stop talking to our DIA people, what do we lose? Saddam loses more, it seems to me."

Without waiting for answers, he said, "If we stay silent now, two things will happen. First, Saddam will know he has gotten away with his crime and has permission to go farther. He knows we're not going to say anything. Tom, I can understand that his gassing Iranian soldiers may not bother many people here. But does no one care about Saddam's gassing his own citizens who happen to be Kurds? We need to think beyond Iran and our distaste for Khomeini and the Islamic Republic. Yesterday Saddam was gassing Iranian troops; today he's gassing Iraqi Kurds. Who will he gas tomorrow? Jordanians? Turks? Kuwaitis?"

Porter's colleagues stared at their shoes. Few officials in Washington ever spoke such plain truth. Instead they fed each other a diet of Iran-bashing. By the simplistic calculations of the day, anything bad for Iran was good for America.

Porter continued, speaking slowly and carefully, "Second, if we don't call out Saddam now, we can kiss good-bye to Hashemi-Rafsanjani's helping free our people in Lebanon. According to Miriam's reports, despite his feeling cheated in the recent arms deal, he's willing to take political risks to help. Not because he likes us, but because he wants to be part of what he thinks is an inevitable shift in Iranian foreign policy.

"Look, we don't have to like Iran to do the smart thing. We've already done enough damage with our earlier silence on

Iraqi chemical weapons and our clumsy attempt last year to blame the Iranians for the Iraqis' missile attack on the USS *Stark*. How many American sailors did Saddam kill then? And what did we gain by putting our heads in the sand? If we don't take a stand, the Iranians will see we have openly allied ourselves with Saddam. In that case, why should they bother to do anything for us? Our actions will come back to haunt us."

Despite his strong words, Porter knew he would lose this battle. He could predict the mushy press statements and messages that American officials would recite while putting their consciences on hold. There would be some nonsense about "condemning all use of chemical weapons."

He worried less about the bureaucratic struggle and more about Nilufar. Whatever her relationship with Ruzbeh – an open secret by now – he knew that after more than eight years in Iran she was close to nervous collapse – even if she somehow escaped being captured and killed. A myopic American reaction to Halabja, particularly after she had heard Ruzbeh's firsthand account and seen his pictures, could push her over the edge.

"Tom, Martin. I'm not going to be silent here. You've all seen the Halabja images on *Nightline*. How many times do we ignore the evidence from our best sources on the ground? I'm glad you mentioned Iran-Contra, because I thought I was being polite by not talking about it. We're heading for another Iran-Contra style fiasco and you don't seem to care. Miriam was right about that three years ago. No one listened then. Now we have both her and Yousef telling us the reality of Halabja. We ignored her once and see where it got us."

Porter looked directly at his colleagues. "Sooner or later, gentlemen, our sucking up to Saddam is going to bite us in the ass. Maybe not tomorrow, but soon. When it does, where will you be? I predict you'll be figuring how to blame the Iranians and how to protect yourselves by finding some State Department or CIA scapegoat."

He paused and heard only silence. "Look, if I can hear something directly from the president, I promise I'll stop preaching and shut up. I won't be happy, but I'll salute."

Verranzo was clearly uncomfortable. He was in an un-equal contest with an experienced professional. He knew he had no sense of the realities in either Iran or Iraq. For him, real-ity was limited to the few square miles between Capitol Hill and the think tanks around Farragut North Metro station.

He turned to Porter and said, "Alright. Let's get it directly from the boss." He stepped out of the Situation Room and called the White House chief of staff. He quickly explained the standoff.

The chief of staff was not pleased. "Tom, the president thinks he has been clear on this. It suits the United States to have the war continue, but not in a way that favors Iran. I know it's not easy, but our bets stay on Iraq."

"Sir, I understand. But Porter feels very strongly. I don't think he'll resign over this, but let's not chance it. He's a disci-plined Foreign Service Officer. If he hears it straight – and I'll grant you, again – from the president, we'll hold him. We need him where he is."

"OK Tom. Let me prepare POTUS. Come to the Oval Of-fice in fifteen minutes. But no fighting in front of the president. He does not like it, so neither do I."

Verranzo led McDermott and Porter up the narrow stairs and opened the door into the West Wing lobby. Through the double doors to the left, they could see the marine security guard on duty just outside. They went down another corridor, past the Roosevelt Room, and waited outside "the Oval."

Even though Porter had been here many times, the history and importance of the room, its contents and that it is where the most important political leader in the world spends his day, never failed to both impress him and make him nervous.

The president was seated at his desk, famously made from the timbers of HMS *Resolute*, an abandoned British ship dis-covered by an American vessel and returned to the queen of England as a token of friendship. The desk was commissioned by Queen Victoria and presented to President Rutherford B. Hayes in 1880 and used by many presidents since. Some of his advisors had suggested he send it to storage because Jimmy Carter had used it, but the president admired UK Prime Minister Thatcher and liked to remind her that he sat at the *Resolute* desk. Porter recalled that to make it more comfortable for a man of his height, the president had the desk raised two inches.

Behind the desk were family pictures, his wife most prominent. At the front of the desk were two of the best-known plaques in America: "It can be done" and "There's no limit to what a man can do or where he can go if he doesn't mind who gets the credit."

Porter, Verranzo, and McDermott were not invited to sit down so they clustered around the president's desk.

"I understand you fellows are having quite an argument downstairs about this terrible gas attack in Halabja, or whatever the town in Iraq is called. The director of CIA has shown me the pictures. Awful. This Mr. Saddam is no angel, that's for sure, but we need to keep him on our side for the long haul. We simply can't let Iran be the boss of the Gulf. Whatever we say in public needs to protect Baghdad. That's a hard call because so many people – think of the children – are dead. But that's my job and that's what I've decided. I'd be glad for your views, but I'm pretty well set on this."

The chief of staff moved forward to signal that no debate was welcome – he had staged the scene Verranzo had ordered up for Porter's benefit and now wanted it over. McDermott made for the door. But Porter turned to the president.

"Sir, thank you for receiving us here and for making your direction clear. As you say, this is a very hard call. May I ask for one addition to your decision?"

It suddenly seemed as if the chief of staff was going to physically stop the president from replying, but the man behind the desk waved him away. Critics might lament his lack of interest in details, but the president understood people, and he recognized Porter needed his say.

"Of course, Alan, I always value your view."

"Thank you, sir. We will of course put out a public statement that reflects your view. But may we also send a personal message from you to Saddam that this must never happen again?"

"Go ahead, Alan, but remember, in the end, he's our man. So easy does it."

They left the Oval Office, each headed his own way.

Porter went back down the stairs toward the White House mess and the situation room. He thanked the Secret Service officer who sat just inside the door and walked out to the driveway between the White House and the Old Executive Office Building, the French Second Empire monstrosity that once was called the State, War, and Navy building. Porter wondered if it was any easier to run US foreign policy when the whole State Department could fit into it.

Porter told his driver that he'd walk the four blocks to the State Department. He left the White House through the Southwest Gate. He looked at the tourists as they gauged him. To them he looked important, but they had no idea who he might be. To him, they looked free of burdens.

Porter walked toward the Octagon Museum, headquarters of the American Institute of Architects, momentarily fantasizing that Alfred B. Mullett, who had designed the Old Executive Office Building might have been run out of the institute on a rail.

But his thoughts kept coming back to Halabja, his deep misgivings about letting Saddam off the hook, and his responsibilities as a Foreign Service Officer, sworn to "support and defend the Constitution against all enemies, foreign and domestic and to bear true faith and allegiance to the same" and the compromises required to be the Undersecretary of State for Political Affairs.

As he crossed Eighteenth Street and continued west on E Street, he wondered if he should resign. Not calling Halabja a crime against US and international law that required sanctions was wrong. But was it wrong enough for him to quit?

He had often thought about where his line was. How much was too much? He had read about the State Department's efforts to keep Jews out of the US during Hitler's terror. How, he thought, could they have refused to let the liner *St. Louis* – with more than 900 Jewish passengers – land in the US when it was in the Caribbean? They sent the Jews back to a Nazi Germany that would murder most of them. The State Department had opposed the creation of the State of Israel in 1947. Would he have stood up to the then masters of the Foreign Service? Thank goodness for those young officers who refused to "go along" and gave visas and support to Jews and others fleeing for their lives from the Holocaust. He thought of Hiram Bingham in Vichy Marseilles, of the officers rescuing Vietnamese colleagues in 1975, and of the Tehran political officers defying orders to give Iranians visas in 1979.

McCarthy's attacks on State, and especially the "China hands," had not deterred him from joining the Foreign Service. Why not? Did he think he would never have to make moral compromises?

He had opposed the Vietnam War, but he had, like so many others, served there and accepted the catechism of government servants everywhere: that he had more influence on the inside than out.

That's what it always comes down to, doesn't it?

Porter walked through Triangle Park's fountains to Twenty-First and crossed Virginia Avenue. He entered State through the old entrance, perhaps hoping he would get some inspiration from the ghosts of Marshall and Acheson, who had worked in offices just above the dark foyer with its WPA mural.

By the time he reached his office on the south side of the building, he was sure of his most compelling reasons to remain undersecretary beyond his love of serving the United States: Nilufar and Ruzbeh.

9

SARHADDI

TEHRAN
MARCH 1988

On March 23, what Porter most feared happened. On the late edition of BBC news, Nilufar heard the State Department spokesman say, "There are indications that Iran may also have used chemical artillery shells in this fighting." He went on to say, "We call on Iran and Iraq to desist immediately from the use of any chemical weapons."

Nilufar thought there must be a mistake until she heard the same report on other stations. Radio Baghdad gloated that the Americans had confirmed Saddam's claims that the Iranians were using chemical weapons. She called Mehrdad, who was almost too stunned to speak. "Yes," he told her. "I've heard it. They have taken leave of their senses."

Hashemi-Rafsanjani was furious. He screamed on the phone at Iranian diplomats in Europe and the United Nations. He told the information minister to ensure foreign journalists in Iran immediately got their Halabja stories into international TV and newspapers. He ordered the foreign minister to organize a press conference and make sure to include both Phillipe Tehrani from AFP and Patrick Tyler from the *Washington Post*. He sent Nilufar to the conference and told her to give him frequent summaries of reporting and commentary in the foreign media.

Iranian press, radio, and TV reporters needed no urging to dish out extra servings of vitriol against the United States. They displayed graphic pictures and wrote headlines like "Reagan

Approves Gas Attack on Kurdish Women and Children" and "America in Open War against Innocent Iraqis and Iranians." The ideologues of the newspaper *Keyhan* wrote editorials full of thinly veiled attacks on Hashemi-Rafsanjani. They criticized those "traitors to the Islamic Revolution and the Imam who deal with allies of the mass murderer Saddam."

At the foreign ministry press conference, Nilufar gave no sign she knew Phillipe or any of the foreign reporters. None of the journalists, all of whom were men, had the temerity to approach a heavily veiled Iranian woman. As soon as possible, she left Ruzbeh a signal for a safe house meeting.

The next day, when they met at the Behnam Alley apartment, they were in no mood for lovemaking. She asked him, "Ruzbeh, what do we do now? I am furious. Disgusted. We've been used. As soon as I heard the State Department's announcement, I began writing my final message to Porter. But I decided to wait until we talked."

He shook his head and said, "What has happened confirms all those crazy things we used to hear from our Iranian relatives when we were growing up. They would rant and rave about how the Americans betrayed Iran, manipulated the Shah, and stole our wealth. Then they would go on about how the Americans deserted their servant and ally the Shah when he got in trouble and could no longer serve their interests."

"Yes, we both can recite that script by heart. I used to tell myself, 'These people – our Iranian relatives – wallow in self-pity and absurd conspiracy theories.' Well, maybe they were right.

"Ruzbeh, I'm finished. I've been here almost nine years and now it seems to have been for nothing. We put our lives in danger every day to tell our government the truth, and no one is listening. Of course Porter sends us nice words about how much he values our work. How empty that all sounds now. Shame on us for believing him. We've wasted our time."

"Dear Nilu, I'll support you whatever you decide. I haven't been here as long as you, but how could I feel differently, especially after what I saw at Halabja."

After a pause, he added, "Besides, I'm here only to help your mission. That's my only job. Why should I stay without you? You are right. Why should we keep doing this if no one cares?"

She almost reminded him he had recently added another, more intimate function to his mission, but this was no time for wisecracks. "Ruzbeh, I've given this a lot of thought. We'll send a joint message to Porter. Brief and polite. I'm certain he understands what idiocy this is, but he must have lost some bureaucratic battle at home. But I no longer give a shit about his battles. We report what we see and hear, and if people choose to ignore us, who cares about their reasons? I'm done making excuses for them."

"You're right about that. After we send our message, we'll prepare to leave Iran. It may take some time, and we'll have to be careful. We want to make sure we leave in ways that don't raise suspicions or threaten our relatives and friends here. I don't think we're in immediate danger. I can have AFP reassign me. You can leave to take care of a sick relative in the US. If we run now, we leave behind serious problems."

Nilufar took a deep breath. "Good. So that's settled. I was afraid you might try to talk me out of leaving. Let's have supper and we'll write our message."

Ruzbeh felt the tension and anger leave the room. He looked directly at her, took her hand, and smiled. "Before we start working, there's one more thing. When we get home, do I have your permission to ask my aunt, my father's sister, to call on your parents for *khaastegaari,* a marriage proposal? They'll ask your father and mother officially to agree. We have to do this right. We should respect traditions.

"And, dearest Nilu, do you know what else I discovered? It seems our two families have a feud going back three generations. I don't know the details, but about eighty years ago one of your ancestors swindled one of my ancestors in a business deal. At least that's our version of the story. Since then our two families have not spoken to each other. Some of the older generation would never let me marry a Rastbin, although I doubt they know why. I don't know if my father or your mother is even aware of the feud, but our marriage could finally bring a reconciliation. Especially if we do it right. Of course we could just get married in some Virginia courthouse, but that wouldn't do anything to bring the families together."

Nilufar said nothing for a while and then returned his smile. "Well, what a nice surprise, Mr. Tehrani. And what a novel way of proposing! I can't wait to see you as a proper Iranian suitor. You will sit there with your aunt and your parents, smelling of cologne, stiff in your best suit and new haircut, and say nothing, while I serve tea and look down at the floor. I don't see my mother making problems, like haggling over the marriage settlement. That's not the way she and I were brought up."

"That's too bad. What's a proposal without the two families bargaining over the settlement?"

Nilufar again turned serious. "We'll need to decide about our careers. I don't see much future for me in the Foreign Service. What am I going to do after this? And I certainly don't see myself as some dutiful 'trailing spouse' following you around the world and pretending you work for the State Department while you sneak around at night doing things you can't tell me."

"No, Nilu, that's definitely not you. And I don't see myself working any more for the agency. *In ham baraaye haft poshtemun kaafi bud* (This has been enough for seven generations)."

Ruzbeh had foreseen a long evening and had bought chicken from a nearby KFC franchise. The shop looked like its American original, although the locally raised chicken tasted better. To protect themselves against trademark lawsuits, the Iranian owners had dropped one Persian letter and moved a dot on another and rechristened it "Kabuki Fried Chicken." Nilufar found bread, tomatoes, and cucumbers to complete the meal. Ruzbeh's French contact had somehow secured a bottle of decent white wine. They opened it and toasted their engagement.

They finished their message about 1:00 a.m. and Ruzbeh promised to send it via MRCS the next day. His leaving was out of the question, and they fell onto the quilts and made love until morning. A relieved Nilufar felt she had resolved so much and that, for the first time in many years, she had a clear view of a future life of her own choosing. They just needed to survive for a few more months.

For the Undersecretary: Joint message from Miriam and Yousef,

We were surprised and distressed by American official statements about the Halabja attacks. What we heard from the State Department spokesman contradicts what Yousef saw firsthand in Iraqi Kurdistan and the testimony of other Iranian, Iraqi, and third-country observers.

Eyewitnesses are unanimous that the Iraqis killed at least five thousand Kurdish civilians at Halabja on March 16 with poison gas. The photographs, videos, and firsthand accounts all support the above judgment. Blaming both sides equally does not accord with the facts and amounts to a transparent effort to placate a mass murderer. By doing so America loses any pretense of neutrality and whatever credibility it once had among either the Iranian people or government.

Putting aside questions of morality and truth, our explicit, pro-Iraqi position now prevents Speaker Hashemi-Rafsanjani from making any efforts on behalf of the American prisoners in Lebanon. For him to do so now would be political suicide. He remains vulnerable to attacks from his Iranian enemies, who have not forgotten his role in Iran-Contra and suspect he is still making secret deals – involving large commissions – with the Americans.

Although we understand there may be policy reasons for taking this morally dubious position, in good conscience we cannot continue our mission in Iran under these circumstances. We are arranging for orderly and safe exits from Iran as soon as conditions permit. As far as we know, neither of us is in immediate danger of discovery. We will create plausible reasons for leaving and make sure our contacts and family members do not fall under suspicion. We expect to be out of Iran by the first of August.

With respect, Miriam and Yousef

Porter struggled over how to answer. What could he tell them? What comfort could he give? Should he provide more high-minded advice about the moral compromises required to serve the nation?

At first he wanted to reassure them how much he valued their work and how well he understood their obvious disappointment. He could describe the harsh choices they would always face as professionals. He thought about sending them a brief account of the bureaucratic infighting that had ended in the American government's shameful action. He wanted to urge them to keep calm and not take any rash decisions.

In the end, he did none of those things. Within a few hours of receiving their message, he sent the following seventeen words: "Understand. Agree. Let me know if you need help getting out. Stay safe. See you both soon."

TEHRAN
LATE MARCH, 1988

As soon as Ruzbeh had applied to AFP for a transfer, Nilufar asked to see Hashemi-Rafsanjani.

"Sir, I want to thank you for giving me this chance to serve in your office. When I came back to Iran almost nine years ago, I never imagined I would be dealing with these challenges. It's been a privilege to work with you."

"Ms. Rastbin, you have served our beloved country very well. I wish all of our educated young people were as conscientious and as committed to the revolution as you. It's no secret that many of our best and brightest have left the country. It's a shame they wouldn't give the new system a chance. But if we can raise a new generation of educated, pious believers like you, our country and our Islamic Republic will be in good hands. I'm hopeful."

"Sir, thank you for the kind words. I regret to say that I've had bad news from my family. My aunt's husband in the United States has been diagnosed with Alzheimer's. Their grown children are working in different cities, and my aunt desperately needs help. She's close to a nervous collapse. It's a horrible disease and she can't leave her husband alone for a minute.

"You know I lost my parents when I was young, and my aunt was a second mother, especially when I was living there as a student. I have to help her. I'd like to ask your permission to leave."

"We'll be in difficulty without you, but of course you need to do this. I'm sorry to hear about such a tragedy. How long will you be gone? I hope you can come back soon."

"With Alzheimer's we can't know. I would like to be able to tell you I'll be back in six months or a year. But who knows? However long it is, I cannot abandon my aunt under these circumstances."

Hashemi-Rafsanjani was visibly disappointed, but he knew well the demands of loyalty in an Iranian family. No revolution could change those. "Ms. Rastbin, of course we will miss you here, but I understand. Mr. Niku will help you with whatever permissions you need so you can travel without problems. When do you need to leave?"

"Not immediately. For the moment, my cousin – my aunt's daughter – is there, but she has her own children in another city, and cannot stay beyond this coming July. If it works for the office, I will stay until late July or early August. There are a few projects I need to finish."

"I'm grateful you can stay until then. I will instruct Mr. Niku to provide whatever help you need.

"Both you and Mr. Niku have been very kind. I also wanted to thank you for helping my friend, Ms. Dowlatabadi, with the adoption of the orphan from Halabja. From what I hear, she's an amazing little girl. You have made both mother and daughter very happy."

"You know that your friend and I are both from Rafsan-jan. Her grandfather, the late Seyyed Abbas Dowlatabadi, was one of the most learned and generous men of the region. At his own expense, he paid for the education of dozens of young boys and girls from the villages. Her father, Seyyed Ali, has always been close to our family and there are marriage and business connections between us. As for your friend, Ms. Nazanin, she has sacrificed so much for the revolution, that what I did for her was not important at all. I want all our young women – including my daughters Fa'ezeh and Fatemeh – to follow your examples."

When Nilufar left her boss's office, she understood his message. Behind all of the flowery language, he was telling her: "I am repaying you for your honesty, hard work, and discretion. Stay close to Nazanin and you will have my support."

TEHRAN
LATE MARCH 1988

The KGB resident's office at the Soviet Embassy in Tehran was nicer than most of the others in the drab, architecturally undistinguished communist compound on Bobby Sands (formerly Churchill and Stalin) Street. In 1981 the authorities had renamed the street to honor the IRA activist who starved himself to death in a British prison. In an ironic touch, near the head of the street, a resourceful entrepreneur had named his modest café "The Bobby Sands Snack Bar."

It was hard on everyone to live and work in the same place, but that was the way the Politburo ordered it, not just here, but in Soviet embassies around the world. Fewer defectors trumped the desire for privacy and the chance to grab a few unsupervised family moments every time and everywhere. "Besides, this setup makes my job easier," thought Revmir Gorokhov, as he looked around his office. "At least I have Russian furniture and not that horrible Iranian jumble."

Gorokhov was a believer. Aged sixty, he had been recruited for the KGB after his military service in the Great Patriotic War. His parents had been believers as well. They had survived purges and show trials. Indeed, his first name was a neologism for "*revolutsiya mira*," world revolution. Tehran would be his last assignment. He had a dacha outside Leningrad where he hoped to live quietly and walk each day in the forest.

He was intrigued and not a little worried when his best communications officer, Bonderev, had asked to see him. He hoped it was not another trail of illicit jabber between embassy employees. He no longer got the slightest titillation from listening to their extramarital couplings.

Bonderev knocked and entered. Gorokhov waived him into a seat in front of his desk.

"What is it, Gennady Mikhailovich?"

"I am not sure, sir, but I have identified repeated electronic bursts which have the exact same electronic signature and last the same amount of time. They come from various parts of Tehran. Using a new machine we have from Moscow, I am able to trace one end of the transmission to the vicinity of the French Embassy. I notice them mostly on Sundays. Not all the time, but a majority."

"Gennady Mikhailovich, you have done well. What do you think you are hearing?"

"I believe the French have an agent at work in Tehran and this is the way he reports."

After Bonderev left, Gorokhov decided to use this information to reconnect to Revolutionary Guards' intelligence officer Gholam-Hossein Sarhaddi. The Soviets had a liaison arrangement to help the Revolutionary Guards; they both sought to push America out of the region. Recently he had been able to give Sarhaddi only Moscow's boring analyses on this or that international development. This discovery was more like it. Operations was what kept him going until his reward at the dacha.

TEHRAN
APRIL 1988

Sarhaddi looked again at the latest report from the agent Hamidifarr in Paris. *"Khaahareshro Gaa'idam*! *(*I'll fuck his sister!*)* What am I supposed to do with this? Who is this in Tehran? What do they know? Who have they bought? How do I find them? Where do I start?"

Sarhaddi called into his office the three clerks who reviewed airport landing cards. One focused on the few Iranians who could still travel. Another on foreign diplomats. The third, on foreign travelers, especially journalists.

"Traitors and spies still threaten the revolution," he told them. "We are looking for a foreign agent who wishes to bring down our revered and beloved leader and promote the interests of our enemies. You have never failed us. Do not do so now. Do not stop your work until you have names for me."

Two weeks later, as spring was warming Tehran, Sarhaddi walked Gorokhov to the door, thanked him insincerely for his important visit, his commitment to Iranian-Soviet friendship, and, more sincerely, for his information. He knew the Soviets were no friends of Iran, having invaded with the British in August 1941 and then crudely pressed for a share of Iranian oil and a big slice of Iranian territory after the war. But there was enduring truth to the maxim "the enemy of my enemy is my friend" and so it was their common cause against America created today's bond. "That's good enough for now," thought Sarhaddi.

As soon as he returned to his office, he called for the man in charge of airport landing cards. Sarhaddi told him to search all the forms again for anyone with a connection to France.

"Are we looking for an Iranian or a foreigner?"

Sarhaddi snapped, "None of your business, you ass. Just look at the cards. All of them."

For two weeks, everyone in the office looked. And looked. There were forms on the floor, forms on the desks. Mountains, piles, of forms. They dreamt of forms in the few hours Sarhaddi allowed them to sleep.

One afternoon, a young recruit came to his chief with a paper and a look of hesitant satisfaction.

"Sir, perhaps this is something to see."

The card read: Phillipe Tehrani. Iranian passport Number 830-637, issued Iranian Embassy Paris. AFP correspondent. First entered Iran December 1984.

Sarhaddi immediately called Reza Dehghaani, the Revolutionary Guard chief of internal surveillance.

"What do you know about the French AFP correspondent?"

"His name?" an exasperated Dehghaani replied. Just like Sarhaddi to try to put me off balance, thought Dehghaani. Sarhaddi had been a creditable wrestler in school and that tactic remained part of his game.

"Phillipe Tehrani. A name you should know."

"Of course I know it. He's part Iranian. We have had him under surveillance several times over the last four years. He seems to be what he says he is. He went to Halabja with the other foreign reporters a few weeks ago, and his reporting was helpful."

No one – not even you – is what they say they are, thought Sarhaddi. How can we have such a moron in charge of watching enemies of the state?

"You need to get a team of watchers on him right away. Follow him everywhere. Do not let up for an instant. We need to know where he goes, what he does, who he sees."

"Why the sudden worry?"

"I cannot tell you, but I am sure of this: you won't want to explain to a Revolutionary Court why you didn't do this immediately. Report to me every morning," Sarhaddi barked as he hung up.

TEHRAN
MAY 1988

After almost four years of living two lives in the physical and psychological hothouse that was Tehran, Ruzbeh Parvizi was very aware of his surroundings, in tune with his environment.

Failure to pay attention, he had learned at the Farm and had confirmed every day since arriving in Iran, would mean the end of his mission or his life. Security was everything, now even more so since he and Nilufar had become lovers.

He knew something was not right these past few days. Too many people close by. Too many familiar-looking faces. Too many of the same pairs of shoes, even as seemingly random passersby had different clothes. He had sensed surveillance once or twice during his time as Phillipe Tehrani, but nothing like this. He stopped using the MRCS. He stuck strictly to his AFP work. He saw Nilufar only at the safe house and less frequently, which pained him greatly.

Could he and Porter have foreseen any of this when they had first talked in his office? He was in love. Now he was hunted. His American side focused on having a plan of action to save himself, Nilufar, and their mission. His Iranian side asked what fate awaited him and whether he could do anything to change it.

USS *VINCENNES*
PERSIAN GULF
MAY 1988

Captain Will Rogers III and his crew were honored to serve on the *Vincennes* and proud of their ship's power and history. The *Vincennes* was a modern Ticonderoga-class guided-missile cruiser, equipped with the new Aegis combat system. The heart of this system was the powerful, three-dimensional, electronically scanned array radar, which could simultaneously track several dozen targets thanks to its pair of radar-guided 127mm turrets and two batteries ready to rapidly fire off the sixty surface-to-air missiles.

The *Vincennes* had a proud lineage. Named for the Revolutionary War Battle of Vincennes, won by George Rogers Clark in 1779, it was also the namesake of the eighteen-gun sloop of war *Vincennes*, which had played a key role in the Navy's famous US Exploring Expedition, led by Lieutenant

Charles Wilkes, which had cruised the Pacific from 1838 to 1842.

The *Vincennes* had received urgent orders to proceed to the Persian Gulf from San Diego six days after the US guided missile frigate *Samuel B. Roberts* hit a mine as part of Operation Earnest Will, the US effort to protect Kuwaiti tankers in the Persian Gulf from Iranian attacks. The *Vincennes* arrived on station to provide Aegis cover to the effort to extract the *Roberts* through the Strait of Hormuz, a mission the assembled Navy vessels successfully completed.

TEHRAN
JUNE 1988

For over two and a half months a report from Dehghaani had come every morning. His men had followed Phillipe Tehrani everywhere. They had reactivated the listening device in his apartment. Working with the KGB, they had listened for the bursts.

Nothing.

Of course, Sarhaddi had expected nothing from Dehghaani's amateurs. Sarhaddi assumed that if Monsieur Phillipe Tehrani had survived this long he must be a skilled agent with professional handlers.

But – with proof from surveillance or not – Sarhaddi decided that defending the revolution – and advancing his career – required quick action. He had given these next steps serious thought. If he was wrong about Tehrani, so what? Right or wrong, there would be one fewer arrogant, westernized parasite to worry about.

Sarhaddi had never met Tehrani, never read his reporting, but he hated and envied everything he represented – cosmopolitan ways, Western education, sophistication, and mastery of foreign languages. The fact he was also fluent in Persian further infuriated Sarhaddi. He told himself, "Our martyrs didn't die so such people could walk our streets, pretend to be superior to Iranians, publish lies about us, and paint the rest of us as ignorant fanatics." If his plan worked, he would endear himself to the ruling clerics for striking a blow against the Great Satan. He would also crush someone whose very existence reminded Sarhaddi of his inferiority.

His plan was too sensitive to discuss on the phone. The enemy with its advanced technology would certainly be listening. To put his plan into place, he made two visits, one to Undersecretary Hossein Eslami at the Foreign Ministry and the other – during a quick trip to Bandar Abbas – to the commander of Iranian Revolutionary Guard naval forces in the Strait of Hormuz.

TEHRAN
JULY 1, 1988

The ambassador of France had already waited forty minutes for the undersecretary to receive him. Fifteen minutes, that's just Iranian time, thought Pierre de Montréal. Forty is a calculated snub. But what is the nature of this Persian diplomatic message?

"The undersecretary can see you now," oozed an assistant. "Please follow me."

"Ambassador, please come in. I trust I have not kept you waiting," Eslami extended his long-fingered hand. Eslami was of medium height, about thirty-five years old, with a noticeable gap where a front tooth was missing, He spoke fluent English learned during a sojourn, ostensibly as a student, in Utah before the 1979 revolution. De Montréal recognized the privileged skin of a man used to having others do the hard work, not, he knew, unlike his own.

"Oh, no, Mister Undersecretary, I had just arrived." Let his staff explain that, thought de Montréal.

Without bothering to conceal his insincerity, Eslami said, "Ambassador, I have an unpleasant duty to perform, especially in light of the special relationship between France and the Islamic Republic."

"I can't imagine what that might be, Mr. Undersecretary."

"There is an Iranian citizen, a Mr. Phillipe Tehrani, who is correspondent for your news service Agence France-Presse. He has worn out his welcome in Iran. We are tired of him, his hypocrisy, and his provocations masquerading as journalism. His reporting promotes divisions among our simple but believing citizens. He seeks to divide our nation by his lies and his innuendos."

The attack on Phillipe caught de Montréal by surprise. His DGSE officers had given him no warning that the Iranians were suspicious. Other Iranian officials had praised Phillipe's recent work, especially his eyewitness reports from Halabja. There had to be some deeper game. "In France, we have a free press, Mister Undersecretary. Mr. Tehrani works for Agence France-Presse, not for me. What do you think I can do about him? Expelling him will hurt the image of your country not just in France, but throughout Europe. You need more friends in the world, not fewer."

"Mr. Ambassador, please do not tell me what we do and do not need. We are both professionals. That is why I asked you here. We do not intend to expel Mr. Tehrani. Indeed, since he is an Iranian citizen we cannot expel him. But we would be completely within our rights to arrest him. If we did so, you would have no right to consular access. As a mark of respect to you, however, we ask you to order him to leave Iran immediately."

"On what possible grounds?"

"On the grounds that it serves neither of our interests – speaking as professionals, of course – for us to make public what we know of Mr. Tehrani's activities in my country. Activities, shall we say Ambassador, which, I am informed by others in my government, go far beyond his AFP responsibilities. We are not seeking a crisis with your country. We are asking you to help us avoid one."

"Do you have proof of this outrageous accusation, which is false, I assure you."

"Ambassador, I represent a sovereign country. I need no proof. I have only the certainty that I am doing what is required to protect my nation. I believe in French this is called *'raison d'état,'* which you should understand better than anyone. We want Mr. Phillipe Tehrani out of Iran as soon as possible."

Eslami checked some papers. "I know it is difficult to find seats on planes going abroad, but as a special favor we have booked him on an Iran Air flight to Dubai the day after tomorrow. I am told his Iranian passport is in order, and I will guarantee there are no difficulties at the airport. Please, Mister Ambassador, do not make this harder than it is. But please make sure he leaves. If he does not, the consequences will be serious both for our two countries' relations and for Mr. Tehrani personally."

Ambassador de Montréal arrived back at the French Embassy on Neauphle-le-Château Street (formerly Avenue France) and asked his secretary to get Gerard Rouleau immediately.

When the chief DGSE officer reported to the ambassador's office, the Belle Époque fantasy of some Quai d'Orsay civil servant architect, de Montréal described his meeting with Eslami.

"I think they mean business," de Montréal said. "He's got to go."

"But Ambassador, this is not our operation. Tehrani is a CIA officer and he is working with and protecting someone extremely valuable to them. The Americans have shared the intelligence, and it is of the highest quality and very valuable to us. We make it possible for him and his agent to do their work. We cannot make this decision unilaterally."

"I am sorry for the Americans and I know how well you and your predecessors have managed this difficult case for four years. It's a shame we will lose the intelligence, but we must protect our own interests in Iran. Our companies have sales to make. We hosted Ayatollah Khomeini in 1978 and '79 and we do not want to lose any remaining goodwill. I do not want France connected to this espionage, especially when, in the end, we are just the postman. I will take responsibility. Inform Tehrani. Get him on that flight Eslami identified."

De Montréal paused and looked at his colleague. "I'm truly sorry to see him go. But we really have no choice. Remember, the Iranians hold a powerful trump card. They have threatened to arrest him if he stays. If they do, we have no recourse. Under their laws, he is an Iranian citizen and we cannot help him. Eslami didn't mince words when he told me that.

"One more thing: you may tell the CIA what has happened only after the plane is out of Iranian airspace. We need to give them a *fait accompli*. Am I clear on that?"

"Yes sir. With all respect, I think you are wrong but you are clear," said Rouleau. He left the ambassador's office as quickly as possible to arrange an emergency meeting with Phillipe Tehrani.

The DGSE station in Tehran sent the agreed emergency signal to Ruzbeh in the old-fashioned way, since he had given up on the MRCS. Chalk marks on dumpsters. Half-opened window shades in safe houses. He had seen one and, while trying to make sure he was not being followed, arrived at safe house #3, near Palestine Square. He had never been to this meeting place because it was for use only in an emergency.

Rouleau was already seated in the living room.

With no preliminaries, he told Ruzbeh, "You have been exposed. I don't know how. The Iranians demand you leave immediately. They have offered us a deal: there will be no noise if you are on the Iran Air flight to Dubai the day after tomorrow. My ambassador has accepted this arrangement in the interests of France and to prevent your possible arrest. I have your ticket. I had no choice in this matter and neither do you. If you do not go, you will be arrested and have no protection from us. We have been proud to support you, but this is the end. I wish you luck and wish the same to your asset. We must not linger. *Au revoir*, Phillipe."

"But you cannot decide this yourselves. I must consult Langley."

"No, this is the end for us. By tomorrow morning we will have cleaned all of our safe houses and will have no connections to you, traditional or otherwise. Do not try to contact us. Please go now."

Ruzbeh knew this day might come, but it was still a shock. In reality, the Iranians were forcing him to leave only a month before he was already planning to go. He had to tell Nilufar he was leaving and warn her he had been exposed. He could not simply disappear.

As he shook hands with Rouleau, he asked him, "I have one last favor to ask. Can you keep one of the safe houses open for another twenty-four hours? This one may not be secure any more. The one on Kheradmand Street – near Amjadieh Stadium – is the best. I know you have your orders, but if I leave without notice, my asset will imagine the worst and panic. I'm sure you understand."

Rouleau nodded his head. "I will begin clearing the other places and think of something to tell the ambassador about why there was a delay on the Kheradmand Street house. *Bonne chance, cher* Philippe.

On his journey back to the French Embassy, a question kept nagging Rouleau: Undersecretary Eslami did not think this up himself. Who gave him orders? In his office, Rouleau reviewed his conversation with Ambassador de Montréal. "He ordered me not to contact the CIA until the plane takes off, but he did not say anything about the British," he said to himself.

He sent a secure and urgent message to his British counterpart in Tehran. As a show of professional courtesy, might the MI6 station ask the signals intelligence establishment at GCHQ Cheltenham for a list of phone calls made to undersecretary Eslami's MFA office between June 25 and July 2?

When the results arrived a day later, one entry made Rouleau scream in frustration: "I knew it was that bastard!" Gholam-Hossein Sarhaddi, the Guards' counterintelligence officer working against the French, had called Eslami on June 30. Eslami summoned the French ambassador the next day to order Philippe's expulsion.

TEHRAN
JULY 2, 1988

Nilufar saw Ruzbeh's emergency signal, a chalked number four on a wall near her Amirieh apartment. Early the next morning a taxi dropped her on Forsat Street, not far from the safe house.

When she arrived at the apartment, the two embraced quickly but she sensed bad news.

"Nilufar, it's over for me. We don't have much time. I have been exposed. I'm almost certain I wasn't followed here, but we should be out of this apartment in fifteen minutes." He then told her about Rouleau's message and the Iranians' demand that he leave the next day.

"I had to plead with my French contact to keep this place open today so I could tell you. It'll be cleaned out before noon."

He squeezed her wrists. "As far as I know, the Iranians haven't connected us. You didn't see anyone following you?"

"No. And if I had, I wouldn't have come. You're right, we need to get out of here now."

"Look, *azizam* (my dear), I'll go back to Washington from Dubai. I'll start making wedding plans, although I won't do much until you come."

"I will leave as soon as I can, but don't think I should panic and run. I told Hashemi-Rafsanjani's office I would be leaving in late July. I'll keep to that schedule. I'll be on a flight out in three or four weeks."

"OK. We should go now. I'll leave first. Goodbye for now until Washington. Then we'll do a proper Iranian wedding with the *sofreh* (cloth), mirror, sugar cones, the band, the fat singer, the bad-taste comedian, and enough food for an army."

He brought out a delicate gold chain and a pendant with the phrase *Raaz-e-sar besteh-ye-maa bin* (See our deepest secrets) engraved in fine calligraphy.

As Nilufar admired the gift, she said, "Dear Ruzbeh. I've always loved this verse from Hafez." She recited the words, "See our deepest secrets, how every moment they are sung to the flute and tambourine, at the entrance to yet another bazaar."

"Hafez understood. Try as we might, our deepest secrets will never stay hidden. I was hoping to give you this at a more suitable time. Wear it now, so the words of Hafez will protect you."

She took his hands and looked into his face. "It's exquisite. And there's one more thing. When we get married, it's going to be a shotgun wedding. I'm a month pregnant. If we wait too long, it'll be obvious."

As she kissed his face, she asked, "What about this? If we have a boy, we name him 'Behnam' after the street where we made him. If a girl, we call her 'Nazanin' after the keeper of our secrets. Agree?"

"*Chashm* (on my eyes). We could call her 'Massoumeh' of course. How about that? I've come to like that name."

"Go. *Khodaa be-ham raahet* (May God go with you)."

After he left, she broke down and wept silently. Because lives depended on her keeping calm, she quickly composed herself, dried her eyes, put on her coverings, and left the apartment.

BANDAR ABBAS
REVOLUTIONARY GUARD NAVAL COMMAND
HEADQUARTERS
JULY 2, 1988

The Guards' captain told his fast gunboat commanders: "I don't know why so I cannot tell you. All I know is that Sarhaddi is a very important person in Guards' Intelligence with powerful friends. He has ordered us to do this in the name of the revolution, and so we will.

"Tomorrow, July 3, beginning at 0600 you will take your boats and crews and move aggressively to harass a group of oil tankers headed to America's Arab lapdog Kuwait. You will continue this effort until we have lured the American warship *Vincennes* into contact with our fast boats. You are not to attack it – it's a powerful ship – but just evade it, even if it attacks you. In fact, once it enters our waters, you should return immediately to base. This Sarhaddi says our mission is to make the captain and crew of the *Vincennes* nervous and fearful of our power. Sarhaddi wants to scare the Americans into violating our territorial waters. If they fire on you, our leaders in Tehran will denounce their open aggression against the Iranian people. Go now and prepare yourselves and your men."

MEHRABAD AIRPORT
TEHRAN
JULY 3, 1988

After snaking through the long line in the hot and humid departure area, Phillipe Tehrani put his passport on the counter of the immigration officer. He could detect no special recognition. Exactly as he had when he arrived four years ago, he tried to control his breath. He hoped an attitude of frustrated indifference would see him out of Iran, to the path home and a new life.

The immigration officer handed back his stamped passport and boarding card. Iran Air 655 to Dubai via Bandar Abbas was at gate four, ready to board.

As Tehrani left passport control, Nazanin watched him from behind a curtain in the women's section and wondered how Nilufar would manage.

BANDAR ABBAS AIRPORT
IRAN

One hour and forty minutes after takeoff, Iran Air flight 655 landed at its scheduled stop in Bandar Abbas.

Ruzbeh Parvizi went through the possibilities. They can ignore me. They can pull me off this plane and I will disappear forever. He thought of Nilufar and again tried to control his breathing.

Nearly half of the passengers got off and new travelers came aboard. Parvizi watched those who passed his aisle seat in row eight. All were seated. Just as he began to relax and think about his next moves in Dubai, two men in Revolutionary Guard uniforms armed with AK-47s, came aboard and pretended to scan the crowd

They then walked directly to seat 8C.

"Passport."

Parvizi held up his Iranian document. One of the men studied it and handed it to the other, who nodded his head as if to confirm some information moving silently between them.

He handed the passport back to Parvizi without another word and the two men walked off the aircraft.

The Bandar Abbas tower cleared IA 655 for Dubai and the Airbus A300 began to accelerate down the runway.

As the plane climbed out of Bandar Abbas, the copilot asked if he should monitor the civilian or military emergency frequencies.

"Don't bother," the pilot responded. "It's only a thirty-minute flight. We'll be fine."

PERSIAN GUILF
JULY 3, 1988
USS *VINCENNES*

The *Vincennes*, escorted by the frigates *Sides* and *Montgomery*, was cruising near Abu Musa Island headed northeast toward the Strait of Hormuz. From there it would escort a convoy of oil tankers headed for Kuwait, protecting them from Iranian attack. The gossip in the fleet was that Captain William Rogers and his crew were looking for an opportunity to prove themselves.

The USS *Montgomery*, sailing beside the *Vincennes*, fifteen years older than the modern Aegis ship and not in the same technological universe, first detected a flotilla of thirteen Revolutionary Guard gunboats at 6:30 a.m. and determined they were maneuvering to attack a group of tankers fifty nautical miles from the American escorts.

Captain Rogers on the *Vincennes* ordered action stations, increased speed, and headed to engage the Iranian boats. For two hours the cruiser traveled northeast to intercept the Iranian boats. Its course brought it close to the naval exclusion zone decreed by Iran. By 8:40 a.m. the *Vincennes* was forty nautical miles north of its assigned position.

A Middle East Task Force (METF) watch officer in Bahrain called Rogers and asked him to resume his regular course. Rogers answered that he had sent the ship's helicopter on a reconnaissance flight and could not turn back without it. A few minutes later, the helicopter was hit by bursts of automatic weapon fire as it flew over the Iranian boats. Rogers invoked the right of self-defense and requested authorization to pursue the gunboats, which were moving north toward Iranian waters. Unable to assess the situation near the strait, the METF officer gave him permission to do as he thought best.

At 9:39 a.m. the *Vincennes* opened fire on the gunboats, which seemed to be making a disorderly retreat. Two minutes later the *Vincennes* entered Iranian territorial waters, but its crew was so absorbed by the chase that they did not notice.

On board the *Vincennes,* when the officers realized where they were, anxiety replaced the excitement of combat. By entering the enemy's territorial waters, the ship was now exposed to a legitimate attack. Some of the officers began to wonder if the Iranians were luring *Vincennes* into a trap. Rogers ordered his crew to cease fire so the helicopter could land and the ship could turn back toward international waters.

Almost immediately after takeoff from Bandar Abbas at 10:17 a.m., Iran Air flight 655 was detected by the *Vincennes*'s radar, whose transponder initially classed it as a "civilian contact." The Airbus, which was following the airway for commercial aviation, was still ascending to reach its cruising altitude of 14,750 feet for the short flight southwest across the Strait of Hormuz. But several of the *Vincennes*'s operators misinterpreted radar signals and determined that the plane was descending while gaining speed, the standard profile for an air attack against a ship.

The young officer responsible for the interception system looked at the transponder again, which now classed the contact as "civilian or military," adding to the general confusion. Could the aircraft be an Iranian Phantom or Tomcat posing as a commercial flight? The Bandar Abbas civilian airport also served as an air force base for about ten of those fighters. The memory of the Iraqi fighter's missile attack on the USS *Stark* just over a year earlier was on everyone's mind. Thirty-seven of their Navy comrades had been killed and twenty-one injured. The incident also ended the captain's naval career.

At 10:20 a.m. the *Vincennes*'s radio operator sent a warning to the approaching aircraft over two international emergency frequencies. He received no answer.

At 10:22 a.m. the *Vincennes* sent another message over both emergency frequencies, asking the approaching aircraft to identify itself, warning it that it would be shot down if it entered a safety zone of twenty nautical miles from the cruiser, still sailing in Iranian waters.

At 10:23 a.m. the cruiser sent a final radio warning. Again, no response. One minute later, Rogers gave the order to fire. The man responsible for carrying out the order was under so much pressure that he pushed the wrong button several times until a more experienced noncommissioned officer showed him the right one; two SM-2 missiles immediately hurtled out of the ship and sped toward the Iranian Airbus at three and a half times the speed of sound. The plane disappeared from radar screens at 10:25 a.m.

TEHRAN
JULY 3, 1988

By noon in Tehran, IRNA (Islamic Republic News Agency) was reporting fragments of a story that a US warship had destroyed a civilian airliner in the Persian Gulf. By 2 p.m., the news agency had identified the plane as Iran Air 655 and that, although no wreckage had been sighted, sources in the Iranian government were saying the plane was missing and presumed lost.

At the airport, Nazanin heard the news and told her supervisor she was suddenly ill, a convenient but terrible truth, and needed to go home immediately. She made her way to Hashemi-Rafsanjani's office to find Nilufar.

Gholam-Hussain Sarhaddi heard the news at Revolutionary Guard headquarters. He felt some sympathy for the 289 innocents on IA 655, but he hoped the French, and whoever was helping them, or whoever they were helping, would get the message: "Don't fuck with the Islamic Republic." But he decided, given the heavy loss of Iranian life, that he would not play up his "achievement" to his superiors. At least not right away.

He also ordered his watchers at Mehrabad to pay close attention to departing passengers over the next thirty-six hours.

Ambassador de Montréal heard the news from Rouleau, his intelligence chief. "That bastard Sarhaddi, working through his friend at MFA, had me send that boy to his death. And he killed 289 others. I do not know how we will repay him, but we will. We have long memories," he told Rouleau.

"Gerard, tell me one thing. Do you know who Tehrani's agent was? Who he was working with and protecting?"

"I do not," he lied. "I suspect it was a woman."

"May God protect her."

Nilufar was translating an article from *Le Monde* about UN-sponsored negotiations for an Iran-Iraq cease-fire when Niku told her, "The Speaker needs you in his office immediately."

She found Hashemi-Rafsanjani standing alone near his desk looking very serious. Without preliminaries he said, "Ms. Rastbin, I will be direct. Because of the respect I have for you, I will tell you this: you must leave Iran now. Get on the first flight. I won't say more, but please believe me when I say you must do this. I am telling you this as a friend of yours and your family. If you have any problems leaving, Niku can help."

Amazed, Nilufar asked him, "Sir, what is happening?"

"I will say no more. Don't wait. And when you reach Washington, please give my best wishes to Ambassador Porter. Now go and may God protect you."

A shaken Nilufar staggered out of the Speaker's office and found Nazanin waiting at her desk.

"You must come with me now," Nazanin whispered.

Still dazed by Hashemi-Rafsanjani's words and wondering what could be going on, she asked her friend, "What has happened? Why have you come here?"

"I will tell you, but you must come with me now."

The two women made their way to the street. Nazanin steered Nilufar to a quiet stand of trees and took her hands in her own. She began to weep.

"Dearest Nilu, I don't know how else to say this. An American warship shot down an Iranian airliner in the Gulf this morning. Phillipe was on that plane. Our boats are searching the area, but there are no survivors. I am sorry. I do not know what to say."

Nilufar knew she had no time for grief, no time for fear. She had to act. She could mourn later. She held Nazanin's hands tightly. "Nazanin, I need your help. I cannot explain everything. Maybe someday in another Iran or in another lifetime. *Dastam be daamanet* (I put my life in your hands). Will you save me?"

"Tell me what I can do for you, my dear sister."

"Meet me at the airport at five this afternoon. At the Turkish Airlines counter. Have all of your airport passes. Please do not ask me any questions, because I do not have any answers. Now I must go."

Nilufar cut short the countersurveillance protocol Ruzbeh had taught her, and went to the Iranshahr Avenue safe house that she and Ruzbeh had established without informing the DGSE or CIA. Just as she had suppressed her emotions on hearing about Ruzbeh's death (and so many others), she could spare no feelings remembering the love she and Ruzbeh had shared in this small apartment. She told herself, "Whatever will become of me, one thing is for sure. I am done with this life forever."

Nilufar pulled the tiles off the wall behind the big armchair in the living room and found the box with $10,000 cash and the US passports that Ruzbeh had carefully placed in the wall. They had planned that, in an emergency, they would take this money together. Fate had not been so kind.

She called Mehrdad at his Foreign Ministry office. He told her, "What we know for certain is that the plane was on its plotted course, climbing to its cruising altitude for a thirty-minute flight to Dubai. It had reported nothing unusual when Bandar Abbas controllers lost contact."

On the radio she heard the announcer reading President Reagan's statement. "The course of the Iranian civilian airliner was such that it was headed directly for the USS *Vincennes*, which was at the time engaged with five Iranian Boghammar boats that had attacked our forces. When the aircraft failed to heed repeated warnings, the *Vincennes* followed standing orders and widely publicized procedures, firing to protect itself against possible attack."

She could not control herself. She somehow reached the toilet and vomited until she lost everything in her stomach. Then she continued heaving until she fell exhausted and trembling on the tiles.

When she had recovered enough to stand and walk to the kitchen table, she composed a final note to Undersecretary Porter.

> Ambassador,
>
> When you read this message you will know about the destruction of Iran Air 655. You may also know that RP was on that flight. What you do not know is that RP had become the love of my life and my future husband. Now he is gone.
>
> Sir, for almost nine years I have done what you asked me to do for the United States in Iran. It was my honor to do so. But this life is over for me. Perhaps at some time in the future we can meet and I can tell you how much I have appreciated your commitment to me and to a peaceful future between my country – America – and the land of my heritage.
>
> I will leave Iran as soon as I can. I do not know what I will do or where I will go after that. Please do not try to contact me.
>
> M

She next wrote a note to her Tehran family that would be delivered in the secret way they had long ago agreed if there was an emergency. She hoped they would understand. She prayed her presence since November 1979 would in the end cause them no harm. She hoped God and politics would allow her return someday to say proper thanks.

Nilufar put a few personal items in a carry-on bag. She dressed in her heaviest chador, one she had used when she worked at the airport. She distributed the cash in three pockets hidden in the folds and her still brand-new US passport in a fourth. She destroyed Ruzbeh's passport and her own US diplomatic passport, with its Tehran entry stamp of November 4, 1979.

She forced her memories to the bottom of her consciousness, looked around the house once more and went out the door to visit the sweetshop – which she had secretly preserved for emergencies – for the last time.

Ninety minutes later, Nilufar found Nazanin at the Turkish Airlines counter.

"I will buy a ticket on the eight p.m. flight to Istanbul. I will go to passport control and then to security. I may need help. Watch over me," Nilufar said firmly.

"I promise."

The clerk at Turkish Airlines paid hardly any attention to Nilufar's purchase. She had decided in the taxi on the way to the airport that buying a round-trip ticket would cause less suspicion than one-way, and she had the cash. She had chosen Turkish Airlines because Turkey was one of the few countries Iranians could visit without a visa. Her plan was to get to Istanbul, disappear for a few days, and figure out what to do next.

Nilufar did not notice the two men who watched her leave the THY counter and fell in behind her as she moved toward passport control. They did not know who she was, but their instructions were to keep an eye on all travelers. They had not done much on their shift and chose Nilufar as their random target.

Nilufar approached passport control. She had been in and out of Iran over the years to meet Porter in Dubai and was confident of her Iranian document. The inspector from border security flipped through the pages, checked the entry and exit stamps and looked at the picture, at Nilufar, and back to the picture.

"Why are you traveling alone? Do you have permission from your father, husband, or brother to travel?"

Nilufar produced a notarized letter in Persian from her uncle, the patriarch of the Rastbin family, which she had also hidden in the safe house for an emergency, giving her permission to travel.

"I am going to Istanbul to have a medical procedure that is common to women but one that men do not wish to hear or know about. Perhaps you are different. Should I tell you about it?"

"Be on your way, sister," the border policeman said as he pushed back her passport.

Nazanin silently returned to her spot behind a curtain, smiling at the simple but effective explanation.

As she approached security, the two men who had watched her move through passport control decided they needed to do something to justify themselves to the boss. As Nilufar stepped up to the screening enclosures, one of the men stepped in front of her, and, without touching her, steered her to a set of booths away from the main area.

"Passport."

"Where are you going and what is the reason for your travel?"

Nilufar repeated the story from passport control, but it had less impact on these two.

"Come with us." They led her to a small, musty office furnished only with a metal desk, a telephone, and a few metal folding chairs. One of the security men said into the phone, "Get me Mr. Sarhaddi at Guards' Security. He asked us to check travelers, and we have someone here he will want to question. Her name is Massoumeh Rastbin."

"How dare you," barked Nazanin as she burst into the room flashing her airport badge. With four of them inside, it was cramped and tense. "How dare you," Nazanin repeated. "Get away from this woman of virtue and away from me. She works directly for Hashemi-Rafsanjani. Should I call him now and tell him how you behave with devout Muslim ladies? Shame on you both."

"Madam, this is not your business. It's a Guards' security matter. Mr. Sarhaddi will be here soon to interrogate this woman."

Resisting panic, Nilufar passed a telephone number to her friend and told her loudly, "Call Hossein Niku in the Speaker's office and explain the situation to him. He will not be pleased."

Pushing past the two officers, Nazanin picked up the phone, dialed a number, and spoke urgently. She passed the receiver to one of the men saying, "Hashemi-Rafsanjani's chief of staff wants to talk to you."

The women could not hear what Niku was saying, but the security man kept repeating, "Yes, sir. I understand, sir," and "Immediately, sir."

Nazanin led Nilufar to the gate.

Sarhaddi could not believe his good luck. He decided he would be in no hurry to reach the airport. "I'll take my time. Let the high and mighty bitch wait and worry," he thought. He looked forward to extracting slow revenge for so many humiliations and watching her sob and beg for mercy. When he finished with her, he would turn her over to his guards who would enjoy completing her degradation.

Two hours later, when Sarhaddi reached Mehrabad, Nazanin had gone home, the two security men had found urgent business elsewhere, and Nilufar's plane was 34,000 feet above Lake Van.

WASHINGTON
JULY 4, 1988

There were no longer any days off at the State Department. Not Sundays, not Independence Day, August, or Christmas. Porter looked out the window at the crowds gathering on the Mall for the fireworks show later that evening. He would be on the eighth floor of the State Department building hosting the diplomatic corps for hamburgers, hot dogs, ice cream, and the greatest view of the fireworks in Washington.

But it was Iran Air 655 on his mind. At this stage in his life and career he no longer wondered how things like this could happen. They just did, especially where there was uncertainty and men with weapons. He had trained himself not to get caught in the inevitable controversies about what went wrong. Let the admirals sort that out in the investigation to come. Porter's job as a diplomat was to defend US interests. His responsibility as a human being was to protect Nilufar and Ruzbeh.

The executive secretary of the department had convened a task force in the seventh-floor Operations Center. Consular officers would be trying to find out if any Americans, or "AMCITS" as they called them in a way Porter always thought disrespectful, were on board the doomed flight. Desk officers would be writing situation reports to their deputy assistant secretary bosses who would be drafting recommendations for next steps to mitigate or take advantage of the crisis. He would soon be reading their proposals and would either take an immediate decision or consult with the secretary or the president.

Earlier that day the president had made his statement noting a threatening Iranian plane. As far as Porter knew, whoever wrote it for the president had not spoken to the State Department, but had used the Pentagon's language.

But for the few moments, before the next phone call from the NSC or the undersecretary for policy at Defense, Porter could think only of Nilufar and Ruzbeh. Among the many burdens that came with being "P," their safety remained his heaviest.

He sat looking at the Lincoln Memorial from his private office in the back of the ceremonial cavern. He looked again at Nilufar's picture. He usually found the mahogany wall panels natural and calming. But today all he wanted was to know where his Foreign Service Officer and her CIA agent protector, handler, and probably much more, were. His imagination about what might be happening to them was no help in keeping his professional serenity.

Porter called the task force director, a senior consular officer who had learned after many crises how to convey both confidence and competence.

"No, sir, we so far have no reports of any Amcits on the plane," she reported. "Yes, sir, we have been in touch with the Iranian Interest Section here in DC to express our condolences and offer to share information. No surprise, I suppose, they seem uninstructed and scared to talk to us. We have also sent a message to the Swiss, who look after our interests in Iran, to ask for any information on Amcits."

"Thank you," said a subdued Porter, recognizing that he did not have to convey any "leader's optimism" to such a senior and savvy Foreign Service colleague. To her subordinates, she would report the substance of his call in just the right way.

"If there is any more news, let me know at any time. Don't wait for the sit rep at the end of the shift. And please thank everyone on the task force for their effort. I will come by in person in my way upstairs to the reception.

The secure phone rang. It was George Blessey from CIA.

"Alan, I have very bad news. The head of the DGSE station in Washington was just here. He told me Ruzbeh Parvizi was on Iran Air 655. He said the Foreign Ministry, on the orders of Revolutionary Guard intelligence, had told Ambassador de Montréal in Tehran that Ruzbeh – or Tehrani as they knew him – needed to leave before the security forces arrested him. They directed him to that flight. He had no idea why no one alerted us in real time. I lost my cool and said his service was complicit in the cold-blooded murder of our officer and almost 300 other innocent people. He reminded me that it was our ship that shot down the plane. I doubt he'll be back for a while. What a fuckup. I am very sorry."

"I am sorry about Ruzbeh and I don't mean to be unsympathetic, but did he say anything about Nilufar or 'Miriam'?" pleaded Porter. Was she on the plane too?"

"Nothing. I don't know how much the French knew about her. They did know that Ruzbeh, under his Philippe Tehrani identity, was running an agent. We won't know more until the Iranians release a passenger list."

Porter put down the receiver. He felt an overwhelming guilt. Had she survived all those years in Iran only to be killed by Americans on her way home?

Leaving Nilufar in Tehran in 1979 was his idea. In 1984 he had interviewed Ruzbeh in this office and sent him to Iran. He had felt the thrill of reading nine years of the most astonishing intelligence – and did not parry the accolades for his foresight when all was going well. But how many times did he tell himself, "Let them come home. Enough. They have done their service and then some." But he did not act, and now he was responsible for one death and perhaps many more.

Porter alerted the secretary and the deputy. They agreed he should go to the White House and tell the president that Ruzbeh was dead and Nilufar missing. Both were sympathetic, but not sorry that job belonged to him.

After his meeting with the president, Porter called Farzaneh and David Hartman. He told them everything he knew minus Ruzbeh and said he would let them know the minute he had any news. They were outwardly calm and polite, but did not let him off the emotional hook.

ISTANBUL
JULY 5–7, 1988

Using her American passport – to ensure she had an entry stamp for Turkey – Nilufar passed through security at Istanbul's Atatürk International Airport without incident. She threw her Iranian passport and clothing in the trash in the women's toilet before passport control. She put on a thoroughly Western outfit while maintaining the modesty shown by most Turkish women, both as a show of respect and to maintain as much anonymity as possible.

She took a city bus to the *Kapalıçarşı*, Istanbul's grand bazaar. From there she looked for a place to stay and found a room in an Ottoman wooden building converted to a small hotel called the *Mavi Ev*, the Blue House. Her Turkish hosts were hospitable but, unlike Iranians, not curious or prying. To them, she was another foreign tourist in their magnificent city.

Nilufar spent the next day walking in the bazaar. She was immune to the calls of the carpet dealers and gold merchants that she should come in to their shops for a cup of the apple tea served with every sales pitch. "*Büyürün* (Come in). Looking is free," they said. "Looking is far from free," she thought. "Just look at me."

Nilufar needed the time and the physical activity to weigh her options. Maybe she should go to the consulate and tell her story and get help. But that would put her back in the machine's grip.

Several hours later, she had come to know what seemed both right and secure. She went to the closest Turkish PTT office, bought a chit to use the telephone, called her parents, said she would soon explain everything, and told them she was buying a ticket home, the only place she now wanted to be. She made one request of her mother and father: that they not tell Porter they had heard from her. She was done with the life she had been living. A feeling reinforced a thousand times when Nilufar saw, in a day-old *International Herald Tribune*, the same statement from the White House blaming Iranian provocation for the destruction of Iran Air 655 and a statement from the vice-president saying, "We never apologize."

WASHINGTON
JULY 11, 1988

Nilufar's message through the sweetshop finally made it to Porter. He was shaken by the anger and grief in her message, but at the same time elated to think Nilufar might – must, please God – be alive. But where was she?

Porter called Farzaneh Hartman.

"I have a message from Nilufar. It is some days old but she says she is leaving Tehran. Have you heard from her? Do you have any idea where she is? May I come and see you and David this afternoon and talk to you about what we can do next?"

"Mr. Undersecretary, thank you for calling and thank you for caring about our beloved daughter," said a noticeably uneasy Farzaneh. "I know this is cruel, but for now it is best you not contact us anymore. We are sorry. We know you were do-

ing the right thing for our country and, you thought, for Nilufar. But now we must do the right thing for our family."

"Is she with you? Is she safe? At least tell me that."

"Goodbye for now, sir. We are sorry."

Porter called the consular officer who had been on task
force duty on July 4. In two hours she reported back that
American citizen Nilufar Hartman, using an ordinary passport,
had entered the US at Dulles on a flight from Frankfurt after
transferring from Istanbul three days earlier.

WASHINGTON
APRIL 1989

In the nine months since Nilufar returned, Porter had done everything he knew how to do – at least bureaucratically – to make
things right. With the help of the undersecretary for management, he got Nilufar as much money for her time as an FSO –
including a 25 percent hardship allowance for Tehran – as he
legally could. The State Department retired her with honor, but
the Office of Personnel Management denied her the exemption
she needed for a pension. "Too young and not enough years of
service," they told him.

Porter thought he might see the Hartmans at the CIA
ceremony honoring Ruzbeh's ultimate sacrifice – he became
another anonymous star on a plaque in the agency lobby – but
he assumed the pain and bitterness were too great.

One clear morning in October, Nilufar and her mother
drove to Arlington Cemetery, stopping on the way to buy a
bouquet of flowers and a small American flag. They parked
their car and rode a shuttle to a stop near the Tomb of the Unknown Soldier. From there they walked a short distance up a
gentle rise and stopped before a simple gray monument.

Nilufar laid the flowers and planted the flag in front of a
stone with eight names, the American airmen and marines from
the failed rescue mission, killed in Iran, near Tabas, in April
1980, when a refueling helicopter collided with a C-130 transport. Holding her mother's hand and speaking quietly, she
said, "Dear compatriots. Today I again salute your bravery.

You risked everything to bring my friends home. Like my dear Ruzbeh, you never finished your journey."

Porter finally convinced David Hartman to meet him for tea at the Hay Adams at Christmas 1988. From her father, he heard Nilufar's story and learned Nilufar was pregnant by Ruzbeh and due in March.

With the help of George Blessey at CIA, he knew he could make Nilufar a last offering of respect and friendship.

At the Hartmans' Falls Church home, the birth of Behnam was a moment for joy and a chance to think about the future. One afternoon, as Nilufar was feeding him and his grandparents were catching a few moments rest, a courier arrived at the front door.

"For Ms. Nilufar Hartman from Ambassador Alan Porter."

When she opened the stiff envelope she found a fully filled out and fully legitimate Virginia birth certificate for Behnam Parvizi, born March 15, 1989, the son of Nilufar Hartman and Ruzbeh Parvizi.

Attached was a handwritten note from Porter: "Please accept best wishes for your and Behnam's future. With my great respect and affection, Alan Porter."

PART THREE

SEE OUR DEEPEST SECRETS

TWO CONSPIRACIES

THE PRESENT
VERMONT

Ruzbeh was safely at day camp. Nilufar drove forty-five minutes north on US 7 from Middlebury to the optimistically named "Burlington International Airport." She parked her car and waited at the gates until Porter appeared. The two exchanged hugs and quickly began the ride south.

"How have you been, sir? Do you stay busy in Washington?"

"I'm doing less, especially since my wife Anne died two years ago. I read more history. People don't change. They remain as brilliant, stupid, or greedy as they always were. Ninety percent of our policy problems come from ignorance of history."

"Well, that's always been true in the case of Iran. Will you stay in Washington?"

"My life is there now. But I must say, it's beautiful here. From the plane I could see the Adirondacks, the Green Mountains, and Lake Champlain. I see why you stayed."

"People who say that have never experienced the winters. But it has been a refuge for me. Ruzbeh's murder and what came after crushed me. Friends at State and CIA wanted to help, but I could not be any part of their world. Of course, you understood – you must be part Iranian – and let me find my way out of the horror. And now I am a rooted academic in this remote place."

Porter said nothing, letting Nilufar lift some of her burden.

"My saviors were you, my parents, and my mother's amazing Iranian family. They knew intuitively what I needed. They never asked what I had done or not done. Did they know or care I had blood on my hands? Did they know or care how much misery I had caused while working to serve the United States? If they did, they never said anything. I was family and that was enough. The same with Ruzbeh's Iranian relatives. They are particularly good with our son Behnam and my grandson. That was the help I needed – love without questions or judgments."

"Nilufar, even today only a few people know what you did, how you risked your life every day for nine years. The blindness and ignorance you saw after Ruzbeh's senseless death must have been shattering, but few people could know why you walked away. You did the right thing. And no one could tell them."

Nilufar stopped at a country store along Route 7 and bought sandwiches and soft drinks. In downtown Middlebury she turned left and drove east on State Route 125, beginning a climb over the main range of the Green Mountains toward Hancock. A few miles before the famous Bread Loaf Writers' Center, she pulled off the road at a marker on the right for the "Robert Frost Trail." She told Porter, "There's an easy path to walk here. It's always quiet at midweek and we can find a place to sit, have our lunch, and talk."

After crossing a marsh on duckboard for about ten minutes they came to a bench. Next to it was a plaque with these lines of Frost.

The Pasture

I'm going out to clean the pasture spring;
I'll only stop to rake the leaves away
(And wait to watch the water clear, I may):
I sha'n't be gone long.—You come too.

I'm going out to fetch the little calf
That's standing by the mother. It's so young,
It totters when she licks it with her tongue.
I sha'n't be gone long.—You come too.

"I love this place. They say Robert Frost lived somewhere near here, but no one is sure just where. It reminds me of how Iranians honor poets. The difference is that poets' graves in Iran become shrines, always crowded with pilgrims. Here – lucky for us today – not so. Instead we Americans build monuments to politicians and generals. In Iran no one remembers them. Even the few good ones."

Indicating the Frost poem, she said, "There's a famous verse from Rumi that the translator has rendered into this:

> Out beyond ideas of wrongdoing and rightdoing,
> There is a field. I'll meet you there.

"The English is beautiful, but it's not Rumi. It's Robert Frost and his pasture." In her musical voice she recited the original:

از کفر و ز اسلام برون صحرایی است.... ما را به میان آن فضا سودایی است

Az kofr va z'islam borun, sahraa'ist
Maaraa be miyaan-e-aan fazaa, sowdaa'ist.

There is a boundless plain beyond Islam and unbelief.
For us, in the midst of that expanse, there is endless longing.

"You see? The translator has taken Islam and longing out of Rumi and made something different. Different, but still beautiful. Much more intimate. In Frost's New England there are pastures and fields. In Rumi's Anatolia there were boundless plains."

The two sat silently for a few minutes. The only sounds were birdsong and the flowing creek nearby.

"Nilufar, I don't know where to start except to begin. As we sit in this peaceful spot speaking of ageless poetry, terrible people are making evil plans. Parallel groups in Washington and Tehran are working to provoke a conflict – listen to me, sounding like a diplomat – to start a war between Iran and the United States. They are well organized, flush with cash, and passionate. An awful combination."

Nilufar looked carefully into Porter's eyes. "I love this man," she thought, "but has he lost his grip on reality? Conspirators seeking war? Has Alan Porter been in Washington too long?"

Porter continued. "The Americans call themselves the 'Kalorama Group,' because they meet in Washington, on California Street in the Kalorama neighborhood. They use a mansion belonging to the far right-wing billionaire, John Simeon, whose arms businesses stand to gain from a war. I am astonished every time I say this: The vice president of the United States, Andrea Longton, leads the Kalorama Group. She has long taken Simeon's money and has concluded that war with Iran will open her path to succeeding President McGuire – who promises no more wars in the Middle East – in the next election.

"Longton has recruited Nestor Childress, the deputy national security advisor, Chelsey Bock, undersecretary of defense for policy, Senators Charles McGowan and Elizabeth Montez, three House members, and Peter Mason, head of the 100,000-member group called Evangelicals for American Security. The Kalorama Group meets every week. They tell their aides and bodyguards they are attending a 'foreign policy discussion group.' They hide in plain sight.

"As part of the effort, Childress from the NSC keeps an active channel to the Israeli Prime Minister, Mordechai Ben-Eliezer, thorough an American industrialist who has decided Ben-Eliezer's political success is more important than the long-term safety of five million American Jews. That's why he is silent when President McGuire flirts with the neo-Nazi, alt-right. Bock at Defense is Kalorama's connection to a group of secretive Saudi royals who follow the most conservative form of Wahhabism. They finance the Kalorama Group out of hatred for the young Crown Prince, their fear of Shia Muslims, and their emotional and strategic anxieties about Iran."

Nilufar was silent. Porter wasn't certain if she was weighing his news or ignoring him, preferring the harmonies of wind, water, and birds in the midst of Rumi's "endless plain of longing." Was she even listening, or was she now so far from his world that his worries and urgencies meant nothing to her? Had he misread someone he thought he knew?

She looked at him carefully and replied softly, "Sir, so far I don't hear anything new in what you say. Groups like this Kalorama, in one form or another, have been with us forever. The MEK and its paid American voices – from both political parties and high in the current administration – have been peddling their nonsense for decades. One of its biggest supporters is a former governor of a neighboring state – a true progressive. The Israeli far right and our own far right have been working together and beating Iran war drums for years. Neither could stand the previous president and they made Iran a pretext to attack him.

"The Saudis and their friends in the Persian Gulf have nightmares that we and the Iranians will resume talking. They see us as a divorced couple who never got over each other. They imagine we will somehow get back together and leave them out in the cold. Their fear has reached the point that militant Sunnis in Riyadh will finance the MEK, an Iranian Shia cult that fought for Saddam Hossein. How strange is that? The MEK then invests Saudi money in Americans who will stoke fear for them."

Porter, relieved that she had listened and that she still had the analytical mind he always knew, answered, "Nilufar, you're right as far as all that goes. But this is more than the usual suspects making the usual noises. I'll tell you why an old man came all this way to ask – no, to beg – for your help.

"It's no longer just the same dubious people braying the same nonsense. We have very good intelligence that there is a parallel group of war hawks in Tehran. They call themselves the 'Fifteenth of Khordad Group.' They take the name from the date of Khomeini's violent uprising against the Shah and his 'White Revolution' in 1963.

"What is new is that Fifteenth Khordad has an explicit understanding with those Americans in the Kalorama Group. The Iranians call their plan 'Operation Zeinab.' Fifteenth Khordad and Kalorama are working together and they've agreed on a course of action that will bring the two countries to war within a month. At most two.

"If it were just the deluded Kalorama members wanting to lead the United States into a war, I wouldn't worry this much. I wouldn't be here. War with Iran is not a galvanizing issue for most Americans. President McGuire was not elected to start another war in the Middle East. All the chest-beating about the evils of the Islamic Republic don't mean much outside Washington.

"Of course the Islamic Republic is bad news. It suppress free speech. It rigs elections. It puts opponents in jail and tortures them. It supports terrorism and instability in Syria, Lebanon, and Yemen. Most people reasonably ask, 'So what? How does all that make Iran different from other countries, including some of our friends and allies? The Saudis? The Egyptians? Are Iranian misdeeds worth more American lives in the Middle East?'

"But if there is a provocation, especially one with American casualties, the cries for revenge will be too loud to ignore, even for McGuire. As things stand now, there's almost no way to defuse a crisis. The channels that existed are gone."

"You say these Iranian and American groups have an understanding. How do they talk to each other?"

"They don't. At least not directly. A few Saudis act as intermediaries. They have good contacts among hawks in Washington, some of whom, including the MEK, they finance. The Iranian side, as usual, underestimates the Arabs, who have their reasons for encouraging a war. For one thing, it will send the price of their crude oil soaring. War in the Persian Gulf would stop exports by sea from Iran, Iraq, Kuwait, Qatar, and Abu Dhabi. That's ten million barrels a day off the world market. With their giant pipeline overland to the Red Sea, the Saudis stand to make billions. If thousands of Iranians die in the process, so what? The Saudis consider them heretics anyway.

"As for the Iranians, they cannot imagine anyone – especially Arabs – can be as cynical as they are. Some of the Saudis and Iranians are in business together, and the Iranians find it pays to listen to their wealthy partners."

Nilufar remembered Adil and Morteza, the Arab and Iranian fixers, who decades ago together played all sides so skillfully during Iran-Contra and almost destroyed an American president. It did not surprise her that extremist Saudis and Iranians could work together in a tangle of greed, fanaticism, and self-delusion.

"Tell me about this Fifteenth of Khordad group. Who's in it? What makes it so dangerous? And what does all this have to do with me?"

"I can't give you all the details here, but our intelligence is good. It's a coalition of Iranians who agree on one thing: the need for a war with the US. Different people have different motives, but they were all terrified when relations were improving a few years ago. They were infuriated when they saw American and Iranian officials sitting in meetings smiling and shaking hands; when they learned of regular and professional contacts between ministers and between lower-level officials from both sides; and when they heard talk of further cooperation. To them, all these meant two catastophes: betrayal of the revolution and, even worse, their losing power."

"So why are they worried now? From what I hear, their reasons to worry are gone. No one is smiling, talking, or shaking hands – at least not in public. We're already on the brink of open conflict. We're back to where we were for so long: accusing, insulting, and threatening. I would think the Fifteenth of Khordad people would be happy. Why do they need a war?"

"They won't be satisfied with anything less than all-out war. Short of that, they fear the wheel could turn again and we'll be back to what they fear most – civility and dialogue. It happened once and could happen again. They figure war is the only sure way to kill normalization for good. From what we hear, Iranian public opinion – especially among young people – is against them, and they have to move before they are swept away."

Nilufar thought for a moment and said, "In Persian we say that anyone once bitten by a snake is afraid of a black and white rope. And they do know how unpopular they are."

"That's exactly it. We came close to normalizing a few years ago, and fanatics on both sides are terrified it may happen again. The Fifteenth of Khordad includes some of the supreme leader's relatives, his chief of staff, and the chief prosecutor of the revolutionary court. Their spiritual leaders include the chairman of the Assembly of Experts and the Friday prayer leader of Mashhad and his son-in-law. The son-in-law recently lost a presidential election, but he still controls billions belonging to the shrine there."

Nilufar remained skeptical. "But, seriously, a war with us? It's hard to understand, even for that benighted crowd. President McGuire says a war would be the end of Iran. I know they don't care about their country or the death of millions of innocent Iranians. They've already proved that. But why would they commit political suicide? That's what war would mean."

"Nilufar, they don't see it that way. Even if millions of Iranians die and their cities become ash, they figure they will survive and keep power. They may end up ruling piles of rubble, but they will still rule. That's all that matters to them. They fear losing power so much that they're willing to take down the whole country."

Nilufar, assaulted by buried memories of Iran, remembered the violence, repression, treachery, and greed of her years there. She also remembered the self-sacrifice, bravery, generosity, and kindness of strangers, relatives, and friends like Nazanin. She remembered the blindness of American officials as they made every possible wrong choice. Most of all she remembered the betrayals that had cost the life of her beloved Ruzbeh and had stolen a father from Behnam. She had tried hiding from her past for thirty years; and here was Porter, forcing her to confront it.

"Maybe they're not entirely crazy in Tehran. There must be a warped calculation at work. When I was there, the extremists loved the certainties. Things were simple: Iran was at war with the world and Khomeini's word was law. I remember those years too well. As harsh as they were, there were no doubts, no questions, no debates. The rules were clear. Whoever questioned or opposed you, you crushed them. Whoever walked or talked the wrong way, you smashed them. For most people, their role was either to shut up or march, denounce, and cheer on command.

"Now things have changed. Former true believers are now talking of democracy, transparency, and civil society. The old guard is unhinged. Open enemies they can deal with; but now what do they see? No more certainties. They see new music and art they would have silenced and burned thirty years ago. They see young people ignoring them and their absurd rules. They are not used to being questioned or ridiculed. They don't like what they see but can't stop it.

"They must imagine a new war will bring back their glory days. It will create hysteria they can use. They will condemn opponents as unpatriotic, un-Islamic, and counterrevolutionary. They will use the same tactics that worked for them during the Iran-Iraq war. When I was in the morality patrols, I saw how politicians used us and how we used the war as an excuse to bully other Iranians. I saw firsthand how much misery that war created just to satisfy the ambitions of some cynical old men. Whatever else happened, they destroyed their enemies and ruled, even if they ruined the country in the process."

Nilufar had not intended to recall so much she had wanted to forget. She turned to Porter and added, "And please remember you and I had a part in all that misery. After all, we helped Beheshti crush his enemies and solidify his power. How many died because of what we did?"

As she spoke, Nilufar's bitterness surprised her. She knew her words would tear open old wounds. Thirty years later, the horrors of the past still ripped at her soul. She thought of all the miseries inflicted on Iran over the centuries: invasions, civil strife, pointless wars, misrule, massacres, famines, plagues, and foreign domination.

She remembered her friend Nazanin and what she and her husband had suffered in the Shah's prisons. She remembered Rafsanjan and all those memorials to slaughtered boys who would never know the delights of marriage and family. She remembered the lines of people waiting hours in the cold to buy food, heating oil, and medicine. She remembered Amira and her children, the countless men left maimed and crippled, and the thousands of widows and orphans left destitute. She remembered Ruzbeh's pictures of the gassed Kurdish children in Halabja and America's efforts to whitewash Saddam's crime and blame the Iranians. Most of all she remembered the mangled bodies from the blown-apart Iranian airliner that had carried her beloved Ruzbeh to his death.

Porter made no effort to answer her accusation. Nilufar expected no response. She had made a simple statement of fact: "You and I were also responsible."

He pressed on, hoping his version of the facts would sway his reluctant audience of one. "The Kalorama Group has used its high-profile members to gain supporters in our military and national security agencies. Some of these people are aware of the larger goal, some are not. The Group has engaged editorial writers from around the nation, playing especially on those rightly angry at the Iranian regime's human rights record, suspicious of Tehran's ballistic missiles program, or angry at Iran's support for terrorism in the region. Just like in 2003, before the invasion of Iraq, many newspapers now ask daily why the president has not yet moved militarily to eliminate the 'malign mullahs' regime.

"That's not the worst of it. While Kalorama's friends beat the war drums, its senate and house member friends keep the legislative branch quiet. No questions from them about rushing into a war the Congress never authorized. They genuflect to the administration's interpretation – the same interpretation as all its predecessors, of course – of the War Powers Act.

"The group has used front companies around the world to pay lobbyists to denounce Tehran's transgressions in public and on Capitol Hill. "And as I said, the Kalorama Group's Chelsey Bock, through her Saudi friends, is in contact with the Fifteenth of Khordad group. That, dear Nilufar, is real treason, not the 'fake news' variety our thin-skinned president believes is all around him."

"Sir, how do you know all this? Why not just have the traitors arrested? What does this have to do with me?"

"I cannot tell you how we know about Kalorama and Fifteenth of Khordad – or their connections. You'll have to trust me that we do. This is not like the phony agent 'Curveball's' tall tales of nonexistent stocks of Iraqi WMD in 2003 -- the stories which supposedly justified attacking Iraq. The Kalorama Group works on many fronts. They have learned from the way a small group of determined people inside and outside government pushed our country into war in 2003.

"So why am I here? There are some very senior people in Washington opposed to the Kalorama Group. They include the deputy secretary of state, Lamont Greene; CIA director, Brian DeWolf; and the secretary of defense, Darnell Hobbes. The FBI director, Steve Quoddy, is an ally. They have asked me to play a modest role.

"The challenge is the president. Getting his attention. Keeping it. Asking him to weigh costs and benefits to our nation and not just to what he proudly and repeatedly calls 'my base.' He hates Iran, or at least finds it useful to pretend he does. He hates the previous president's nuclear agreement. He has sanctioned the Tehran government and US and foreign businesses. He has cut off their oil exports. But does he want a war? What he calls his base is against it. He is also heavily influenced by the last person to talk to him on any subject, especially foreign policy. Andrea Longton and Nestor Childress have the inside track in that race.

"You must now know why I am here."

She did. Knowing brought no comfort. After thirty years, Porter had reentered her life to unearth all that past desolation and to warn her to expect more in the future. She already knew what he wanted, but she still asked him, "When you called, I suspected you weren't bringing news of a party. But what does all this have to do with me?"

Porter hesitated to continue. He was exhausted. He had no more arguments. He was on an old fool's futile errand. He was about to ask her to risk her life for her country again. What could he tell her?

Porter knew he was throwing money into a poker pot in hopes of drawing an inside straight. You knew the odds – about twelve to one – but you still paid and sometimes you filled the hand. After all that had happened, how could he be so dense and imagine she would agree? It must have been only her innate Iranian courtesy and respect for age that made her listen to his rantings.

He sighed, pushed in all his chips, and continued. "Nilufar, this group in Washington – the one I told you about – has asked for my help. They had nowhere else to go. I agreed, but what can I do? Now I'm coming to you. They're desperate. We all are.

"In all this evil there is one hope. There are people in Tehran who see things as we do. They don't trust us, but they know what war would mean. A few years ago, they could see a better path for Iran and the United States. Now they want somehow to get back on that road. This president isn't interested in better relations with Iran, but we can buy time until things change – if we manage somehow to avoid a war that will destroy everything.

"My friends in Washington are desperate to contact their Iranian counterparts and offer to act together to stop a war. It's the only way. One side alone can't stop it. That's why they came to me. And that's why I've come to you. Who other than you, Nilufar?"

Nilufar understood very well that in Tehran and Washington a madness was driving both countries to destruction. But understanding was one thing. Returning to the inferno she had barely escaped thirty years before was something else. She had paid her price then. Saving the world was no longer her mission.

In Nilufar, Porter saw Farzaneh, her late mother. Once she decided to leave her old life, that was it. No more discussion. Even if she accepted the mission, it would be the same when it was over: she would turn her back on all of it, including him.

"Sir, with all respect, aren't the Iranians playing us for fools again? Exactly who are these sensible people in Tehran? Do they even exist? It sounds to me we are hearing the same fantasies people swallowed during Iran-Contra in 1985. Remember those nonexistent 'Iranian anti-communist moderates'? All they wanted were American weapons. They played on our fears and scammed us then. They're probably doing it again. I don't have to remind you that I sat in the room while Hashemi-Rafsanjani and his conmen fed that fake ayatollah his lines in a third-rate farce."

All the bumbling, self-delusion, and wishful thinking of past administrations had now come back to haunt Porter and his friends. As much as she respected him, she could not take his account on faith. She would listen politely. Beyond that she would not go. How could she believe him?

"Nilufar, you were right then and you may be right now. Here's what I know: the Iranians involved include former foreign ministers, senior scientists, and even some former presidents. Other members are from the next generations of the elite, the children and grandchildren of the Islamic Republic's founding fathers – Beheshtis, Khomeinis, Motahharis, and Hashemi-Rafsanjanis. Their backgrounds are impressive and they all detest what the extremists are doing. They don't like us or what we've done, but they don't want their country destroyed. If they act together they carry a lot of weight."

Porter played his last card. "My counterpart in the Iranian group – their advisor – is your mother's brother Arash. He's in his eighties now. He retired from the Iranian Foreign Service soon after you left Tehran in 1988. He didn't want to stay in Europe or the US. He and his wife Farideh moved back to Iran to supervise family property and to take care of aging relatives, including Farideh's parents."

Nilufar did not tell Porter that she had occasional indirect news of Arash, mostly through relatives. She had seen Arash a few years earlier when he was able to travel to Istanbul. His mind remained clear as ever.

Porter continued, "He had high-level protection, particularly from the late Hashemi-Rafsanjani, who all that time suspected your connection to me through Arash and Mehrdad Dashti at the Foreign Ministry. I was sorry to hear of Mehrdad's death, by the way. I regret I never met him. As for Arash, until now he's kept out of politics. He teaches political

science at Tehran University and stays in touch with old colleagues. If he's working to stop this conspiracy, the danger is
real."

Nilufar remembered Hashemi-Rafsanjani's saying, "Give
my respects to undersecretary Porter" on her last day in Iran,
just before Nazanin gave her the shattering news of Ruzbeh's
murder. She said only, "As I remember, you and Arash used to
meet, even after he left Washington for Geneva. He would pass
your messages to me through Mehrdad. Are you still in touch?"

"Not really. Then he was taking an enormous risk. It's
more dangerous now. Even his relatives in the US – your cousins – are afraid to speak to me. I know he's involved with this
group in Tehran, but our information about the factions is not
from him. It's too dangerous for us to meet, even in a third
country."

Porter had told his friends in Washington he did not know
if Nilufar would agree to help. He expected skepticism and
wasn't sure he could break through her doubts and anger.
Thirty-five years earlier he could persuade her – a young and
ambitious Foreign Service Officer – to risk her life as his agent
in Tehran. That was then. Now she no longer worked for him,
and he had lost the keys to convincing her. He was speaking to
a different Nilufar.

He went on, "Nilufar, if there were any other way, I
wouldn't be here. We now know that the schemes of the Fifteenth Khordad and Kalorama groups – with Saudi help – are
farther advanced than we originally thought. We imagined we
had at least three months to make contacts in Iran and design a
plan to discredit both groups.

"We don't have that much time. We have a month at most.
There's a plot for Revolutionary Guard fast boats to attack an
American warship in the Gulf. In a few weeks the USS *Gerald
R. Ford*, our most advanced nuclear-powered aircraft carrier,
will be sailing through the Strait of Hormoz. It has escorts, but
one lucky missile hit from a Guards' boat will cause major
damage and casualties. We could even lose the ship."

Nilufar asked, "Are the Guards that good? Can they actually carry off such an attack?"

"Maybe not on their own. But they'll have help that will improve their chances. I hate to admit this, but the Kalorama Group has people inside our military and DOD who will give the Iranians our carrier group's schedule and course into the Persian Gulf. With that information the Guards' targeting becomes much easier. Finding a nuclear carrier in the strait won't be hard. The question becomes: How many fast boats and IRGC men are they willing to sacrifice?"

Seeing Nilufar's shock, Porter told her, "Can you see now why we're so worried? It's hard to accept that our own people could be so depraved. But the Kaloramans are desperate for a war. They'll murder American sailors to get it.

"And when the Guards attack our ships, they will be ready. They're already preparing members and sympathizers to write op-eds and go on every talk show in the country to denounce Iranian provocation and demand swift punishment."

Nilufar could not go back to all that evil. She was ready to tell Porter, "Sir, I'm sorry you came all this way for nothing. You know I left that world thirty years ago. I'm never going back. If blind and self-centered people are going to drag our countries into an abyss, so be it. If they have decided on ruin, I cannot stop them."

Before she could say anything, Porter made his last, desperate plea. "Nilufar, I have no one else to turn to. We need you in Tehran to contact Arash and his anti-war friends. They need to know they're not alone. We need you to take them a message. We are proposing that the authorities in Washington and in Tehran move simultaneously to stop the fanatics. But it has to be done in the next few weeks before some bloody incident makes the war machine unstoppable."

He paused. They both remained silent. He could do no more, and told her, "That's my appeal to you. If you tell me no, that I'm crazy to ask you, I'll tell my friends in Washington that we expected too much."

Nilufar now remembered all she wanted to forget. She remembered the loving hours with Ruzbeh in the Behnam Alley apartment and the desolate years that followed as that same cherished body rotted in the Persian Gulf. She remembered the suicide bombs, the bloody street battles between Revolutionary Guards and regime opponents, and the thousands of young prisoners executed. She remembered the hundreds of thousands maimed and killed in the endless war. She remembered her constant fear of Iraqi Scuds, the torture chamber, and the gallows.

What could she say to Porter? In his desperation he had come to her. How could she reject him? Finally, she asked, "Sir, when do you need an answer?"

He looked at her carefully. "I need to take your 'yes' or 'no' back to Washington tonight. If it's no, then we need to find another way. If it's yes, then we'll start immediately to arrange your mission and build your cover."

The two of them gathered their trash, walked to the parking lot, where, despite the delicious late-summer weather, Nilufar's car remained alone. They did not speak as she drove west toward Middlebury and turned north onto US 7. She found the local public radio station. The announcer spoke of summer gardens, deer, poison ivy, ticks, and an invasion of zebra mussels in Lake Champlain. Nilufar broke the silence as they approached the airport. "Sir, I'll do it. I assume I'll need to come to Washington first. Will I need to pee in a cup again?"

He smiled and said, "Of course you will. Some things never change. Can you be there in two days? We'll need to prepare your documents, create a cover story, and write our message to Arash and his friends. You should be in Tehran as soon as possible. The less time you spend in Washington the better. It's not completely safe for us there."

Porter had one more story from the past. Would she reconsider when she heard it?

"Nilufar, we have asked the French to bring you safely out of Iran when you finish your mission. You need to know that, years ago, by analyzing telephone calls, they discovered that it was Sarhaddi from Revolutionary Guards' intelligence who laid the trap for Ruzbeh and put him on the doomed flight. The French hate him for that. As they say, 'We have long memories and feel intimately connected to you, your success, and your safety.'"

Nilufar was too spent to argue. She would digest this last nugget later. She said only, "I understand."

As he left the car in front of the United Airlines counters, he looked at her carefully and said, "Nilufar, I don't have to tell you how grateful I am. If you had turned me down, I don't know what we would have done. We had no options."

GREAT FALLS, VIRGINIA

As soon as Porter left, Nilufar called her son Behnam in Raleigh and told him, "I need to be in Washington day after tomorrow. I'll bring Ruzbeh with me. Can you drive there and meet us? I know I promised to keep him all summer, but something urgent has come up. I'll be staying with my cousin Iraj and his family in Great Falls."

Behnam Parvizi knew better than to debate his mother. Her question was not a question. She had raised him to expect her unconditional love and protection in return for his unconditional obedience."

She never spoke to him of her past, and when he asked he met silence and evasions. Neither she nor his grandparents would tell him much. He knew his mother had stayed in Iran through the 1980s and returned shortly before he was born. He knew that during her years there she had met his father Ruzbeh – a French-Iranian reporter for AFP who died in 1988 on the doomed Iran Air Airbus. No one mentioned a CIA connection.

A Google search led only to her academic career. He did not know she had gone to Iran in 1979 as a Foreign Service Officer. Nilufar told him only that she went to Iran a few months after the revolution to visit family. When war broke out in September 1980, she decided to stay and care for her widowed great-aunt Zahra. That was all she would say.

As Behnam was growing up, Nilufar insisted he learn to speak and read Persian. He spent as much time as possible with his grandmother Farzaneh and with his father's Iranian relatives in California. He listened to their heated discussions of recent Iranian history: how the CIA-supported *coup d'état* of August 1953 removed the nationalist premier Mohammad Mosaddegh; how Ayatollah Khomeini rose from obscure cleric preaching extreme religious causes to national hero and undisputed leader against the Pahlavi monarchy; and how Russians, Americans, British, and others competed to steal Iranians' wealth and control their destiny.

Most of his Iranian-American contemporaries ignored their parents' debates, which they dismissed as the futile bickering of exiles laying blame on others for their misfortunes. Behnam was different. He was fascinated by the exchanges. He not only learned a rich Persian vocabulary, full of nuance and subtlety, but the arguments opened his eyes to Iran's turbulent history and its cast of oversized personalities. Because no one had a clear answer to the question, "What happened?" everyone had his own ideas, which usually meant hidden hands and bizarre conspiracies.

The young Behnam would ask his mother if he could somehow visit Iran, meet his relatives there, and better understand his origins. She strongly discouraged such a visit, noting that – because of his father's nationality – he would have to travel on Iranian documents. While thousands of Iranian-Americans came and went without incident, there were tragic cases of dual nationals detained for years for no clear reason. When he asked, "Will I ever see Iran?" she answered, "If God wills it."

Two days after Porter's visit, Nilufar and her grandson Ruzbeh flew to Washington. She told her department chair that, because of a family emergency, she would be a few weeks late for the start of classes. Her colleague agreed to arrange for someone to cover her classes as long as necessary.

Her cousin Iraj – who had fled Iran during the bloody strife of 1981 – had earned his degree in electrical engineering and was now near retirement as chief of technical services for Dominion Electric Power Company. He and his wife Parisa – a distant cousin – had bought an elegant house in Great Falls, a Virginia suburb thirty minutes from downtown Washington. Their three children were all younger than Behnam and older than Ruzbeh. The cousins had remained close and everyone doted on Ruzbeh. Nilufar was especially grateful that Iraj had helped care for her aging parents and had kept her secrets, remaining silent about her time in Tehran. He didn't know everything, but he remembered the veiled "Massoumeh", the whispered conversations between her and Mehrdad Dashti, the relative in the Foreign Ministry, and how the family united to hide Nilufar's true identity.

Behnam had driven from Raleigh, and over a meal of eggplant stew flavored with unripe grapes, the talk was of family, children, and news from Iran. Iraj and Parisa had done their best to maintain their children's Persian, but it was difficult to keep the children from using English among themselves or slipping into English when subjects were complicated.

Even without explicit orders, no one spoke of Nilufar's years in Iran. Behnam knew her time there had been difficult, that tragic things had happened, and that his mother spoke little about his father Ruzbeh. He never asked. He respected her wish for secrecy and hoped she would tell him more when the time was right. Iraj also respected Nilufar's wishes, although it was clear to Behnam he knew more than he would say. When Behnam had asked his grandparents about those years, David or Farzaneh replied only, "She needed to stay with Auntie Zahra. You know how close they were. She hadn't planned to stay so long, but with the war and all the problems she felt she couldn't leave. It would not have been right."

Behnam knew enough about Iran's nationality laws to understand the Islamic Republic did not consider his mother Iranian. He also knew enough about his mother never to ask how she managed, as an American citizen, to stay so long in Iran. Those (and many other) questions were off-limits. Instead the family spoke of safer subjects – children, parents, and other relatives.

Parisa asked Behnam, "Why can't dear Ruzbeh stay with us for a while? The schools here in Fairfax County are excellent. It would be a treat for him and his cousins. He's like our own son. No difference for us."

Behnam answered, "I'm sure he'd love to stay. You will all spoil him rotten and he'll love that. But Anita won't hear of it. I should take him home before school starts. We've missed him a lot this summer."

Nilufar asked about her uncle Arash and his family. Iraj told her that as far as he knew, Arash and Farideh, now in their eighties and late seventies, were both well. They had a group of friends in Tehran, mostly retired diplomats, who all lived quietly. Inflation had wiped out the value of Arash's government pension, but they owned their apartment and earned an income from renting some houses and shops. Farideh's parents had died, but she still had numerous brothers, sisters, cousins, nieces, and nephews in Iran. The couple's children, who had grown up mostly overseas, and their grandchildren, were split among Iran, the US, and Europe. Arash and Farideh had no wish to join the Iranian diaspora, but would visit their offspring abroad when the vagaries of exchange rates and" Muslim bans" permitted.

Before the gathering broke up, Iraj spoke privately to Nilufar, "Dear Nilu, at some time – sooner rather than later – you need to tell Behnam the truth about your time in Iran. I don't know everything, but I know much more than he does. That's not right. He's your son and my cousin. I shouldn't have to lie to him. From what I do know, he should be very proud of you and Ruzbeh. You are both heroes. How long are you going to keep him in the dark?"

Nilufar smiled and replied, "Dear Iraj, you are right. I should tell him more. But when? And how? I just can't do it yet. When I want to tell him, I can't speak the words. After thirty years those wounds are still raw."

She looked at him. "Believe me, dear cousin, there are things I did in those years I am still ashamed of. Eventually I'll make peace with myself. But it isn't time yet. There are things I need to do first. But I promise you this. When the moment is right, I will tell you and the family everything. Please give me a little more time."

He took her hand and said, "Of course. Just don't wait too long. You need to deal with the pain. It's hurting Behnam, more than you know. Even young Ruzbeh knows something is wrong."

"Thank you, dear Iraj, for humoring your crazy cousin. I can never thank you enough for keeping quiet about those years. I know it's been hard to hide all that from the family, but I can't tell you how important your silence has been to me."

FALLS CHURCH, VIRGINIA

Following instructions from Porter, the next day Nilufar parked her rented car in a nondescript strip mall on West Broad Street in Falls Church. She entered through a door marked "Ideal Flooring," and took an elevator to the second floor. She found herself in an empty foyer and pushed a buzzer next to an un-welcoming wooden door marked "Receiving."

The space behind the door was a poor advertisement for a flooring company. The carpeting was the kind a developer might use in his "base model" townhouse in some remote, soul-less community far west of Dulles airport. Goodwill Charities would have rejected the scarred and scratched office furniture. The only thing missing, she thought, was a large neon sign say-ing, "CIA Front."

A dark-haired, olive-skinned man of about thirty-five with a narrow tie and no jacket extended his hand. "I was told to call you Nahid. You can call me Gregory." She noticed that, al-though he spoke like an American, he pronounced the Persian name with no trace of an accent.

"Sorry for this place. We had to fix it up on short notice and we don't have even a coffee machine. Our job here is to take pictures for documents that will get you into Iran. My in-structions are to work fast, ask no questions, and report to no one but my boss. After we've taken your photographs, my work is finished. As far as most of the agency knows, this of-fice does not exist. Let's begin."

In another room she found a well-equipped photography studio with expensive printers and a clothes rack with various "Islamic" outfits. "Gregory" introduced her to two technicians and explained, "We'll take the photographs here. We'll do pic-tures for an Iranian identity card, passport, driver's license, and health insurance card. Once we are happy with the pictures, another office will construct your identity and produce your documents. The fewer people who see you the better."

She liked this no-nonsense "Gregory," who seemed both competent and well informed about the Islamic Republic and its ways. If he resented being dragged into this dump to support an unexplained mission, he did not show it.

"We'll do photographs now and send them to our document lab. You'll need to cover your hair." Nilufar looked at a collection of unflattering clothes and chose an outfit that said, "Middle-class Tehran housewife with enough money to travel to Turkey." Once the technicians had taken the photos, Gregory said, "When the documents are ready, someone else will get them to you. You might start thinking about a name and whether you want to go Islamic or Iranian."

When the technicians had done their work, he told her, "If the pictures are good, you won't need to come back here and we won't see each other again. I'm supposed to tell you to be at the Mesquite Grill at the Avenwood Country Club in Potomac tomorrow at 12:30 p.m. A friend will meet you there. I expect it will be a lot more upscale than this place."

Nilufar shook Gregory's hand, and went back down the elevator and onto West Broad Street. As he heard the elevator door shut, Gregory, looking around to make sure he was alone, whispered, in perfect Persian, but in a tone of both contempt and sadness, "*Movaafeq baashid, khaaharam* (Good luck to you, my sister)."

POTOMAC, MARYLAND

Nilufar rarely visited private golf courses or country clubs. The exclusive grounds of this hideaway off River Road in Potomac, Maryland, were what she both imagined and feared. The Mesquite Grill overlooked the eighteenth hole of the golf course. Porter had called the previous evening to tell the hostess she would be there to meet a Mister James Chris. Nilufar was put off by the hunt club surroundings. She stood out rather than blended in. Bad tradecraft, she complained to herself.

James Chris came through the door at 12:35. He was dressed in the Washington, DC, fifty-five-year-old male's travelling casual uniform: khaki pants, brown shoes, blue blazer, button-down long sleeve dress shirt, no tie. An affable, newly retired CIA officer on contract to the agency for jobs like this, he greeted Nilufar and tried to put her at ease.

"Mrs. Parvizi, allow me to say that it is an honor to meet you. You have already done so much for our country. Everyone at the agency was shattered at Ruzbeh's death. We still mourn him. That you would do more is a testament to your patriotism and courage."

"Thank you, Mr. Chris. Your words are very generous. If you have read my file, you will know that is all the flattery I need or can stand. Please call me Nilufar. I am ready to go to work. And, can we please get out of this place?"

"We can. But we do not have to go far. We chose this spot because our friends here let us use a building at the back of the golf course. It looks like a maintenance shed, but in fact it's an excellent place to work privately. At the end of the day, I'll show you how to reach it without having to go through the club's main driveway. Will you please follow me in your car?"

Waiting for Nilufar were Lillian Deal, the CIA officer assigned to the operation, which they had decided to call "Operation 53." She also met Colonel Tom Hanson of the US Special Operations Command, and Ambassador Gordon McLennan, representing – in a bureaucratic miracle demanded by the sensitivity of the operation – both the secretaries of Defense and State. James Chris made the introductions, promised he'd be back to get Nilufar off the property, and disappeared.

What they called "the shed" was a highly secure conference area where the four principals could talk without fear of interruption or interception.

Lillian Deal, a CIA veteran of Iraq and Afghanistan – she had worked against the Iranians in both countries – spoke first, since the CIA would take the lead in this mission. Defense Secretary Hobbes feared that too many people at the Pentagon were Kalorama agents or supporters, and so agreed to a CIA lead. If Special Operations forces were needed, he would personally "chop" them to CIA command. Deal and Colonel Hanson had worked together in Baghdad's Green Zone. They trusted one another and had pledged in front of their bosses that nothing about the mission would become "FUBAR."

"Nilufar, welcome and thank you. Undersecretary Porter has outlined the story and its many complications. I understand you have already begun constructing an identity. I apologize for the shabby facilities yesterday, but 'Gregory' is very good at his job.

"Over the next few days we will give you the best possible identity and cover story. Then we will practice it until it is yours. We will arrange to protect you for the weeks you are in Iran, design a channel for your contact, and figure out an extraction plan. I'd suggest we take each in turn."

They began with her name. She had used "Nahid" yesterday, so it was no longer secure. They settled on "Ziba," a Persian name meaning "beautiful."   It wasn't Islamic, but neither was it the kind of in-your-face Iranian name that screamed "I despise your religion and your regime" or defied the Islamic part of Iranians' identity. For her surname, they chose "Amiri," the Iranian equivalent of "Smith" or "Jones." There were so many Amiris in Iran, she could plausibly deny kinship with any of them.

In a few hours they had a cover story. In her Iranian passport Nilufar would be "Ziba Amiri," born in Tehran August 14, 1954 (23 Mordad 1333 by the Iranian-Islamic solar calendar). On her Iranian identity card her father would be Mostafa, her mother Setareh, both Tehran natives and both deceased. Her Tehrani accent would confirm her background. Her profession was listed as *khaanehdaar* (housewife).   The identity card also listed a husband, Reza, who had died ten years previously. No children. She would enter Iran by air from Turkey, where she had gone for medical treatment. Just in case, they would give her documents from a clinic in Istanbul. Her Iranian passport would need only Turkish entry and exit stamps and an exit stamp from Tehran.

At the end of four intense days in the "shed," they had met Deal's goals. Nilufar was now Ziba Amiri. She had practiced using the covert communications device they had given her, a smartphone that looked like millions of others but was unique in ways that might save her. They had three times done a "tabletop" exercise to model her way out of Iran.

What this well-intentioned group could not give her – for this she would need to return to Porter – was the message for Arash and his allies in Tehran. What, she wondered, could they possibly say that could stop a war far too many wanted so badly?

WASHINGTON

While Nilufar was in her briefings, Porter made discreet contact with former Israeli ambassador to the United States, Eitan Dahan. Dahan had fallen out with Prime Minister Ben-Eliezer, who made it clear that Dahan's "dovish views" made him unwelcome in Israel. He decided to stay in Washington, teaching at American University. Porter and Dahan met at a Peet's coffee shop on E Street near FBI headquarters.

Dahan was not surprised by Porter's story. He had already been approached by a group of Israelis opposed to their government's connection to the Kalorama Group. There are no secrets in Israel; some just don't make it to the newspapers *Ha'aretz* or the *Jerusalem Post*.

What did surprise Dahan was Porter's request that an "off-the-books" covert team from Mossad protect an American agent while she was working in Iran.

GREAT FALLS, MARYLAND

On Wednesday morning at 9:45, Gregory parked his car in the end lot at Carderock, a site off the Clara Barton Parkway, with easy access to the Chesapeake and Ohio Canal National Park. In 1954, Supreme Court Justice William O. Douglas had providentially identified the then-forgotten, storm-damaged, 185-mile canal as a place of singular beauty and history that, preserved, could be an oasis of sanity in official Washington's political and social madness. Walkers, hikers, and cyclists used the canal's towpath where mules once pulled barges of coal from "the West" to Georgetown.

Gregory's job today was to look like others soothing their souls or meeting their Fitbit step goals on the towpath. Under a slight drizzle, he locked his car, put on his blue, hooded, Land's End rain jacket, and walked up the towpath toward Great Falls. He was certain no one had followed him by car. There were few others on the towpath, exactly why he had chosen this time of day.

After an hour's walk, he was at the old Great Falls Tavern, now a small museum and gift shop. He used the bathroom and, as soon as he could, headed back down the canal, looking carefully at those he passed to check again for anyone who seemed either too interested or uninterested in him.

Between mile markers 14 and 13, he took some wooden stairs off the canal that led to the Berma Road, an old trolley line that had once brought tourists to see the falls. He set out down the road toward Angler's Inn.

At an isolated point where the Lock 16 spur trail meets the Berma Road, a man dressed in walking gear that looked to Gregory like it was bought at REI yesterday, fell in beside him.

"I congratulate you," Gregory said to the man he knew only as "Jeff."

"Your information was correct. She is going to Iran. She is creating an identity with an Iranian passport, identity card, and other documents. I took her picture. Here are copies. It's hard to tell from these *hijaabi* pictures, but she looks Iranian, is about sixty years old and attractive. She speaks unaccented American English. I didn't want to give myself away by speaking Persian with her. Others will make her fake documents. I was told her name was Nahid, but I expect that is neither her real name nor her mission cover name. I do not know how and when she will travel. I expect soon, since this was a rush job."

Jeff put Gregory's envelope in his pocket. He said that $5,000 would, as usual, be wired to a bank account in Phoenix which Gregory controlled in another false name.

They walked in silence for a few minutes.

Without turning to look at Gregory, Jeff said, "Thank you. You have done well. You have begun the effort to block this latest effort to stop us. I will take it from here. I will not see you again. Your work is done."

They had by then reached the wooden stairs near the parking lots at Angler's. Jeff, whose real name was Gaston O'Shea, stayed on the Berma Road to reach his car. Within minutes he would be giving Gregory's information to Peter Mason, the Evangelical leader in the Kalorama Group, at an Italian restaurant in Potomac Village. He would then collect his very secular reward.

Gregory was born Enver Atman in Istanbul to an Iranian mother, coincidentally named Ziba, and a Turkish father. He had joined the MEK while a student at Elon University in North Carolina. MEK sympathizers at the CIA had guided him into the agency, where for seven years he had earned a reputation for discretion and competence and had proved invaluable to the MEK's objectives. The organization still nursed its grudges against Porter, whom they blamed for their bloody defeats in Iran forty years earlier. This coming war – and the MEK's taking power – would be their revenge.

He left the road, went down the stairs toward the canal, turned left, and walked back to Carderock. When he reached his car, he put the key in the door and found it unlocked. He was sure he had locked it, but opened the door without any further thought, got in, and put his hands on the steering wheel before he started the vehicle.

Two hours later, Atman – "Gregory" – collapsed in the parking lot in front of a Starbucks off Lee Highway in McLean. A passerby rushed to help him while another called 911. An ambulance took him to the Emergency Room at the Virginia Hospital Center, where he was admitted with the symptoms of a heart attack.

WASHINGTON AND SUBURBS

After a lunch much shortened by the importance of O'Shea's information, Peter Mason sat in the parking lot in front of the

Potomac Village restaurant. On the secure telephone he used
for calling other Kalorama members, he punched in the number
he had for Chelsey Bock at the Pentagon. He gave her Gregory's report as relayed by O'Shea. He would give her the pictures as soon as he could get to a secure scanner.

Bock did not hesitate. Although it was after midnight in
Saudi Arabia, she dialed the numbers for the prince. He answered on the second ring.

He wasted not a minute either, dialing the secure number
he had for someone in Tehran he knew only as Abbas, his contact in the Fifteenth of Khordad group.

Dr. Michael Johnson – a recent medical school graduate
and new medical resident at the hospital – kept checking on
Gregory. Something about the initial diagnosis made him uneasy. He had both a medical and amateur spy novelist's interest
in the recent case of the Skripal family in Salisbury, England.
Mr. Skripal, a KGB defector, along with his daughter, had been
the target of an FSB assassination attempt. The Russians had
poisoned them both with the nerve agent Novichok spread on
the doorknob at their home. Both had become very sick but
survived. Johnson thought he recognized the same pathology.
No one else agreed, but by early evening, he had at least convinced the senior resident to get Gregory into isolation.

At Dulles airport the same evening, two Russian nationals
boarded the Austrian Airlines flight to Vienna. They would be
paid well for smearing Novichok on the steering wheel of a car
at Carderock. The job had been subcontracted to the FSB by
Peter Mason through various cutouts in the European right-
wing movement who admired, as did Mason, the Russian
President's commitment to "Christian values."

By midnight, Gregory was dead.

TEHRAN

Hossein Niku had gone far since his days as an errand boy for
Beheshti, first as a soldier in the Guards, and then as Hashemi-
Rafsanjani's office director. Now chief of staff to Iran's su-

preme leader, he sipped a glass of tea and surveyed other the members of the Fifteenth of Khordad group. When "Sultan," his Saudi contact, had called him a few hours before, Niku knew he had to convey this new message immediately. He sent a coded text saying, "Come immediately to the safe house off Motahhari Street near the Modarres Expressway." Within three hours, six members arrived. Others responded that they were out of town or otherwise unable to come.

Niku was now in his late sixties. He still spoke Persian with the peculiar Qazvini accent Nilufar had detected almost forty years earlier. He had thinning hair and carried multiple wounds from service on the Iraq front. Near Mehran, an Iraqi mortar shell had left him with a severe limp.

The room was dark. The sparse furniture even darker.

Niku came directly to the point. "I'm sorry to have brought you here on such short notice, but my Saudi contact Sultan has sent me an urgent message. We have a serious problem.

"Sultan's Washington source tells him the CIA is sending an agent to Iran to disrupt our plans. He did not have a name, a cover story, or a date of arrival. There is a picture, which he will send me as soon as he has a secure channel."

The revolutionary court prosecutor asked with some irritation, "Are the Saudis and their American masters feeding us lies so we waste time pursuing a nonexistent agent? And if Sultan's story is true, so what? So the CIA is sending another spy. What's new about that? We'll pick him up, tickle him until he talks, and then hang what's left of him. What do we know about this spy?"

Niku replied carefully, "Normally you'd be right and I wouldn't have bothered you. And you're right to be suspicious. It wouldn't be the first time the CIA and their Saudi servants planted a story to send us chasing phantoms.

"But Sultan believes his source and that this isn't just another spy. The Americans are running this operation in very restricted channels outside the regular structure of the CIA. Only a few people in Washington know about it. The CIA has taken extraordinary precautions to keep it secret. Sultan's contact in Washington got lucky.

"He could tell me they are sending a woman who's about sixty years old. She looks Iranian and will be arriving with Iranian documents. We don't know for sure, but we should assume she speaks fluent Persian. We don't have a name. We don't know how she's coming to Iran or when. Probably soon. We'll have a picture as soon as my Saudi contact can send one on a secure line."

"And then what?" asked the prosecutor.

"That's why I asked you here. To find an answer to your excellent question. What should we do?"

Another conspirator, the grandson of the head of the Assembly of Experts, said, "What's wrong with the earlier suggestion? We pass her picture to the Guards' intelligence service and they arrest her at the frontier. We'll find out soon enough what she's up to."

Niku shook his head and thought, "What a collection of idiots!" He drew a breath and said, "We have to assume her mission is connected to our 'Operation Zeinab.' That's what both Sultan and his American contact believe. Why else did they pass us this message so quickly? Why is there so much secrecy? If we spread her picture around, hundreds of people will know we're looking for her. People will start asking questions. Who is she? Why did the CIA send her to Iran? The risk is that the wrong people in high places will find out what they shouldn't know. We risk a disastrous security breach. We can't take that chance."

Musa Vakili, nephew of the Mashhad shrine administrator, spoke out. "I agree with brother Niku. We must be careful. The message is most likely genuine, although there's always the chance it's a trap to make us reveal our plans. The most important thing is that we keep 'Zeinab' a secret until we're ready to act."

Niku was relieved to have found an ally. "Thank you, brother Musa," he said. "Catching the spy is important, but only if we can protect 'Zeinab.' If we raise the alarm now, even if we catch her, we're creating a bigger problem. Can everyone agree with brother Musa?"

Although some still preferred a more direct approach, they deferred to Niku's position in the Supreme Leader's office. They had to admit – reluctantly – that he and Vakili were right.

Niku turned to Hassanzadeh, senior official of the Revolutionary Guard Corps Security Service. Hassanzadeh spoke little, but years of intelligence operations in Iran and abroad had taught him the value of patience. There was always a place for brutality, and everyone in the room knew the Islamic Republic had survived for forty years because it never hesitated to torture and murder its opponents. In this case, however, they would need other methods.

"Brother Hassanzadeh, if we give you a picture and what we know about this spy, can your agents find her? More important, can you keep this search quiet? I don't have to tell you how vital secrecy is."

"Give me the details, and we'll mobilize a special, secret unit within the Guards. We'll watch every frontier post, both land and air. We won't share anything with those Ministry of Intelligence bureaucrats or with passport officials. We can't trust them.

"She shouldn't be hard to find. As soon as we've identified her, we'll follow her to find out her contacts and her mission. Let's assume that she's coming here for something related to Operation Zeinab."

Niku addressed the group. "Brothers, I will brief our Guards' colleague here on what Sultan has told me about this woman. I will give him her picture as soon as I have it. Thank you for your attention and for helping in our sacred mission."

TEHRAN

When Niku had finished briefing Hassanzadeh, he left the safe house and walked toward the Shahid Moffateh metro station on the red line. There he put a chalk mark with a coded time signal on a wall near the station entrance. He was giving a signal that he had an urgent message for a contact he knew as Ali.

Over a year ago, he had been contacted by a former Guards' comrade from the Iraq war. This man had also been wounded and complained bitterly to Niku that those who had sacrificed were now forgotten. Everyone was getting rich except those who had risked their lives and lost their limbs.

Luckily, his friend said, there was a man called Ali who was supporting veterans of the war against Saddam and had money to pay in exchange for a favor now and then. Since working in Hashemi-Rafsanjani's office for four years, Niku had made his way up the Islamic Republic's greased pole doing staff work for mullahs and politicians, finally ending up as the chief of staff to the Supreme Leader. But he had never felt properly appreciated and certainly not properly rewarded.

Niku agreed to meet Ali. And for the last four months he had been reporting the activities of the Fifteenth of Khordad group. He did not know exactly who Ali's employer was, but he could make an educated guess. What was certain was that Ali was paying him very well through a numbered bank account in Zurich. If everyone else can get rich, why not me?

Niku knew it was time to take the money and run. His position in the Supreme Leader's office – a den of snakes and scorpions – gave him no job security. He saw the cynicism and greed of those now ruling the Islamic Republic. He also knew that Fifteenth of Khordad was planning to bring death and destruction on Iranians. He had barely survived Iraqi bombs and poison gas on the southern front, and had sworn he would never face war again.

Over the past few weeks, he had insisted that his children leave the country on the pretext of study or business. He planned to leave with his wife for Turkey before the fighting began, and to use the ample funds in his Zurich account to buy a hillside villa near Bursa. "Let others earn the honor of *shahaadat* (martyrdom)," he thought. "Let the Americans and Iranians murder each other. What's that to me? With luck they'll kill my idiot brother-in-law."

He wrote out his notes from this recent meeting in a three-page message to Ali. He left it taped in a remote spot in the "*Park-e-Mellat*." The chalk mark meant the message would be available six hours after the coded time. Ali would leave his mark acknowledging receipt near the Mir-Daamaad metro station.

Things did not go as planned. After he left the package, there was no acknowledgment. In such a case, his instructions were to wait another six hours, and then retrieve the package. When he returned to the drop area, he found the package undisturbed.

Niku did not know that "Ali" was Ari Benshlomo, an Israeli of Iranian origin, who worked – without the knowledge of the Israeli prime minister – under cover as a Moslem real estate broker in Tehran. There were individuals in Israeli intelligence who saw the alarming results of collaboration among far-right Israelis, the Saudis, the MEK, and the Kalorama Group. They had sent Benshlomo to Iran and established their own channel of intelligence to the director of the CIA. His reports from Tehran, limited to just a few people in the American government, were the basis of Porter's urgent appeal to Nilufar.

The other thing that Niku did not know was that on the day before the Fifteenth of Khordad group's urgent meeting, Ali had been in a serious traffic accident, and, after several emergency surgeries, was still recovering in a Tehran hospital. As a result, he missed his agent's message and Niku had no news from his controller.

It was not the first time Ali had missed a dead drop, and Niku was not going to panic. He would already be in prison if the authorities had discovered Ali. A day after the aborted message exchange, Niku was relieved to have a text Ali sent from his hospital room explaining what had happened.

The next afternoon, the Saudi named Sultan sent Niku a message saying he would send the scanned photo of the American agent via secure email. They arranged for the message to be sent that evening at 8:30 p.m. at which time the Supreme Leader's office would be deserted and Niku could use the secure system unobserved.

The photo arrived clear and detailed. At first, he refused to believe his eyes. He first cursed modern technology; then he cursed the entire fucking universe. Even in modest clothing, even so many years later, he knew the woman in this photo: Massoumeh Rastbin, the woman he had guarded for Beheshti and later his colleague in Hashemi-Rafsanjani's office. What was going on? What should he do?

He quickly decided this foolish woman must have a death wish. But if she was discovered too soon, his own plans would collapse. Hassanzadeh's goons would connect him to this CIA agent if they asked enough questions. He did not care what happened to her, to the Supreme Leader, to the Fifteenth of Khordad group or, for that matter, to the whole damn country. Screw them all. He cared only for his money and his dream house in Bursa. Now he needed time.

He saved the photo on his computer and went to work on Nilufar's picture. He changed the color of her eyes, the shape of her chin and gave her a nose job for which young Iranian women would have paid plastic surgeons a fortune. He saved the altered photo on a memory stick. He then deleted Sultan's email and the attached original photo, using special shredding software to ensure no one could recover it. He calculated he could explain a twenty-four-hour delay without arousing suspicions.

He sent a message to Sultan: "Technical problems in our system. Message was garbled with no picture. Please resend tomorrow at the same time." He then called the Guards' officer Hassanzadeh and told him, "The picture didn't come through. I should have it tomorrow evening. I'll deliver it by hand as soon as it arrives."

Hassanzadeh told him, "We'll need that picture in our agents' hands as soon as possible. Now all we can tell them is to look for a sixty-year-old Iranian woman."

Niku hung up. He would destroy the second picture and share the doctored photo. Would those actions save his life?

NAZANIN

TEHRAN

Nilufar never told Porter that she had stayed in touch with Nazanin for thirty years. After 1983, as Tehran University gradually reopened, Nazanin was forced to transfer from engineering to mathematics when the Islamic Republic banned women from some technical fields. She told Nilufar, "They're afraid of the competition. They'd keep us out of medicine if they could, but even the mullahs' wives need doctors, and they prefer women."

Focused on her studies and her two children, she ended her political activities and left the "discussion group." In 1990, two years after Nilufar fled Iran, she earned a fellowship for graduate work at Durham University in England. She would not leave Iran without her children, so she took both her son Amir and her adopted Kurdish daughter Kazhal. Both children thrived in Durham, and when Nazanin returned to Iran with her doctorate after three years, they were fluent in "Geordie," the often incomprehensible dialect of far Northeast England.

When she returned her family friend Hashemi-Rafsanjani was president. He made her director of science and technical studies in the Ministry of Higher Education. When the reformist Mohammad Khatami became president in 1997, he persuaded her to stay in her post.

Nazanin eagerly promoted women's education, particularly in science and math. But by 2000, she had had enough of the ministry's jealousies and bureaucratic warfare. As long as her patron Hashemi-Rafsanjani was president, no one dared interfere with her work. After 1997, the new president Khatami, with all his good intentions, could not stop those intent on sabotaging her programs for young women. Rivals spread stories about her private life, her religious views, and even revived the old rumor that she and her martyred husband had been Communists.

Nazanin sadly concluded that the Islamic Revolution had done nothing to change most Iranian men's view of women. Men feared what would happen when women and men competed fairly. They knew the numbers. While the median age of girls' marriage was rising, young women were passing the rigorous, competitive university entrance exams at twice the rate of men. Ironically, the Islamic Republic's dress codes had enabled studious girls from conservative families to stay in school longer than they had before the revolution. They were leaving men behind.

Exhausted by the constant infighting and the ministry's misogynist culture, Nazanin accepted a job as professor of mathematics at Tehran University, where the dean of the faculty, her old teacher Dr. Moshiri, had fought off all attempts to "Islamize" his departments.

She never remarried. Her son Amir studied in France, and returned to Iran as a journalist. He had inherited from his late father a skill with words. He now worked as a stringer for AFP, and wrote for several semi-independent Iranian papers and magazines, including the intellectual journal *Andisheh-Pouya,* which waged a constant struggle with the authorities to keep a measure of integrity. He maintained close ties to Iran's independent filmmakers, many of whom were earning international recognition while playing cat-and-mouse with the censors at home. Like his mother, Amir was slight, dark, and intense. Nazanin's daughter Kazhal had grown into a brilliant, dark-eyed beauty. She studied medicine at Shiraz University, finished a specialty in pediatrics in Italy, and now had a thriving practice in Tehran.

Nilufar and Behnam had visited Nazanin and her children when they were in Durham. They also saw both of Nazanin's children when they were older and studying in Europe. During these visits no one talked about the past. The two mothers traded stories about brief flings that had led nowhere. Both of Nazanin's children immediately adored Behnam, and the two mothers fantasized about a marriage between him and Kazhal.

In 2006, after the fall of Saddam, and when Kazhal was nineteen, Nazanin had taken her to Halabja in Iraqi Kurdistan. Through DNA tests, and with the help of the "Halabja Memorial Project," they discovered that Kazhal's biological mother Sahar had survived the 1988 attack and was living in nearby Suleimanieh. Kazhal's father and four siblings had died in the attack, but their bodies were never found.

There was an emotional reunion when Kazhal met her mother and her surviving aunts, uncles, and cousins for the first time since infancy, and learned that her original name had been "Dilnaz." After a few days of hugs, visits, and meals, she told Nazanin, "I love these people, but you will always be my mother. You raised me, you loved me, and made me what I am. I can barely understand Kurdish, and Kurdestan is a foreign place to me. I will learn their language and visit them when I can. But I will always be your daughter."

Six years later she married a fellow doctor, Afzal Khosrowabadi, an Iranian Kurd from Bijar. She learned Kurdish from her husband's family, and visited her Iraqi relatives every few years. The couple's two children, a daughter Rehan and a son Dijle, immediately became the center of Nazanin's life. Amir had yet to marry, and remained totally committed to his journalism. Nazanin did not pressure him to find a wife.

Nilufar and Nazanin communicated through Nazanin's cousin Sediqeh in Northern California, where she was a real estate agent and her husband worked for a computer company. Nilufar knew the family well enough to trust their discretion. As soon as she knew she was going back to Iran, she passed Nazanin a message through Sediqeh: "Your friend Ziba Amiri will be coming soon for a short, family visit. Details to follow."

Nazanin immediately replied. "Understand. Love to see her whenever she comes. Of course she will stay with me."

KHOMEINI INTERNATIONAL AIRPORT, TEHRAN

When Turkish Airlines flight 874 arrived at Tehran's new Imam Khomeini International Airport just after midnight, Nilufar returned to a country vastly changed from the one she had fled thirty years earlier. The airport was clean, efficient, with automated teller machines, car-rental agencies, and modern shops and cafés, although none served or sold alcohol. Those needing a drink would have to go elsewhere and rely on the centuries-old subterfuges that Iranians used to flout laws of kings and clerics.

The airport had a metro station with direct trains to downtown Tehran, over forty miles away. Airport signs, in English and Persian, were clear and helpful. Gone were the scowling, shabbily dressed officials that Nilufar remembered harassing travelers at the old Mehrabad facility. Courteous, professional, multilingual customs and immigration officers wore clean uniforms with name tags; they rarely opened bags and their stations were equipped with up-to-date computers. No one questioned her story or identity documents.

The airport halls displayed excellent examples of Iranian contemporary art. There were of course pictures of Imam Khomeini and the current supreme leader and a few discrete signs reminding travelers of the Islamic Republic's dress restrictions. Uniformed and armed security personnel were visible, but in no greater numbers than in European airports.

"They've learned fast," thought Nilufar. "It's like Dorian Grey. They show a nicer face to the world, but the fiend is still there, even if we don't see it. We may not see the Revolutionary Guards at first, but they're here. They don't wave their weapons anymore which makes them even more dangerous." She reminded herself, "Don't fool yourself, Nilufar. They are smoother and smarter – and more terrifying for that."

She found Nazanin and Amir in the crowd of greeters. After she and Nazanin had kissed and embraced, Amir – who could not touch her in public – took her small bag, filled mostly with "Turkish" gifts for Nazanin and her family. He told them. "I'll get the car and meet you in front of the arrivals door."

When he left, Nazanin pulled Nilufar aside and said softly, "Don't look, but over there someone is watching you." With a nod, she indicated a neatly dressed man of about thirty who was drinking tea and seemed overly intent on something on his smartphone.

Nilufar answered calmly, "Are you sure? He doesn't look like anything special. At my age should I be flattered?"

Nazanin looked at her carefully and said, "Nilufar (or Ziba as I should call you), you've been away too long. We're all experts now at picking out the *az maa behtaraan* (those better than us) from the security services. We can smell them. That one is trying too hard to be inconspicuous. His expensive Italian shoes would cost most Iranians six months' salary. What's he doing at the airport at this hour? He's not meeting anyone. Why does he keep looking at you and then looking away? You're very attractive, but you're old enough to be his mother. He wants to take a photo of you on his phone. Keep your back to him."

"In the old days I would have gone straight up to him and said, 'Sir, why are you staring at me? Don't you have anything better to do than annoy other people's daughters and wives? Don't you have a mother and a sister?' I would have raised a fuss and called the guards."

Nazanin nodded. "Not today. Something else is going on. I'll tell Amir to hurry. We need to get out of here."

NORTHERN VIRGINIA

Gregory's CIA office mates were worried. He was a strange man, but he never missed work. They contacted their supervisor who in turn alerted CIA security. After reviewing Gregory's file, they became anxious and took the usual first step in these cases: checking the local hospitals to see if there had been any odd admissions over the past twenty-four hours.

The autopsy on the body known by the hospital as First and Last Name Unknown got the attention of the entire hospital chain of command. Young Dr. Johnson had been right: Novichok was both the cause of death and now of barely controlled panic among the hospital's senior staff. Thirty minutes after the autopsy was complete, the hospital's director, Dr. Hiram Segal, called every staff member who had dealt with the mysterious and dangerous body to meet him in his third-floor office.

"We need to keep this secret for as long as we can. If word gets out that we have an unidentified corpse killed by a Russian nerve agent, there will be panic. Each of you has been screened, so you can thank any God you pray to that the poison did not spread.

"I have alerted the Centers for Disease Control in Atlanta and the National Institutes of Health in Bethesda. They will consult with the Department of Homeland Security and the director of National Intelligence. I am sure we will soon hear from someone about what to do next. Until then deep breathing, praying, and silence are in order."

When his phone rang, Dr. Segal noticed that the caller ID said only "US Government." When he picked it up, a Ms. Robinson started to talk. He listened and hung up three minutes later.

"We need to go to the morgue. Dr. Johnson, please gather all the records we have on this patient and meet us there."

Twenty minutes later three black cars followed by an all-white ambulance turned right off of George Mason Drive into the hospital grounds. A dozen people in hazmat suits went through a side entrance without a word and went directly to the morgue.

"Where is the body?" barked a voice from a hazmat suit with a blue florescent stripe on the right sleeve.

In ten minutes it was over. The corpse of Gregory, FNU/LNU, Enver Atman, now also in a hazmat suit, was gone. His records went with him. The black cars and the ambulance turned left onto George Mason and vanished into the dusk.

At CIA headquarters later that night, Director DeWolf, who had just returned from a secret visit to Baghdad, was briefed on the case. He reviewed the files. He also noticed he had nothing recent from the Israelis' source in Tehran who was providing such vital reporting from inside the Fifteenth of Khordad group.

A career intelligence officer, he trusted his instincts. The death of Gregory had to be connected to Nilufar and "Project 53." The dead man was one of a small group who had seen her and knew she was part of a sensitive Iran operation. Even without a confirming report from Tehran or elsewhere, he knew.

He then made another intelligence officer's judgment: They had a big problem on their hands. The Iranians knew something about Nilufar and Project 53. What they knew was not certain. Nilufar/Ziba was in Tehran and her operation had started. He would not reverse it. And so, because he was staking everything on Porter and the anti-Kaloramans, and because he wanted more than anything to avoid war with Iran, he kept his assumptions and fears to himself, at least for now.

TEHRAN

At three a.m., Amir's car left the airport road and approached *Enqelaab* (Revolution) Square. The Tehran streets were quiet. Anarchy would begin soon, when millions of Tehranis began their daily combat with traffic and the air pollution that on most days erased their views of the magnificent 13,000-foot wall of Alborz peaks guarding the city from the north.

Nilufar had heard about Tehran's dreaded, lethal *vaarounegi* (inversions) – the result of too many cars, badly refined gasoline and diesel fuel, drought, overbuilding, and incompetent water management – that was shortening the life expectancy of the capital's eight-and-a-half million inhabitants. At this moment she could enjoy the quiet and the cool desert night air. She also noted the absence of curfews, blackouts, and checkpoints.

Nazanin and Amir lived in a comfortable, prerevolution, two-bedroom apartment near Tehran University on Nazari Street, a middle-class neighborhood of low-rise buildings two blocks south of the former Shah Reza – now Revolution – Avenue. Other areas were more fashionable, but Nazanin's university office was a ten-minute walk from her door. Amir lived with Nazanin by choice. He could have found his own place, but refused to let his mother live alone. Nazanin encouraged him to be independent, but he insisted on staying with her.

He told Nilufar, "You can have my room, Ziba *khaanom*. I'm staying with friends and will look in on you and mother tomorrow." Before he left, the three of them sat for a glass of tea, and Nilufar gave them their gifts, purchased in Turkey. For Nazanin, in an Istanbul tourist shop, she had found a ceramic figure of a Mevlana dervish, that, when plugged in, whirled to the sound of a reed flute. "I thought if I gave you this, you might be inspired to make the pilgrimage to Rumi's tomb in Konya.

Nazanin told her, "It's perfect. We'll make the pilgrimage together, God willing. Let's sleep now. I have a class at ten. Sleep as late as you like and then we can talk."

"That's fine. I don't think I should go outside. That business at the airport has me worried. Probably nothing, but who knows?"

"I'll be home just after noon. I'll bring in some chicken kababs. Kazhal and her husband and children will be here for dinner tomorrow. They're looking forward to seeing you."

TEHRAN

Two days later Hassanzadeh called Niku and asked to meet in an unmarked Guards' office at 65 Palestine – formerly Palace – Square. "I may have progress to report," the officer told him. Niku had put off giving the Guards' officer Nilufar's doctored photo as long as he dared. Even twenty-four-hours' delay would slow the hunt and give Niku more time to plan his flight.

When the two met an hour later, Hassanzadeh said, "After you gave me the spy's picture, I circulated copies to a select group of agents who are watching the frontiers. They have strict instructions not to interfere if they see her. Just to follow and report. We're also checking databases to see if there's a match. So far nothing."

"So you're telling me no sightings and no identifications? That doesn't sound like progress to me."

Ignoring the criticism, Hassanzadeh answered, "We acted as soon as you sent us the photograph. Before that we had only the general information you gave us: an Iranian woman in her sixties."

Niku was cautious. It appeared Hassanzadeh was looking to blame him for the Guards' failures. "So what is this progress you mentioned?"

"Two nights ago – about one in the morning – an agent at Imam Khomeini Airport picked up a possible. He wanted to take a photograph on his smartphone, but the woman was covered and kept her back to him. He didn't get a good shot, but we're working to enhance what he gave us. He did get a better picture of a second woman – the one who met her at the airport. We still don't have an ID for her, but we're working on it."

"What made your agent suspicious? She can't have been the only sixty-year-old Iranian woman who's entered the country recently. Anything special about her?"

"Not really. She arrived on a Turkish Airlines flight from Istanbul with very little luggage. It was just the agent's instinct that something wasn't right. The way she kept her back to him. The way the other woman looked at him. The way they left the airport quickly."

"Do you think they identified him as an agent? Unfortunately our countrymen have become experts in picking out your security men. They're neither popular nor subtle."

Hassanzadeh again ignored the insult. "Possibly. He insists not, but, as you say, some of our people are less than skilled at surveillance."

Hassanzadeh showed the pictures. "Here's what your source Sultan sent us; here are the two women at the airport."

Niku studied the three photos. "It could be the same person, but how can we be sure without a face? What do we know about the other woman? She's covered as well, but she too looks to be in her sixties. Small and dark, as far as I can see. Hard to make out."

"If we can identify her, she will be our best lead to the mystery woman. Of course it's still a long shot that she's the one we're looking for."

Niku was relieved the Guards had so little to go on. "Let them chase shadows," he thought. "It will keep them busy."

To Hassanzadeh, he said, "Thank you, brother." Please let me know as soon as you learn anything more."

As he left the Guards' office, Hassanzadeh thought, "What a shit Niku has become. I remember him from the war. He was a good man then. We were all idealistic, ready to die for our religion, our country, and each other. Now he lords it over me because he works in the leader's office."

That afternoon Hassanzadeh got a call from Qasem, the Guards' officer responsible for investigating the airport photographs. "Sir, can I come to see you? I would like to brief you on the women in the pictures. Hassanzadeh replied, "We can't meet here. Too many people around. I'll come by your office in thirty minutes."

TEHRAN

At Nazanin's apartment the two women ate a lunch of chicken kababs, raw onions, flat bread, Russian salad, and *dough*, the chilled, fermented yoghurt drink that helped Iranians endure the hot, dry summers of the plateau.

Nilufar, now Ziba, told her friend, "We have lots of Iranian kabab places in the US now. One of the benefits of the revolution, I guess. One is even named "Moby Dick," if you can believe that. Remember its tongue sandwiches in the old days? There's a special taste to the food here they can't duplicate in the US."

Nazanin looked at Nilufar carefully. "The children and grandchildren will be here this evening. The grandchildren may show up early. We should talk now while we have the chance. Nilu dear, I never expected to see you in Iran again. What's happened? What brought you here? Just your being here has made me happy. But very worried too. Tell me, *Che khedmati az dast-e-man saakhteh-ast?* (What service to you is in my power?)"

Nilufar put aside her food and spoke. "First, I apologize for putting you and your family in difficulty. I never thought I would return, at least as long as these criminals are in power. I had to be convinced. And it wasn't easy. Here's what I can tell you. Excuse me if I leave out some details for your own safety."

She gave Nazanin the outlines of Porter's story. She told her how Iranian and American zealots, encouraged by others with their own agendas, were conspiring to push the two countries into war. She also spoke of what she had learned subsequently during her time in Washington. "Of course we're used to being enemies. Most people can't remember things any other way. We've been threatening and insulting each other for forty years, but this time it's different. If it hadn't been, I would never have come back. Now some very dangerous people on both sides are working together. They don't care if millions die."

Nazanin didn't seem surprised. "It's odd you tell me this. There are rumors here about a group of fanatics planning for a war. There's nothing specific and no names. There are hints of Saudi and Israeli involvement as well. To be honest, I didn't believe these stories. We Iranians love to build conspiracies, the more complex and far-fetched the better."

"Nazanin dear, I wish it were just, as we say, 'weaving together a thread and the sky.' But this is real and serious.

"We're desperate. I need your help. If we can't stop these plotters, in a month or sooner Iran and America will be at war. How many innocents died in the war with Iraq? This time it will be much worse."

Nazanin was silent for a few seconds. "I should have guessed you hadn't come for a wedding. After what happened then with Ruzbeh...." Her words trailed off.

"Nazanin, you can help me. I need to reach Arash Rastbin, my mother's brother, as soon as possible. You remember he used to work for the Foreign Ministry. I can't approach him directly, but I have an urgent message for him from friends in

America. If I can get my message to him we may just be able to stop a tragedy."

She grasped both of Nilufar's hands. "Of course I'll help. How do I find your uncle? What do I tell him?"

"I have a home telephone number, but it's not safe to call him. He teaches political science at the university. Could you reach him there?"

"I'll go to the university tomorrow and find him. What is the message?"

"Tell him that his late sister Farzaneh's daughter is here and needs to see him immediately, but discreetly, for just five minutes. I'll meet him at the Tahouri Bookstore across from the university's main gate. It has to be very soon. I'll have a written message for him there. Of course he may be suspicious. If he hesitates, use the name 'Massoumeh.' He'll remember it. If he still refuses, you can tell him I'm carrying an urgent message from 'Porter.' I hope you don't need to say that, but I absolutely must meet him.

The next day Nazanin was lucky. She called the political science department in the morning saying she needed to see Professor Rastbin about a student. The secretary told her he would be teaching a class at two p.m. Nazanin asked for the classroom number, saying she needed to meet him only for a minute.

She met him outside his classroom and passed Nilufar's message. If Arash was surprised, he did not show it. He asked her only, "Are you Professor Nazanin Dowlatabadi?" When she answered yes, he said, "Well, I have heard much about you from my niece. The whole family owes much to you." He told her he would be at the bookstore at 4:30 p.m.

At the apartment, Nilufar carefully wrote out Porter's message in both English and Persian. Having veiled herself carefully, she walked north on Moniriyeh Javid Street, and turned right onto Revolution Avenue. Before reaching the bookstore, she crossed the avenue and walked north on Vessaal Shirazi Street. After seven short blocks, she turned left into Behnam Alley. Number 36, the safe house where in 1988 she and Ruzbeh had become lovers, was gone, like that part of her life. Instead there was a deluxe, six-story condo building. Relieved that she did not have to face that delicious, agonizing memory, she returned south on Vessaal Shirazi, and reached the bookstore at 4:15. She asked the salesman for a newly published translation of Arthur Miller's classic, *Death of a Salesman*, a play always popular in Iran. The salesman found the volume and asked her, "By the way, *khaanom*, have you seen Mr. Farhadi's film *The Salesman*? The two main characters – a Tehrani husband and wife – are actors in this play." When Nilufar told him she hadn't seen the movie, he said, "Well, in Iran you won't see it in the cinemas any more. I'm sure your local DVD man can get you a copy." She thanked him and moved to a quiet corner of the store where she could pretend to look at the book.

Arash entered a few minutes later. When the two saw each other, they fought back their impulse to embrace and have a proper reunion. Instead they spoke formally, like professor to former student. She called to him, "Professor, here is the book I was speaking about. The translation by the late Sanatizadeh is a few years old, but it's just been published."

Also speaking loudly, he answered, "Well done, my sister. Many thanks. Please let me see it." He moved to the corner where the two of them could speak softly, while pretending to look at the book. She spoke to him softly. "*Da'i jaan* (dear uncle), there is a letter inside the book. It's an urgent message from Porter for you and your friends. I need to meet with them to explain its contents and to receive an answer. Can you arrange it?"

Arash nodded. "How do I reach you?"

"The less contact we have the better. The telephone isn't safe. Better we work through my friend Professor Dowlatabadi in the university math department. You've obviously met her. I trust her with my life. Tell her when, where, and how I can meet your group. Read the letter and you'll know why I need to see them. It's urgent."

"*Chashm, Nilu jaan* (Of course, dear Nilu). Please make sure that Dr. Dowlatabadi is at the university during the next few days. I will have a message."

The two of them walked toward the door. Speaking in a normal voice, Arash said, "Please, *khaanom*, tell me how much I owe you for the book." In the same tone, Nilufar answered, "It's nothing at all, sir. Consider it a small gift from a grateful former student. I have to leave now, but I hope you enjoy the new translation. It's very well done."

After she left, he pretended to browse for another ten minutes. He left the store, turned left, and boarded an eastbound yellow line metro at Revolution Square station. He rode it a few stops to *Darvazeh-ye-Shemiran* station near his home.

Opening the letter, he found Porter's message written in both Nilufar's English handwriting and in her clear and elegant Persian script:

My dear friend and colleague Arash,

You are reading this letter thanks to the courage of your amazing niece. She was at first reluctant to return to Iran, the scene of so much misfortune. It was not easy to persuade her. Once she understood the circumstances, however, she volunteered for this dangerous mission upon which the fate of millions depends. I am part of a group of like-minded patriots in Washington. We are former and active-duty government officials. All of us wish to avert a catastrophic war between our two countries. This message is from me, but it represents the views of the group.

Our goal is to frustrate the efforts of the so-called "Kalorama Group," a coalition of extremists: American hawks, right-wing Israelis, Saudis, and Iranian exiles who – for different reasons – aim to provoke a war within the next few weeks.

This group is cooperating – through Saudi intermediaries – with extremists in Tehran who call themselves the "Fifteenth of Khordad Group." The two groups are well advanced in their planning. If not stopped, in the next few weeks there will be a bloody incident involving American and Iranian forces in the Persian Gulf. In the aftermath, the drive to war will be unstoppable.

According to our information, the plan is to provoke a clash in the Persian Gulf between an American aircraft carrier and naval units from the Revolutionary Guards. Shore-based Iranian missiles will also be involved.

We know that you are part of a similar-minded set of patriots in Tehran. You and your colleagues are, like us, working to stop a plan that, if successful, will involve the United States in a pointless, destructive war and bring ruin to your beautiful country.

We must stop this plot. We can do so if we are willing to act together against our enemies. Doing so will not be easy. We will need an unprecedented level of trust and cooperation between two governments that have demonstrated neither for forty years.

My proposal is this. We both will approach our respective leaders within a week with evidence of this conspiracy. I cannot speak for Iran's Supreme Leader, of course. We pray he is persuadable.

Our president is no friend of the Islamic Republic. He makes his hostility clear at every opportunity. Stronger than his dislike of Iran, however, is his insistence that no one is going to push him, as others pushed an earlier president, into a futile war in the Middle East.

We can persuade him to stop this plot if he knows you will do the same. Of that I am 95 percent certain. When we do, you will receive a sign that he is ready to act. We will make sure that one of his speeches includes a coded message indicating he is prepared to move within twenty-four hours against the conspirators. When that happens, we will expect a similar coded response from the Supreme Leader.

Arash, my friend. I ask that Nilufar meet with your allies as soon as possible to vouch for the truth of my message. Of course I leave it to you how you persuade the other members of your group and how they persuade the Supreme Leader. We know he neither likes nor trusts the United States. I can only hope that he, like our president, does not want a disastrous war and does not want others forcing his hand and making life-and-

death decisions for him. She will send me the necessary signal when you and your friends agree to this plan.

Arash, I ask you to trust me once again. The matter is urgent. We have only a few weeks left and there is no time to argue over details.

Your good friend,
Alan Porter

TEHRAN

Hassanzadeh met Qasem and his investigators in a secure conference room. Two civilians working a laptop and projector were introduced as experts in photo identification. Qasem told his boss, "There are none better in Iran."

Hassanzadeh nodded and told the two men, "Brothers, I am at your service. Please describe what you have learned, but be brief and remember I am just a simple soldier and not well-versed in your technology."

Using a laptop, the senior technician projected three photographs – two from Imam Khomeini Airport and one sent from Washington via Sultan and Niku – on a large screen. "You can see the airport agent's photograph of the passenger from the back doesn't allow identification. None of our enhancement software can help. As you can see, for the second woman – the one who met her at the airport – we have a photograph of her face."

Hassanzadeh interrupted, "Who is she?"

"We don't know yet, but we will identify her soon."

Hassanzadeh fumed and swore to himself, "Why am I condemned to work with idiots? What am I going to tell that bastard Niku?" Barely controlling his anger he turned to Qasem and said, "We've already seen the photos. We know all this. Now you've brought me here just to tell me again you can't identify either of the two women at the airport."

In the same angry tone, he asked, "Well, what about the woman in the Washington photograph? Can you do any better with that?"

Humiliated in front of the two technicians, Qasem swallowed his embarrassment and pointed at Nazanin's face. "The welcomer is obviously not the woman in the Washington photo you gave us. We're working to identify her, the small, dark one. But so far nothing. As for the other woman – the traveler and possible spy, as soon as we identify her friend we can find her. Then we can compare her with the Washington photo. I'm confident we can do all that soon."

Meeting hostile silence, Qasem continued, "So far this is the best lead we have from our agents. Will you give me more men to work on this case?"

"Of course. As many as you need. There's a smart and dangerous spy out there and we have to stop her. Find her. Now."

Qasem asked the two technicians to leave. When he was alone with Hassanzadeh, he told him, "I'm sorry for that little charade. I know I didn't tell you anything new. You were right to be upset. I didn't intend to waste your time, but there's another reason I asked for this meeting."

Hassanzadeh was still cold, but now curious. "What's the problem? Good news or bad?"

"Not sure. Probably not good. Our technicians think someone has doctored the Washington photo. Their newest software can detect such things. They may be able to restore the original picture, although that is very difficult. Could we get another copy of the photograph without the changes?"

Hassanzadeh thought while he digested the news. He would have to ask Niku, the only one of the plotters who could talk with the Saudi contact "Sultan." No one else could reach him. "Can your men tell us when or where it was done? Here or sometime before it arrived in Tehran? In Washington, for example?"

"They don't know and probably can't figure it out. What do you think it means?"

Hassanzadeh did not answer. But he and Qasem both understood. Either someone in Washington or Riyadh was deliberately misleading them in a subtle double game or they had a traitor in their midst. In either case, they had a problem.

MACLEAN, VIRGINIA
CIA HEADQUARTERS

When CIA director Brian DeWolf saw the message from Jerusalem, he immediately called Porter. "Alan, please come here as soon as you can. We need to talk."

Porter arrived forty-five minutes later. DeWolf gave him a single sheet of paper covered with exotic security markings. "Alan, so far I've spoken only of an 'excellent source' in Tehran reporting from inside the Fifteenth of Khordad group."

After a pause, the director continued, "Here is the latest from that source, whom the Israelis call 'David.' Read it and then we can talk. I can tell you that David's reporting comes only to me through Israeli friends I knew during my time as station chief in Tel Aviv fifteen years ago. They feel as we do. They are terrified at what their zealots are planning. They have their own man in Tehran who is running David. They know my views, so they share his reporting. Very few Israelis – and no one in their cabinet – know about this source and perhaps only one person there knows his true identity. They have told me he's a key figure in the Fifteenth of Khordad group. So far his reporting has been 100 percent accurate.

"Oh, and Alan, former Ambassador Dahan is part of this group of Israelis. You were crazy to go to him to set up your private security detail for Project 53, but by God you were lucky."

Porter read the message.

> To: Director CIA WashDC
> Most Urgent
> Message from Tehran/Source David.
> For Your Eyes Only
>> Via Saudi contact "Sultan" Fifteenth of Khordad group last week learned that CIA is sending a female agent to Iran on mission most likely intended to neutralize "Operation Zeinab." Sultan told his Fifteenth Khordad counterpart that information and agent's photograph came from a well-placed Washington source.

Using the agent's picture supplied by Sultan, Ebrahim Hassanzadeh, Revolutionary Guards officer in the group, has undertaken to identify the agent and stop her mission. He has assigned several hundred Guards' personnel to watch air, sea, and land frontiers for someone matching her description.

Guards have not yet identified agent from her picture, but four days ago they spotted a suspect at Khomeini International Airport arriving on a flight from Istanbul. They were unable to photograph or follow her, but they did photograph a second Iranian woman who met her at the airport. So far they have not identified either woman.

Hassanzadeh and his men have given highest priority to identifying the two women and matching one with the photograph from Washington. He claims the Guards will have at least one identity within forty-eight to seventy-two hours.

Will report further on status of investigation.

"Holy shit," Porter gasped. "They have a picture of Nilufar. What do we do now?"

Before the director could answer, Porter asked the obvious question. "Last week? Four days ago? Why are we hearing about this just now? By now she could be dead or chained up and screaming in a cellar somewhere. We told her not to use her encrypted phone except for the most urgent calls. We know she made contact with her uncle two days ago and delivered our message, but after that we've heard nothing."

"Alan, the delay was just bad luck. The Israelis tell me their man in Tehran had a traffic accident. He was in the hospital for a few days and lost contact with David. There's some good news. When they did exchange messages, David told his handler that he had doctored the photograph of Nilufar and delayed sharing it with Hassanzadeh for twenty-four hours."

The implications of the message tore at Porter. The Iranians were aware of Nilufar's mission, even if they had only an altered photo. Had he sent Nilufar into a trap? Had he sent her to Iran only to be tortured and killed? Aloud he asked, "Brian, how did the Iranians get a picture? I assume we're talking trai-tor here. I'm tempted to send her an abort signal right now. If she's still free, she needs to get out of Iran while she still can."

"You do that, Alan, and our mission is finished. How do we stop the 'Zeinab' plot? If the guards have arrested her, your abort signal won't help. Nothing will. You're right to worry, but from David's message it looks like she still has time to convince Arash's friends. If she runs now, where are we?"

"At least I should warn her; but I do not want to do it from here," Porter said as he headed for the door. "You must keep me informed," he said as he dashed out of the director's office and to the elevator.

Porter got into his car, which he had parked in the VIP lot in front of CIA headquarters, and turned onto the George Washington Parkway headed north. He took the early turnoff into Turkey Run Park, and drove to an isolated parking area. He put in the code for Nilufar.

"Sir?" a startled Nilufar answered.

"They know we have sent a woman to Tehran. You must speed up your work. God bless you and keep yourself safe."

He cut off the call. It was an especially long drive home.

After Porter left his office, DeWolf tried to piece the story together. Where was the leak? What was the motive? Who benefited? He reviewed the last few weeks in his mind, search-ing for an anomaly, an unanswered question, a loose thread.

The mystery man killed by Novichok.

He called in his chief of staff. They needed to find out more about Gregory and fast.

Four hours later, the director knew he was looking at an-other case where compartmentalization had kept them from what they needed to know. Gregory was Enver Atman. Enver Atman was an MEK agent. The MEK was allied with Kalo-rama in the push for war. Nilufar was in immediate danger. And what else had been compromised?

After two short calls, the director took his elevator to the parking area, got into his armored black Chevy Suburban and, with his escort SUV following, headed for Porter's home to meet him and Steve Quoddy, the FBI director. They needed a plan.

TEHRAN

Driving a battered Iranian-made Peugeot, Arash's daughter Elaheh picked up Nilufar, as arranged, two blocks from Nazanin's home. The two made their way north to a new high-rise apartment building close to Vanak Square. "My father will meet you here. He will call me when you need to go home."

She didn't need to explain to Nilufar that a man – even one as old as Arash – with a woman in his car risked being stopped and questioned by some guardian of public morality – or by someone in search of a bribe. Even in today's more relaxed Islamic Republic, it was unwise to test the authorities' moveable red lines. Yesterday's yes could be today's no.

Arash met her inside the door of the building and they took the elevator to the eleventh floor. "I gathered as many friends as I could. I told them it was urgent. The key people are here. Our host is a good friend from the Plan and Budget Organization. I won't introduce them to you. Everyone here has studied and worked abroad, and it might be better if you used English. I don't know why, but when we hear Persian from an American we get suspicious. We don't trust a foreigner who speaks it too well. Of course we don't trust each other in any language.

"One more thing," he told her. "At this time, in this place, there's no reason for you to hide your identity. That my own niece has brought Porter's message is a sign of its urgency."

Nilufar nodded, "Whatever you believe will work, dear uncle."

When they entered the well-furnished apartment, Nilufar saw eight men, ranging in age from forty-five to seventy. They all deferred to Arash, the senior member of their group. There was no other woman present. They looked at veiled Nilufar with curiosity, and, always cautious, did not offer to shake her hand.

After tea was served, Arash began. "Dear friends and colleagues. I apologize for the short notice, but – as I indicated in my message – the matter is urgent. It turns out that the Americans are confronting a group of extremists similar to our own "Fifteenth of Khordad." They are so worried about a war that they have taken an extraordinary risk."

He paused for a few seconds to see the effect of his words. "Allow me to introduce my late sister Farzaneh's daughter, Dr. Nilufar Hartman, professor at Middlebury College in Vermont. At great risk to herself, she has left her family and work in the United States and under cover of a false identity brought us an urgent message. The message is from an old friend and colleague, Ambassador Alan Porter, former undersecretary of state for political affairs. It was with Ambassador Porter's help we were able to stop the MEK in the 1980s when they were plotting a Stalinist bloodbath in Iran. They tried to assassinate him in Washington, and nearly succeeded. We owe him a lot, and we must take his message seriously."

Arash then read Porter's message to them in English and Persian. Before anyone else could speak, Nilufar began. Speaking in English, she told them: "Gentlemen, I thank you for coming tonight and listening to my dear uncle Arash. I can testify only that what he says is true. As for me, as an American I love my country. I also love Iran, my mother's country. I will do all I can – including risking my life – to make sure our two peoples are not dragged into a pointless war with hideous suffering."

Their reaction was an unsympathetic mix of male condescension, suspicion, and disbelief. She told herself, "Well, Nilufar. You knew this was going to be hard."

To the group, she said, "Let me repeat what my uncle has told you. Porter's message is the truth. A week ago I was with him in Washington when he composed it. Unless our two leaders find a way to act together, there will be a tragedy. There is not much time. Ambassador Porter and his colleagues need an answer from you."

The reaction of Arash's friends to Nilufar and to Porter's letter, if not welcoming, was predictable. They ignored Nilufar and spoke to Arash.

One said, "So your friend in Washington expects us to convince the Supreme Leader to cooperate with the American president against other Iranians? How does he advise us to do that?"

Another added, "The Supreme Leader hates everything American. He particularly despises this president. Senior officials in his administration support the MEK – the same traitors who crippled the leader forty years ago."

A third said, "I have a hard time believing this message isn't a trick. Can you imagine the leader's reaction? I can hear him now. 'How stupid are you to believe such a transparent American plot to set us against each other?'"

Nilufar sat silent and Arash listened patiently to his colleagues. Finally, after all had voiced their objections, he said, "Gentlemen, all you say is true. You raise valid questions. The message could be an American plot. The Supreme Leader will never believe it. He will never agree to cooperate with this American president."

After watching his friends nod, Arash continued, "Yes, perhaps all correct. But ask yourself this. If the letter is genuine, as I am sure it is, what choice do we have? I know Porter well, and I know two things: this letter is from him and he is being honest."

Arash continued, "What happens if we do nothing? What happens if we make no effort to convince the leader? How much blood and destruction will be on our hands?"

Arash turned to Nilufar. "My dear, do you have any words for our friends?"

Nilufar knew she needed their attention and that an appeal to reason would not work. She removed her *hejab*, and looked at their shocked faces. Then she switched to Persian and said, "Gentlemen, I risked my life to come to Iran. Why? Thirty years ago the man who was going to be my husband was murdered here. Americans killed him on the Airbus over the Persian Gulf. What's left of his body is still there. This is the most

painful trip I have ever taken. I would never have come back
on a fool's errand or in an attempt to deceive.

"Be sure of this. I am not a donkey to be led around by
others or to imagine I can fool you. Neither are you donkeys to
be tricked by some false message. I came because I love my
mother's magnificent country and I know that you do as well. I
came because together we can stop a tragedy. If you don't
agree with my uncle Arash and to Mr. Porter's proposal, then
fine. I will tell him now that my mission is a failure and will
leave Iran tomorrow morning. I'll will tell him you do not trust
him."

She had read these men perfectly. Their hostility vanished.
They had a hundred reasons to reject Porter's proposal; but, as
Iranian men, they could not ignore an appeal to their honor and
chivalry from a woman ready to defy the rules of the Islamic
Republic. Now the matter was personal. Answering her in Per-
sian, they said, "*Khaanom-e-mohtaram, khaahesh mikonam,
naaraahat nabaashid.* (Respected lady, please don't be upset).
Maa az avval nemikhaastim be shomaa bi-ehteraami konim
(We never intended to show you disrespect)."

Arash took his cue. "Dear niece, please excuse my friends
for their harsh words. They have no intention of upsetting you.
Porter's message came as a surprise to them. They are all
thoughtful and serious people. We are worried and perhaps we
reacted too quickly. We all love our country and want the same
thing. Please allow us a little time to discuss all this and consider our response. It's late. I will call my daughter to take you
home."

Switching back to English, a new Nilufar – now serene,
confident, and conciliatory – told them, "I apologize for becoming emotional. I have not slept well for days. Of course,
please take the time you need to consider your answer. I know
there is a lot to discuss. And thank you for your kind attention
to me and my dear uncle."

With exchanges of mutual respect and affection, Nilufar
covered herself and took leave of the group. She and Arash
rode the elevator to the ground floor. They didn't speak until

the elevator doors shut. He said, "Well done, my dear niece. You were magnificent as the *za'ifeh* (helpless woman)."

"What do you think, uncle? Will they agree?"

"Of course they will. What else can they do? It may take a few more hours. They'll posture, wave their arms, grumble, and complain. But that's all for show. They are not stupid. Once they've swallowed their pride, they'll do what they must. Of course we'll need to figure out who will convince the Supreme Leader and how. It's going to be a long night." As she rode south on Vali Asr Avenue toward Revolution Square with her cousin Elaheh, Arash returned to the apartment to "continue the discussion" as he put it. It was, as he predicted, a long night.

TEHRAN

"Brother Hassanzadeh, this is Qasem. We need to meet. We've identified the second woman at the airport."

"Excellent, brother Qasem. I'll be right there."

As he rode to his meeting, Hassanzadeh considered his next move. He was convinced a spy inside the Fifteenth of Khordad group had doctored the spy's photograph. The alternative explanation – an American or Saudi double cross – seemed unlikely. What would be its purpose after planning for "Zeinab" had gone so far? Although the group had not dealt directly with the Americans, until now they had kept their word and performed as promised.

If the traitor was Iranian, Hassanzadeh had to be very careful. Whoever it was would already be reporting Fifteenth Khordad's activities to the enemy. Hassanzadeh asked himself what he should do now with the identity of the second woman and the report of the doctored photograph. So far he had said nothing. If he shared what he knew with the group, the traitor would learn he had been discovered and warn his foreign employers. He had to keep these discoveries secret. But how?

When he entered Qasem's office, the two technicians were absent. The officer sat alone at his desk with the photographs and a file in front of him.

"Thank you, brother, for coming so soon. Let me tell you what we've learned." Qasem pointed to the picture of the small, dark woman at the airport. Our technicians couldn't identify her from databases, but we had some luck. We didn't need technology. It turns out that one of our officers recognized her. Four years ago, when he studied at Tehran University, she was his math professor."

Hassanzadeh cursed and thought, "Another damned intellectual. They will destroy the Islamic Republic. We let them keep stabbing us in the back. We should have shut down the universities for good and shot all the professors." Turning to Qasem, he said, "So who is this traitor?"

"Her name is Nazanin Dowlatabadi. Full professor of mathematics at Tehran University. Former director in the Ministry of Higher Education under that useless Khatami. Here is her file. You can see our airport photograph and her university ID photos from our files. It's clearly the same person."

"I can see that. What else do we know about her?"

"She has strong revolutionary credentials and is the widow of the martyr Karimpour. She and her husband were student activists before the revolution. He was tortured to death under the Shah and she spent almost four years in prison. After the revolution she ran the women's *komiteh* at Mehrabad Airport. During the Cultural Revolution, with the universities closed, she served in Tehran with the women's *gasht*, the morality police. When the universities reopened, she went back to her studies. At that time she was briefly part of a so-called 'religious-intellectual' discussion group, but there's no trace of any political activity for the last twenty years. She spent three years in England getting her doctorate, but our agents there never reported anything suspicious. She observed strict *hejab* and spent her time studying and taking care of her two children. No political activity there either."

Hassanzadeh felt swamped in useless information. Still patient, he asked, "Have you found anything to link her to a CIA operation against us?"

"That's the interesting thing. On the surface I have to say no. But we have discovered something very odd. Dowlatabadi is originally from Rafsanjan, and has family connections to the late President Hashemi-Rafsanjani. One of our senior archivists worked for him in the 1980s when he was Speaker of parliament. He remembers Dowlatabadi from that time and says she was very close to a translator in the Speaker's office named Massoumeh Rastbin. Our man says he remembers the woman well because she was very devout, American-educated, and spoke several foreign languages fluently. An exceptional person."

Hassanzadeh didn't see where Qasem was going with this history. "So thirty years ago madam professor had a friend in Hashemi-Rafsanjani's office. So what?"

"Our officer remembers that one day this Ms. Rastbin suddenly disappeared and was never seen again. It happened in July 1988, just after the Americans murdered the 300 passengers on the Iranian Airbus. She just vanished. The odd thing was, Hashemi-Rafsanjani himself never asked about her and stopped anyone from searching for her."

Qasem pointed to the pictures in Nazanin's file. "Sir, it may be nothing or it may be important. In this file there are some old reports and photos from England showing Ms. Dowlatabadi with an American friend called "Nilufar Hartman." When our archivist saw that woman's picture, he was almost certain that Nilufar Hartman and Massoumeh Rastbin are the same person, although the pictures from England are more than twenty years old and she is not wearing Islamic dress."

Hassanzadeh thought for a minute and asked, "So do I understand this? Last week your madam professor of mathematics meets a traveler from Istanbul at the airport – someone who might be a CIA spy. We also learn that thirty years ago she was a friend of a mysterious Ms. Rastbin who worked in Hashemi-Rafsanjani's office, and disappeared suddenly after July 1988. Then the same woman reappears a few years later with a different name as an American visiting Ms. Dowlatabadi in England."

"That's correct. So far we've found nothing in our file searches for this Massoumeh Rastbin. If there are records, they're rotting in a warehouse somewhere. I showed our archivist the spy's picture from Washington, but he couldn't make an identification. Whoever doctored the photograph made it unrecognizable."

Hassanzadeh asked, "Can your technicians tell where it was altered?"

"Not with certainty, but they suspect it was done in Iran. Unfortunately they cannot undo the process."

Hassanzadeh knew the truth was hiding just out of sight. He had a collection of suspicions, probabilities, and educated guesses. He had pieces of a thousand-piece jigsaw puzzle that almost fit together. On the other hand, Qasem's information was the best they had. Even if it was vague, he had to act on it. But he had nothing but bad choices. If he reported what Qasem told him to the group, he would be helping the traitor protect himself. If he did not, others would accuse him of bad faith and hidden motives. He silently cursed this unknown spy whose actions endangered him and all associated with "Zeinab". He turned to Qasem. "Who else knows about all this?"

"Only the two of us. The others in my office know just a few pieces."

Hassanzadeh knew he needed both to take action and hide what he knew from the traitor. He came to a quick decision.

"Thank you, brother Qasem. You have done excellent work. Here's what I want you to do. You know where this professor lives and works?"

"Of course."

"Then watch her home, and put bugs in her house, her office, her computers, and her telephones. Follow her everywhere. Do it now. I don't care how many men it takes, but for God's sake, tell your men to be discrete. You don't want to scare her. She cannot know we suspect her.

"One more thing. I want to hear from you every day, or more often if necessary. You can reach me any time in my office or my home. Use the secure mobile. You will report only to me. Do not discuss this case with anyone else. I don't have to explain why."

GEORGETOWN

After the MEK assassination attempt in American University Park thirty years earlier, Porter and his wife moved to a townhouse in Georgetown, between Holy Trinity Church and Georgetown University. He liked that there were young people around him even if he tired of the noise on the weekends.

DeWolf and Quoddy arrived at almost the same time. Porter suggested they take a short walk onto the Georgetown campus where they could talk in the open air. They entered the grounds at Thirty-Seventh and P and sat on a bench tucked behind the Gothic building which houses the registrar's offices with a small memorial fountain to the left and a statue of the Polish hero and later Georgetown Professor Jan Karksi. That the bronze Karski was seated next to a chessboard with a game in progress seemed appropriate.

The CIA director took them through what he now knew about Gregory. "We've been had in a big way."

"No shit," said Quoddy. "What now?"

Porter looked at the two younger men. 9/11 had been their formative crisis. Watergate was his. What they faced now was an assault from the inside against the root systems of government. The result could be a physical attack on Americans and their allies from an outside power who wished us no good. If this provocation succeeded, many would die for the profit and aggrandizement of a few.

"I need to see the president," Porter said. "I must convince him to stop the conspiracy against our country and prevent a confrontation that will lead to war. You two look astonished. Maybe I should not be surprised. You have taken many risks up to now, but you still have careers. Leave the president to me. I have nothing left to lose except Nilufar, and I'm not going to lose her. She's everything to me. But what I need from you two is a parallel effort. You need to be ready to arrest the Kalorama traitors."

THE WHITE HOUSE

From home, Porter called retired General John Byrne, the president's chief of staff. Porter had met Byrne years earlier, when Byrne was an army colonel serving on the Joint Staff at the Pentagon. Both men recognized the utility of staying in touch over the years of promotions.

"John, I have never asked you for anything since you have been at the White House, but our country is in danger and I am desperate. I must see the president and I need to do so immediately. No one else except you can be in the Oval Office. That includes the vice president and the national security advisor and his deputy. I cannot and will not tell you more on this line or before we enter the Oval. You have to trust me."

"Alan, I know you are a patriot and I admire your service to our country as a Foreign Service Officer. But you realize who you are and what you have done are huge negatives with the president."

"Of course I do. This is not about me. I am expendable. This is about the nation we both serve and love."

"Be here at 1700. I'll have you cleared in at the Southwest Gate. Come in through the lower entrance that leads to the Sit-Room. Take the back stairs and meet me in the West Lobby. And, Alan, wear fireproof underwear."

"Who the hell are you and what the fuck are you doing here?" President Martin McGuire shouted at Porter and Byrne as they stepped into the Oval Office. Two televisions on the wall were showing the same news channel.

"Mr. President, I am Alan Porter. I am a retired Foreign Service Officer. I am here because…."

"Alan Porter. Charter Member of the Swamp. Georgetown address. My base and I despise you Porter; but you already know that, don't you? And you also know I am not the first to sit in this office and distrust you and your globalist friends. Lyndon Johnson hated you because you got him into the Vietnam War. And for what? Almost 60,000 American dead so now we can have a trade deficit with Hanoi? Nixon hated your class and so you and your deep state allies destroyed him. Now you're here to screw me."

"I came to warn you of a conspiracy inside your administration which is making common cause with a group of criminals in Iran to start a shooting war – which you do not want – between our two countries. The plan is for the Iranian Revolutionary Guards to attack the aircraft carrier USS *Gerald R. Ford*, which is now on course to the Persian Gulf.

"John, most times I think you are the dumbest person in Washington, but you can now drag both of your asses out of here and please don't come back."

"Sir, I will not leave until you hear me out," Porter said.

"Go tell it to the vice president," McGuire barked.

"That's the problem. She's leading this treachery, sir. She wants you sucked into an unpopular, drawn-out war with Iran so she can replace you."

McGuire looked directly at Porter for the first time. "Keep talking. This had better be good."

Forty-five minutes later, Porter had made his last appeal, shown his last evidence, tried one last time to make a connection to the scowling president, who sat with his arms crossed, and often seemed simultaneously intently interested and irredeemably bored.

"What do you need me to do?" McGuire finally said, his voice full of suspicion and hostility.

"I need you to give me permission to take any action in your name that I must to stop this treason and avoid a war with Iran," Byrne responded.

"You have it. Go ahead. But if this gets screwed up, I'll say I never knew either of you."

The president returned to watching television.

WASHINGTON

At one thirty p.m. in Washington, ten p.m. in Tehran, Porter's secure phone buzzed. Nilufar told him, "Sir, the friends have accepted your proposal. They will meet the Supreme Leader this evening. They wanted to know what signal they should expect to hear from President McGuire."

"Please tell them that tomorrow – pending the leader's agreement to the plan – the president will be making a speech at a rally in West Virginia. Most of his speech will be about how he is saving America's coal industry. Near the end he will say, 'America first, America last, America always.'"

Nilufar repeated the line, and said, "Let's hope he gets it right."

Porter disconnected the call and said a silent "Amen." He then called Chief of Staff Byrne. "John, the friends there have agreed to our plan. They're meeting with the Supreme Leader tonight."

"Can they convince him? He's a hard case."

"Our person in Tehran thinks they can. They wouldn't go ahead with the meeting unless they thought they could persuade him. It'll be crucial that we've already convinced McGuire. In any case, I hope she's right. If he doesn't agree or wants to bargain, we're all in very deep shit."

"So what's next, Alan? The USS *Gerald Ford* is nearing the Strait of Hormoz. If we can't make this plan work, we'll have to try and turn her around. I don't even want to think about asking the Navy to do that. It would be easier to make the president believe in global warming."

"I'll let you know as soon as we have a 'yes' from Tehran. We've told the Iranians about the signal in his West Virginia speech tomorrow. Can you assure me it'll be there and he won't go off script?"

"Of course he'll go off script. But we'll get it in. He's actually become fascinated by the whole plot. At the same time, he's brooding over the Kalorama Group's treachery. He's furious at them. He thought they were his allies. I heard him say, 'Who do they think they are? Didn't they get it when I fired that idiot of a National Security Advisor? They'll learn only I get to decide when we kick rag-head ass in a fucking war.'"

TEHRAN

Eight hours later, at two a.m. Tehran time, Nazanin called Porter. "Sir, the Supreme Leader will act. He's ready to move against the Fifteenth of Khordad. He's speaking to a meeting of teachers tomorrow evening, which will be around midday your time. If he hears President McGuire's message in his speech, he'll say toward the end 'Iran will never again be colonized' (*Iraan digar har gez este'maar nakhaahad shod*)."

"How did they convince him?"

"It wasn't so hard once the leader realized an Iranian clique, including the MEK, was plotting with Americans, Zionists, and Saudis. He detests them all. Arash and his friends had allies who knew how to make the case.

"They never said he would be cooperating with McGuire or accepting an American proposal. They didn't give him all the specifics, but presented the plan as an Iranian idea that the Americans were forced to accept. They told him the president was afraid of a resolute Iran and that he was backing down in the face of Iranian steadfastness. The leader also liked the idea of showing everyone who's in charge."

"Good. You stay safe and be careful. We'll talk later about getting you out."

Nilufar's phone buzzed twenty minutes later. Without any preliminaries Porter told her, "Nilufar, don't speak. You must run. Now. Both you and Nazanin have been exposed. The Revolutionary Guards are watching her apartment and probably bugging it as well. Better you not say anything while you're there. I can't tell you how I know, but I do, and I'm sure of it. Get somewhere safe, and when you can speak, let me know where."

She woke Nazanin and put a finger to her lips indicating silence. She gave her a note, saying, "We've been identified. The Guards are watching us. We have to go somewhere safe. Now."

Nazanin nodded. She made a quick call, spoke a few words, and then began packing a small bag. She scribbled a note to Nilufar. "Amir will be here in an hour. We'll go to the farm near Rafsanjan."

Nilufar pointed to the last three words and made a questioning gesture. Nazanin answered with an emphatic "yes" movement of her head. She wrote, "We can talk when we're in the car."

Nilufar gave a nod of agreement and began gathering papers, money, and clothes.

An hour later the two women were waiting in the foyer when Amir's Renault stopped in front of Nazanin's building. Carrying their small travelling bags, they walked the few steps to the car.

Nazanin told her son, "Don't stay here. Drive toward the railroad station."

As he pulled out, a green Suzuki followed him along Nazari Street toward South Kaargar Avenue. They did not notice a yellow Peugeot exit a garage and follow both cars.

Amir knew better than to say anything except to agree with his mother. Nilufar asked, "Well, my dear sister, you obviously have a plan. What is it?"

"We'll go to the farm, but not directly. There's a train for Mashhad at nine twenty this morning. It arrives about ten this evening. If anyone asks, two middle-aged widows are making a pilgrimage to Imam Reza. Nothing remarkable in that. From Mashhad we can get an overnight bus across the desert to Yazd. From there to Rafsanjan, it's about four hours on the bus. We'll be there day after tomorrow."

Nilufar thought for a few seconds and replied, "Two questions. Somebody's following us now. How do we get away from them? And if the Guards have identified us, they know where you're from and where you might go."

"Amir can lose them in Tehran traffic. Any driver here knows how to do that. As for tracking us to the farm, going there should buy us time. They know I'm from Rafsanjan, but very few people know about the farm. My family hid it from the Guards after the revolution."

Nazanin continued, "If I understand what you're doing, and if your and your uncle's plan works, in a few days we won't have to worry about these guys following us. By the time they figure out where we are, *kaar az kaar gozasht* (it will be too late)."

Amir drove his Renault south on Kaargar Avenue through the beginning of Tehran's morning rush hour. Drivers weaved in and out of the smallest openings, changed lanes with no signals, and made turns from anywhere. Shared taxis slowed and stopped as hopeful passengers yelled their destinations. Trucks and busses spilled diesel fumes into the already polluted air. A chorus of horns arose from cars whose paths were hopelessly blocked. Pedestrians crossed anywhere, with death-defying maneuvers through moving traffic. Helpless traffic policemen blew their whistles, waved their arms, and watched the chaos. A normal day on Tehran's streets.

Amir searched for a side street where he could lose the Suzuki. He didn't mind ignoring one-way signs (everyone did), but he feared ending up in a blind alley. Before he could find an escape, the yellow Peugeot suddenly accelerated and turned in front of the pursuing Suzuki and came to a dead stop. The Peugeot's driver got out, threw up his hands, and called, "Sorry, brothers, my engine just died." One of his passengers walked up to Amir's Renault and said, "Go as quickly as you can."

Watching the growing traffic jam in his rearview mirror, Amir continued south toward the railroad station. He told his riders, "I don't know who it is, but someone just helped us lose that Suzuki. The Guards have almost certainly ID'd this car, so you'll need to switch as soon as possible. I'll get a taxi to take you the rest of the way. When you get to the station, mix with the crowds, and get on the train as soon as you can."

TEHRAN: REVOLUTIONARY GUARD HEADQUARTERS

Hassanzadeh knew he could no longer trust the Fifteenth Khordad group. He strongly suspected Niku, its titular head, of being the traitor. No one else had seen the Washington photograph before Niku brought it to the Guards. Inquiries found no problems with secure photo transmissions to the Supreme

Leader's office in the forty-eight hours before Niku handed over the doctored picture.

He also knew he could not work alone. He needed help to stop this betrayal and protect Operation Zeinab. He asked Musa Vakili of the Mashhad Shrine organization and Yazdani, the revolutionary court prosecutor, to meet him privately. He explained to them what Qasem had told him about the doctored photograph, about Nazanin, and about the strange story of Nilufar Hartman, aka Massoumeh Rastbin.

He told them, "We checked passenger arrivals, and we found a woman named 'Ziba Amiri' on the flight from Istanbul. She matches what we know about the Washington spy. Her passport was good but, when we checked, we found no record of her ever leaving the country. As far as we know, 'Ziba Amiri' does not exist."

Yazdani's response was predictable. "So let's arrest them all. We'll find out soon enough who they really are."

Hassanzadeh answered, "We've just now made the connections. We're certain that Massoumeh Rastbin, Nilufar Hartman, and Ziba Amiri are the same person. Whoever she is, our Professor Dowlatabadi is helping her."

He looked at his colleagues. They did not need him to spell out why they were meeting secretly without their chief. "If you gentlemen both agree, I will give orders to arrest both of them immediately."

As they both nodded, an aide came in the room. "Sir, you're needed urgently in the communications center."

Hassanzadeh was furious when he returned ten minutes later. "The bitches have fled. Someone was helping them and blocked our follow team on South Kaargar Avenue. Now they've vanished."

"We'll find them. We've identified the car they're riding in. We'll put every man we have on the case. We'll check every town. They can't hide for long."

A few hours later, searchers reported seeing Amir's car, without its passengers, on the road to Tabriz and the Turkish frontier. Hassanzadeh told his men, "He's probably going to meet them somewhere and take them to the border. Keep following him until he leads us to those women."

As an afterthought, Hassanzadeh said, "And alert our agents in Rafsanjan. Send them more men. Dowlatabadi is from there, and they could make a run in that direction."

MASHHAD, IRAN

The train to Mashhad was full of pilgrims traveling to celebrate the birthday of the twelfth imam, the most festive day in the Shia religious calendar. At ten p.m., when the train arrived, the city was illuminated and crowds of pilgrims and local families were enjoying sweets and music at impromptu street parties. Nilufar and Nazanin found beds at a clean but modest hotel between the railroad station and the city's famous shrine. The owner would never presume to ask these two pious, middle-aged ladies for identification.

Even if the Guards knew they were in Mashhad, they would have great difficulty finding them among the hundreds of thousands of Shia visitors – Iranians, Pakistanis, Iraqis, Afghans, Kuwaitis, and Bahrainis – who had flooded the city for the holiday.

The next morning, the two women, after a breakfast of sweet tea, bread and jam, found a transport office. Using false names, they bought tickets for Yazd on a bus leaving at six that evening. Traffic on that desert route always traveled by night. No one asked for identification.

As they walked through the crowded bazaars near the holy shrine, Nazanin heard a man's voice whisper, *Khaanom, sigheh mishi?* (Madam, are you ready to be a temporary wife?) A furious Nazanin turned quickly and saw a short man with a torn coat, greasy hair, run-down shoes, and a food-stained shirt. She was about to strike him, when Nilufar grabbed her arm. "Not here. Not now. I'd like to tear out his liver, but it's too dangerous. We can't bring attention to ourselves."

Instead they gave the pimp a look of pure contempt, and entered a jewelry shop selling the exquisite turquoise and lapis of Khorasan. The pimp went in search of better prospects. The shopkeeper was a genial, elderly Mashhadi, who was delighted to have two such respectable women as customers. After some small talk, he served them tea.

Using the honorific Iranians give bazaar merchants, Nazanin asked him, "*Haaji aaghaa,* do you know that man in the torn, brown coat? Did you see him annoying decent women? He's lucky he still has eyes in his head."

The shopkeeper sighed and answered in a voice full of disgust. "Of course I know him. Everyone does. He's famous as Sha'baan the Procurer. He's one of Musa Vakili's men. Vakili is nephew of the shrine administrator, and related through him to Mashhad's Friday prayer leader. His local nickname is 'J.B.,' for *jaakesh-baashi* (chief pimp).

"That family is already rich from stealing shrine money. It makes itself richer by brokering temporary marriages for pilgrims. They employ an army of pimps. They find poor, desperate widows and divorcees. With millions of visitors a year, that's serious money. All the big shots get their cut and no one interferes in that filthy business.

"By the way, you did well by not confronting him. He doesn't look like much, but *paartiyesh kheili koloft-e* (he has very powerful protectors). No one would dare take your side in public."

As they sat, they heard a commotion outside. They saw a group of men marching through the bazaar waving signs and shouting "*Doroud bar Vakili. Imaam-jom'eh qahremaan-e-maast. Saazeshgaraan doshmanaan-e-maas*t. (Hail to Vakili. The Friday prayer leader is our champion. The compromisers are our enemies.)"

Their host quickly pulled down the iron grate outside and locked the shop. "Excuse me, ladies, but there are hoodlums in the bazaar looking for an excuse to smash and loot."

"Why are they demonstrating?" asked Nilufar.

"They're supporting Mashhad's Friday imam and his family, including that J.B. – the Vakili I mentioned. He has his own gang that marches and shouts on demand. They're well paid and can get rough.

"Last night there were rumors in the bazaar that J.B., the same head pimp, is in trouble in Tehran and might be on his way out. Of course a move against him is a move against his whole rotten family. I for one would be happy to see them go, but it's not likely. The family is close to the Supreme Leader, who's a Mashhadi as well."

The two women exchanged looks and said nothing. If the shopkeeper was right, the Supreme Leader was already moving against Fifteenth Khordad. After the demonstrators had moved on, Nazanin and Nilufar each bought a gold necklace set with the beautiful local stones. In an unspoken understanding, the jeweler set a reasonable price and there was no bargaining. As they were leaving, he told them, "Dear ladies, you should be careful. An hour before you arrived, plainclothes security men were going through the market showing pictures and asking about two women around your age. They told us to report if we saw anything."

Without giving them a chance to react, he said, "Don't worry. I'm not a snitch. If you can wait a few minutes, I will call my nephew Abbas and he'll bring his car to the bazaar entrance. You'll need to walk only about fifty meters. I'll walk with you. He'll take you to our house and keep you there as long as necessary. I will call my wife and she will be expecting you. You are obviously honorable, pious women of good family and as long as you are in Mashhad, it is my responsibility to keep you safe."

Before the women could thank him, he said, "There's no need for thanks. I detest those people. This is just my duty. I ask only one favor: that in the future you not speak badly of us Mashhadis and our city. Forget about that pimp you met. Please remember that there are still many of us here with *gheirat* (a sense of honor). I want you to have good memories of us."

MASHHAD, TABAS, YAZD, RAFSANJAN

Nazanin and Nilufar spent the rest of the day at the jeweler's home with the women of his family. They passed time resting, drinking tea, and gossiping. They women shared the jeweler's low opinion of Mashhad's Friday imam and his family. The jeweler came home for lunch and reported more rumors from Tehran, more disorder in the market, and more plainclothes security men searching for two "women counter-revolutionaries"

Abbas drove them to the station, and the bus for Yazd left on time. As the travelers settled down for the overnight trip across Iran's great central desert, Nilufar sent a brief signal to Porter giving their location and status. About one a.m., after passing through the ancient oasis town of Tabas, the bus pulled into a service plaza on Route 68 for a rest stop. Some passengers continued to sleep, but Nazanin and Nilufar both stretched their legs and washed with the brackish water of the area. Nilufar grasped her friend's hand and said, "Come with me."

She led Nazanin to the edge of the plaza. They stepped off the pavement and walked ten meters into the sandy desert. As they left the artificial light of the bus and truck stop they saw the millions of stars that illuminate the endless deserts of Iran.

"What is it, dear Nilufar? Why are we here?"

"Nazanin *jun*, join me in saying a prayer. Eight brave men died here forty years ago. We should remember them."

The women stood shoulder to shoulder as they recited the *fateha*, the powerful opening verse of the Qur'an. "...It is Thee we bow to, and it is from Thee we seek help. Guide us on the straight path." One by one Nilufar pronounced the names of the dead Americans from Operation Eagle Claw, the ill-fated 1980 mission to rescue the embassy hostages in Tehran: "John Harvey, George Holmes, Dewey Johnson, Richard Bakke, Harold Lewis, Joel Mayo, Lyn McIntosh, Charles McMillan." The two women ended their vigil together with: "*Khodaa rahmateshaan kone* (May God have mercy on them). *Ruheshaan shaad* (May their souls be joyful)."

The next morning from Yazd they took the first bus available to Rafsanjan. In the afternoon, when they reached the terminal on Azadi Street, just south of the city, Nazanin's nephew Javad rushed them into his car. "Security men are looking for you," he told them. "Amir called me and explained everything. By the way, they're still following him on the highway to Tabriz. That's good. He'll keep them distracted. We'll hide you in town until dark and then drive to the farm. The Guards don't know about that place and they'll never manage the road at night. So far there's no one up there."

RISEH (near Rafsanjan)

It was after midnight when Javad, Nilufar, and Nazanin, having crawled over the mountain roads, arrived at the farm. They were exhausted but fear kept them intently focused. They did not dare turn on a light in the house. Javad had driven the last five kilometers without headlights, with only the moon and stars to show him the twisting road.

Nilufar's secure phone chirped.

"Do not speak," Porter said. "In fifteen minutes look outside. Two red flashes. Two white flashes. Three blue flashes. Recognition signal 'Franklin,' You reply "Rochambeau.' Go with this team. They will help you."

Porter disconnected the call.

"Nazanin, I am about to be taken away by friends. You must come with me. You are in danger here. Do this for me."

"My dear sister, I know you mean well and I will never forget what we have done together. But Iran is my home. My children are here. I have made my way so far and I will make my way again. This is my fate. I cannot deny it."

Nilufar pleaded but Nazanin was firm. She would stay.

"Please dear friend, think about this at least once more."

Two red flashes. Two white flashes. Three blue.

Seven men in commando fatigues with the tricolor on their sleeves came to the door.

"Franklin," said their leader.

"Rochambeau," Nilufar replied.

"Madame Hartman, please come with us."

Nilufar gave Nazanin a fierce embrace and stepped into the starlit night. The French commandos from the Seventh Parachute Regiment surrounded her and she went into the night toward two waiting cars. She was gently directed to the rear of the second one. The commando who sat down next to her laid his Uzi on his lap.

They then paused. The commandos in the first car urged that they move and move now. But a door opened in the second car and one of the French soldiers dashed back to Nazanin's door. He pressed a piece of paper into her hand and sprinted back to the car.

Both vehicles headed onto the curving road. When they reached the main road that led south to Sirjan and Bandar Abbas, they began to move at high speed.

"Madame Hartman, we are honored to be your escorts. We know only a small part or your story, but we thank you. We are headed to a beach outside of Bandar Abbas where we will entrust you to our brothers from the US Navy. Please try to sleep now if you can."

In the darkness behind Nazanin's farmhouse, the four members of the Israeli security team that had covertly shadowed Nilufar since she had landed in Tehran, and had kept Porter regularly and fully informed of her whereabouts, received an urgent order to stay in place for forty-eight hours and do whatever was required to keep Nazanin and her family safe.

Nazanin unfolded the paper the Frenchman had given her. As she looked into the night she asked her questions. The darkness and her friend's absence revealed her answer. She made two phone calls.

BANDAR ABBAS

Eight hours later, the tiny convoy arrived outside of Bandar Abbas. They had evaded or bribed their way through several checkpoints during the night. Since they carried their own petrol, there was no need to stop in public places.

They pulled into a decrepit villa overlooking the sea that a French agent in the town had rented. It was as safe a house as they could manage this far from a DGSE base. "We will need to stay here until dusk," said the team leader.

The villa's feeble air-conditioning was no match for the suffocating heat and humidity of the Persian Gulf coast. A dazed and sweaty Nilufar sat in the main room and looked at the sea. It was just after 10:00 a.m.

BANDAR ABBAS
IRAN AIR 655.
RUZBEH

She wept from both exhaustion and sorrow; she wept to release the tension of the past few days; she wept for the many years she had lived alone since Ruzbeh's death; and finally she wept for the future. Nazanin's. Her grandchild's. Iran's. America's.

She got up and went to the window. Ruzbeh, you died here. I am to be rescued here as you were not. Please forgive me.

Just after 7 p.m., she went with her French escorts to a small bay five miles from the villa. They stood very close to the cliffs hoping to stay out of sight in the gathering darkness.

As they waited in the still, wet air, she walked alone to the edge of the water. She removed the gold chain and its "See Our Deepest Secrets" charm from her neck. She spoke quietly. "Ruzbeh, my beloved, I know you died near this place. I have worn your gift for thirty years. You gave it to me when we last saw each other in Tehran. Please accept it now as an eternal memento of our love. I regret I could not bring our son Behnam here, but perhaps in the future, so he knows what a great man his father was."

She said a silent prayer, kissed the necklace, and threw it into the sea.

They heard the Zodiacs before they saw them. More coded flashes were exchanged. A Navy Seal team came ashore, fully armed and wearing night vision goggles.

"Ma'am," we are here to take you home."

Nilufar turned to the French commando team. "Will you be coming with us?"

"No, madame, but thank you. We will find our own way home. Is there something more we can do for you?"

There was. Nilufar asked for this just as her feet touched the water off Bandar Abbas. "I will never forget what you risked for me. I wish you success and a safe return."

Nilufar was helped into the Zodiac and eight minutes later she was aboard the American Navy destroyer USS *Kidd*, which would take her to Doha, Qatar. From there she would travel to Vermont on a US Air Force G-5 from the American airbase at Al Udeid.

TEHRAN

Gholam-Hossein Sarhaddi was happy in his retirement. He was proud of his service to the Imam and to the revolution. He had managed both to avoid the Iraqi front and to extort enough in bribes and hush money to buy a comfortable apartment on Africa (formerly Ministers') Street. He took his grandchildren to the local park. He had no regrets.

He had just turned off the evening TV news when he thought he heard a sound at the fire escape. He went to look but saw nothing. When he returned to his easy chair, he found himself looking at three men dressed in black. The one pointing a gun at him said quietly, "This is for Iran Air 655. This is for Philippe Tehrani. This is for Ambassador de Montréal. Above all, this is for Nilufar Hartman. We have long memories."

The silenced weapon puffed three times and Sarhaddi fell bleeding to the floor.

The three men joined the four who had provided cover and protection outside the apartment. Their leader told them that, in fact, they had just been given another assignment. No killing this time, but another rescue. Together they walked into the dark street. Early the next morning, with five passengers, they headed south toward Rafsanjan and Riseh.

ABOARD THE USS *GERALD FORD*. THE STRAIT OF HORMOZ

"Officer of the Deck, what is our status?"
"No hostiles in any direction, captain."

"Very well. Proceed at speed and on course as ordered."

MIDDLEBURY, VERMONT

Porter and Nilufar sat for a long time in silence in the garden of Nilufar's house. There was both too much and too little to say.

Porter broke the silence. "While you were flying home, the FBI raided the Kalorama Group as they met in the house on California Street. The director had tipped off some of his friends in the press. The pictures of these people in handcuffs with coats over their heads almost made the whole thing worth it. The next day in Tehran, we detected a shake-up in the leadership."

When Nilufar said nothing, he continued, "One odd thing. We know what happened to almost everyone in Fifteenth Khordad. Some were shot immediately. Some are in jail. Some will be managing sugar factories near the Pakistan border. But a key figure in the group, a man named Hossein Niku, the head of the Supreme Leader's office, has disappeared. And when he did, our reporting from Tehran stopped. Makes you wonder."

As Porter spoke, Nilufar realized she no longer had much interest in this story. Except that she could not help remembering the damaged Niku, who had saved her thirty years before, and who now, for whatever reason, had saved millions by his treachery. She said nothing to Porter, but said to herself, "Makes you wonder. Indeed it does."

The last few weeks seemed a detour that had brought no personal resolution to her loss or any extra meaning to her service to the United States. She wanted to be with her grandchild, teach her students, and be left alone with her memories of Ruzbeh and what might have been.

"Thank you for everything you did for me, Alan, using his given name for the first time. I do not mean to be rude, but I will bid you farewell here. Have a safe trip back to Washington." She walked to her house and closed the door behind her.

Porter sat for a few more minutes and drove to the airport. Nothing ever ends the way we imagine it will when we start, he thought.

Nilufar looked with love, relief, and fascination at the guests sitting in her kitchen. Nazanin, her children Amir and Kazhal, her son-in-law Afzal, and her grandchildren Rehan and Dijle had arrived a week after Nilufar's return to Vermont.

After Nilufar left, Nazanin called the number the French commando had given her and asked for help. She summoned her family to join her at the farm. The Revolutionary Guard detachment, acting on orders that were never cancelled, eventually found her farm and sent a team to arrest her. They arrived fifteen minutes after her children, but the Israeli security team was waiting and killed them in a brief firefight. The French commandos had appeared at almost the same time and took control of the rescue operation. The Israelis executed their own exfiltration plan and were in Jerusalem by daybreak. Nazanin and her family were smuggled out of Iran two days later on an aircraft owned by the French oil company Total.

They stayed in a safe house outside of Grasse in southern France for a week and then, at CIA Director DeWolf's direction, were brought in an unmarked CIA aircraft to Burlington where they would be resettled.

For now, with the grandchildren playing in the basement, everyone else was content to drink tea from the modern glass samovar Nilufar had found online and let the past recede into the coming dusk. The only sounds were low conversation, bubbling water, and the clack of dice and backgammon pieces.

EPILOGUE

VERMONT. ONE YEAR LATER

Nilufar usually spent Thanksgiving with Behnam and his family in North Carolina. This year she assumed her role of matriarch, and hosted Behnam, Anita, and Ruzbeh along with her cousin Iraj, his wife Parisa, and their three children. Nazanin, Amir, Afzal and Kazhal, and the two grandchildren, joined the group.

After her escape from Iran, Nazanin stayed in Middlebury, where she soon found work in the college's math department. In a few months she became one of the school's most popular teachers. She told Nilufar, "Math is math, students are students, and university politics are much the same everywhere. But I love the freedom I have here as a woman. Maybe one day in Iran…"

It wasn't easy for Kazhal and her husband. They both found jobs at the hospital in nearby Glens Falls, New York, but still faced the long and demanding process of repeating much of their training before they could practice in the US. Their two children learned English quickly, and were star pupils in the local public schools.

Parents and grandmother Nazanin ensured the children maintained their Kurdish and Persian. Kazhal's birth mother Sahar visited from Iraq. During her three-month stay, she took over running the house, cooking, and caring for her beloved grandchildren, who adored hearing her call their mother by her original name, "Dilnaz". Nazanin's teaching schedule was light enough that she too could provide badly-needed help to her daughter.

Amir was studying for an advanced journalism degree at the University of Vermont in Burlington, and there were reports of a friendship with an Iraqi Kurdish refugee woman there. Nazanin told him, "I won't pressure you, but another grandchild would be wonderful. When you give the word, Auntie Nilu and I are ready to visit her family for the *khaastegaari* (marriage proposal)."

After dinner, which, in addition to turkey and sweet potatoes, included rice with sour cherries, a walnut and pomegranate stew, and other Iranian delicacies, Iraj brought out his violin, Amir his *dombak* (drum), and Kazhal sang Persian and Kurdish songs.

After she finished with a spirited version of the Kurdish favorite "*Asmar*", Behnam spoke to the group. "Obviously we have much to be thankful for this year. What a joy it is to be together with family and friends!

"But something is still missing. For the past year, Ruzbeh has been asking me, 'Why did Mama Nilu leave us? Where did she go? Why won't she tell me?'"

He turned to his mother. "*Maman*, isn't it time you tell us your story? All of us are full of your delicious food. We've heard our lovely Kazhal's sweet voice. Now we need a good story to make this day perfect."

Nilufar had finally decided, but she first made the necessary show of reluctance. She said, "I don't want to bore you. It's a long story, and not that interesting. I'm afraid I'll put you to sleep."

The guests knew their lines, "No, no, we insist. We're dying to hear everything. Please tell us."

Finally, she gave in. "Well, if you insist. First, let me say how happy I am that you are all here." Turning to Behnam, her face wet with tears, she said, "My dear son, how pleased your father would be to see all of us together. Kazhal, last time he saw you, you were fourteen months old and had just come to Tehran. He would be so proud of you."

After a deep breath, she turned to her grandson, and began. "Dearest Ruzbeh, this story is for you. It begins forty years ago in Washington. That was before I met your grandfather and ten years before your father was born.

"One day I had a telephone call..."

About the Authors

Marc Grossman.

Ambassador Marc Grossman served as the Under Secretary of State for Political Affairs, the State Department's third ranking official, until his retirement in 2005 after 29 years in the US Foreign Service. As Under Secretary, he helped marshal diplomatic support for the international response to the attacks of September 11, 2001. He also managed US policies in the Balkans and Colombia and promoted a key expansion of the NATO alliance. As Assistant Secretary for European Affairs, he helped direct NATO's military campaign in Kosovo and an earlier round of NATO expansion. Ambassador Grossman was the US Ambassador to Turkey 1994 – 1997.

Ambassador Grossman was a Vice Chairman of The Cohen Group from July 2005 to February 2011.

In February, 2011 President Obama and Secretary of State Clinton called Ambassador Grossman back to service as the US Special Representative for Afghanistan and Pakistan. Ambassador Grossman promoted the international effort to support Afghanistan by shaping major international meetings in Istanbul, Bonn, Chicago and Tokyo. He provided US backing for an Afghan peace process designed to end thirty years of conflict and played an important part in restoring US ties with Pakistan. He returned to The Cohen Group in February, 2013.

Ambassador Grossman is Chairman of the Board of the Senior Living Foundation of the Foreign Service. He is a Trustee of the German Marshall Fund of the United States, the UC Santa Barbara Foundation, and Robert College of Istanbul. Ambassador Grossman is Vice Chair of the American Academy of Diplomacy. In 2013, Ambassador Grossman was Kissinger Senior Fellow at the Johnson Center for the Study of American Diplomacy at Yale University.

Raised in Los Angeles, California, Ambassador Grossman has a BA in Political Science from the University of California,

Santa Barbara and an MSc in International Relations from the London School of Economics and Political Science.

John Limbert

During a 34-year career in the United States Foreign Service, Ambassador John Limbert served mostly in the Middle East and Islamic Africa, including posts in Iran, Iraq, Sudan, Guinea, Algeria, Saudi Arabia, and the United Arab Emirates. He was president of the Foreign Service employees' union, the American Foreign Service Association (2003-2005), and ambassador to Mauritania (2000-2003). In 2009-2010, on leave from the Naval Academy, he served as Deputy Assistant Secretary responsible for Iran, in the State Department's Bureau of Near Eastern Affairs.

After retiring from the State Department in 2006, he was Class of 1955 Professor of Middle Eastern Studies at the U.S. Naval Academy, where he taught history and political science until retiring in 2018. In the academic year 2015-16 he held the Gruss-Lipper fellowship in Middle East policy at Princeton University's Woodrow Wilson School.

A native of Washington, D.C, Ambassador Limbert attended the D.C. public schools and earned his B.A., M.A., and Ph.D. from Harvard University, the last degree in History and Middle Eastern Studies. Before joining the Foreign Service in 1973, he taught in Iran as a Peace Corps volunteer in Kurdistan Province (1964-66) and as an instructor at Shiraz University (1969-72). He has written numerous articles and books on Middle Eastern subjects, including *Iran at War with History* (Westview Press, 1987), *Shiraz in the Age of Hafez* (University of Washington Press, 2004), and *Negotiating with Iran: Wrestling the Ghosts of History* (U.S. Institute of Peace, 2009).

Ambassador Limbert was among the last American diplomats to serve at the American Embassy in Tehran. He holds the Department of State's highest award – the Distinguished Service Award – and the department's Award for Valor, which he received in 1981 after fourteen months as hostage in Iran. He and his wife, the former Parvaneh Tabibzadeh, currently live in New York City. They have two children and four grand-children.